In a Gilded Ca

By Susan Apple

CW00859954

Published by Susan Appleyard 2016

Some Principal Characters

The Wittelsbachs of the Royal House of Bavaria:
Maximilian II, King of Bavaria.
Elisabeth Ludovika, (Elise) Queen of Prussia – the king's sister.
Sophie Friederike, Archduchess of Austria – the king's sister and Franz's mother.
Ludovika, (Mimi) Duchess in Bavaria – the king's sister and Sisi's mother.
Ludwig II, King of Bavaria 10th March 1864–13th June 1886.

The Wittelsbachs of Possenhofen:
Duke Maximilian Josef, Duke in Bavaria – Sisi's father.
Ludwig Wilhelm (Louis) – Sisi's brother.
Helene, (Nené) Princess of Thurn and Taxis 24th August 1858–16th May 1890 – Sisi's sister.
Elisabeth, (Sisi) Empress of Austria 24th April 1854-10th September 1898.
Karl Theodor (Gackel) – Sisi's brother.
Marie Sophie (Madi) Queen of the Two Sicilies 22nd May 1859-20th March 1861– Sisi's sister.
Mathilde Ludovika (Spatz) Countess of Trani 5th June 1861-18th June 1925 – Sisi's sister.

The Imperial House of Austria:
Archduke Franz Karl – father of Franz Josef.
Franz Josef, Emperor of Austria.
Maximilian I, Emperor of Mexico 10th April 1864-19th June 1867 – Franz Josef's brother.
Archduke Karl Ludwig – Franz Josef's brother.
Archduke Ludwig Viktor – Franz Josef's brother.

Chapter 1 – June 1853

She had always known the hills were alive. Sometimes she could see their exhalations drift across their faces like a gauzy veil, and when she lay in the sweet summer grass she could feel the beat of their hearts, in perfect harmony with her own. Giants they were, mighty and eternal. In summer, on their backs and shoulders they wore garbs of multi-hued green, and in winter they slept under a snow-white carapace and all the creatures that made their home on breast and brow nestled with them for a long, long sleep until spring came and woke them with her warm breath.

It was summer now, and the sweet smell of crushed grass was in the air. A group of children played on a grassy plateau overlooking the blue waters of Lake Starnberg. Some of the boys were engaged in a lively game of football, while the girls wove garlands from wildflowers they had picked or tossed balls or hoops. They were noble children from the castle and peasant children from the villages that dotted the shores of the lake and had freely mixed all their lives. Sisi lay in the grass gazing at the sky. 'Stay out of the sun – it will blight your skin,' her mother warned her constantly. Her mother enjoyed the outdoors too, but on sunny days she always wore a veil. Sisi thought the sun on her face was one of life's small treasured pleasures.

She loved the mountains when snow draped the peaks. She loved the hills, the forests that cloaked them and the high meadows with their tiny Alpine flowers, the smell of pine, the crunch of needles under her feet. She loved the lake, where she swam and fished, and Possenhofen Castle, her family's summer home.

She was Her Royal Highness Princess Elisabeth Amalie Eugenie, Duchess in Bavaria, but known to all as Sisi. She didn't think of herself as a royal princess, and hardly ever behaved like one. She wasn't doing anything as she lay there, not even thinking, hardly breathing, just being. She was aware of the giants beneath her and the tiny creatures that scuttled and crawled around her, about their busy labours in the dark, moist places of the earth. The grass was growing, springing up where it had been trodden down by small feet, reaching for the sun, and the distant trees hummed with pleasure.

Into these lovely sensations came the sound of her dog's excited yapping. Bummerl wasn't very big, but he had an annoying voice. Sitting up, she looked around and laughed. With his head and knees tucked in to form a perfect ball, one of the boys rolled down the hill, gathering speed as he went, with Bummerl yapping behind him. The watching girls shrieked and applauded. Before reaching the path beyond which the hill continued precipitously, the boy flattened himself out horizontally and after two more revolutions came to a stop. On the path, Duke Maximilian and some of his friends came into view.

"Papa!" Sisi called and skipped down the hill followed by some of the others.

"Hello, children!" the Duke roared, as they swarmed around him.

Her father was Maximilian Josef von Wittelsbach, Duke in Bavaria, loud and boisterous, and determined to live life to the fullest and in his own manner. A nobleman born, but with no connection to the ruling house except through his wife, he had no function at the royal court in Munich and was able to live as a country gentleman and allow his children a degree of freedom they would not otherwise have had. Eight years earlier he had received his royal status, only because of his wife's kinship to the king, but it hadn't changed him or his lifestyle.

Sisi adored him in spite of his flaws. She knew if she stuck a hand into one of the capacious pockets of his tweed jacket, among other interesting items, she would be sure to find a flask of whisky. He was drunk so often he had to be carried to bed, or he would disappear and be found sleeping it off in the stable or kennels. But when he was drunk he was funny and more affectionate than usual, and Sisi loved him no less for it. What shocked her more than his drinking was that he was not a faithful husband. At noon every day he had luncheon in his rooms with his illegitimate daughters, whom he loved as much as his legitimate issue. At fifteen-years-old, she understood that her parents' marriage was not a happy one and why.

Inserting herself between the Duke and the artist, Herr Bruckner, at his side, Sisi slipped her hand into her father's.

"There's the end of an interesting discussion," Herr Bruckner grumbled, with a glance that seemed to suggest her manners needed improvement.

4

"Papa, where are you going?"

"Wherever my feet take me. Sisi, why are you not at your lessons?" Max asked but with no trace of anger.

"Baroness Wulfen was talking about geography again." Sisi *hated* geography. She couldn't sit through a lesson without fidgeting and longing to be outside. More than once, Baroness Wulfen had threatened to tie her to the chair.

"What, don't you want to learn about the rest of the world? It's an interesting place." Herr Bruckner popped his monocle into place and peered at her as if she belonged to some new and fascinating species.

"The only place that interests me is Possi."

"Max, you should take the child in hand. My children could name all the capital cities of Europe by the time they were eight."

The Duke released her hand to drape an arm across her shoulders and give her a quick squeeze. "Sisi will be who she is, a child of nature, and I wouldn't change a thing about her."

Sisi gave him a warm smile. She knew she was her father's favourite, although she didn't know why. It would have been natural if Ludwig Wilhelm, his heir, was his favourite or Nené, her elder sister, who was so beautiful and accomplished. But no, Sisi was his favourite, and everyone knew it.

Birds twittered and warbled under hanging boughs that blotted out the sun. The duke's manner of walking was almost aggressive. He flung his walking stick out in front of him and gave the distinct impression that he would trample underfoot anyone or anything that got in his way. Sisi loved to hike through the hills with her father, exploring new places or visiting old favourites; or taking out the rowing boat to fish in the lake, sometimes just the two of them, sometimes with other family members. She always made a point of wearing sturdy shoes when out walking with her father.

She walked with her mother too. The Duchess enjoyed the outdoors, but she wasn't as adventurous as the Duke and preferred well-worn paths. She would never dream of clambering over rocks or lying on her stomach beside a woodland pool to see what was revealed in its shady depths. Not that walking with the Duchess wasn't fun, but her preference was to explore the wildflowers and fungi along the way. She would say: "Surely this plant has never grown in this spot before." Or: "Look at the size of this alder. It was no taller than me last year." She could lead anyone to the spot where the best mushrooms grew or where the wild apple trees stood and knew the names of everything that grew in the immediate area. The duke and duchess never walked together.

Eventually, the village children fell away, and Sisi was left with her youngest sisters Sophie Charlotte and Mathilde Ludovika, and Bummerl the dog. When old Manfred went by with his hay cart, bound for the castle, the two girls and dog hopped aboard and waved goodbye to their father, who strode purposely on. As the cart trundled onward, pulled by a donkey Ludwig Wilhelm said was as old as its owner, Manfred kept the three girls entertained by telling them far-fetched stories of his donkey's relationships with his other animals.

Possenhofen stood on the shore of Lake Starnberg. It was not a very imposing castle as castles went, but was pretty enough with its gleaming walls pocked by many windows, red tiled roof, and ivy and flowering vines clambering in rampant profusion around the portico. Gardens and terraces overlooked the lake while the stables and other utility buildings clustered to one side, enclosed within a shield of tall trees and undergrowth. The whole sat in the protective lap of the giants.

Every morning when Sisi rose she would go to the window, throw open the shutters and look out to see what the weather was like but also just to gaze at the lake, to see its mood. Was it tranquil and smiling with diamonds scattered on its surface? Was it grey and stormy? Was it turbulent? At night, when the moon laid a silvery path across the water, the sight never failed to stir her heart to wonder.

Manfred let the younger girls off at the front before driving around to the side with Sisi and Bummerl still on board.

Sisi wanted to visit her horse and Bummerl wanted to visit his dishes of food and water kept outside the kitchen door. Tethered to a post beside the stable was the Imperial rider's horse. He had been coming to Possenhofen quite regularly for several months. *He will be sorry to have missed Papa*, Sisi thought. Mama won't ply him with whisky. *She might offer him a cup of tea.*

"Shall I saddle Valour up for you, Princess?" the head groom asked.

"What time is it?"

Taking the watch out of his waistcoat pocket, he studied the face for a moment. Valour nickered softly; he recognised her voice. "Half-past four, Miss."

"Good. Then I shall have time. But don't trouble yourself. I shall saddle him."

Her horse greeted her with a whinny of delight and a toss of his fine head. The grooms rode him once a day, but they didn't ride him as she did, giving him his head and letting him run. Nor did they love him as she did. Sisi believed that in his great equine heart, Valour understood this.

Her earliest memory was of a groom handing her up to her father as he sat on his great hunter. One hand held her in place while the other shook out the reins and the horse walked out of the stable yard, down the avenue bordered by lawns and beds full of summer flowers. A lone cow had wandered in and was munching contentedly at the grass. Her father let her hold the reins for a short time until the horse began an erratic pace that had them both bouncing in the saddle. He said the horse didn't know her hand, which she hadn't understood then.

"All right, Sisi?" her father asked as he increased the pace to a trot.

"Faster!" she cried. "Faster! Faster!" Bouncing in the saddle as if the rise and fall of her little bottom could move the horse to greater speed. Her father laughed his great boom of a laugh.

Up they went towards the sweep of hills that she had only seen through her bedroom window or the window of the carriage as they arrived or departed, along paths used by farm carts and shy animals. To ride through the dappled shadows of the giant firs and pines, to smell the tang of fallen needles and damp earth, to be out in the open with the wind in her face was a wonder such as she had never experienced before. Her father increased the pace to a canter so that the horizon moved in great leaps and bounds and the ground rushed by under thudding hooves. Her sister Nené, three years her senior, had been coaxed into her father's saddle on one occasion, but she was so fearful she had not even got out of the stable yard. Then she had to take riding lessons on a tiny pony, a groom walking her slowly round and round on a leading rein. Sisi was eager to take riding lessons, but she wanted nothing to do with tiny ponies or leading reins. Clinging to the pommel, she shrieked in fearful joy, held firm and safe against her father's solid chest.

Higher they went up winding paths, past fields already showing the tender green of crops, into deep dank woods and out again, skimming across the breasts of the giants until her father brought the hunter to a halt where the hillside, clear of trees, dropped away. Sisi had her first view of Possenhofen from on high, its mellow bricks gilded in the sunshine, the cow a black dot on the lawn. Behind the castle was the shimmering lake, with the red roofs of houses around its shores peeking out between clusters of trees. It was the most beautiful sight Sisi had ever seen.

"You own all this, Papa?" she had asked in wonder.

A laugh rumbled out of his chest. "No, not all. There is Possenhofen, the village we own." He pointed over her shoulder. "And see there? The big building across the lake, that's the king's summer palace. It's a fine place."

"Not so fine as Possi." Even at four-years-old, Sisi was quite sure there was no finer place in the world than Possi.

All the children of Possenhofen learned to ride, but none learned so quickly nor as well as Sisi, not even the boys. By the age of five she was riding her own mount – a tiny pony, to her dismay – following behind her father or one of the grooms. At the age of eight, she had a full-size horse, and at ten she was allowed to ride out entirely alone. At fifteen she had two handsome riding habits and was teaching Valour to do tricks. She'd had her tumbles, sometimes accompanied by tears, but she always got back on her mount immediately and tried to hide her bumps and bruises.

....

Sisi returned to the castle in plenty of time for supper after an exhilarating ride and was passing the drawing room when she heard her father's loud voice.

"Dammit, Ludovika, I have a right to know!"

And her mother's voice in the tone she reserved for her husband, cool and impersonal as if she was speaking to an unsatisfactory servant. "And you shall, all in good time. I won't have you spoiling things."

8

Her mother, Ludovika, was a Wittelsbach of the royal house, one of eight daughters of King Maximilian and the only one of the seven surviving to adulthood who had not married into royalty. Sisi's father was a Wittelsbach also, but from a merely noble branch, and Ludovika never let him forget it. Ludovika didn't love Possi as Sisi and her father did; she deplored the threadbare carpets, cracks in the walls, worn upholstery, and scuffed floors. But to Sisi, it was a warm and hospitable house where children could romp without adults getting upset about ruined finery. Ludovika also deplored the wildness of her children. There was a time when she had tried to instil some courtly refinement in her family, but with eight children and a husband who indulged them and refused to chastise them and was often away from home, she faced an uphill battle. She had long since given up, often retreating to her room with a migraine to escape the turmoil.

Ludovika despaired because none of the Bavarian aristocracy ever came to visit. She blamed it on the shabby furnishings, her ill-behaved children, her husband with his loudness and bonhomie, his bawdiness and eccentricities. She relieved her loneliness by writing letters to her many sisters, collecting clocks and walking.

Sisi continued up the stairs without pause. Arguments between her parents were nothing new. No, they weren't arguments really, not anymore. They had got past that stage to a beleaguered tolerance of each other, punctuated by the occasional brief but passionless flare-up. In spite of appearing not to like each other and having nothing in common except a love of music, they had managed to produce ten children at regular intervals, eight of whom were still living. The eldest, Ludwig Wilhelm, was twenty-one, and the youngest, Maximilian Emmanuel, was only two, leading Sisi and Nené to giggly speculation as to why their parents kept having children when, after the birth of a second son, they didn't need to.

Nené, whose proper name was Helene, was in the room she and Sisi shared, dressing for dinner with the help of the maid they also shared.

"Oh, Miss Elisabeth!" the maid said in mild reproof.

"You are a mess," Nené said frankly.

"I've been riding."

"No, you've been galloping. You've been setting poor Valour at every stream and wall and hedge you could find, haven't you? Ladies don't ride like that, Sisi."

At eighteen, Nené was the oldest daughter of the house. Life had changed for poor Nené in the last few months. While they were residing in Munich for the winter a bevy of dressmakers and milliners had descended, and Nené found herself the recipient of lots of new clothes, while Sisi had to make do with her sister's old gowns to replace the ones she was fast growing out of. What's more Nené's lessons were stepped up and included such things as dancing, deportment and manners. Sisi knew all the attention was because her sister was expected to make a grand marriage and she was being prepared for that eventuality. She had badgered her mother to tell if there was a prospect in the offing and who he might be, but Ludovika was tight-lipped.

Nené was a natural lady, refined, charming, always carefully coiffed and elegantly dressed. Her lovely face required no artifice. She was everything a mother could want in a daughter. Sisi thought her wonderful if a little too 'proper'.

And Sisi was a natural hoyden. She didn't mind in the least all the attention her sister was getting, for while mother and governesses were focussing on Nené, she was free to roam the hills, to play with her friends, and to daydream about a certain handsome count who was on her father's staff. So much in love was she that she had once hidden behind a hedge to get a glimpse of him. But they were seen holding hands, and he was sent away to rejoin his regiment. Her heart was broken. Though she had known he wouldn't be considered a suitable match, that hadn't prevented her from daydreaming. She still thought of him occasionally with a wistful sigh.

Glancing in the dressing-table mirror, Sisi had to admit her sister was right. Her long, thick braid was windblown, little wisps of hair sticking out all over, and there was a smudge of dirt on her nose. Not that it mattered. She had plenty of time to wash and change her clothes, and there were no guests expected for dinner, only some of her father's friends as usual and some visiting cousins.

Sisi had been growing her hair all her life. It was her pride, and she would not allow scissors anywhere near it. According to her mother, she popped into the world with a head of thick golden curls. By the age of nine it had darkened to light brown, and now it was a rich chestnut with golden highlights. Nené's colour might be most people's preference, being dark blonde, but Sisi preferred her own; it had more life. When loosened from its braid, it hung like a majestic cloak, shimmering in ripples and waves, past her buttocks. It sparked like a fire, flowed like a dark river.

Every night she and Nené stuffed their braids into a net. They had discovered while very young that if they failed to do this, they would find themselves lying on each other's hair, resulting in a sleepy tussle to get the trapped hair free. In the morning, she had the maid brush it down its long length – brush and brush until the woman complained her arm ached – and then it was braided once more. Even so confined it was lovely, thick as her forearm and gleaming with health. Also, there were twice monthly rituals of washing, oiling, rinsing, drying and then more brushing.

All of this was a burden on the maid who swore she had the forearm of Hercules, and on Sisi herself. The pulling and tugging she endured, her neck muscles braced against the vigour of the brush strokes, and the patience she had to summon when she could have been outside roaming the hills, was a daily torment. Not to mention that such a vast amount of hair was a physical burden. But she wouldn't be without it. It was her glory.

When her thirteen-year-old brother Karl Theodor wanted to annoy her, he would threaten to steal into her room one night and cut off all her hair until she was as bald as an egg.

Even with her hair neatly braided and her face clean, Sisi knew she wasn't as beautiful as her sister. Her eyes were the colour of topaz, yet with a melancholic cast to them, surmounted by slender eyebrows, nose regular, mouth small but full-lipped, with shadowed indentations at each corner hinting at smiles yet to be born. Each feature was pretty enough, yet somehow the whole did not make her as beautiful as Nené.

Supper was at eight in the family dining room and a very informal affair. On the walls caribou and various species of deer that Max had hunted in Bohemia and Moravia and a lion he had shot in Egypt, looked down their lofty noses at the boisterous throng. There were often animals below too. One had to be careful not to step on a stray tortoise or a kitten.

Whether there were guests or not all the children were present and permitted to talk, which they often did at piercing levels. The

11

servants were free to remonstrate with a child who did not eat their vegetables, or slopped food on their clothing. When Karl Theodor began to lob balls of bread at his older sisters, it was one of the serving men who took his bread away. The servants only referred to family members by their royal titles in company. The duke and duchess would ask them about a sick parent or a child away at school, amid a babble of young voices and the clatter of dishes and cutlery. It was a very relaxed atmosphere. No one stood on ceremony.

When dinner was over the duchess rose. It was the sign that the children could scamper off to their evening activities before bedtime at ten o'clock. "Nené, Sisi, come with me. You too, Maximilian," she added, and sailed out of the room, leading the chosen ones into her small and cosy sitting room, where they settled themselves on furniture made comfortably lumpy by many years of use.

Some of Ludovika's collection of clocks lined the mantelpiece. The centrepiece was an ornate ormolu creation in the shape of a horse-drawn chariot with a figure of Victory standing in the car and the clock face displayed on the wheel. Every hour, from so many rooms in the house that the noise was inescapable, a variety of chimes and bells would resound.

Sisi and Nené sat together on a sofa while their parents took the two chairs. Bummerl curled on the worn carpet for a nap and Ludovika's little dog leapt into her lap.

Max took his pipe and tin of tobacco from his pocket. "Do you mind?" he asked the duchess.

"Yes," she said with a glare, "I do. If you must smoke that smelly object do it elsewhere."

With a resigned sigh, the Duke returned his beloved pipe to his pocket. Sisi loved the smell of her father's pipe. It lingered in a room long after he had left it, an essence of him. It was much nicer than the cigars some of his friends smoked.

"What is this about, Ludovika?"

To her everlasting – and often expressed – disappointment, Ludovika had been bound to a nobleman without a drop of royal blood and a penchant for drink and low women. The diminution of her status had hurt then, and it still hurt. She also compensated for a bad marriage by collecting clocks and studying geography, but she knew nothing of politics and cared less. Her children were her life, and she was very close to them.

Speaking directly to the girls, she said, "Your Aunt Sophie writes that to strengthen the empire's diminishing authority over Prussia, she is keen for closer ties within the German Federation. To achieve this end she hopes to find a bride for the emperor from among suitable German princesses."

That rules us out, Sisi thought. *We could never be thought a suitable match for the emperor.*

"There have already been two proposed matches that have fallen through, with Prussia and Saxony and now... well..." Ludovika smoothed her skirt as if she was nervous "Bavaria has always been one of the empire's staunchest allies in the federation. Your Aunt Sophie and I have been corresponding for some time concerning the prospect of a marriage between the House of Wittelsbach and the Imperial House. We are invited to Bad Ischl to join the celebrations for the Emperor's birthday and to enable him to meet our dear Nené." She beamed at her eldest daughter.

Simultaneously and without conscious volition, the two girls' hands crept towards each other and clung. Nené's hand had always been there to help a little sister across a rough piece of ground, to caress her when she cried. Now it was Sisi's turn to offer comfort or support or whatever Nené needed. She glanced at her sister, who looked stunned. Her eyes were wide and perhaps a little frightened. Her father's face was grim.

"So that's what you and Sophie have been cooking up?" he growled. "And not a word to me about it!"

"Please try to remember that it is a great honour just to be considered. Even you must see that it would be a brilliant match."

"I tell you this, Ludovika, Nené will be free to marry him or not as she chooses. I'll not have her coerced."

"How does one refuse the Emperor?" Ludovika asked with saccharine sweetness. She gave him a moment, but he had no answer, and she turned her gaze back to her daughters. "Sisi, you will go with us to Ischl as company for your sister, and who knows... perhaps we'll find a husband for you while we're there."

Nooo! It's too soon! I'm not ready.

In the spring of that year, Sisi had accompanied her mother to Dresden so she could meet Prince George, the second son of the

King of Saxony. Sisi had been terribly downcast during the entire time. Even Ludovika wasn't optimistic that the visit would be productive, and she was soon proved right. Sisi had neither the blood nor the dowry to catch a prince. She couldn't wait to get home. That visit taught her how it felt to be a commodity put on display for prospective buyers.

"I want to marry for love."

Ludovika looked at her as if she had grown two heads. "Don't be foolish, Sisi. That's childish nonsense. You are a princess of Bavaria. People of our rank do not marry for love, but to refine the family's prestige through an ideal connection. Put all thoughts of love out of your head, or you'll only break your heart."

"When is the Emperor's birthday?" Nené whispered.

"The eighteenth of August. I know this has come as a bit of a shock. None of us had reason to expect such a grand alliance for you. But you have two full months to adjust to the idea. In the meantime, the two of you will need new ball gowns and they must be made in the latest Viennese style, not by provincial Bavarian standards."

Max snorted. "Aye, trick 'em out for the marriage market. Put a ribbon round their necks and parade them before those worthless monarchy-loving parasites."

"You don't have to go if you don't want to!" Ludovika snapped at her husband.

"I have no intention of going. I wouldn't want to see a daughter of mine as Empress. She'll be a showpiece. She'll lose her individuality, her independence. She'll become a cypher, a clockwork person. Wind her up, and she'll dance for you, going round in the same circle over and over."

Sisi gave her sister's hand a little squeeze. *It doesn't have to be like that.*

"I'm sure we all know your views, Max," Ludovika said. "Pray excuse us from hearing them again?"

Max lurched to his feet. "I need a drink. There's a bad taste in my mouth."

When the door had closed behind her father, Sisi rose. "May we be excused now, Mimi?"

"Yes, go along." Ludovika looked rather baffled that neither girl had shown any excitement. "You'll see, Nené, once you have accustomed yourself to the idea, what a glorious future awaits you."

Their hands only separated once they got to the door. They walked upstairs at Nené's sedate pace rather than Sisi's headlong rush. From their father's rooms came the sound of loud male voices. Max liked to surround himself with intellectuals. He had what he was pleased to call a round table comprised of like-minded men who enjoyed philosophical and political discussions. Among them were scholars, artists and anyone he found of interest regardless of their station in life. Erudite discussion tended to deteriorate as the day wore on and the empty bottles mounted. In the evenings their voices could often be heard in all parts of the castle, laughing uproariously and bawling out songs accompanied by Max on his zither.

The two girls didn't speak until they were in their room and sitting side by side on the edge of the bed they shared. Nené still looked dazed, as if she'd taken a blow to the head.

"How do you feel about marrying the Emperor?"

"I don't know. How would you feel?"

"I don't know." They both laughed, but it was nervous laughter. A moment later Nené's eyes flooded with tears. Sisi slipped an arm around her. "If you marry him, I shall miss you terribly."

"But only for a little while. Mimi is sure to find you a husband at Ischl. Perhaps Karl Ludwig. Would you like to marry him?"

Sisi had met the Emperor's younger brother five years earlier, and the two had got along famously and had corresponded ever since. Karl was nice enough, but she didn't really want to marry anyone. It would mean having to leave Possi, and that thought was even more intolerable than being parted from Nené.

"At least if you married the Emperor and I married his brother, we would still see each other – on state occasions!"

"Of course, the Emperor might not accept me," Nené said bracingly. "And you and I will end up with nothing more than Viennese-style ball gowns with which to amaze the good people of Munich."

Sisi couldn't imagine why he would not love Nené and desire her for his wife. She would make a perfect Empress. It was as if she was born for the role.

The news didn't remain the province of the four in Ludovika's sitting room for very long, and every day poor Nené had to suffer the well-meaning felicitations of friends and staff and the teasing of her younger siblings as if the imperial crown already rested on her fair head. But day by day, she came to a quiet acceptance that a glorious future just might await her.

In bed at night, before they fell asleep, Nené confided her nervousness to Sisi, but as the days wore on, excitement began to replace the nervousness, even if a large part of that excitement was stimulated by the prospect of appearing, however briefly, at the imperial court. Ludovika wrote to family and friends in distant parts requesting their recommendations for a dressmaker who was up to date on the fashions of Vienna. A whole month had elapsed before a woman arrived, an expatriate Parisienne with two apprentices in tow, sent by the Queen of Saxony, another of Ludovika's sisters, who designed and created four of the most sumptuous ball gowns the two girls had ever seen. It was not enough, the dressmaker insisted. If they wished to make an impression, they must have morning gowns and tea gowns and new riding habits. They must have gowns for every possible occasion, and the vital accessories to complement them: shawls, shoes, fans, gloves, parasols, hats and veils and corsets, capes and coats. Although they worked long hours, the dressmaker and her apprentices couldn't possibly make all the clothing she deemed indispensable in time. So a three-day-long shopping spree to Munich was organised, with the Parisienne sorting despairingly through ready-made clothes and having to settle for the less-than-perfect, and Ludovika repeatedly having to reassure her that this was indeed one of Munich's finest couturiers.

During those heady weeks, Ludovika received so many invitations she couldn't possibly accept them all. Banquets and balls, teas and musical evenings were held in Nené's honour as if she had already been chosen as Empress. Nené, who had been out in society, sailed through these events graciously and with such self-possession that her little sister was in awe. Sisi relied on her shy smile when someone engaged her in conversation and otherwise tried to efface herself as much as possible.

Between the fittings, shopping and socialising, for Sisi especially, there were crash courses in deportment, manners and imperial protocol. Archduchess Sophie provided the latter from afar,

16

her increasingly frequent letters admonishing her provincially-raised nieces how they must behave if they were not to make fools of themselves. Sisi was also given lessons in recent political history so that she wouldn't appear a complete ninny if someone struck up a conversation with her. Dancing and deportment masters arrived. For Nené there were further instructions from the Archduchess about what she must do to make herself pleasing to the Emperor.

During the last days of July and the first of August, the two girls forgot about the Emperor and Bad Ischl. All they could talk about was their new clothes.

Chapter 2 – August 1853

A series of unfortunate incidents disrupted the trip to Bad Ischl. An aunt died just before the family left and they had to observe mourning, which meant the ladies must travel in black gowns. Ludovika decided that once they arrived it would be permissible to wear the court dresses bought at such cost without being disrespectful to the dearly departed. Ludovika suffered terribly on the journey, the bounce and lurch of the old carriage gave her constant headaches. The trip was interrupted when she had one of her migraines and needed to rest for a day. She fretted that the delay would upset all Archduchess Sophie's carefully laid plans for their reception.

Squeezed into the back seat between her governess and the maid, Sisi spent a great deal of the journey leaning past one or the other to look out the windows. She was thrilled by the breathtaking peaks, Alpine lakes and animal sightings as the carriage rolled around the shoulders of mountains, across high trestles and occasionally plunged into deep valleys. Nené read, only glancing up occasionally to smile when Sisi pointed out something of interest.

The small town of Bad Ischl swelled every summer to accommodate the aristocrats, who followed the Emperor wherever he went. Shops and houses built of yellow stone, with overflowing flower-boxes outside the windows, lined cobbled streets clogged with horses, carriages of all sorts, and foot traffic. Shopkeepers hailed passing prospects. Housewives strolled by with laden baskets. Urchins darted about dodging wheels and hooves. Smart gentlemen on handsome horses tipped their hats when they saw the occupants of the carriage. Ladies peeped from under their parasols.

When they arrived at their hotel, two days before the Emperor's birthday, there was no sign of the carriage carrying their luggage and the duchess's ladies-in-waiting. The bellman had nothing to carry up to the suite Sophie had engaged for them, which consisted of a sitting room, two bedrooms and a bathroom. It's sure to arrive soon, the two girls assured their mother, who was inclined to pessimism. It's not a catastrophe.

A huge bouquet of flowers stood on a table and beside it a heart-shaped box of chocolates with a card attached. The flowers were from the Emperor in welcome, but the chocolates were from Karl Ludwig and for Sisi alone. She had once told him that she adored chocolate. It pleased her that he had not forgotten.

With her mouth full of chocolate, she darted to a window where there was a spectacular view of the mountains.

What now? Ludovika wondered. How did one proceed? Should she send one of the hotel staff to the palace to alert Sophie of their arrival? She had sent a telegram from their last inn to inform her sister they would be here today. Should they wait to be contacted? Or go to the palace themselves? No, no, that could not be the correct procedure.

Never had Ludovika felt so unsure of herself. Unlike Max, she was not well travelled. Here in a hotel in Bad Ischl, she keenly felt her provincial roots and her ignorance of the world outside her Bavarian homes. She was out of her element. She had unknowingly become 'countrified'

She stretched out on the overstuffed sofa with a sigh of relief. Nené leaned over her.

"Are you getting a headache, Mimi?"

"Yes, I think so. Tell Sisi to stop banging about, will you?"

Sisi was exploring every cranny, opening the doors to cupboards and closets and closing them none too quietly, exclaiming over her finds. Nené returned to her mother with a cold cloth to lay on her forehead. In the bathroom, Sisi had found some lavender water that Nené sprinkled on the cloth.

"Wouldn't you rather lie down on one of the beds?" Nené asked.

"I don't think I could move, dear. No, I shall be all right."

It isn't a migraine, she told herself firmly. *It's just my nerves. That long journey, the vital importance of the next few days, seeing Sophie again...* For as long as she could remember she had been in awe of her sister, who was three years older. Even as children, Sophie had dominated. She had made a brilliant match when she wed the second son of Emperor Franz, whose fourth wife was her eldest sister, making Sophie daughter-in-law to her own sister. Ludovika still smiled to think of it, of all the family jokes. Emperor Franz's heir was Ferdinand, who was sickly and feeble-minded. After the revolutions of 1848, Ferdinand abdicated and was presently living in retirement in Prague.

Sophie's husband was expected to rule in his turn, but she had different ideas. Politically astute, strong-willed – she had been described as the only man in Schönbrunn – first, she helped get rid of Chancellor Metternich, who was 'the power behind the throne'. Then, passing up her chance to become Empress, she persuaded her husband to step aside in favour of their son, Franz Josef. Ludovika admired her sister greatly and wanted to please her, but she was also, she admitted to herself, a little bit intimidated by her.

"Sisi, is there any sign of the other carriage?"

"I can't see the street from here. But there's a man in the garden with an enormous dog. What will we do now, Mimi?"

"We'll just wait here until the other carriage arrives. We can hardly be presented to the Emperor like this, can we?" That was best, and she would just rest a bit before the excitement began. "Why don't you two go into the bathroom and tidy yourselves up?"

They must have been very quiet about it because she was awakened from sleep by a knock at the door. As Ludovika sat upright and patted her hair, Helene went to open it. An older lady in court dress, with a knobbed chin crowned by a rather large wart, sailed into the room and made a graceful curtsy to the three drably dressed duchesses. A younger woman, plainly dressed, followed her, carrying a tapestry bag.

"Permit me to introduce myself. I am Countess Sophie Esterhazy-Liechtenstein. Her Royal Highness, Archduchess Sophie was informed of your trouble by the hotel manager and sent me to render what assistance I may."

"How very kind of the Archduchess." Ludovika spread her hands in a helpless gesture. "We are as you see us, Countess: dishevelled by long travel, no change of clothing, not even any toiletries. We are not fit to meet the Emperor." Her voice trembled a little on the last words. It was all so disheartening. She was very cross with Sisi who had splashed her clothes when helping the groom water the horses. The stains were still visible.

"Well, let us see what can be done." The Countess glanced at the two girls. "Duchess Helene? With your kind permission, we will endeavour to make you a coiffure that will turn heads. Please be seated."

The young woman placed the bag on the dressing table, and Nené sat on the stool in front of it.

20

"What lovely hair you have, Duchess Elisabeth," the countess said to Sisi. "Marie here is the Archduchess's hairdresser. I'm sure it would give her great pleasure to create something special for you, but I am afraid we must leave you to see to it yourself. Here are brushes, combs and pins, everything you might need."

"Thank you. I am accustomed to braiding my own hair."

They all went to work. The hairdresser unpinned Helene's hair and loosened her braids. The maid helped Sisi brush out her masses of hair and then, after braiding, piled it on top of her head with the help of a few pins. The style made Sisi look more mature.

"Can you tell us, Countess, what is planned today?" Ludovika asked.

"Certainly. You are invited to join the archduchess for the *Jause* in her rooms at five o'clock."

"Will the Emperor be present?"

"But of course."

Ludovika's gasp of dismay was quite audible. "Can this first meeting not be put off until tomorrow? My daughters and I would feel so much more at ease if we were properly dressed." If only Nené had a lovely dress to wear. Mourning didn't become her at all. What kind of impression would she make? Black suited Sisi better. She looked very appealing in her simple high-necked dress. Helene looked... severe. *Oh, where were the carriages?*

"Do not concern yourself, Duchess. I assure you His Imperial Majesty will be nothing but pleased that you honour your lost loved one by wearing mourning. He is eager to meet... all of you."

....

In one of the imperial carriages, with the double eagle of Austria painted on the side, bowling along towards the villa the imperial family rented for summers in Bad Ischl, Countess Esterhazy adopted the role of tour guide. Between reminders to the girls how they must behave in the presence of the Emperor, she pointed out the town hall, the opera house, the River Traun and named some of the high peaks. In the sixteenth century a salt mine had been built, followed by a salt evaporation pond. Thriving on salt production, the town became a popular spa with the aristocracy. Along the river, grand mansions sat in splendour behind perfectly manicured lawns and crystal fountains, some in baroque style or evoking a bygone age with pillars, pediments and porticoes.

The Eltz villa, built of yellow stone, brilliant in the sunshine, was no more imposing than some of its grand neighbours. Once inside, everyone they came across bowed or curtsied and then peered covertly to catch a glimpse of the one who might become their Empress. Ludovika thought they must look like a trio of crows led by a bird of bright plumage. Her sense of inferiority increased.

The Countess conducted them up a broad set of curving marble stairs. Mounted animal heads hung on every wall they passed, complete with a little brass plate that told what the animal was, where and when it had been shot. "The Emperor's hunting trophies," Countess Esterhazy explained. Ludovika thought it a little overwhelming.

Liveried footmen opened doors before them, and they entered an opulent drawing room with dark red walls almost obscured by gilt pilasters, gilt-framed paintings and mirrors and a seventeenth century Gobelins tapestry depicting the finding of the True Cross by St. Helen. No animal heads. A series of French doors opened onto a balcony. The marble fireplace drew Ludovika's eyes. The mantel was laden with a number of family photographs. Hung on the wall above was a portrait of the Archduchess when she was younger. *One ought not to display pictures of one's youthful self,* Ludovika thought, gazing at the golden ringlets now faded to grey, the smiling mouth now in a perpetual droop.

Sophie Friederike Dorothee Wilhelmine, Archduchess of Austria, was there with her sister, Sisi's godmother, for whom Sisi was named, Queen Elisabeth Ludovika of Prussia, known in the family as Elise. The two were very much alike, with long noses and round eyes. In Elise those eyes made her look perpetually astonished. Sophie's gave the impression of being always alert.

Sophie seemed to fill the room with her presence. She wore a gown of dark red satin that was almost the same shade as the walls around her and that showed off her meaty shoulders. A triple strand of huge pearls hung around her neck and earrings with three matching pearls dangled from her ears. With her was her husband Franz Karl, a person of no significance in the lives of his son and wife.

22

After greeting Ludovika with kisses on both cheeks, Sophie went to Nené and took her face between her hands.

"Ah, you are as lovely as reported. I cannot tell you how much my son is looking forward to seeing you again." She kissed Nené on the brow and turned her beaming face to Sisi. "And this is little Elisabeth, all grown up. You will soon be as lovely as your sister, I have no doubt." Sisi also received an absent-minded kiss on the brow before the Archduchess turned her attention back to Ludovika, who meantime had greeted her other sister and bewailed the fact that their luggage had not yet arrived.

"It is a most distressing circumstance in which you find yourselves," Sophie said. "I do wish they would put in a railway between Vienna and Munich. The journey would be made so much faster and more comfortable. And luggage wouldn't get lost. Still, we must make the best of it. The ball is to be tomorrow night. I do hope your trunks will have arrived before then. In fact, I shall send someone to discover what has happened. But Franzl will brook no delay. He wants to meet you all today." She cupped Nené's face in the palm of her hand. "I cannot think he will find Helene anything less than agreeable, no matter her dress."

Ludovika fervently hoped that would be the case.

"He will be here shortly. He resides with the mayor. Unfortunately, the villa isn't big enough for both of us and our suites. There simply isn't anything better. And we all love Ischl. My children have been coming here in the summer since they were small. It is the one time of year we allow ourselves to relax."

"I am permitted to drink beer," Franz Karl put in, "which is denied me in the Hofburg."

There was time for only a brief exchange of familial pleasantries before the Emperor was announced. "Don't be nervous, children," Sophie said, and all the ladies, except her, sank into curtsies.

Two of his brothers, Archduke Maximilian and Archduke Karl Ludwig, Sisi's epistolary friend, followed him in. Karl Ludwig's eyes glanced around until he saw her. Sophie made the introductions, first Ludovika, then Nené and then Sisi. Ludovika couldn't help but note the broad smile that Franz Josef gave Sisi. And when they were making somewhat stilted conversation over their Dresden cups, it was to Sisi that his eyes continually strayed. Nené looked frozen with nerves, her cheeks paler than usual.

Sisi didn't notice the Emperor's regard. So nervous was she in the midst of so many important people that she could not bring herself to eat any of the dainty cakes arranged so enticingly on silver plates and hardly dared more than a glance at the Emperor.

Karl Ludwig sat beside her on a plush sofa, but even he made her feel shy. He would be about nineteen now, she calculated, no longer the boy she had briefly known. Naïve as she was, it didn't escape her notice that he was looking at her adoringly.

"Thank you for the chocolates. You remembered."

"Of course. Will you have a cake?" Karl beckoned to a footman standing by with a silver plate.

"Thank you, no. I am so nervous I can't eat a thing."

"No need to be nervous. We're only people. I'm so glad you're here."

Up to that point, she'd had no trouble at all obeying the oft-repeated injunction: "Do not speak to the Emperor unless he speaks to you." But he did speak to her. After a brief conversation with Nené, he asked if she liked what she had seen of Bad Ischl. Since he could not remain sitting while the Emperor stood, Karl Ludwig relinquished his seat and walked off with a rather angry backwards glance. Franz Josef sat beside Sisi.

She looked down at her knees and focused on keeping her hand steady so that the cup didn't rattle in its saucer. "It is a very fine town. And the surrounding area, the mountains, are beautiful."

"We must arrange an excursion to Katrin," Franz Josef said, to a chorus of enthusiasm from the others.

"What is Katrin?"

"It's an Alpine pasture almost five thousand feet high. It's not the highest point, but a gondola runs up there, and the views of the Salzkammergut Mountains are stupendous."

"It sounds lovely. I've never been in a cable car. Is it quite terrifying?"

"Quite," Franz said but chuckled.

There was a brief pause before Sisi said, "I have been mountain climbing with my father."

"You... Such a young girl. You hardly seem..."

"Oh, I am very strong and agile. The highest I climbed was Kreuzspitze in the Ammergau Alps. It wasn't really a very high mountain at seven thousand feet, and we had guides who taught us what to do and kept us out of trouble. It was quite exhilarating."

She peeked at the Emperor through her lashes, just long enough to see that he was better looking than she remembered, without the prominent nose or protruding under lip that her father said all the Habsburgs had. He had blue eyes, pleasant features, auburn hair and a rather thick lower lip under a neat moustache. He cut a graceful figure in his general's uniform. She hoped he was only astonished and not shocked.

Franz switched his attention to Nené. "And you, Cousin Helene, do you like to climb mountains, too?"

"No, sir. I'm afraid I lack my sister's adventurous spirit."

"An adventurous spirit is not an asset in a young girl of good breeding," Sophie said. She had been chatting with her sisters, but obviously also listening. "What were you thinking to let her?" she demanded of Ludovika, who had no answer.

Franz turned back to Sisi. "What else do you do in Bavaria?"

"I like to hike in the hills, swim and fish in Lake Starnberg. I pick wild fruits and herbs and mushrooms with my mother. Best of all I like to ride my horse. He is very spirited. Sometimes I spend all day outdoors and my mother will be cross because I've missed my lessons or luncheon." She didn't mention spending time with peasant children or playing childish games, sure that would shock the Emperor as it did some of her royal Bavarian relatives.

"You have allowed her to become a tomboy," Sophie hissed, loud enough for everyone to hear.

"My brothers and sisters and I have had a very happy childhood, Aunt," Sisi said mildly.

Before Sophie could respond, Franz said: "I gather you like the outdoors?"

"Yes. I don't suppose you have time for any of that," she replied, her voice soft with sympathy.

"Not much, no." Franz didn't elaborate. "What do you do in the winter?"

"We move to Munich. When it snows, we go for sleigh rides, sometimes with friends, so there's a long train of sleighs racing giddily through the city, and we stop at a café to drink hot chocolate.

Everyone's noses are red. There isn't much to do in winter." She very carefully took a sip of her tea with a reasonably steady hand. "I love Christmas, though. I love the smells of pine boughs and roasted apples floating in the wassail bowl and the Yule log burning in the hearth and the bright red berries and glistening leaves of holly and how everyone tries to be nice to one another, even when they're usually not, just because it's Christmas." Feeling she had said enough about herself, Sisi ventured timidly, "What do you like to do?"

"I? Oh…" Franz Josef paused. Sisi had the unhappy impression that he was trying to think of something. "I like to ride too."

A military band struck up in the garden, which helped to break the ice. Soon the company was singing the refrains from the latest operettas. Franz Karl made feeble jokes and smiled amiably at his nieces. Ludovika and her sisters chattered incessantly.

For the rest of the *Jause*, while not neglecting Nené and Ludovika, Franz was most attentive to Sisi. He was as pleasant as any humble gentleman, speaking to her about her likes and dislikes and her life in Bavaria as if nothing could interest him more, and showed such delight in her company that Sisi was able to relax in his presence.

Chapter 3 – August 1853

At precisely three-thirty, Eugen Ketterl, *valet de chambre*, awoke the Emperor with the formula: "I fall at your feet, Your Majesty. Good morning."

"Good morning, Eugen." Franz stretched and thought about the coming day, which filled him with an extraordinary sense of well-being. It was not very often he awoke in such good spirits. God had given him an onerous responsibility, and he applied himself to it diligently. And now God had answered his prayers and given him a girl he could love: the adorable Elisabeth.

He had been unable to sleep the previous night for thinking of her. It had taken no more than one brief afternoon, and he had fallen head over heels. Part of it was her beauty: those amber eyes, those infinitely kissable lips, that astonishingly abundant hair worn like a crown, and that so-charming hint of a double chin. Helene was beautiful too, but hers was not the rich, vibrant beauty of Sisi. Talking to her had only confirmed his initial impression. She was so different from any girl he had ever met, sweet and serious by turns, fresh and refreshing, and so disarmingly guileless in a world where direct speech was submerged beneath layers of florid courtesy.

After putting on a Chinese patterned dressing gown over his nightshirt he went to the washstand, where Eugen handed him his toothbrush already laden with powder. Eugen was the man who lived most closely to the Emperor and, although faultlessly unobtrusive, was never more than a call away. He was the head of a household of fourteen people who were the personal servants of the Emperor.

The bath attendant entered carrying a rubber tub, followed by a number of lackeys carrying pitchers of water. The bath attendant amused Franz. He didn't like being awoken before three-thirty, so he drank schnapps to help him stay awake until it was time to fulfil his duty. This habit meant that he was sometimes so drunk there was a danger that he and Franz would end up in the tub together. Still, he was a good fellow. The water was less than tepid, but Franz did not complain. Although as much of a stickler for protocol as his mother, he was tolerant of his servants' little failings.

While Ketterl was shaving him, he reflected upon the *Jause* of the previous day and the impression little Elisabeth had made on him. Then he went to his prayer stool where, after his routine prayers, he asked for guidance in the decision he was about to make, although he was quite sure, with or without the direction of the Almighty, his decision was already made, and it was the right one.

Meanwhile, Ketterl laid out his clothes for the beginning of the day: his habitual mouse-grey uniform.

By five o'clock he was in his study, where he read the documents his secretary had neatly stacked on the left side of his desk, from incendiary bulletins written by dissidents to top secret reports on the doings of his fellow monarchs to state papers requiring his signature. The work was interrupted by Ketterl with his breakfast, which he ate while listening to the daily report of Count Grunne, who was chief of the army, concerning matters of war. Ketterl then went to lay out his next suit of clothes.

"You can put those away," Franz said when he returned to his bedchamber. "I won't be going hunting today." He had wanted to go hunting, the Salzkammergut Mountains being rich in game, but he had to take care of more pressing business.

The valet was too good a servant to show his surprise. "A uniform then, Your Majesty?"

"Yes, the dragoon, I think." Franz had been given a military training as a boy and, at the age of thirteen, had become a colonel of dragoons. It was a proud moment in his young life, and the uniform was one of his favourites.

"Very good, Your Majesty."

Franz glanced at the clock. If he judged right, his mother would have finished her toilette. He wanted Elisabeth for his wife, and he wanted his mother to understand that no matter what she and her sister had planned between them he would have no other. He was in face a little nervous. He had never gone against his mother's advice before.

....

"Good morning, Mother." A smiling Franz fairly bounded into Sophie's salon.

"Franzl, this is a surprise." Seated at her writing desk, she tilted her face for his customary kiss. Her ladies withdrew to other tasks. "Is there something urgent you want to speak to me about?"

28

"The Jause, yesterday – did you think it went well?"

"As well as can be expected, I suppose. They were ill at ease, of course, which is only natural."

"I found Elisabeth quite charming."

Sophie didn't mistake Franz's meaning. When she looked up at him, he glanced quickly away, but he was still smiling. It was good to see him smile. He had assumed burdens at such a young age that would have tested and disheartened more experienced men; smiles had become strangers. Once he had protested to her: "Must I do without my youth?" But only once.

"Didn't you find her enchanting? How sweet she is. She's as fresh and unspoilt as a budding almond, and what a magnificent crown of hair frames her face. What lovely soft eyes she has, and lips like strawberries. She is so innocent. I don't believe she suspected the deep impression she made on me."

It wasn't like Franz, usually so prosaic, to speak so poetically. Sophie had noticed that his eyes often strayed in Elisabeth's direction and that he gave more of his attention to her than to Helene, but she hadn't realised that the attraction went so deep. After the *Jause* Karl Ludwig had said to her: "Franzl likes Sisi better than Nené. You will see, she is the one he will want to marry." And Sophie replied: "What utter nonsense! As if he would look at that little monkey."

"Don't you think that Helene is intelligent, that she has a beautiful, slender figure?"

"Well, yes, a little grave and quiet, certainly pleasant and nice, yes, but Sisi… Sisi… such loveliness, such exuberance, like a little girl's, and so sweet. I have never met a girl as enchanting. I think she would make a perfect Empress."

Alarmed, Sophie said, "Franzl, don't do anything rash. You've only just met this girl."

"It would be an unkindness to delay, don't you think? Helene has certain expectations. And have you noticed the way Karl looks at Elisabeth?"

Sophie was quite bewildered. It seemed to her that Helene was more beautiful, more sophisticated and poised than her sister. Elisabeth did seem childlike. Yet two of her sons were smitten with the younger girl. She would have been happy to see her married to Karl Ludwig, but not to Franz!

"But she is unsuitable. She's a hoyden. Viennese society will never accept her. You would do her a great disservice, as well as yourself. And me. And the empire!"

Franz had a look on his face that she recognised, and her heart sank. It said his mind was made up and he would not listen to reason. He put an end to any further argument by saying, "I love her, Mother. If I can't marry Sisi, I shall never marry."

Sophie could not believe her level-headed son had fallen in love at first sight with a girl not yet sixteen, who knew nothing of the world. And he thought she would make a perfect Empress!

Franz was no stranger to women. Sophie had arranged his first liaison with a girl from the theatre. Count Grunne was dispatched to choose one. The girl was bundled into a carriage, smuggled into the palace and as discreetly smuggled out again in the morning. On one occasion, to give the boy more confidence, a meeting had been carefully arranged with a girl from a good (but not noble) family so that it appeared accidental and the rest left up to Franz. There had been a few affairs discreetly played out, and a near-betrothal to one of Elise's daughters, but he had never spoken of love before. Of course, he was still very young, and the young tended to be impulsive.

"Very well. But I beg you, Franzl, do nothing for a few days. Spend a little time with her. Get to know her better." If she gave him some time he would see that Sisi was immature, with none of the social skills essential for an Empress, while Helene had already acquired polish. Then he would come to his senses.

"I won't change my mind. But I will wait – a little time."

"I thought you were going hunting today." He had dressed in one of the more than two hundred military uniforms he owned.

"I couldn't hunt or do anything until this matter is settled." He kissed her hand and went to the door, pausing there to say, "I didn't know such happiness existed." He was still smiling as he went out.

Sophie's ladies swarmed around her, exclaiming at the news. Queen Elise said: "It is good to see him so happy."

Sophie stared at the letter she was writing without seeing it. He wasn't born for happiness, her Franzl. No royals were. Shoemakers, perhaps, bakers and ostlers and physicians, might find a little happiness here and there between life's disappointments and disasters. But kings and queens were meant to rule, to put duty above

30

all else. That had been one of the guiding principles of her life. She had inculcated it into Franz.

He wasn't born to be Emperor. He owed his status entirely to her. And the revolution. It began in 1848 in France, that cradle of upheaval, an organic and spontaneous upsurge of unrest that swept across Europe like some dread disease, pulling rulers down, changing boundaries, terrorising whole populations amid calls for liberty, democracy and equality.

Nationalism was the war cry in Hungary, Italy and Bohemia on the outskirts of the empire. In Berlin, when the king and queen had been forced from their palace to salute the bodies of slain revolutionaries laid out in the courtyard, the Queen had remarked: "Only the guillotine is missing now." The revolution came to Vienna with an uprising of students and workers. A mob stormed the gates of the Hofburg. The mutilated body of the minister of war was hung from a lamppost outside his ministry. The imperial family were forced to flee to Innsbruck in the Tyrol. It was inconceivable that such things should happen in Vienna, the gayest city in the world, where the people danced in parks and public squares under colourful Chinese lanterns to the music of its great sons, Schubert, Haydn and the Strausses. Where the balls of the elite went on until dawn in gilded salons under a thousand pinpricks of light from gigantic chandeliers. When the madness was over, the streets of the city were torn up, buildings pocked by bullets, scorched by flame, many families in mourning, but the imperial throne, though tottering, was still the seat of the Habsburgs.

Emperor Ferdinand, a pitiful epileptic, was encouraged to abdicate, and his brother, Franz Karl, persuaded by Sophie to step aside in favour of their son. So there was a new enlightened ruler, Franz Josef, eighteen-years-old, who would usher in a new era. Josef was added to his name at this time to distinguish him from Franz I and also to associate him with Josef II, the reformer, still revered in Vienna. He was cheered whenever he went abroad. The revolutionaries would not be executed, he promised, but it was a promise he couldn't keep. They were executed, jailed, or forced to go into exile. He promised a constitution and freedom of the press, but these promises were promises of expedience. And the lone voice raised in approval was drowned out by the grumbles.

31

In spite of a strong military presence, the fires of revolution continued to flicker, particularly on the outer fringes of the empire. Earlier that year there had been serious disturbances in Hungary, which was demanding secession from Austria, and in Northern Italy. In Milan, during Carnival, Italian Nationalists attacked Austrian soldiers. The revolt lasted only a few hours, during which ten Austrians were killed, many more wounded. Several were pinned to doors by long nails driven through their flesh. Sixteen of the ringleaders were rounded up and executed, another forty-eight given prison sentences.

When Franz Josef donned the imperial crown, Sophie said on more than one occasion, that she would not interfere in matters of state, but would be happy to sit by and observe current policy calmly and with confidence, because she knew the empire was in good hands after thirteen years without an effective ruler. That had proved impossible. Franz might be firm about choosing his bride, but when it came to complex political issues, he was sometimes indecisive, sometimes stubborn. He was unable to see potential consequences and analyse options with any more than a mediocre degree of discernment. Sophie remained at his side, his principal adviser. She had to. He still needed her. As some had observed, it was she who ruled the empire. It was never her intention or wish to rule through her son. But she firmly believed that only the strong hand of youth could save the empire.

In February that year it was Franz Josef who had almost paid the ultimate price for unpopular policies. At the same time as the uprising in Milan, while the Emperor was out walking, a Hungarian tailor, who supported the cessation of Hungary from Austria, had come out of the crowd and managed to get close enough to Franz to stab him in the neck. Franz was seriously wounded but very courageous. The first thing he said to his mother after the incident was: 'Now I am wounded like my soldiers. I like that.'

The assassination attempt shook Sophie. Never before had a Habsburg been assaulted in such a manner. It proved that revolutionaries, subversives, gone underground, were beginning to raise their heads again. The movements that had sparked the revolutions of '48 were still alive in Italy and Hungary. Sophie hated both peoples.

....

In planning the seating for the family dinner that day, Sophie had in mind to show Franz that Elisabeth was unused to adult conversation and unfitting for the role of Empress. She arranged to have Elisabeth sit beside the ageing and partially deaf Prince of Hesse, while Nené sat in the seat of honour between Franz and his father. As she hoped, Sisi was unable to converse with her adult companions and sat through most of the meal in miserable silence. Sophie noticed that Franz, while making polite conversation with Helene, couldn't take his eyes off her sister.

Sophie wasn't about to give up. At the ball the following night, she reasoned, the sophisticated Helene would shine, while Elisabeth... If she had her way, Elisabeth would be nowhere in sight.

She suggested to Ludovika that Elisabeth was too young to attend the ball the following night and ought to remain at the hotel. Ludovika wasn't blind; she could see what was happening and readily agreed. But when Franz found out he insisted in the strongest terms that Sisi must attend the ball.

Chapter 4 – August 1853

To everyone's relief, the luggage had arrived the previous evening with the duchess's ladies. Fresh from a much-needed bath, Sisi dressed in her combinations, a one piece garment of fine wool that reached the knees. The next item to go on was the corset, steel boned and a required aid for the twenty-inch waist to which ladies aspired. Looking at the garment as if it were a viper, Sisi rebelled.

"Why do I need to wear that… that steel fortress? I already have a twenty-inch waist." She knew it was torture to wear because ladies always complained about it, even though they wouldn't be seen beyond their bedchambers without one.

"It is an integral part of your foundation garments. The sooner you get used to it the better." Countess Esterhazy, who had been instructed to take the Bavarian party under her wing, looked cross. "It also helps to promote correct posture."

"You do slouch sometimes," Nené said from across the room. She had already dressed in a silk camisole and lawn knickers. The two ball gowns were spread out across the bed. "In any case, your stockings have to be fastened to your corset. You don't want them falling to your ankles while you're dancing, do you?"

Sisi giggled at the image this conjured up.

"And before you ask," the countess added, "you do have to wear stockings. Come now. With all the excitement, you'll soon forget you're wearing one."

"Oh, very well." Sisi took hold of the bedpost the way she had seen Nené do many times, but the maid didn't have to pull the laces very tight because she did have a sylphlike figure, with small breasts and a tiny waist. Over her shoulder, she said: "It seems impossible that one can be excited and frightened at the same time, but I am!"

Both girls had had a dancing master intermittently while they were growing up, but Sisi was as little interested in learning to dance as she was in geography; until her mother told her the rest of the world was of the opinion that Bavarian ladies weren't good dancers. Then she had resolved to learn, onerous as it was. But she had never danced without a master to correct and guide her. She could only hope that no one would ask her to dance and she wouldn't make a fool of herself.

Nené's hair was dressed, and tendrils of ivy threaded through to add a whimsical touch. Sisi's was braided; some of the braids formed into loops at the back of her neck and the rest piled on top of her head. She thought the style made her look much more grown up. After hairdressing, the gowns went on, very carefully to avoid upsetting the work of an hour. Nené's was white silk, off the shoulder, which was the current fashion.

"Oh, Nené, you look lovely!" Sisi sighed.

"But so do you. Sisi, you are truly beautiful," Nené said, and she sounded sincere.

Sisi skipped to the full-length mirror. She was pleased with what she saw. Her pale pink dress was a simple style with a high neck, and her elaborately arranged hair was glorious. Nené came up behind her and smiled. Then Sisi saw that compared to her elegant sister, she looked rather childlike. The Emperor would surely fall in love with Nené tonight – if he hadn't done so already.

"You see?" Nené said kindly. "You'll break so many hearts at the ball."

Already dressed and coiffed, Ludovika came in carrying her jewellery box. "Now, my loves, we must attempt the impossible and gild the lily."

She wasn't wearing any jewellery herself but gave her girls the first choice. Diamond earrings for Nené. The matching elaborate necklace was rejected because the Duchess and her ladies agreed that a young girl's throat needed no adornment. When the Duchess tried to choose earrings for her younger daughter, Sisi declined.

"I have the very thing for you." Ludovika produced a diamond arrow, which she carefully fitted into Sisi's hair.

Sisi examined her reflection and finally pronounced, "I like it very much!"

"Well," said Ludovika, sounding slightly breathless, "are we all ready? Let us go."

The carriage was waiting. The ladies climbed in carefully, and carefully arranged their gowns to avoid creasing as much as possible. The yellow façade of the villa glowed in the mellow light of torches and lit windows as the carriage rolled to a stop outside the pillared entrance. Following an usher, they swept up the broad steps into the ballroom. Sisi's eyes grew wide as she tried to take it all in, gilt and glitter, huge chandeliers, corniced ceiling with a painting of, among other elements, cherubs with trumpets, a castle, a sea with boats, and around the edge trees with shy animals peeking out. The parquet floor, shining like a lake in the sun, was large enough to accommodate fifty dancing couples comfortably. Elegant couches dotted the sides of the room, bracketed by potted plants. Liveried footmen stood by with trays of champagne. At one end a twenty piece orchestra tuned up; at the other, a series of French doors opened onto a terrace and the cool, wet night.

The smell was rather unpleasant, a mixture of various perfumes and lotions, the Macassar oil some men had taken to using on their hair, and body odour.

People crowded the sides of the room. The Bavarians caused quite a stir when they entered. Eyes gleaming, women whispered behind their fans. Men stared appraisingly and leant their heads together. It seemed everyone knew why they were there or at least guessed. It was well-known that Franz Josef was looking for a wife. Sisi wanted to hide. She hated people staring at her. But it was worse for Nené. She was the focus of all eyes.

Ludovika took possession of an empty couch. Sisi sat close beside her mother and slipped a hand into hers. Nené sat on her other side. Sisi didn't know where to look. Sisi felt overwhelmed by it all: the dazzle of gold and jewels, the rudely staring eyes, the noise, a constant thrum, punctuated by loud male laughter, shrieks of female laughter and the scrape and twang of musicians tuning their instrument; above all that oppressive smell.

It was a great relief when the Emperor entered, looking extremely dashing in a uniform with military decorations. The archduchess was on his arm. Those seated rose and, in unison, everyone curtsied and bowed amidst a rustle of fabric and crinolines. Franz Josef made a gesture that gave everyone permission to rise. Now all eyes were on him and his mother as they proceeded down the room and sat on the chairs provided for them beside the orchestra.

Soon it will be Nené entering on the Emperor's arm, Sisi thought. She formed a mental picture of them together, which made her smile.

"Am I to be allowed a glass of champagne?" she asked her mother as they resumed their seats.

"Perhaps one, and later. It will make you even giddier than you already are." Ludovika began to fan herself rapidly.

Sisi pouted. "I am not in the least giddy. Am I, Nené?"

"I prefer to think of it as exuberance," her sister replied loyally.

The two girls sat out the first dance. As the music for the second struck up, a polka, Archduchess Sophie approached the trio with a young man in tow.

"Permit me to introduce Count Hugo von Weckbecker, His Majesty's aide-de-camp."

To Sisi's complete surprise and consternation, he held out a hand to her. "Princess Elisabeth, may I have the honour of this dance?"

Acutely embarrassed, she dipped her head. "Forgive me, sir, I… I'm afraid I've never danced without a dancing master to guide me. I don't know how I shall manage."

He smiled. He had thick black hair, with a narrow moustache and a blue-black chin. Sisi thought he looked rather like a pirate.

"I am quite sure you will manage very well." He had hold of her hand and urged her forward into the mass of reeling dancers. "A suggestion, if I may, Princess. Just let yourself go. The polka is not a structured dance. It is a dance for throwing yourself at the moon. Are you ready? Then we're off!"

Somehow Sisi kept up with him, even enjoyed herself and once or twice smiled in answer to her partner's smile. But as soon as the music stopped, she thanked him and dashed back to her seat beside her mother before he could escort her. Nené had not been asked to dance, and the Emperor still stood beside his mother's chair.

"I thought you were going to refuse him," Ludovika scolded, still fanning herself. "That would have been the height of bad manners."

The Emperor approached and bade them good evening. *Now he will ask Nené to dance*, Sisi thought. But he didn't. When he held out his gloved hand, it was towards her. "May I have the pleasure of this dance, Princess?"

She wanted to advise him that he really should dance with Nené, but she could hardly refuse him. Feeling herself blush, she placed her hand in his and allowed him to lead her onto the dance floor, aware that everyone's eyes were on them. The whispering behind fans began again.

It was a Strauss waltz, a dance that required holding, a dance for lovers where one was supposed to look dreamily into the eyes of the other. Sisi kept her eyes fastened on the point of Franz Josef's immaculately barbered chin.

"Do you like to dance, little Cousin?" he asked her.

"Yes, Your Imperial Majesty, but I'm afraid I'm not very good at it. This is the first ball I've attended. Nené has been to many balls. She is a much better dancer than I."

"I must disagree with you. You are a graceful dancer, light as air."

"Your Imperial Majesty is very kind."

He was an excellent dancer, and she followed him effortlessly. In his arms she felt as if she were floating, her feet barely touching the floor.

"It's quite a mouthful, isn't it?"

"I beg your pardon?"

"'Your Imperial Majesty.' I would be pleased if you would call me Franz."

Sisi dipped her head in confusion. "Oh! I couldn't. I... It would not be... appropriate." She had been told to call him "Your Imperial Majesty" in public; "Sir" was acceptable on informal or family occasions, but never to use his Christian name.

"I insist. And, with your kind permission, I shall call you Sisi. That is what your family call you, isn't it?"

"Yes, Your... Yes."

When the dance ended, he did not release her gloved hand but led her to the side of the room, the opposite side from where her mother sat. They stood beside a huge potted eucalyptus. She hadn't looked at him once throughout the dance.

"I wish I knew what to say to put you at ease," he said earnestly.

Then she did look at him, startled. He had been so kind to her, and she was afraid she had hurt his feelings. "Oh, it's not you, sir. Truly. It's just... Nené has been out in Munich society, but I haven't. I'm not used to so many people."

"Would you like to go out onto the terrace? Get away from all the noise for a while?"

Before she could answer, he had tucked her hand under his arm and led her towards the French doors. She cast a frightened glance in the direction of her mother and Nené, but couldn't see them for the dancers. Why hadn't he danced with Nené? Why was he paying such attention to her? It was thrilling but also embarrassing. How could anyone so handsome and important be interested in someone as insignificant as herself?

It had rained earlier, spoiling the plan for dancing on the lawn and releasing the smell of the earth. The night air was cool and damp. A few other people were on the terrace, but it was far from crowded. The balustrade was of gleaming marble, with red and yellow hibiscus in marble urns arranged around it. A series of shallow steps led down into a dark garden area still dripping with moisture. There were no lamps on the terrace, only the spill of light from the ballroom. Franz released her hand. They stood side by side looking at the sky.

"When I was a child," Sisi said, "I believed the stars were formed by God pricking the fabric of the sky to allow the light of Heaven to shine through."

"That's charming. What do you believe now?"

"My governess told me what stars really are. She often reduces things of beauty and wonder to the prosaic in the name of education."

"What a pity. Things of beauty should never be spoiled." Franz smiled. "I have something for you." Unpinning the nosegay from his lapel, he offered it to her rather formally. "Will you accept this with my deepest respects?"

"Thank you, Your... Thank you, Franz. It's beautiful." She brought it to her nose: three scented pink rosebuds surrounded by a spray of tiny white flowers. But her confusion magnified. Why was he giving her flowers? What did it all mean? Why wasn't he on the terrace with Nené?

Franz looked down at his feet for a moment, then looked back at her. "I suppose I should return to my guests. Duty calls. Shall I escort you back to your mother, or would you prefer to remain here a little longer?"

Yes, please go and dance with Nené. "I would like to stay here for a while."

"In that case..." He sought her hand and carried it to his lips before turning to the light and the music inside. He glanced back at her before disappeared into the crowd.

It was very romantic: the music, the rustle of ball gowns, the flash of jewels, the handsome Emperor in his white uniform, his breast covered in ribbons and medals and orders, his kiss on her hand – her overactive imagination was carrying her off to undreamt of realms.

As soon as he was gone, three people rushed up to her in a most unsettling manner.

"How fortunate you are, Princess," a lady who didn't come close to the desired wasp-waist said.

When Sisi didn't answer, a florid gentleman added, "My stars, I don't think the lady understands the significance of the nosegay."

"The Emperor gave it to me." She hadn't realised that everyone on the terrace had been watching the Emperor, just as they always watched him.

"It means you are the chosen one," the second lady said.

"Chosen for what?"

Disconcertingly, they went off into peals of laughter, which only ended when Queen Elise came out of the ballroom, and they rushed inside. Sisi felt herself flush.

"It's true then: he gave you his nosegay," Elise said. "Oh, my darling!" She gave her niece a hug. Sisi looked distressed. "Come, let me take you back to your mama."

Two other ladies now sat beside Ludovika, and a fair sized crowd had gathered around. Elise steered her niece away, but there was no avoiding it. Sisi was the focus of all eyes, the subject of a susurration of whispers. Some of the dancers paused to stare at her. Some even tried to engage her in conversation. Elise fended them off and made for the cloakroom, where comfortable couches offered tired guests the opportunity to rest and relax. The room was empty apart from an attendant. "Let no one else in," Elise ordered and sank into plump pink cushions, tugging Sisi down beside her.

"You don't understand, do you?" she asked sympathetically, as she pinned the flowers to the bodice of Sisi's dress. Sisi shook her head. "The presentation of the nosegay means that the Emperor has chosen you to be his bride."

Sisi's heart leapt in her chest in a most unpleasant manner. "No! That cannot be! He is to marry Nené."

"Everyone thought it would be Nené – as the eldest, she was the obvious choice, and she was your mother's and his mother's choice

– but even at your first meeting it was quite apparent that Franz was smitten with you."

"Really?" She had noticed nothing except that he was kind. Even tonight when he had escorted her out onto the terrace, she thought he was only being thoughtful in getting her away from the crowd, and she had taken the giving of the nosegay as an impulsive but meaningless gesture towards the little sister of his intended bride. But she couldn't explain, even to herself, why he had chosen her to partner him in his first dance of the evening.

"Ah, you are so innocent and modest. But you don't look very happy. This is a great opportunity for you."

"You must be wrong, Aunt. I won't make a good Empress. The way I've been brought up… I've always been free to do things that people of my class usually aren't allowed to do, or choose not to do. I don't want to leave Possenhofen. I'm not ready to marry anyone." She felt a bubble of panic rising in her. Elise took her hand and squeezed it.

"It's perfectly natural to feel overwhelmed, darling. You are still very young… but that is good. You'll grow into your role, and Franz will help you. He is very kind and patient. I cannot imagine him keeping you away from your family home if you wish to go. I'm sure you will be very happy."

Sisi gave her aunt a hesitant smile. "Yes, he does seem very nice."

"You know, Sisi, when I was growing up, it was understood by my sisters and me that we were political pawns and would marry the men chosen for us by our parents. We were forbidden to read love stories, even in the classics, for fear they might confuse our young minds. And yet many of us suffered broken hearts before we married."

"I know about my mother. She fell in love with Prince Miguel of Braganza who later became King of Portugal, but they were not allowed to marry. Instead, she was forced to marry my father, who was in love with a woman of no rank. They have not lived happily together. Mother once told me: 'When one is married, one feels so abandoned.'" She couldn't remember how many times she had heard her mother say that or something similar.

"Until you children came along. Children are a woman's great blessing. Your Aunt Sophie was equally unfortunate. She didn't

41

want to marry Archduke Franz Karl. She too had been in love with another man. But when she realised there was no choice she determined to be happy with the Archduke."

"But you, Aunt, I've heard yours is a true love match."

"Not at first. They seldom are at first. But my husband is a good man whom I love and respect, as I believe he does me. Your parents have set you an unfortunate example, but you see, dear, it is possible to find love in marriage. It just doesn't happen all at once. Do you think you could love Franz Josef?"

"I'm sure I could. If only he weren't the Emperor!"

Elise nodded her understanding. "All those ladies out there envy you, for they must defer to you. Even your Aunt Sophie must yield her place as the first lady in the empire. She is quite taken with you too, you know. She told me she finds you charming and unpretentious. It is not easy to win Sophie's approval." Elise sought Sisi's hand and patted it. "Granted, it won't always be easy. Some of your duties will be onerous but think of all the good you will be able to accomplish as Empress. You will be in a position to improve the lives of many people. You are most fortunate."

"But he hasn't proposed yet. He will change his mind when he knows me better."

Elise's laughter rang out like the tinkle of silver bells. "Oh, darling, why do you persist in thinking you're less than you are? Humility is a virtue only in moderation, and it's misplaced in you. Allow yourself a little pride. When we go back into the ballroom, lift your head, look all those people in the eye and say to yourself: I am to be your Empress!"

"I will try. Thank you, Aunt."

"No need to thank me." Elise gave her a mischievous smile. "I'm merely currying favour with my future Empress."

When they returned to the ballroom, Sisi was relieved to see Nené dancing with the Emperor, and they were smiling at each other. Outranked, the two ladies on the couch with her mother relinquished their seats, and Elise shooed the others away adroitly. "The princess is feeling a little faint. Kindly allow her some breathing room."

Ludovika glanced at the nosegay, then at Sisi and shook her head, looking faintly bemused.

The carriage ride back to the hotel began in silence. It was very late, and all three were tired. Sisi stared out the window. She felt as if she were being swept along in a fast flowing river where she had no control over what happened to her. Into what sort of life was she being carried? Her aunt had said she was fortunate but was she? And why hadn't Franz asked her? He had declared his intention to everyone present, but he hadn't actually asked her. And did she have any choice or was her fate sealed? All she ever wanted was to marry a nice count, preferably Bavarian, have children and a normal life. Someone like Count Richard. She had never dreamed of being an Empress. What if she said no? She imagined that would cause a scandal of epic proportions. There was a frail bough hanging over the river to which she could cling. Franz hadn't actually asked her.

The lights of the villa were behind them, and the carriage rolled into the street. Sisi could stand the silence no longer. "Please, say something."

"I am relieved," Nené said simply.

Ludovika massaged her temples. "It is not what I expected, but it is an illustrious marriage. You should be proud."

"And you?" Nené probed.

"Oh, I don't know! I'm so bewildered! Perhaps everyone misunderstood the significance of the nosegay. Yes, perhaps that's it!"

"He truly loves you, Sisi," Nené said warmly. "Anyone can see that. And he's very handsome and nice. Don't wish away your good fortune."

Sisi glanced at her sister's pale face in the darkness of the carriage. "And you don't mind, really?"

"I don't think I would like being Empress and I'm relieved I won't be."

She was being brave, Sisi thought. Nené hadn't quite been jilted, but she had come to Ischl believing she would be chosen as the bride of the Emperor and the entire court and even the Bavarian court had expected it too. She must be feeling at least a little demeaned Franz had chosen her younger and less accomplished sister instead. Sisi resolved to be especially nice to her from now on.

Chapter 5 – August 1853

"I am pleased to see you with such a hearty appetite," Franz Josef said when Sisi asked for another helping of boiled beef with chive sauce.

"I have been so nervous throughout the last two days that I have hardly eaten anything. Now I'm famished."

The occasion was the family dinner to celebrate the Emperor's twenty-third birthday. Aside from family members, some of Franz's adjutants were present and two ministers: Alexander Bach, minister of justice and the red-faced foreign minister, Count Ferdinand Buol-Schauenstein. Thirty velvet covered chairs surrounded a huge table laden with Meissen dinnerware and flowers arranged in low sprays in order not to impede the diners' view of each other.

Sisi was permitted to sit next to the Emperor in the middle of the table with the archduchess on his other side. She presumed this was the seat of honour and was made acutely self-conscious by her occupation of it. Ludovika and Nené were at one end. Nevertheless, Sisi ate with gusto.

"I hear you are an excellent horsewoman," the Emperor said to her.

"Papa says I have the seat of a Cossack."

"We must ride together sometime. I have a fine stable here. I'm sure we can find something that will suit you."

"That would be nice."

Between making small talk with Franz, she overheard snatches of a conversation between Sophie and the two ministers, enough to gather there was trouble between Russia and Turkey.

"His motive is clear and has nothing to do with religion. He is a bombastic autocrat with notions of expansionism," Sophie said while vigorously chewing.

"All this concern about the mistreatment of followers of the Greek Orthodox Church in Turkey is so much balderdash," justice minister Bach's deep voice rumbled. "Specifically he wants to occupy the Dardanelles, which would allow Russia free passage from the Black Sea to the Mediterranean."

"Does this concern Austria?" Sisi whispered to her other neighbour, Count Grunne.

"Very much so. If Russia becomes a presence in Europe, she will rival the power of Austria, as well as challenging England's supremacy in the Mediterranean. And Friedrich Wilhelm must be wondering if Prussia will be next."

"Will there be war?"

"It is a real possibility. A Russian emissary handed a note to the Turks claiming a Russian protectorate over all the Christians living in the Ottoman Empire. Of course, the Sultan refused. Then the Czar moved his soldiers into the principalities of the lower Danube – an act we see as unprovoked aggression."

"It is an impossible dilemma," Sophie continued. "Nicholas supported us in suppressing the Hungarians. Without his help, the revolt would have lasted much longer. And yet doesn't the moral imperative compel us to aid the sultan?"

Bach mopped his mouth with a pristine napkin. "France and England will certainly come out on the sultan's side, but, dear Madam, may I suggest the choice has little to do with morality."

Count Buol gave a little snort of laughter. "I heard an amusing tale from the British ambassador. Nicholas wrote to Victoria that he wished only to aid the sultan, whom he calls the sick old man on the Bosporus. Upon hearing this, Sir John Russell, head of the Foreign Office said the sick man would undoubtedly expire through the kind ministrations of his well-wishers."

"Victoria has never liked him," Sophie said.

Buol spoke directly to Franz. "As apostolic Emperor, does Your Majesty's conscience permit you to make common cause with the Turks?"

Franz pushed a morsel of leftover *erdapfel* around on his plate. "It is a devilish question."

The foreign minister flung down his napkin. "Our ingratitude will know no bounds!"

"Well, let us not burden our guests with such heavy talk," Sophie said with a smile at her niece. "This is a happy occasion. Let us drink a toast to the health of His Imperial Majesty."

The diners rose en masse and raised their glasses. The toast was repeated in a roar of voices. "Health to His Imperial Majesty!"

"Now I am stuffed like a goose for the table!" Sisi said as she put down her fork, which made Franz laugh.

....

Later that day, on the way back from an excursion to St. Wolfgang's Church, with its painting of the Devil, Sisi and Nené asked if they might walk a little way. The barouche they shared with Franz and the Archduchess stopped to allow them to alight. Below, the Traunsee appeared from time to time, dotted with fishing craft, while rocky cliffs towered above them on the far side. The river flowed away through a series of hills that looked like rumpled green cloth.

"You must like them very much to sit for so long in the barouche!" Sophie observed.

Franz was watching Sisi pick wildflowers in the hedgerow. "She is like a rosebud, unfolding in the rays of the sun." He turned to face Sophie. "Mother, will you make enquiries of Aunt Ludovika, tentatively, if Sisi will have me? I don't want any overt pressure put on her, you understand. My situation is so difficult that, God knows, it is no pleasure to share it with me."

Sophie, who had once longed to be Empress, said: "But my dear child, how can you think that a woman would not be only too happy to lighten your situation with her charm and cheerfulness?" She glanced at the two girls, one so mature and ladylike, the other so much the daughter of that ill-bred Maximilian. She'd had her heart set on Helene.

"Are you quite sure?"

"I've never been so sure about anything."

Sophie sighed. Since Franz was so determined, she consoled herself that there was no harm in replacing the elder girl with the younger if it would make him happy. They were both Catholic, both her nieces, young, nice looking, and with luck would prove as fruitful as their mother. And Sisi was young enough that she could be moulded to fit the role of Empress.

Franz turned to watch Sisi again. "I love her so much already."

....

Early the following morning, Ludovika received a note from Sophie. She clutched it to her bosom in an amalgam of happiness and something that made her heart thud uncomfortably. She was worried about Sisi. How could Sisi go from being a child romping through the hills of Possenhofen to one of the most prestigious – and demanding – positions in Europe? How could she give up the freedom she had been accustomed to all her life? What would those haughty aristocrats of Austria make of her? They were such narrow-minded people, living in a closed world prescribed by wealth, titles and sixteen generations of noble blood. Frivolity and scandal pervaded their conversation; they gorged on gossip. Surely they would despise Sisi: her background, her cheerful exuberance, the fact that she was not one of them. They would show no tolerance for the mistakes she was bound to make as she learned how to be an Empress. But, as she had said to Max, how did one refuse the Emperor?

And what would Max have to say about it? He had declined the invitation to Ischl and went off to the French Riviera instead. With a companion, of course. Ludovika thought him a fool. Just because he was so low on the social ladder was no reason to keep his family down with him. Marriage to the Austrian Emperor was an unlooked-for honour for the house of Wittelsbach, yet the prospect had angered him. His anger would only increase when he learned the intended bride would be Sisi, his favourite, the one who shared his love of the outdoors and many of his outrageous opinions. And how could Franz Josef be so... so contrary!

Only Nené was in the sitting room, reading quietly. Sisi was out walking with Baroness Wulfen.

Here was an opportunity to reveal the substance of the note to Nené, but Ludovika wasn't going to put herself through the ordeal twice. Nené was too well-bred to ask about the letter; Sisi would have asked.

"Is anything wrong, Mimi?" Nené was a very perceptive young woman.

"No, dear, just a slight headache." Ludovika did, in fact, suffer migraines, but she all too often used headaches as an excuse to escape or to mask other upsets. Refusing any ministrations, she went to lie down in her bedroom and rehearse how she would tell her daughters. When Sisi returned, Ludovika was no nearer to finding the right words.

The girl was bursting with the sorts of little adventures she inevitably encountered, the sights she had seen and the people with whom she had talked. She chattered away, while Ludovika smiled and nodded, and finally said: "Well, I am glad you had such a good time, dear. I have something to tell you…" She faltered, looking at the two expectant faces. Pulling a handkerchief from her reticule, she touched it to her nose. She had found it useful always to have something to do with one's hands. "This morning I received a note from your Aunt Sophie. In it, she says the Emperor wishes to marry Sisi."

There, it was out. Ludovika shook her head in bewilderment because she still didn't understand it. Unable to look at her daughters, she took refuge in fussing with her handkerchief. The girls were silent, as were her ladies, waiting no doubt for someone to take the lead. The silence went on too long. It was as if she had announced a death and everyone was numb with shock. She felt compelled to say something – anything.

"Are you pleased, Sisi?"

"Yes, Mimi," she replied, sounding very uncertain.

"I am happy for you, Sister," Nené said.

Sisi turned to her. "Are you really?"

"Of course I am. If the Emperor had chosen me just because our mothers wanted it, we would not have been happy together. But he has chosen you because he loves you. You are fortunate."

"Oh, Nené!" Sisi dropped her head onto her sister's shoulder for a moment, and a tear rolled down her cheek.

That was Nené – uniquely magnanimous. "There," said Ludovika, "now it is all settled. We can be joyful."

Her own joy was unequalled, tempered only by her concern for Sisi, so young and inexperienced, so unprepared for the life that awaited her – a life that was the antithesis of her first fifteen years. At least Sophie appeared to like her, and that meant a great deal. Ludovika would be able to hand her dear daughter over to one who would be as a second mother.

It was at this point that the Emperor arrived. Sisi was overcome with excruciating shyness all over again and kept her eyes on the carpet as Franz, like any common suitor, went down on one knee before her.

"Princess Elisabeth, you would make me the happiest man in the world if you will you do me the honour of becoming my wife," he said, very formally.

"Yes," Sisi said softly and peeped at him through her lashes.

Franz sprang to his feet and took her hands, drawing them against his chest. "My dear precious girl, I cannot express how happy you have made me. I am convinced that you possess all the virtues and all those properties of mind and heart that will ensure continued happiness for the rest of our lives together."

Sisi smiled faintly. "I am happy too."

Franz turned to Ludovika. He was beaming and Sisi... Sisi was hiding away in depths her mother had never noticed before.

"Aunt, I can't tell you how happy your daughter has made me," Franz said.

Such trite words, Ludovika thought, *never before so sincerely spoken.*

When he glanced at Sisi, she smiled back at him, and when his gaze moved elsewhere, the smile disappeared in a second. *Is she happy?* Ludovika wondered. *Is she only loving the idea of love?* She had claimed to be in love once before, with a youthful member of Max's staff, and when he had been sent away, she had remained in her room for three days, eating nothing and writing maudlin poetry. That had been just this last March. Girls of her age fell in and out of love so easily.

....

Dressed in a simple sprigged muslin dress and a straw hat, Sisi on Franz Josef's arm was escorted to the villa for breakfast with Sophie and other family members. Ludovika wasn't alone in watching the young couple closely. Everyone seemed in the best of spirits now that the matter was decided, except Karl Ludwig. Poor boy, he looked as if he had lost the love of his life.

At eleven o'clock, the party walked to the parish church. Somehow news of the engagement had spread, and a crowd of cheering people had gathered in the small square before the church. It was a noteworthy moment when, at the door, Sophie held back and allowed Sisi to precede her. As the future Empress, Sisi now outranked the archduchess. Most likely, Ludovika thought, Sisi never noticed the gracious gesture. She had her eyes down, only peeking up occasionally as necessary. On this occasion, it was not the handsome Emperor in his military uniform, with his hand resting on the hilt of his sabre, who was the cynosure of all eyes, but his future bride. Members of the congregation strained their necks to see her, bobbing and weaving. Sisi reacted to all this attention by shrinking into her shell.

His eyes filled with tears, the priest welcomed them as musicians played the National Anthem. After the benediction, Franz Josef took Sisi by the hand and said to the priest: "I beseech you, Reverend, bless us. This is my bride."

Ludovika said to the person next to her, who happened to be Count von Weckbecker: "My daughter is facing a hard task. She is ascending the throne straight from the nursery. The ladies of Vienna will judge her severely, I'm afraid."

Even in provincial Munich, the royals and nobles looked down on eccentric Max and his family. It would be so much worse in Vienna, where the populace – a mix of many races – regarded anyone not Viennese, as not quite good enough, and the aristocracy measured everyone, not by character or accomplishment, but by bloodlines.

The Count confirmed her thoughts when he gave her a sympathetic smile but no reassurance to the contrary.

After the church service, the entire Imperial Suite was presented to their future Empress. Among them was the adjutant general, Karl Count Grunne, one whose judgement Franz valued. Ludovika had heard talk of this man. Rumour said he was the Emperor's mentor in matters concerning women. He had the longest side whiskers she had ever seen. They seemed to sprout from his cheeks horizontally and, she estimated, as much as four inches long, with a pink bubble of chin peeking between them. He also possessed a thicket of eyebrows. On the other hand, the top of his head was as hairless as an egg. He was of middle age and correctly formal, but a little later Ludovika saw him wink at Sisi, which drew a smile from her. One could see he approved mightily of Sisi, who greeted him, like the others, pleasantly but shyly.

Outside, the crowd had grown. Although it was Sunday, the shops were open and selling blue and white ribbons, the colours of Bavaria, and the yellow and black banners of the Habsburgs hung from windows and flagpoles. People threw bunches of flowers into the carriages and shouted Sisi's name in the streets. The crowds frightened her, so although she continued to wave bravely, she was almost in tears. Ludovika suggested taking her back to the hotel to rest, but dinner had already been arranged.

"It is a pity Sisi is so delicate," Sophie remarked to her sister.

Dinner was in Hallstätt, a small picturesque village nestled on the shores of the Hallstätter See. Mountain peaks guarded the salt mining operations begun three thousand years earlier, and now a mainstay of imperial finances. Franz pointed the sights out to Sisi while the rest of the party stood apart and sighed over young love in such a beautiful setting.

They went for a drive through the lovely landscape before returning to Ischl, which meantime had donned a celebratory cloak. Candles and lamps in the Austrian and Bavarian colours lit streets thronged with people in festive mood. On the Siriuskogl, multi-coloured lanterns created a bridal wreath enclosing the initials FJ and E. Musicians played in the parks and squares and outside cafés.

A cheer swelled as the imperial party appeared on a balcony. Looking out at a small town's jubilant outpouring of devotion to the Emperor and its benevolent welcome of the future Empress, Ludovika was moved to tears. Her daughter too was in tears – not for the first time that day. When the people saw the Emperor drape his military cloak over the shoulders of his future bride to protect her from the cool night air, their cheering reached a crescendo. *It will be all right,* Ludovika told herself. *He loves her so much.*

Bavarians, typically, were in bed by ten o'clock and up by six, but no one wanted this day to end. Sisi charmed everyone with her shy glances and gentle manner. The Wittelsbachs didn't get back to their hotel until past midnight.

....

The two girls fell into their separate beds and lay quietly for a time. Wide-eyed, Sisi gazed at the ceiling, trying to sort out her feelings, which were in a bewildering state.

"What a day!" Nené murmured. "Are you tired?"

"Yes, but I'm sure I won't be able to sleep."

"No, I wouldn't if I were in your shoes. It was very exciting."

Sisi turned on her side to face her sister. "It was also..." she paused, searching for the right word, "painful. How will I ever bear it, Nené? Sometimes I think I can be happy because Franz is kind.

51

And then we go to church, and the people stare so! I have the awful feeling that they are a many-eyed monster that wants to devour me."

"You always had too much imagination. It will get better. You'll have lots of people to help you. Aunt Sophie will teach you everything you need to know. I admit, when I thought I was to be her daughter-in-law, I was a bit intimidated, but she seems kind. And Franz Josef adores you."

Everyone seemed to agree that she was most fortunate. Aunt Elise had told Sisi that in the royal and noble houses of Europe were girls, and their parents, with aspirations of marrying the Emperor. He would have been a catch without the imperial diadem, so young, handsome and charming, with none of the mental and physical feebleness that had afflicted his father and uncle. And yet, a shy girl from Bavaria had managed to capture his heart without even trying.

Chapter 6 – August 1853

In the morning the *Weiner Zeitung* carried an official announcement. Ludovika read it to her daughters. "His Imperial and Apostolic Highness, our most gracious Lord and Emperor, Franz Josef the First, during His Majesty's stay in Bad Ischl, offered his hand to Her Most Serene Highness, Princess Elisabeth Amalie Eugenie, Duchess in Bavaria, after obtaining the approval of His Majesty, King Maximilian II of Bavaria, as well as their Serene Highnesses, the parents of the Princess-bride, and entered on an engagement. May the blessing of the Almighty rest on this event, so happy and joyful for the Imperial House and the empire."

"Has Papa approved?" Sisi asked.

"Telegrams were sent out yesterday by the imperial secretariat. I presume permission was obtained from your father, the king and the pope. Their blessing is a mere formality. One doesn't say no to an Emperor."

"No," said Sisi, "I suppose not."

Breakfast was in the hotel dining room. Even there Sisi could not avoid the stares, the sight of women bending their necks to whisper, the simpering smiles. Ludovika chose a table in a corner and Sisi was able to sit with her back to the room.

She had to rush off afterwards to sit for an illustrator who was going to do a sketch of her.

Sisi was touched that Franz sat nearby to keep her company. This was the first opportunity they'd had to be alone – or almost alone – if one ignored the illustrator, which she tried to do.

"When the next official statement is sent out to Vienna, my curious subjects will see a representation of how beautiful their future Empress is," he said.

"Franz, may I ask something of you?"

"Anything, my dear one."

"Has it been decided when the marriage shall take place?" Without waiting for an answer, she rushed on. "It's just that… well, everything is happening so quickly, and I would be so grateful for a little time to adjust and to prepare myself. I am looking forward to becoming your wife, but I know I would benefit from a few more months of maturation. I'm sure your mother would agree with me."

"If that is your wish – of course. They will be very long months for me."

"Thank you, Franz." A deferment – Sisi tried not to show her relief. "Now, you must tell me about Vienna."

"Ah, where shall I begin? It lies on both sides of the Danube, a beautiful river. We shall live at Schönbrunn and the Hofburg. There are many stately buildings, and churches, St. Stephen's Cathedral, many museums and of course the opera and theatres."

Very prosaic, Sisi thought. *He has no imagination.* That's what her father had said about him: unoriginal and unreflective. Perhaps that was due to his upbringing. Unlike her he would never have been allowed to dream, to wonder, to stray from the strictly defined paths of ritual and tradition, of rigid duty, into realms of fancy.

"I have never been to the theatre. Do you go?"

"Occasionally, when time allows. I prefer the Burgtheater. Three Mozart operas premiered there."

"What colour is it?"

"Colour?" Franz looked confused.

"The walls – inside, I mean."

He didn't know. Poor man. Had he never looked for shapes in the clouds, marvelled at the stars, stomped on an iced puddle to see the pattern of the cracks?

"Do you have a favourite opera?"

"I'm not all that keen on the opera," he said as if admitting something shameful. "If I had to choose I would say *The Magic Flute*."

She wasn't surprised. The libretto was in German, and the antagonist of the Queen of Night, Sarastro, represented an enlightened monarchical ideal. Perhaps that was something to which Franz aspired.

"That's mine, too!" Sisi lied, and they smiled at one another as if they had discovered something wonderful. She and Nené had agreed that it was all right to tell little lies, the sort that didn't hurt anyone. But never, never to each other. The truth was, she liked Italian operas and her favourite was *The Marriage of Figaro*, although it was slightly naughty.

"My father plays the zither." She looked at Franz to see his reaction to this piece of news, but his expression was no more than mildly inquiring. "He plays it very well too. Once he played on the top of the pyramid of Cheops in Egypt. And he writes and publishes music, mostly Bavarian folk songs." One summer he had taken her with him when, disguised as a strolling minstrel, he wandered between fairs and small villages, playing his zither while Sisi danced and shook her tambourine. Later she had collected the coins thrown at them. She always loved being with her father.

She didn't mention this to Franz, but he cleared his throat and said: "An unusual man, your father." He was trying to be gracious, but the disapproval seeped through.

Sisi lapsed into silence. After a while, she said: "Tell me about the Viennese people. What are they like?"

She'd already had her father's version. 'They think because they live at the centre of the empire, that makes them superior. They live in a polyglot city, yet they do not integrate. They keep their bloodlines as pure as the Habsburgs. Mind you, they love music, so long as it doesn't make any demands on their brain.'

"They are my children," Franz said rather pompously. "They are not frivolous, but they love pleasure: walks in the park on Sundays, music and of course the opera."

He doesn't know them, Sisi realised. Her father had also said: "Franz Josef looks down from his godlike height on a city that doesn't exist, a Utopian chimera, superimposed on a never-ending Viennese ball. That is what a monarch does. Go out and get his hands grubby? Talk to the man in the street? Never!"

She had eaten in the homes of her peasant friends. Helga's father made the most delicious bratwurst. If she ate what was on her plate he would urge another piece on her and if she ate that another piece appeared, along with words like: "You could do with a little more flesh on your bones, Princess." She had finally discovered that the only way to avoid stuffing herself with an excess of bratwurst was to leave a piece on the plate with a declaration that she was too full to eat another bite – which was usually the truth.

"I had a happy childhood," she said. "My only regret is that I didn't pay enough attention to my lessons. I used to sneak away to roam in the hills or ride my horse. I love being outdoors. What was your childhood like?"

"My education began when I was six. That was when I was taken away from my governess and nurses and given an official instructor. Aside from the three Rs, I learned German and French, geography and religion. When I was older, I learned Hungarian, Czech and Italian, drawing, chemistry and political history – a lot of political history. When I was in my teens, I began to receive military training: to understand manoeuvres, signals, strategies, weapons and the functions of the four military branches. When I was thirteen, I was appointed colonel of a regiment of dragoons." He smiled at her, pleased and proud. He was also becoming quite animated. "My mother had given me a wonderful set of hand-painted toy soldiers when I was about four. I added to them over the years until I had a representation of every Austrian regiment. I played with them a lot, to the point where I knew every button on every uniform. I still have them, every single one. Perhaps you'd like to see them when you come to Vienna?"

"Yes, that would be nice."

Sisi felt rather sad for him. She had asked him about his childhood, wanting to know if it was happy or lonely or strict. His response was a litany of his education. "Did you have any playmates?"

"My brother, Maximilian. We're still chums."

No mixing with boys beyond the charmed circle. No outside influences. Did he ever play with a hoop or a ball? Was he ever given a spontaneous hug? Was there ever a time when he wasn't carefully watched? No wonder he was such a...a closed person.

"Finished!" the illustrator announced. "Though I say it myself, it will melt the heart of anyone who views it." Beaming, he held the portrait towards the sitter.

"It's wonderful!" Franz said. "A very good likeness. We must have Schwager paint you, my dear. He has done my portrait."

....

"We are grateful to Your Royal Highness for making the Emperor happy," Countess Esterhazy said at yet another ball.

"You will have to be very patient with me for a while," Sisi replied, as she watched the dancers whirling around the ballroom.

Countess Esterhazy, Sisi had come to realise, was not only a lady-in-waiting but also a close friend of the archduchess's, in the same way that Count Grunne was the Emperor's close friend, which made them both very important members of the Viennese court. She wondered who would become her intimate as Empress. Certainly not anyone she knew. She couldn't imagine Hedwig or Helga, the girls who were her usual playmates in Possi, being invited to wait on her, and she suspected that even ladies from the noble families in Munich would not be quite good enough. Her closest companions, the ones who would replace Hedwig and Helga, would be chosen from among the high aristocracy, Austrian ladies whose impeccable bloodlines were branch or root of the Habsburg family tree.

Sisi started at a sudden noise like a barrage of gunfire. The dancers continued without pause. The Countess laid a hand on her arm. "It's only firecrackers. That will be the Emperor's brother, Karl Ludwig's, doing. He is enamoured of the horrid things."

Ludovika clamped her hands over her ears and fled the ballroom. Her nerves were constantly on edge. She was proud at the great honour done her daughter and at the same time, fearful that the burdens her new responsibilities would impose on her would crush Sisi. Excusing herself, Sisi went after her mother and found her in the archduchess's bedroom.

"Mimi?"

"I don't know why people like those dreadful things. Do you remember in Possi when Karl got his hands on some? It took us an hour to get the dogs settled. Even the horses were distressed."

"Mimi, is it time we went home?"

She longed to wrap herself in Possi's simple pleasures, the soothing rhythms of the giants' heartbeat, the placid lake. To walk in the hills alone, or with Papa, listening to his philosophies on life, or in the company of people with whom she could be herself – not some puppet princess inserted with dizzying suddenness into a role she neither understood nor relished. Possi would restore her equilibrium.

"I hate to be the one… Everyone is having such a good time. I hate to bring it to an end."

"Is Nené happy?"

The Duchess shook her head. "It is hard for her. She is happy for you, really she is. But she feels the humiliation of being passed over."

Sisi understood this. Nené was the older daughter, eighteen already. She should be the one betrothed to the Emperor, not her little sister, who everyone could see still had so much growing up to do. But Nené would never say anything to distress Sisi.

"Then, please, Mimi, let us go home."

Ludovika looked wistfully at her. "It is hard for you too, my pet. And yet I am pleased with your manner when you speak to so many strangers and, in spite of your embarrassment, maintain such calm."

Sisi felt tears sting her eyes. "I don't know how much longer I can bear it."

"This is just a foretaste of what is to come. Like all of us, you must learn to bear what God sends."

"I know I must. I will do my best."

During the time the Wittelsbachs spent in Bad Ischl, Franz had demonstrated his tenderness for her in many thoughtful little ways. One day he took her by the hand and led her out into the gardens where a swing had been erected. The seat was of polished wood, and the chains and frame were intertwined with ribbons and garlands. Sisi sat, and Franz stood behind, pushing her until she soared into the air, in a froth of lacy petticoats, laughing gleefully. They were almost alone in the garden, no mothers, no siblings, no adjutants, only a few strollers trying to look as if they minded their own business. When Sisi rose from the swing and thanked him, Franz tipped her chin up and kissed her on the mouth for the first time. It was a quick and gentle kiss, made no demands on her, and she found it pleasant. Thus it was: from girl to woman in a heartbeat.

When they went for drives in a magnificent coach drawn by five horses, the usual coachman was replaced by Count Grunne because Sisi felt more comfortable with him than a stranger. There were other gifts, almost every day, usually of jewellery, including a tendril of diamonds and emeralds which could be woven into her hair. Franz was very proper and circumspect and treated her with great consideration for her shyness.

Three balls were held at the villa, where Franz and Sisi whirled around the floor, smiling into each other's eyes, and Nené danced with the Emperor's handsome aides. Party followed party as the elite of Bad Ischl attempted to outdo each other in feting the happy couple. There was a shooting expedition in the mountains, picnics, and an alfresco dinner party aboard an illuminated barge while fireworks shot stars into the sky and Franz and Sisi's initials surmounted by a crown blazed on a mountainside in letters of fire.

Sisi had no idea that life for the Austrian court wasn't always like this. At first, it was all very exhilarating, but the round of festivities, the late nights, meeting new people with whom she was expected to make small talk, and endless sittings for her portrait became too much for her. She had noticed too that Sophie had a gimlet eye, and it was almost always on her. So much was expected of her, though she bore it all stoically and Franz was usually at her side, easing the way.

She went to sit beside her mother and was gathered into her embrace. Tears glistened in her eyes, but she didn't give in to her sadness. Her mother's arms soothed her. It seemed a long time since she had been held like this.

....

"When I return to my desk-bound existence in Vienna, with its cares and troubles, I will be happy just thinking of you. I'll even enjoy sitting for Schwager since it will remind me of your sittings here. My thoughts will cling with infinite longing to Bavaria."

In response to these tender sentiments, Sisi said: "I will write often. If you don't have the time to write back, I will understand."

The parting took place in romantic Salzburg, festively decorated for the purpose. On the eve of departure, Franz gave her another gift, a pearl studded choker with matching earrings. And Sophie announced a very special gift for the betrothed couple.

"I have bought the villa in Ischl where you met, and intend to enlarge it to make it a more fitting residence for an imperial family. When you return next year, after the wedding, it will have a very different floor plan."

"How kind you are!" Sisi cried, overwhelmed by gratitude.

Chapter 7 – October 1853

Sisi sat in her bedroom reading the latest letters from Vienna, brought at least once a week by smartly uniformed couriers. Franz's letters were all full of endearments and accompanied by yet more gifts: a diamond brooch in the shape of a cluster of rosebuds, a blue velvet cloak with sable trimmings and matching muff, a miniature portrait of the Emperor and much more. None gave her as much pleasure as a talking parrot from the menagerie at Schönbrunn.

"I shall call him Peter," she announced and carried him to her room. From where he was promptly banished after Nené complained about the noise he made when she was studying.

From Vienna, the Archduchess applied herself to the task of erasing the old Sisi and creating a new, more suitable one. Her letters were full of instructions thinly disguised as guidance and recommendation. It soon became clear that she disapproved of everything about Sisi: her character, education, upbringing and general behaviour, even her teeth. Along with gifts of her own, she sent Sisi a tin of whitening paste.

Sisi threw the latest letter down. "I shall never be able to please her!"

Nené sat at her desk beside the window, with books open. Her education in the schoolroom was complete, yet it seemed to Sisi that her sister actually enjoyed learning. She was trying to perfect her French now.

Sisi rose and went to the window. A mist lay on the lake, tinted pink by the rising sun. Birds were flocking in the trees ready for their journey south. The last of the roses were fading in the garden. Those were signs of autumn, which meant the family would soon move to Munich. She had spent her last summer in Possi. She longed to be outside, to enjoy once more the colours and smells of summer, to run barefoot in the grass with the dogs bounding along beside her.

As if reading her thoughts, Nené said: "You must apply yourself, Sisi. You cannot spend all your time daydreaming. Would you like me to help you learn the Emperor's titles?"

"No! There are hundreds of them."

"Not quite. You will learn if you practise, practise, practise."

"Well, I won't, won't, won't." Sisi ended with a giggle.

She looked around the room with its familiar objects: her ink-stained desk, the bed with its faded muslin hangings, the threadbare carpet on the bare wooden floor, the pictures on the walls, crude, childish drawings mostly of dogs and horses. All suddenly were so dear. The clocks in the house struck nine o'clock.

"What are your lessons this morning?" Nené asked, dropping a hint.

"Austrian history and the protocols of the imperial court – a basic introduction – followed by Italian. Why must I learn Italian?"

"Because Italy is part of the empire. If you go there it would be nice to speak to the people in their own language and to understand what they're saying, don't you think?"

"But then, why must I learn French. France isn't part of the empire."

Nené sighed. "Because every accomplished person should speak French. It is a sign of good breeding. Do run along, Sisi. You'll be late."

"I haven't read Franz's letter yet." If Sophie's letters demoralised her, Franz's always cheered her up. He wasn't one for flowery phrases, she had learned, but every line brimmed with love and longing. She unfolded the letter. "Nené!" she shrieked. "Franz is coming! He'll be here Friday. He's going to see Possi!"

"Oh," Nené said quietly, "I wonder what he'll make of us all."

Late for her lesson, Sisi snatched up a book and dashed past the dining room. Her father was there eating breakfast.

"Papa, you're back!" She gave him a kiss.

Sisi could understand why her father was popular with the ladies. She thought him handsome in a rugged sort of way. He was tall and straight, with streaks of grey hair at his temples and a moustache that tilted up almost cheekily at the ends.

He looked down at himself, shoulder to shoulder. "Yes, it appears that I am."

"I'm so glad. You'll be here when Franz comes."

"Franz? Here? When is he expected?"

"He should be here within a few days, but he has to stop in Munich to pay his respects to the king."

"Ah, that's unfortunate. You know I always go hunting in Silesia at this time. Can't disappoint the fellows, you know." One of 'the fellows' his usual hunting companions, was the son of a local tavern keeper.

"Papa! You can't possibly go hunting when the Emperor is coming. It would be an unforgivable insult. If you do, I shall never speak to you again!"

"Oh, very well then. I shall make the sacrifice for your sake."

Realising he was teasing her, Sisi pulled out a chair and sat beside him. "Why don't you like Franz, Papa?"

Max put down his knife and fork and pushed his plate away. "It's not the Emperor but the institution I dislike – the monarchy. It has outlived its usefulness and is now nothing more than an extravagant showpiece that is a drain on the economies of Austria and all the countries under its boot. Furthermore, Franz Josef is an absolute monarch. He has control of the army and the police. He doesn't even have a prime minister. There is a parliament, but he has made sure it has no power. He makes the laws. All power is in the hands of one man."

"But, Papa, the Emperor was chosen by God to rule over us."

Max snorted. "That's what he would like us to believe. But if God chose all monarchs it has to be said He has made some odd choices. Franz Josef has not earned the right to rule over millions of people by merit."

"Forty million," Sisi supplied. Her Aunt Sophie had told her that.

"It was only because of his birth, the luck of the draw, like a lottery."

"That's true of us too. The lottery made us aristocrats and not peasants."

"Exactly. If people are elevated above others, it should be according to their merit and abilities. Even us. If you and I, Sisi, had not been born princes, we would have been performers in a circus."

Sisi smiled at him. It was true. "Well, no one can say your views are self-serving. What would you like to see in place of the monarchy?"

"Democracy – rule of the people by the people. As in America…"

Sisi put her chin on her fist as she listened to her father's description of the government of America. Instead of being educated at home by a tutor like most boys of his rank, her father had attended an academy in Munich among boys from many different walks of life, where he was exposed to camaraderie and competitiveness and the role models of teachers with unfettered minds. Sisi suspected that was where he developed many of the views others called liberal.

"But common people don't know how to rule. Kings are taught the business from an early age."

"Aye, and who has taught Franz Josef? His mother and Chancellor Metternich – both rabid monarchists. He's probably never heard terms like democracy, nationalism, self-determination, and if he has you can be sure he hasn't explored them. Well, he may be the Emperor, but he's only one little man. He can no more deflect the movements of reform than he can stop the waves rolling against the seashore."

"Nationalism – that's what Count Mailath is talking to me about." Count Mailath was not a university professor like her other tutors, but a friend of her father, who had engaged him to give her lessons in Austrian history, of which she knew little.

Max nodded approvingly. "Interesting man, the count. You may yet turn into a good little liberal."

"Don't be silly, Papa. I'm about to join the monarchy."

"Don't remind me," he said sourly.

Sisi rose. "I must go. I have a lesson with the count this morning, and I'm late."

She had lessons three days a week from Count Mailath, who read to her from his *History of the Austrian Empire*. To Sisi, he was a very old man, short and stout and always with messy hair, but interesting and with an amusing delivery. Others came to sit through his lessons including Ludovika, Nené and Karl Theodor, as well as some of the other tutors. Sometimes they lasted far into the evening.

The count was a Hungarian who lived in a shabby apartment in Munich. Although criticised by his compatriots as being pro-Austrian, his book and his teachings were very much from the Hungarian point of view, so he was criticised by Austrians also.

"Nationalism, the idea of nationalism, once planted in fertile soil, cannot be cut down. A limb might be cut off here and there before it flowers, but the rootstock will remain strong because it is fed and watered by the desire for that most ideal of human conditions: liberty."

"Few can understand the long-term consequences," the French tutor objected.

"But, sir, monarchs have the right to make choices, be they right or wrong, and can they be sure of the consequences of a wrong choice? All we can do is make determinations based on the needs of today."

"Metternich said: 'Monarchy is the only form of government that appeals to my mentality.'" The French tutor was a great admirer of the former Austrian chancellor.

The count peered at his interlocutor over his steel-rimmed pince-nez. "Do you think it possible there is something wrong with his mentality?" he asked, with such perfect delivery that his audience laughed.

Sisi thought a great deal about what her father had said, along with what the count taught. Freedom, the right to make their own choices, to determine their own fate – that's all the peoples of the empire wanted, just as it was what every individual wanted. She wondered if there was some way to balance the two.

....

Three artists were sent from Vienna to paint her portrait before Franz was satisfied that one was good enough to be shown publicly. While she was sitting those long hours, her mind was not allowed to be idle. A tutor would always be with her trying to improve it.

Crammed between sittings and lessons, the preparation of a suitable trousseau took up many long hours. Dozens of seamstresses worked on new gowns, coats and undergarments and all the necessary accessories. Sisi flaunted herself before a full-length mirror in her finery, occasionally also wearing some of the jewels Franz had given her. Nené and their twelve-year-old sister, Marie Sophie, ran out of superlatives to describe how she looked.

There were also calls from royal relatives and the Munich elite, who had never before thought to visit Possi and eccentric Max and his wild bunch of children. Sisi was expected to practise her manners and conversational skills with people who she understood were trying to curry favour with the future Empress, or glean a bit of gossip to pass along to their friends over tea and iced cakes in the drawing rooms of Munich. It was very difficult for her. She found their conversation banal, superficial and sometimes spiteful, and she was often at a loss how to respond.

On one occasion she received some guests with her parrot on her shoulder, just to see what they would say. Of course, no one said anything. At least not in her presence.

"I know they can be a trial," Ludovika said without sympathy. "Think of them as another lesson. They will teach you social skills. These are very necessary to you."

Sisi pulled a face. "Those people have nothing to teach me. They are hypocrites and favour-seekers."

It was a glorious autumn day when Franz came to visit. Sisi rushed out of the house when she saw his entourage arrive. Ludovika ran behind her, calling: "Sisi, don't run!" By the time she reached the door Sisi had slowed her steps and emerged decorously. Family members crowded behind her. Franz walked from his carriage and kissed her hand. The family dogs sniffed around him.

Then he swept her into his arms and kissed her repeatedly. When he released her, she said breathlessly: "Your Majesty, welcome to Possenhofen."

"I couldn't wait to see you again, my darling angel. I made it to Munich in thirty-one hours. I dare say no one has ever done that before."

Although his entourage was relatively small, most had to find lodgings in the village. Ludovika fretted that he would find Possenhofen boring.

"Mimi, no one could be bored at Possi. There is so much to see and do here."

But in fact, Franz spent long hours with Count Grunne, attending to business, which she presumed had something to do with the trouble in the Balkans and the couriers that came almost daily. She had no idea what the Balkan situation was and little idea of the burdens Franz shouldered as Emperor, but she wanted to know since her Aunt Sophie often used expressions like 'share his burdens' or 'relieve his cares'.

One day she found Count Grunne sitting alone and smoking a cigar on the terrace that overlooked the lake, and seized her chance. He rose at once and bowed, reclaiming his seat when she sat.

"Count, can you tell me what is happening in the Balkans?"

"To put it simply, Princess, Czar Nicholas claimed Russian protectorate over the eleven million followers of the Greek Orthodox faith living in Turkey because he says they are badly treated. He fools no one. His real purpose is to get control of the Dardanelles, which would allow Russia free access from the Black Sea into the Mediterranean. But the sultan could not accept that and has declared war."

"Have Britain and France joined?"

"The British fleet has been standing by at the Dardanelles for weeks. France will certainly join because Louis Napoleon wants to curry favour and gain recognition. Queen Victoria mistrusts him as an ex-Carbonaro." Tactfully not waiting for her to admit her ignorance, the count added: "A Carbonaro is a member of a secret society active in Italy, France and Spain."

"I see. Has there been an engagement yet?"

"Yes, the Russian fleet annihilated the Turks, with the result that the British ships have sailed into the Black Sea."

"But what will the Emperor do?"

"He is in a difficult position. During the revolutions of '48 Russia came to Austria's aid in putting down the last and most stubborn resistance in Hungary. The Emperor feels he owes Nicholas an enormous debt, and yet he cannot tolerate a Russian presence in the Danube provinces. He has ordered troops to Galicia to prevent a Russian invasion and ordered Nicholas to withdraw from the occupied Danubian principalities, which sent the czar into a paroxysm of fury. His Majesty was sorry to do it. He said he had stabbed a good friend in the back and felt wretched about it."

"But his priority is to protect Austria, isn't it?"

"Yes, and he does not want to lead the empire to war. We are only just starting to recover from the effects of the revolution. His Majesty is trying to remain neutral."

"I am sure he will do what is right."

He smiled at her. "In politics, it is not always possible to know what is right."

When business didn't occupy Franz, he fell under the spell of Possi. Sisi was delighted when she was withdrawn from lessons, fittings and sittings to keep him company as they romped on the lawn, throwing balls and hoops and cheering the younger children as they turned somersaults, with the dogs yapping around them. When an impromptu football game began, Franz descended several degrees in dignity to play on one side, Max on the other, while the aides-de-camp who had accompanied the Emperor looked on in amazement. To the surprise of the older members of the family, the Emperor and Max got along very well together.

Giving the other children strict orders that they were not to follow, Franz and Sisi walked in the hills, hand in hand, as she showed him her favourite places, and went on exhilarating rides, always with a few of the imperial guard at a discreet distance.

When Sisi protested that they were perfectly safe, Franz replied: "I'm afraid it's something you will have to get used to. You cannot be allowed to go beyond the walls of the palace without a guard. There are madmen everywhere, who see themselves as patriots. Look at this." He pulled the collar of his coat down.

Sisi's hand went to her mouth. What he revealed was a livid red scar on his neck.

"It happened earlier this year. I was out walking on the old walls. A madman, a Hungarian, came out of the crowd and stabbed me. One of my adjutants saved me from a fatal wound." He looked away, across the lake to the dark mystery of the tree-covered island rising from the still water. "That was the day I lost my youth."

"Oh, I never knew!" Sisi cried. How ignorant she was.

"So now I am wounded like my soldiers." Franz smiled. "But that is why we must be careful not to expose ourselves to danger."

They were in a particularly beautiful spot overlooking the lake, with the hills beyond in violet shadow. Franz took off his greatcoat and laid it on the grass. They both sat, and Franz put an arm around her shoulder. The wind had the teeth of winter. Their noses and cheeks were pink with cold, but at least they had left the noisy children behind and all but one of the dogs, and had a little time alone. Almost alone.

"I love you very much," he said. "I love you so much I can hardly believe my good fortune. When I am at my desk, snowed under by state papers, beset by a hundred cares and worries, all I can think about is the earthly paradise I found in Ischl this year. I cannot wait for the day when we will be together. When we're apart, I can't stop thinking about you. Every day I love you more."

"I love you too." She was sure it was true.

He tried to kiss her, but Sisi pulled quickly away with a shy glance towards the guardsmen who were looking anywhere but at them.

Franz chuckled. "You'll soon forget they are there."

"No, I won't," she said. "I won't ever."

Chapter 8 – Winter 1853-Spring 1854

It was winter now, and dusk was a violet mantle with the faint blush of a fading sunset lingering where the snow was pristine. The stars appeared one by one. Sisi stood at the open window of the library, looking out into the street, 'people-watching' as she called it. Snowflakes drifted lazily. She had said a tearful goodbye to Possi, to the hills and the lake, the romping grounds of her childhood, not knowing when or if she would return.

Farewell, you quiet rooms,
Farewell, you ancient castle...

Her mother had assured her the Emperor was not the kind of man who would prevent her from visiting whenever she chose, but she knew when she returned it would not be as a girl but as Empress Elisabeth – an entirely different sort of person. When she left this house, it would be as if Sisi had never been.

Now she must impress the broad Ludwigstrasse on her memory, and the Müncheners, the housewife with her shopping basket labouring home in snow trodden to slush; the gentleman in his tall hat, perhaps thinking of a warm fire; the maid hurrying from the house opposite – did she have a beau waiting for her? – the child crying until nanny came along and hauled him away by the scruff; the black and white dog sniffing its way along the pavement. There were no street lights in Munich, but the lanterns of passing carriages and sleighs helped avoid many accidents. In the windows of the palaces opposite lamp- and candlelight bloomed.

She thought about the *Englische Garten* wreathed in snow, and skating on the frozen Isar, and nights when her father would bang on bedroom doors, drunk and merry, shouting: "Come, children! Come on a sleigh ride with your old papa!" They would jump from bed, stuff their feet into boots, wrap themselves in blankets and hurry out into the crisp night air, for if they weren't quick he would go without them. Being with him was always an adventure. They would huddle together on the seat, snowflakes tingling on their faces, while he whipped up the horses and careened off into the white night, bawling out a song, or telling a story over his shoulder. Ludovika put an end to such nocturnal adventures when the sleigh overturned and five children went sprawling in a tangle of limbs. Their fall softened by snow and the blankets and rugs they were wrapped in, so that the only injury, apart from an assortment of bruises, was to little Sophie, who suffered a broken wrist.

Sisi had never liked Munich as much as Possenhofen, nor the people they mixed with as much as the simpler folk of Possi, but now she felt a tenderness for the city and the Müncheners. They were her people and Munich, the city of her birth, was where she had spent so many happy Christmases. During the revolutions of '48, the royal family had come to stay with them because Max was so much a man of the people that they had felt safer in his palace.

As soon as the family arrived in Munich, the invitations began to pour in. Strangers came to call. Sisi felt as if she was on display. Everyone wanted to meet her. Wherever she went, people stared as if she was an object to be assessed and admired. Nené had been to balls in Munich with her mother along as a chaperone, but Sisi had never been out in society until she was suddenly thrust into it that winter. It was excruciating to be the object of so much attention, but, as everyone constantly reminded her, she must get used to it. She was determined to do her best.

Sisi moved away from the window and curled up in her father's favourite armchair beside the fire. It was a luxury to find herself alone and unoccupied. If the library had a lock, she would have used it.

Her father was well travelled and well read, possessing a library of twenty-seven thousand books between his various homes, many of them about history; few were novels. She loved this room, as warm and welcoming as an old pair of slippers: the dark panelling and worn carpet, the aura of snug masculinity, the smell of musty old books and pipe tobacco. Even when he was on one of his trips and hadn't used the room for weeks, her father left behind the sweet aroma of his presence.

She picked up her notepad, dipped a quill in the inkpot, and wrote:

O swallow, lend me your wings,
Take me along to far-off fields;
How gladly would I loose my chain,
How joyfully the binding band.

It wasn't that she didn't love Franz. She did. But she couldn't look forward to spring and the April wedding. She was overwhelmed by the honour, dazzled by the allure of a crown, yet she hadn't set foot in Vienna and already all the preparations and Aunt Sophie's never-ending strictures were beginning to weigh down her spirit. She dreaded what awaited her in Vienna, of which she'd had a foretaste in the last weeks. Sometimes at night, after a particularly gruelling day, Nené held her while she wept in desolation for the life she had lost and the one she feared awaited her.

The doorknob rattled, and Max entered. "Hello, Sisi."

"Hello, Papa."

"How was your lesson today?"

Her father had not attended any of the lessons of the little Hungarian. Shortly after Franz had returned to Vienna, Max had gone hunting in Silesia and had recently returned for Christmas and her birthday.

"I like Count Mailath very much. Why doesn't Franz like Hungarians? He says they are gaudy troublemakers."

"And the Czechs are bothersome louts, the Italians tricky intriguers, the Serbs and Croatians unwashed barbarians," Max added wryly. "Ah, my sweet naïve Sisi, did you think your husband-to-be was the gallant cavalier you met at Bad Ischl, the dashing hero with the impeccable manners who swept you off your feet? He is more, and he is less." Max took an end of his handsome moustache between thumb and forefinger and gave it a twist. "The better question would be why your Aunt Sophie doesn't like them because he has absorbed her opinions since birth. Initially, it was mere prejudice because she saw them as barbaric. Well, let me be honest, the Habsburgs are contemptuous of all the races they rule over, Germans, Slavs, Italians, Magyars, Romanians, Jews, because they're not Austrian. But when the revolutions came, the Magyars held out longer than any other people and cost the empire a great deal of money and lives. Did your tutor tell you about the reprisals?"

Sisi shook her head. For some reason, her heartbeat had accelerated. Reprisal was a word that didn't fit the Franz Josef she knew.

"No, he wouldn't because it would mean speaking against the empire and that he would never do. In Italy, some women who were heard singing patriotic songs were beaten with wooden sticks. Then a bill was presented to the local magistrate for the replacement of broken staffs and the cost of bandages."

71

"That's terrible. Did the same thing happen in Hungary?"

Max poured himself a glass of cognac, sat in the armchair across the fire from Sisi, put a match to his pipe and expelled a cloud of smoke. "And worse. As I said, they held out the longest. They declared Hungary a republic and Franz Josef dispossessed. It took the intercession of Russia and a combined force of three hundred and forty thousand men to quash the resistance of a poor country of five million people. From the Austrian point of view, their punishment fitted their crimes. When someone advised Field Marshal Schwarzenberg that clemency might be the wiser course, he replied: 'I agree, but first let's hang a few.' And so they did.

Max swirled his cognac and took a sip. "It was a reign of terror. Thirteen Hungarian generals were executed and many lesser officers imprisoned. The tribunals handed down over a hundred death sentences and more than seven hundred prison sentences. They couldn't find any incriminating evidence against the then premier, who tried to commit suicide by stabbing himself in the neck, so they shot him. There was one Austrian in particular, General Haynau, who had a lust for blood. Schwarzenberg and even the Russian leaders tried to rein him in, but nothing could stop him abusing women, shooting men. He shocked Europe. Well-born women who spoke against Austria were publicly whipped. Some of the officers who surrendered to the Russians were executed. Even the czar was outraged, and he is not a compassionate man."

He fell silent. Sisi stared into the fire and fighting tears.

"Perhaps Franz didn't know about it. Hungary is so far…"

"You will find that nothing happens in the empire without his knowledge. He works hard. He reads every directive, every memorandum from his advisers. He signs the orders. I will say this, though. He was little more than a boy at the time, in possession of a throne that has belonged to the Habsburgs for four hundred years, and it had almost toppled. Twice, he and his family were forced to flee. He is not by nature a cruel man, I am sure of that, but he was frightened. Fear is a greater motivator than hate. Instead of bandaging the wounds, he thrashed heedlessly about at those who threatened him. He knew no better."

Sisi wanted to believe he suffered a young man's dread that he might not be able to hold the precious legacy left to him by his predecessors. And there was the fear of defeat too – unthinkable to a young man.

"Oh, Papa!" She flung herself to her knees beside her father's chair and cried into his lap, not knowing herself whether she wept for the young Franz or shattered Hungary.

....

Franz arrived in time to celebrate Christmas with its fragrant wassail bowls and carol-singing, sprigs of mistletoe and wreaths of holly, and the twin spirits of the sacred and the profane. The twenty-fourth was Sisi's sixteenth birthday. Franz gave her a diamond tiara, a portrait of himself set in a jewelled bracelet, and a bouquet of red roses from the conservatories at Schönbrunn. Sophie sent a small silver breakfast service for use while travelling.

Sisi wore the tiara that night when she and Franz went to the Munich Royal Court Theatre. They entered to such a tumultuous reception that she was overcome by embarrassment. Even while the play was in progress scores of opera glasses were turned in the direction of the royal box.

On the following night, the king and queen held a ball at the Residenz. Sisi spent most of the evening on a dais between Franz and King Maximilian, while the old men of the diplomatic corps were presented. She spoke graciously the stilted phrases she had been taught: "How do you do, sir?" "I hope you are enjoying the ball..." followed by a word or two about their country or their sovereigns if she could bring anything to mind.

Franz looked on with a rather fatuous smile, while couples whirled around the dance floor. "You did very well," he said to her afterwards, but she was glad it was over. Introductions to important people were still an ordeal for her. She couldn't get used to the idea that she was more important than any of them.

Once the festive season was past, the circus came and as usual set up boxes and orchestra seats in the courtyard of the palace on Ludwigstrasse. Max, who was always home for Christmas and the circus no matter how far he might wander, enjoyed doing stunts on horseback to an appreciative crowd. Usually, Sisi joined him because she was proud of her horsemanship, but this year she only wandered among the circus people, accepting their reverential greetings and awkward congratulations.

Couriers arrived from Vienna every day bringing news of the worsening situation in the Balkans. Once again Franz was forced to leave precipitously. He was gone, and she felt more and more distanced from the life she had once lived and loved.

....

As the weeks went by Ludovika watched her daughter sink deeper into despondency. She recalled the previous year when Sisi and Nené had new gowns made for Bad Ischl: the shrill excitement, which was only to be expected of two teenage girls. Now, when Sisi had fittings of the most fabulous gowns Munich had ever seen, she was like a mannequin, turning, lifting her arms on command, with no interest at all. When new gloves or new shoes arrived, it was Nené and Marie who exclaimed in delight while Sisi remained unmoved. Her trousseau would go to Vienna in twenty-five large trunks. The only thing she took any interest in was her riding habits.

To Sisi, all this represented undreamt of luxury, but Ludovika knew that it was not a suitable trousseau for a future Empress. When displayed in Vienna, as was the custom, the courtiers, who cared about nothing but appearances, rank and wealth, would look upon it, and Sisi, in disdain.

She did her duty, however, by accompanying Ludovika on formal visits to the Residenz, where she was required to sit at Queen Marie's right hand and make polite conversation. And there were ceremonies to be attended

Franz came again in March. This time the most splendid gift came from Sophie: a diamond tiara inset with opals and a matching choker and earrings. His mother, he informed Sisi, had worn them on her wedding day and he hoped she would do the same. They were among the most precious of the Habsburg family jewels.

There were parties every night as the elite of Munich vied for the Emperor's attention. "Only another month and she will be mine," he would tell people, making Sisi blush.

When he left, she wept bitterly.

What little time she had of leisure she spent alone, often writing poetry that expressed feelings she seemed unable to share with her family.

She was becoming prickly, too. When the Emperor sent pearls that would have reached to her knees if worn in a single strand, she remarked that pearls were suitable for a dowager, not for a young girl. Oh, and the fuss when she had suddenly declared she would not go to another ball or soiree, she would not shake another hand, nor smile at another person who, until six months ago, hadn't wanted to make her acquaintance.

Ludovika knew what was troubling her daughter because she had the same concerns. "If only he were a tailor!" was Sisi's lament. She was happy and unhappy at the same time, causing an inner turmoil that manifested itself in aberrations of character. It was wonderful to be in love and to be loved in return but to love the man, his country and his people, to exchange a simple life for one of extraordinary demands and restrictions was too much for a young girl to handle with any degree of equanimity. All Ludovika could do was to offer Sophie, who had gone through more or less the same thing as a bride, as an example of proper behaviour.

Ludovika would have to accompany her daughter to Vienna of course, which was a great undertaking, such a grand court, the large family gathering, Viennese society, the parties… Neither of them was made for all that. Even thinking about it gave Ludovika a headache.

She had tried to persuade Sophie to postpone the wedding until June when, with much of the aristocracy gone to their summer homes, it would be possible to dispense with some of the events surrounding the wedding. The answer was an emphatic No! An Emperor of Austria did not get married every day, and not one iota of the festivities would be excluded simply because of the future Empress's unreasonable fears.

"I don't like to think of Sisi's moving away, and I would wish to postpone the moment forever," she said to Max in early April – April, when the days were getting longer, but for Sisi, shorter.

Max shook his head, looking sad and suddenly older. "She's already gone from us."

Chapter 9 – April 1854

On April 20th the entire palace staff was lined up to see Sisi off. Her eyes misted as she hugged some, shook hands with others. But she was unable to hold back her tears when she had to part from her youngest brother and sisters, who were not old enough to accompany her.

She had asked to be allowed to leave without an official ceremony, but the King of Bavaria arrived to see her off, along with his predecessor, Ludwig I, who had been forced to abdicate due to a scandal. All Sisi knew of the matter was that it involved a low woman and missing royal funds. It was a subject avoided by the Wittelsbachs. With them were their wives and other family members. A crowd filled the Ludwigstrasse, waving and cheering. Sisi stood in the open carriage and waved her handkerchief in the graceful way her dancing master had taught her. Her younger sisters, Madi and Spatz handed her a bunch of wildflowers they had picked from beside the river. Once again her face was bathed in tears.

"Do try to look happy, Sisi," her mother whispered as they took their seats in the state carriage. Max, Nené and her eldest brother Louis shared the back seat. Gackel sat on the box and sang the songs of their childhood in his clear, sweet voice. A year ago, Sisi would have joined in, but now she was quite sure her new dignity would not allow it. She couldn't help herself. Despite the beauty of the spring day, tears were streaming down her face as they drove out of Munich.

At Straubing, where the steamship *Franz Josef* waited, there was a reception by the grey-bearded dignitaries whose stolid hearts pulsed a little faster at her youth and beauty. She shook hands with a rheumy-eyed old soldier, his medals weighing him down, who called her a fairy princess. Little girls offered her bouquets and received a kiss in exchange. Bells rang. Brass bands played the national anthems of Austria and Bavaria. A gun salute accompanied her up the gangway, along with two Bavarian ladies who were to wait on her during the voyage.

She went aboard into a flower-decked dreamland. A rose arbour with a seat offered a charming place for her to retire to, and garlands of entwined roses looped over the ship's rail to hang down the sides.

Tubs and vases of flowers stood everywhere. Sisi was enchanted, but she couldn't imagine what the sailors thought of this floriated fancy. Her spirits rose as the ship pulled out into the channel.

The river was empty; no other traffic was permitted that day. The steamer passed through festively decorated towns. A general holiday had been declared for schoolchildren and workers. Those who had come to say goodbye to their princess lined the riverbank.

Sisi stood at the bow rail, waving her handkerchief until her arm ached, smiling until she felt her face would be permanently creased. They had come out to see her; perhaps some had travelled far. She did not want to disappoint them.

The following afternoon, the steamer docked at Passau on the Austrian border, where a triumphal arch had been erected. Two more flower-decked steamers escorted her through upper Austria. At six o'clock the ships docked at Linz and there waiting on the dock to greet her was Franz. This meeting was not part of the programme and she wondered how many noses he had put out of joint by acting so spontaneously. She laughed for sheer joy when he bounded aboard and took her in his arms.

The town had arranged a splendid reception. Shyly, Sisi gave her hand to the governor and burgomaster and the local aristocracy. Choirs sang, and military bands played. The guilds put on pageants and little girls in their Sunday best offered flowers until her arms were laden. Later that evening at the Linz Theatre, there was a performance of *Die Rosen der Elisabeth*, followed by a torchlight parade with music. At four thirty in the morning, as fireworks sizzled into the night and exploded in a display of dazzling colours, Franz escorted Sisi to the burgomaster's house where she was to spend the night. He had to take his leave so that he could be in Nussdorf, the little village where boats discharged their passengers for Vienna, to greet her in the morning.

The ships got under way the next morning at eight o'clock and Sisi, though exhausted, was back at her post soon after, fluttering her lace handkerchief, smiling. She kept a wary eye on the sky. It looked as if rain would spoil the day.

By the time the ship arrived in Nussdorf, the sky had cleared, and the sun was shining. Sisi chose to wear a pink lace gown with a crinoline and a matching hat laden with roses. It seemed to her that Vienna must be an empty city, so many people crowded the lower slopes of the Leopoldsburg that it looked like a field of multi-coloured flowers. Their roar of welcome was drowned out by the thunder of cannon as the ship nosed towards the landing stage.

She could see Franz wearing one of his military uniforms, white tunic, black trousers, his chest glittering with gold braid and decorations, a hand resting on the hilt of his sabre, so tall and straight and handsome. Franz always held himself so rigidly she wondered if he wore a corset – as some men did, she knew, especially those who wished to disguise an over-indulged stomach. The ship had hardly come to a standstill before he jumped aboard, took her in his arms and kissed her, accompanied by a barrage of cheers from tens of thousands of throats.

"How was the voyage?" he asked as he led her down the gangway.

"Wonderful but tiring."

"You do look pale."

"I'll be fine after a little rest."

It was such a warm and exuberant welcome, she couldn't help smiling. After alighting, she bowed in the direction of the Leopoldsburg, and another great cheer went up.

"They love you!" Franz shouted. "As I do!"

Sisi kissed the hand of her aunt and future mother-in-law. Archduke Franz Karl, her future father-in-law, kissed her on the cheek. Then came a bevy of imperial relatives, members of the House of Habsburg-Lothringen, some of whom she had already met at Bad Ischl. Meeting new people was harrowing for her, but having Franz at her side always eased her nervousness.

Carriages were waiting. Franz rode in the first with Max, Sisi in the second with Sophie, Ludovika in the third with Archduke Franz Karl, with the rest of the family members following.

As the procession passed through several districts, each with its triumphal arch, Sisi smiled to see blue and white, the colours of Bavaria, in striped awnings on the streets, flower-women selling posies of hyacinths, forget-me-nots, and narcissi. Even the horses that pulled the fiacres wore rosettes of blue and white. Women sported blue and white hats and the Bavarian and Austrian flags hung side by side from balconies. The streets were thronged with happy laughing people, waving their own little flags.

Over the strains of music from street musicians, Sophie's conversation was a litany of must dos and must not dos, to which Sisi responded with an occasional nod or murmur of agreement while keeping her smile fixed in place and waving to the crowds.

They paused briefly at the Hall of Triumph, which was like a fairy temple, with mirrored walls, colourful hangings and flowers. On the left were the Viennese municipal council among the high clergy, the high military, ministers and provincial governors. On the right were the delegates of foreign nations and their ladies. Sisi particularly noticed the Hungarians, men with handsome black beards, wearing national costumes decked with gold and precious stones. For colourful elegance, they outshone the other nations.

Empty carriages jammed the approaches to Schönbrunn. By the time the procession turned in through the wrought iron gates the sun was setting. The guards presented arms. Sisi could see Franz ahead with his arm bent in a salute. Ranks of people jammed the lawns on both sides of a long avenue that led to the vast façade of the baroque palace. Sisi's heart quailed. There were more than fourteen hundred rooms, Sophie told her. It was a place in which one could easily lose oneself.

Franz himself opened the carriage door, helped her out and led her into the palace. In the Great Salon, a vast hall, another crowd of people, princes, prelates, ministers and generals awaited introduction to the bride. All spoke German, but some had the thick accents of faraway places. Then the Emperor's younger brother, Archduke Maximilian Josef introduced the Habsburg and Wittelsbach families to each other. Lined up and waiting to be presented in ascending order, were Sisi's staff. First and foremost was her chief lady-in-waiting, Countess Esterhazy-Liechtenstein, Sophie's dear friend, who had already shown herself to be as punctilious in her adherence to 'the way things are done' as the Archduchess. Sophie had picked each and every one of her staff from her ladies-in-waiting to her grooms. The two ladies who had accompanied her from Bavaria were dismissed with parting gifts.

Franz led her on a tour of the imperial apartments, followed by a large crowd, eager to catch every word. She learned to her astonishment that he was a man of simple taste. His study was small and utilitarian, the furniture rather plain. On one wall was a portrait of Franz and beside it the sketch done of her in Bad Ischl. His bedroom contained a single bed with an iron bedstead and a thin mattress. The imperial bedchamber was altogether different, with a huge bed and furnishings of a dark gleaming wood Sisi had never seen before.

"Jacaranda wood," Franz informed her. "It is a gift from the guild of carpenters."

She couldn't help comparing it to her charming little bedroom at Possi, with its scuffed walls and well-worn bed hangings. It was all so overwhelming.

What struck her most forcibly was the silence. Lush carpets smothered footsteps, doors closed without sound, and even when people spoke it was in hushed, reverential tones. No laughter of children, no servants singing, no music...

Later, in her salon, between showing herself on the balcony to the cheering populace and the planned banquet that she knew would continue until late, she was about to rest on the chaise, when Countess Esterhazy handed her a voluminous document entitled, *Ceremonial Procedure for the Official Progress of Her Royal Highness, the Most Gracious Princess Elisabeth.*

"Her Imperial Highness humbly requests that you read and memorise it before tomorrow, Your Royal Highness," the countess said.

Sisi flipped through the pages and laid them on the floor beside her. "I would like to rest now if I may."

The Countess stooped to pick them up. "Very well, Your Royal Highness." Not even centuries of impeccable breeding could quite disguise the disapproval in the words.

....

Under grey, depressing skies, Sisi rode in a ceremonial procession from Schönbrunn to Augarten Palace, the traditional place from where imperial brides went to their wedding. For the occasion, she again wore a pink gown shot with silver thread, with a train, and a new wedding present from Franz, another diamond tiara. Throughout the previous day, she had not had a moment alone with him, or a moment to herself.

Accompanied by her mother, she travelled in a glass carriage with the panels painted by Rubens and pulled by eight white

Lipizzaner horses, their manes braided with red and gold tassels, and white plumes on their proud heads. White-wigged footmen in full imperial regalia walked alongside. The procession included the carriages of other court members, six imperial trumpeters on horseback, pages and forerunners in gold and black, mounted guards, the auxiliary bodyguard with colours and drums, grenadiers and cuirassiers. But Sisi was in no mood to appreciate all the magnificent ceremonial.

By this time, she was exhausted. The banquet the previous night had gone on until after midnight, and in all that time Sisi had not been able to relax her vigilance because every eye was on her and not all – few in fact – were well disposed towards her. Everything in the Austrian court was done with such precise attention to detail, and yet no one seemed to care that she got enough rest so that she was able to play her part in the proceedings with the poise expected of her. She imagined that to the members of the court she must appear gauche and apathetic, and not in the least what they would expect in a future Empress. Perhaps she would grow into her role. The trouble was first impressions were hard to eradicate.

As she entered the Augarten, she wondered how many other Habsburg brides had crossed this threshold, and how many had been as terrified as she was. She supposed there were many, and most were unloved. At least she had that – at least she had Franz.

She had no duties for the rest of the day, she was advised. But no sooner had she settled on a sofa with her feet up and the comforting presence of her mother and sister than Countess Esterhazy entered and requested she study two more documents: *Most Humble Reminders of the Procedures for the Wedding of...* The other, nineteen pages long, was a list of the various ranks of the guests and precisely how they were to be received and greeted.

'I can't possibly memorise all this,' Sisi protested to the countess.

The Countess compressed her thin lips. "May I humbly recommend Your Highness make an effort? An error in protocol can cause grave offence."

Advice was always offered 'humbly' or 'respectfully', but obsequiousness could not hide their pride or the disdain in which the members of the court held her.

She hardly slept at all that night, but she knew there would be no rest for her the following day, her wedding day. Refusing the lavish breakfast that servants brought in, she settled for a slice of toast and a cup of coffee. The first order of business was a bath. Ludovika and Nené came to her room, but they were not allowed to help. This was a matter of protocol. A bevy of maids and the ladies-in-waiting did the actual work. Countess Esterhazy gave the orders. It was she who selected the soap, lotions and the perfume that Sisi disliked.

The bath shirt that had shielded Sisi from critical eyes was stripped from her before she stepped out of the bath. One of the ladies towelled her dry while another wrapped up her hair. Another draped her in a soft robe, and yet another knelt before her and humbly begged her to lift her feet so she could fit the slippers.

She was allowed to do nothing for herself. When at her dressing table she reached for a pot of hand cream – merely to sniff it – a countess was quick to reach it first and offer it to her. They flitted around her constantly, like gaudy butterflies.

"Are you excited?" Nené asked as Sisi sat in a chair with her hair hanging over the back.

Sisi pasted on a smile. "Yes," she said for the benefit of others. But when she looked inside herself all she could find was nervousness so intense it bordered on terror. Today she would marry the Emperor of Austria. She wondered if Franz was also nervous. He was accustomed to grand occasions, of course, but he had never married before. Was he wondering now if he had made the right choice?

Her official hairdresser was called forth and began the long process of brushing and untangling the strands of her hair until her scalp tingled. The Countess handed her the nineteen pages of protocol for the reception of the guests, with a respectful request that she continue to study it. Ludovika and Nené took their leave, curtsying to Sisi as they did so and backed away three steps before they turned.

The ladies meanwhile were busy laying out all the items of apparel she would need. The gown was on a dressmaker's dummy. Sisi had never seen a more fabulous creation. There was an overdress, and an underdress of white and silver moiré, both heavily embroidered with myrtle flowers, and three layers of sleeves. The first was a close fit, decorated only at the cuff, the second wider and matching the embroidery of the overdress, the third just capping her upper arms, with a deep slash. A small bouquet of white roses and myrrh flowers had been prepared and pinned at the tapering waist. Finally, the diamond and opal tiara Sophie had given her would hold the diaphanous veil in place. She would also wear the earrings and choker. When she was fully dressed, the ladies spoke to her as if she was a real person for the first time, exclaiming over her beauty and the beauty of the gown. Looking at herself in the full-length mirror, Sisi saw what she had never seen before: that she truly was beautiful, at least as beautiful as Nené.

Even sour-faced Esterhazy smiled at her.

Outside, the procession was forming up: men in uniforms or their best top and tails, women in the crinolines Empress Eugenie had made fashionable in Paris. Horses and carriages took their places.

Sisi emerged from the palace into the sunshine and such a roar from the people when they saw her it was almost like a physical blow. She began to weep. The closest were so close she could see the expressions on their faces. The noise went on, rolling in waves across the packed platz, like the thunder of some thrashing colossus. She wanted to run back into the palace and hide from those tens of thousands of eyes.

"Highness," Esterhazy whispered. Just that one word with no particular inflexion, but it was enough that Sisi took hold of herself, spread her lips in a trembling smile and went forward.

Again she travelled in the glass coach with her mother, followed and preceded by the dignitaries of the empire. The coach rolled over the new bridge, which had been named for her. A score of pretty young girls dressed in blue and white greeted her with showers of rose petals. The Graben, an area of luxury shops, banked with flowers, and through the Kohlmarkt, the streets were so congested that the coach could only move at a snail's pace. People broke through the cordon of soldiers and police to get a closer look at her, shouting all the time, "Long live our Empress!"

Vienna was a riot of colour. Flowers carpeted the roads, window-boxes spilled over and garlands hung from lampposts. The blue and white flag of Bavaria, the red and white of Austria and the black and yellow of the Habsburgs, hung over the streets. Copies of

83

Sisi's picture were on display. The people roared out their delight, forgetting in these moments of glittering pageantry the high unemployment, poverty, the poor harvest of last summer and that Austria hovered on the brink of war.

The carriage came to a halt outside the church of St. Augustin, the parish church of the Hofburg. Sisi was shown to a small room where Sophie was waiting with her mother. Sophie gave her a close inspection, smoothed out her skirts and pronounced herself satisfied.

In the two days since arriving in Vienna, Sisi had not had a moment alone with Franz. She wanted nothing more than to go back to her simple, uncrowded life. But she drew back her shoulders. Her ordeal was almost over.

When she entered the nave between her mother and future mother-in-law, a gasp went up from the congregation. Murmurs of admiration accompanied her down the red carpeted aisle as the elite of Vienna craned their necks to catch a glimpse of Franz Josef's bride. Standing before the altar with Count Grunne, Franz turned to watch her and his love shone in his face for all to see. For Sisi, that look made everything else bearable.

Almost a thousand people were packed inside. Ten thousand candles and crystal chandeliers overhead reflected off gold and jewelled tiaras and necklaces, decorations on military uniforms and glittering fabrics. Assisted by seventy bishops, the cardinal performed the marriage service. Sisi gave the responses in such a soft voice that few could hear her, but Franz spoke clearly and confidently.

An exchange of rings, a kiss, followed by a salvo of gunfire from outside, and it was over. Or almost. First, they had to endure a long and rambling address by Cardinal Rauscher, who was famous for his long sermons. In the stifling atmosphere, Sisi was desperately afraid she would faint. She kept turning towards her husband, sending him a message with her eyes, but Franz appeared oblivious.

They left the church amid the pealing of bells and a fanfare of trumpet and kettle-drums to walk to the Hofburg with hands clasped. Sisi was surprised to find it was evening. *I will forget that I am the Empress of Austria, she told herself. I will only remember that I am Franz's wife, and then perhaps I will be able to get through the rest of this day and the years that follow.*

Chapter 10 – April 1854

The Hofburg was the seat of imperial government, with more than twenty-six hundred rooms. Sisi found it even more overwhelming than Schönbrunn. At least the imperial apartments, newly and magnificently refurnished by Sophie, were comparatively modest in size and number. Sophie drew Sisi's attention was to the precious objects with which Sophie had adorned the rooms: pictures, porcelain, statues and clocks from the collections of the Imperial House. The tapestries, rugs, curtains and furniture had all been personally picked out by Sophie, who was never slow to blow her own trumpet.

"I chose only domestic products in order to promote local trade," she said with pride. "You see, we think of every little thing that might contribute to Your Majesty's comfort and happiness."

But Sisi was shocked to discover there wasn't a bathroom in either the Hofburg or Schönbrunn. In Possi there was always the lake to bathe in, and in Munich her father had installed a *hammam* after returning from his travels in the East.

After a short time, the machinery of court ceremonial swung into motion. Further introductions to various groups in the Throne Room was followed by the ceremony of the Kiss on the Hand. All the ladies of the empire above a certain rank packed the audience chamber, hundreds of them in their family heirlooms and shimmering silks, to claim their right to kiss the Empress's hand, among them her mother and her mother-in-law. When Sisi saw them all, she was overcome and fled to an adjoining room where she burst into tears. In the audience chamber, the ladies waited, whispering to one another behind their fans, not at all impressed by this behaviour.

Sophie hurried after Sisi. Ludovika followed and took it upon herself to close the intersecting door. Sisi had flung herself down on a couch and was shuddering uncontrollably.

"Elisabeth!" Sophie snapped. She had instructed Sisi to call her Madame Mere. "Come along now. You are showing disrespect to people who have travelled far distances to do you honour."

"It surely cannot be right that I must submit to having my hand kissed by ladies who are old enough to be my mother or my grandmother."

"Young as you are, you are now the highest in the land and must accept their homage."

"I can't…So many people…"

"What? They are the most illustrious subjects of our great empire, not a mob. They will approach you one at a time. All you have to do is sit there. How hard can that be?"

"Please, Aunt, may I not be excused…"

"No, you certainly may not." Sophie's voice was becoming strident. "Some of these ladies had hopes of marrying the Emperor themselves, but he honoured you. You have duties to fulfil, and you must discipline yourself to it. You cannot just run off like a child because you are expected to do something you don't like."

Ludovika edged Sophie aside, sat down and took Sisi in her arms. "It will be all right, my pet," she said, as Sophie glared down at her. "Remember, Franz chose you to be his Empress. You are superior to all the ladies out there. Remember, too, that you are a Wittelsbach. We are an indomitable breed." She produced a handkerchief and mopped Sisi's tears. "There, now. When you are ready, you will go back in there with your head held high and do those ladies the honour of receiving their salutations."

Eventually, Sisi declared herself ready to return.

"You must speak to each one," Sophie reminded her. "No one is allowed to speak to you until you address them."

Ludovika opened the door. Sisi took a deep breath and went through. The room went quiet enough to hear the whisper of her sprigged muslin gown rustle as she resumed her seat. One by one the ladies came forward, curtsied, kissed her gloved hand, which was resting on a satin pillow, and waited uncertainly a moment or two before retiring. Sisi didn't know what to say. She didn't know them at all beyond their titles, which were forgotten as soon as she heard them. So she remained silent, and the ladies backed away with indignant looks they didn't try to hide. Finally, at Sophie's direction, Countess Esterhazy went among them to pass the word that they should address a few words to Her Majesty if they felt so inclined. Even so, Sisi was able to respond only in the terrified whisper of a frightened little girl.

Among those who were waiting, Sisi caught sight of her cousins, Adelgunde and Hildegard, and a genuine smile bloomed. When they came forward, she didn't give them the opportunity to kiss her hand, but rose to her feet, smiling and extending her arms for a hug. Subdued titters rose from among those who witnessed it. Sisi knew at once she had erred again and froze.

Sophie reacted with outrage. "Empress, you must resume your seat." Her voice was a furious whisper.

"But, Madame Mere, these are my cousins. We always greet each other with an embrace."

"That was fine for a princess of Bavaria. You are now the Empress of Austria and cannot behave as you wish. Resume your seat at once."

Docilely, Sisi sat down and allowed her cousins to kiss her hand.

The ceremony lasted for two hours. When it was over, Sophie, who had recovered her temper, delivered a chilly rebuke. "The purpose of ceremonial is to demonstrate the power of the Crown. When you depart from established procedure, you undermine that power. Today, you were about to deny two young women the honour of kissing your hand. I repeat: the honour! For the sake of familial affection, you would have insulted them and diminished them in the eyes of their peers."

"I'm sorry, Aunt. It was just…" She glanced at Franz, hoping he would speak up for her.

"We all know you meant well," he said.

She felt the tears welling in her eyes. *I will not cry*, she told herself. It seemed she had done nothing else since her arrival in Vienna.

"I gave you documents to study," Sophie went on. "Where in there did it say anything about embracing your cousins? Hmm? Protocol, Elisabeth! It is a matter of everyday practice."

"I'm sorry I disappointed you. I will try to do better."

Ludovika slipped an arm around her slender waist. "You are doing very well," she said, before adding in a harder voice to Sophie: "It is a lot for such a young head to bear, isn't it?"

But Sophie would not bend. "She will have to learn to accustom herself to it."

. . . .

The newlyweds went in an open carriage to watch the illuminations in Michaelerplatz. Whole streets had been turned into ballrooms. Musicians played outside the cafés and on street corners, and the Viennese danced the night away to the latest Strauss waltzes. The great houses were illuminated and their gardens thrown open to the public.

Upon returning to the palace, there was the wedding banquet to get through. It began at ten o'clock. Sisi hadn't eaten anything since toast that morning – so long ago it seemed now – and although Franz tried to tempt her she still couldn't eat. Her stomach felt tied in knots in dread of what was to come. Her mother had told her what was to happen, but she couldn't imagine such intimacy with a man, not even with Franz, who she was sure would be kind and gentle. It all seemed horribly embarrassing, and sordid, too.

'It is a woman's duty,' Ludovika had said. 'It is especially important that you give your husband a son, an heir to the empire. We all must go through it, and we all get used to it in time.'

She had often seen animals rutting without paying much attention, but one day after this little talk with her mother, she watched a stallion and mare that had been put into a field to mate. The stallion was violent in his approaches, and the mare wasn't always appreciative. Sometimes she tried to nip him, before giving in and letting him have his way. Or perhaps the nipping was part of the mating ritual. *I know nothing*, Sisi thought in despair.

"Just lie still and let Franz take the lead," her mother advised.

She sat beside Count von Weckbecker during the banquet. While Franz was engaged elsewhere, the count did his best to engage her in light conversation. She assumed he was trying to distract her from dwelling on what was to come and thought it awfully kind of him. She kept looking at her mother and sister. They were seated far from her.

It was past midnight when Sophie put an end to the festivities: "I think it time for the bride to retire. She looks exhausted."

Sisi rose. Everyone at the table rose simultaneously. Franz took her hand and kissed it. "I will be with you shortly," he said softly. Sisi blushed in embarrassment.

Preceded by twelve pages with candelabra, Sophie and Ludovika escorted her to the imperial bedchamber. It was a beautiful room with blue silk wallpaper, a huge crystal chandelier, porcelain vases filled with flowers, shiny parquet flooring and the most magnificent bed Sisi had ever seen.

"This was Maria Theresa's bed," Sophie said with considerable pride. Half a year ago Sisi hadn't known who Maria Theresa was, but now she knew she was a Habsburg Empress who had ruled after her husband's death and was still revered in Vienna. It was Maria Teresa who had turned Schönbrunn from hunting lodge into an imperial palace.

Tactfully, Sophie then disappeared into an adjoining chamber. It was entirely due to Sophie's knowledge of Sisi's shy nature that putting the bride and groom to bed was done so discreetly, rather than being attended by half the court, as was often the case. Even so, two lady's maids undressed Sisi. Raised to be independent, and extremely shy, she found it excruciating to be dressed and undressed by strangers.

It was the first time she had had an opportunity to talk alone with her mother since arriving in Austria, but she didn't take it. She was so tired and afraid that if she started talking she would also start crying. Her mother's joy in the honour of having a daughter as Empress of Austria, she knew, had been entirely eclipsed by pity. There was a chance Ludovika might start crying too, so their words to each other were banal.

"The wedding ceremony went well, I thought," Ludovika said.

"It was very hot."

"Seventy bishops! Such excess!"

"Yes."

"You make a very handsome couple."

"People say that about all brides and grooms."

"Don't be cynical. It doesn't become you. And you know it's true."

"What shall I do with my hair, Mimi?"

"You had better take it down. It's traditional. After tonight you may leave it braided and under a night cap."

Not until Sisi was in bed, reclining among a mound of pillows and clutching her mother's hand, did Sophie return.

"Do your duty, child," she said and leant over to kiss Sisi on the brow. "I will let him know you are ready."

When Ludovika tried to move away, Sisi clung to her hand. "Mimi…" Almost she said, *Don't leave me*. How ridiculous! This was something she had to do alone. There was no one to encourage or advise her, and no one to rebuke her if she didn't get it right.

A knock sounded on the door. How polite he was. Sisi slid down in the bed, hiding her face in her hair, and peeped at him only long enough to see that he had put aside his uniform and was wearing a claret-coloured silk dressing gown. How odd to see him thus, like an ordinary man, not at all like the Emperor of half of Europe. She peeped again. Sophie had followed him.

Ludovika disengaged her hand and kissed Sisi on the crown of her head. "God bless, my darling," she whispered and went to the door, where she waited for Sophie to join her.

Sophie looked as if she wanted to say something meaningful, but settled for, "Good night, children."

They were alone. Franz sat on the side of the bed. Sisi's heart was thumping against the cage of her chest.

"Come out of there," he said playfully.

When she didn't move, he brushed the hair away from her face to expose one cheek. She turned her face into the pillow. After further coaxing, she rolled onto her back. Franz peeled the covers away from her. Sisi was wearing a satin and lace confection that had been created especially for the occasion, but she still felt terribly exposed. She resisted the urge to pull the bed covers back up around her shoulders, and cowered and shivered inside the shell of herself. As Franz got into bed, she was relieved to see that, although he had removed his dressing gown, he wore a nightshirt.

"How do you like married life so far?" he asked in an attempt to lighten the mood.

Sisi couldn't speak. She merely gave a quick jerk of the head.

"I think it splendid. I have looked forward to this day for so long. Do you remember the day we met in Bad Ischl? I knew then, the moment I saw you, that I wanted you for my wife. We will be so happy together. I can give you anything you want. Anything in the world. You just have to name it."

It sounded to Sisi almost as if he were pleading with her. When he touched her – a light touch on her shoulder – she cringed.

"Are you afraid?" he asked gently.

She nodded again, not daring to look at him.

He was silent for some moments. Then: "Perhaps tonight we could just kiss and cuddle. There's plenty of time. We have the rest of our lives."

The tension went out of her body as if evaporating through the pores of her skin. "That would be nice."

But it wasn't nice. It wasn't like those occasions when Franz had kissed and held her before. She could sense his restraint, and in spite of her innocence, she knew when that restraint began to weaken.

She eased away from him. "May we sleep now?"

"Of course, my dear, sweet wife. But, Sisi, you must…do your duty. There are princes of the empire inside your body waiting to be born."

"I know. It's just…I'm terribly tired tonight."

Although she was exhausted, Sisi slept badly. The next morning, she was having breakfast with Franz in the cosy room adjoining their bedchamber when Sophie and Ludovika walked in. Sisi rose to embrace her mother, who then suggested to Sophie that they leave. Always the soul of courtesy, Franz invited them to stay and have some breakfast, and Sophie was quick to accept.

Barely was she seated when Sophie leant over to Sisi and inquired archly: "How well did my son perform last night?"

Sisi glanced wildly at her mother, her husband, and the hovering servers. Embarrassment stung her cheeks. "Madame Mere, I…" It was on her tongue to tell her aunt that it was not her business, but of course, it was. It was everyone's business. Instead, she excused herself and left the room, her breakfast barely touched.

Before the day was out the news was all over the palace that the imperial marriage, on which so much time and effort and hundreds of thousands of gulden had been spent, that grand pageant of ceremonial, so glamorous and matchless that the watching world had sighed in wonder, had not been blessed by the crowning ritual of consummation.

It was not until the third night that Sisi resolved to get the ordeal over. Although at first Franz tried to be patient and gentle, there came a time when he lost himself and turned into someone without restraint, without tenderness. She found the process both humiliating and painful.

"Did I hurt you?" When it was over, he became his usual caring self.

She shook her head and edged away from him. Her mother had warned her that it always hurt the first time but after that it would become easier.

The next morning they were invited by Sophie to join the rest of the family for breakfast. Sisi protested; she couldn't bear the thought of facing them when they would all know...

"It will please Mother. And it will please me." Franz said. There never was any gainsaying Sophie.

As soon as they entered Sisi caught a swift look between Franz and his mother that conveyed everything Sophie wanted to know.

"My dear children!" Sophie exclaimed. Each received a kiss on the cheek, Franz beaming, Sisi miserable with embarrassment. Later, one of Sisi's chambermaids came in and leant down to murmur something to Sophie, who nodded and waved her away.

By noon the entire palace knew that the marriage had been consummated. Sisi wanted nothing more than to hide in her rooms, but that was impossible. She was the Empress. Sophie had said she must show herself to as many people as possible. "Why?" she had asked.

"Because you are the Empress."

Chapter 11 – April-May 1854

A week of festivities had followed the wedding, interspersed with official duties. Franz attended to his paperwork and met with ministers every day, and Sisi had her first official engagement. She stood between her husband and his mother to receive foreign delegates in an audience. When the Hungarian deputation entered, she was wearing a Hungarian national costume, a pink dress with a black velvet bodice and a pretty apron like a bouquet of roses, trimmed with lace. The delegates beamed their approval.

In a few short days, Sisi was introduced to some of the abstruse and inflexible rules of the court. Because she spent so long on her feet, she had diligently searched among over one hundred pairs of shoes for a comfortable pair, which she wore at the reception of the delegates and on several other occasions. But when she wanted to wear them for a gala dinner, Countess Ugarte, the most condescending of her ladies-in-waiting, informed her that she had already discarded them.

"But that's absurd! They were hardly worn."

"With respect, Your Majesty, it is the way things are done. The Empress cannot wear a pair of shoes more than six times."

Since Countess Esterhazy was not in the room, Sisi thought she might have her way in this. "What happens to the shoes when you discard them?"

"I believe they become the perquisites of the maids. Shall I ask Countess Esterhazy about it?"

Defeated. Sisi sighed.

"No matter. Fetch me another pair of shoes, please."

At a state dinner for a hundred guests, in a small gesture of defiance against the sometimes ridiculous iron-rimmed protocol of the court, she took off her gloves to eat and laid them in her lap. She heard a gasp from someone and looked up to see Sophie glaring at her. Since men and women were seated alternately and that same protocol forbade one to speak with anyone but an immediate neighbour, neither Sophie nor any of the other women present were able to "humbly" correct her.

Franz was on one side of her and Count von Weckbecker on the other. The count said, "Forgive my presumption, Your Majesty, but it is the custom for ladies to wear gloves at the table."

Sisi smiled at him. She liked him very much. "I know, and if I could see any good reason for the custom I would be wearing them still. Can you think of a good reason, Count?"

He smiled back at her. "No, Your Majesty."

After dinner, when she was changing into another less formal gown, Sophie came in and dismissed her ladies. Sisi stiffened, guessing that it was permissible for an archduchess to rebuke an Empress only if there were no witnesses. Not that it mattered; her ladies would be listening beyond the door, which was wide open.

"Why did you take your gloves off at the table? You know better."

"Madame Mere, I…I do not understand some of your customs. It makes no sense to me to wear gloves when eating… and so I thought…"

"These customs, as you call them, have been practised by the Habsburgs since the days of Maria Theresa, if not before. They may seem trivial and meaningless to you, but they are crucial in demonstrating the power of the Crown. They raise us above the common herd."

"I do understand the necessity of protocol and ceremonial. Truly I do. But, forgive me, Aunt, some of the customs are trivial."

The Archduchess stiffened. "You mean like discarding shoes once you have worn them six times?"

Sisi was not surprised that Sophie had learned of the incident. She already knew that everyone around her reported her every move to the archduchess.

"The monarchy won't fall because I wear shoes more than six times, or if I take my gloves off to eat. Handling a knife and fork, even glasses, wearing gloves makes one clumsy."

Sophie stiffened at the implied criticism to the hallowed protocol of the court. "Your Majesty evidently thinks you are still in the Bavarian mountains. If you wish to be happy here, you must learn to fit in. It is not for us to change hundreds of years of tradition to suit you. I hope that is understood?"

"Yes, Madame Mere."

"Most young girls would have gratefully received such a magnificent honour, even enjoyed it," Sophie muttered as she moved away.

Thinking about the incident, Sisi realised that what her father had told her was true. Sophie was regressive and repressive. Change was anathema to her. Sealed in her palaces, where she was the supreme mistress, she was unable to see that the world around her was changing, and with it people's perception of monarchy; absolutist rule was as outdated as the periwig. The common people wanted a voice. The worst of it was, she had inculcated her views into Franz. When he came to bed that night, she complained to him of Sophie's bullying.

"Be guided by her, my dear one," he said. "She knows what's best."

Shedding his robe, he climbed into bed. He looked at Sisi but didn't touch her. The touching would come later. It always did.

"My poor darling, you are exhausted, aren't you?"

In her mirror that night, she had noticed pale mauve shadows under her eyes. The sight had horrified her. "It is just that I am not accustomed to so much… It is too much!" It wasn't only the social engagements, one after another, each requiring a change of clothing, while Countess Esterhazy delivered a lecture about what was expected of her: when she must stand, sit, what she must say, what she absolutely must not do. The worst of it was the strain of trying to remember it all, to behave correctly, and the furious face of Sophie when she failed in some small detail, as she so often did.

"It has been such a busy week."

"But you enjoyed the circus, didn't you?"

"Oh yes, it was wonderful."

It had been a beautiful spring day, a national feast day, and it seemed the whole of Vienna had turned out to enjoy the spring sunshine. The venue was the Prater, the former hunting ground of the Habsburgs that Emperor Joseph II had given to the Viennese for their pleasure. Now there were kaffeehauses and cafés, leafy walks, beds of flowers, as well as an amusement park and the racing stables of the aristocracy. Her father had often spoken to Sisi about Herr Renz, who was the king of circuses, and Sisi loved every moment of the performance. They sat under a marquee, sipping champagne, in full view of the crowd. Her father was there too, and Sisi noted that he wasn't looking as glum as he had since his arrival in Vienna. He had told her that she would have to visit him in Possenhofen in future because he couldn't abide the court.

"I'll tell you what," Franz said. "I'll cancel all our engagements and we'll go to Laxenburg for a week or two. There are two palaces there, a castle and a thousand acre park for you to roam. The castle occupies an island, and its gardens are a replica of an English landscape, with several artificial ponds. You'll like it there and be able to get more rest."

"You mean, like a honeymoon?"

"Yes, just like a honeymoon."

"That would be lovely, Franz! When can we go?"

"Shall we say…in two days after your family has left?"

He reached for her then, and she welcomed him into her arms. It would be wonderful to have some time together without a bevy of attendants and every minute of every day circumscribed. How delightful to breakfast together without Sophie being present or to take a walk through the spring woods, just the two of them, her hand tucked into his arm.

The conclusion of the wedding festivities meant the end of her family's sojourn in Austria. With so many demands on her, it saddened her that she'd had so little time to spend with them. Now they were all going back to their peaceful country life and leaving her among strangers, in an alien and unforgiving environment. She wanted to go home. But there was no home for her among them. Home for her now was somewhere she didn't belong.

It was a tearful farewell. Sobbing, Sisi waved her handkerchief and they hung out of the carriage windows until the streets of Vienna swallowed them up. She ran back into her apartment and hugged her beloved dog Bummerl to her. He was all that remained with her from her old life.

. . . .

Franz was a dear man. Although he was as much a stickler for protocol and tradition as his mother, his tastes were simple. His private rooms were simply furnished and decorated with family portraits. He referred to himself as the first servant of the empire, and indeed, he was diligent in the performance of his duty. King

97

Maximilian was regarded in Bavaria as a good king, but Sisi was quite sure he didn't spend six or seven hours at his desk every day.

Franz was always courteous, never failing to thank a servant for the smallest service, and had never been known to lose his temper. He only made two demands of those about him: the greatest degree of silence possible and strict punctuality.

Sisi knew he was trying to please her: the gifts, this "honeymoon" to Laxenburg. Every day he told her how much he loved her. But presents and loving words could not compensate for an absent husband. She was shocked to wake up that first morning and find him gone. Not only from their bed but the palace. It was only then she realised he had chosen Laxenburg because it was close to Vienna. He had gone back to work and would return in the evening.

What was a honeymoon for one?

It was almost funny, she thought, as she began her morning toilette. Her mother had had to put up with her father's mistresses, while her own chief rival was her husband's desk! He could not bear to be parted from it for long.

She had hoped to leave her ladies behind. There wasn't one among them she felt to be a friend. On an occasion when Sophie had heard her laughing with Countess Paula Bellegarde, she had warned Sisi that it was unwise to develop personal ties with her attendants. If she did, they would be dismissed. She wasn't allowed to do anything for herself. If she were to pour herself a glass of water, Countess Esterhazy would deliver a sharp reprimand to her ladies because they had neglected their duty in not anticipating the Empress's wishes. Franz kept telling her that she was the highest in the land and had only to command to be obeyed. Yet when she had asked for a glass of beer, Sophie was there to remind her again that what was permissible for a Bavarian duchess was not suitable in an Empress. Sisi sighed for the days when she could drink beer and was able to put on her own shoes – a shabby pair, if she chose!

There were compensations. Even if Franz couldn't be with her, she would have some time to herself. The windows revealed a sodden landscape, but when the weather improved she hoped to slip the ladies and walk in the gardens with only Bummerl for company. And then, perhaps, a ride. She hadn't sat on a horse since arriving in

Vienna. Or perhaps she could have someone row her across to the island.

Her hairdresser was looping her braids around the crown of her head when Sophie came in to spoil her half-formulated plans. Oh, it wasn't a honeymoon for one, after all. The omnipresent mother-in-law was there!

"Good morning, Your Majesty." Sophie entered followed by her ladies-in-waiting. She was always in the best spirits in the mornings, before the trials of the day and a recalcitrant daughter-in-law soured her mood.

"I... was not expecting you, Madame Mere," Sisi said, trying to hide her vexation.

"It is not such a great distance from Schönbrunn. It occurred to me I ought to come and keep you company."

Sisi's heart sank to her feet. It was bad enough not having Franz here without her having to suffer the company of Madame Mere and her ladies, with their acidulous faces and unpleasant gossip.

"My goodness, all that hair. I still find it hard to believe it can all be confined atop that small head. Have you ever considered having it cut to a more manageable length, my dear?"

Sisi's hair was her glory. Released from its braids, it was a shining and abundant cascade that tumbled to her knees. Braided, it could be wound about her head or looped into coils of any length she chose. She would never have it cut.

"No, Madame Mere, Franz loves it."

Sophie smiled archly. "Well, Franz has left you in my care, so this would be a good time to begin your education as a Habsburg Empress."

All day long Sisi was in the company of a circle of women, Sophie and her ladies and her own ladies. Some of them brought embroidery hoops and bent their heads together in whispered conversation in order not to intrude upon the interminable lectures of the archduchess. She began with the history of the Habsburgs, relating the achievements of the Emperors but failing to mention their disasters, their less than heroic peccadilloes, their naughty little sins. Occasionally, one of the other ladies was invited into the conversation, but mostly it was the Archduchess, droning on, and on, and on...

Sisi sat with her back to the window, so she couldn't even look out at the depressing sky. She tried to concentrate on her aunt's words, but occasionally her mind wandered to beloved Possi. Her feet skipped over the breasts of the giants; she heard the birds twittering in the trees like gossipy women, the susurration of the breeze among the leaves; felt the cool water of the lake closing around her body. *Oh, but had I never left the path...* It would become the first line of a poem. She brought herself back to the present, to the recounting of Maria Theresa's gift to her husband and country of sixteen children. Thinking of Possi, dreaming herself back there, was always accompanied by an unbearable wave of homesickness.

Franz was back by six o'clock in time for a light supper, but the honeymooners were not left alone for their only shared meal of the day. Sophie and Count von Weckbecker were also present. In answer to Franz's questions, Sisi was forced to pretend she'd had a wonderful day. In fact, she had never set foot out of doors and it had been the most soporific day of her life. Sometimes after supper, weather permitting, there was time for a walk in the grounds, but never unaccompanied.

The pattern was set. Confined indoors by almost incessant rain, Sisi spent her days with the archduchess and her ladies. Even when she was able to walk in the garden, they were there, as constant as her shadow. When she went for a ride, two of her younger ladies, as well as guards, accompanied her. An excellent horsewoman, and daring, she rode as if she were riding away from Vienna home to Possi. When the guards caught up with her, the captain gently and humbly pointed out that if anything were to happen to her, it was they who would suffer the consequences. Sisi apologised and sighed, hearing another door clang shut. And then, upon her return to the palace, there was another lecture from Sophie to be endured about how it was unsuitable for an Empress to go out riding in the forest.

One of her duties at this time was to write letters of thanks to heads of state who had sent wedding gifts. Sophie provided drafts. Sisi only had to copy them. Before being sent on their way, Sophie read them and sent back anywhere Sisi had dared to deviate from the exemplar.

When Franz arrived in the evening, she was often depressed and homesick, particularly if Sophie had come that day. She hated to complain to Franz, knowing – or guessing – how burdened he was with the business of the empire, but after four days of misery she decided upon a plan.

"Do you have to go back to Vienna tomorrow?" They were finally alone in their bedroom, the door closed, the lamps turned down.

"I must, I'm afraid. World affairs do not stand still during a honeymoon."

"Then, perhaps I could come with you? I won't distract you. I'll just sit in your study and read. At least we'll be together."

"That sounds most awfully boring. I thought you were enjoying yourself here, enjoying the peace and quiet."

"I am but... Oh, Franz, I haven't even seen the island yet. I've only been able to ride once. My days are so confined! I miss you. We don't even have our evening meals alone. Your mother –" she lowered her voice "– she is so strict. She makes me feel I can't do anything right."

Franz sat on the edge of the bed and drew her down beside him. With his arm around her, she let her head fall onto his shoulder. "When I was a little boy I wanted to be a soldier. I cried when Mother told me I couldn't because one day I would be the Emperor. She had believed it even when old Emperor Franz was alive, and she began to groom me then, employing Chancellor Metternich, as one of my tutors. She couldn't stand the man – him with his three Austrian wives, and three French and three Russian mistresses – but she knew he was a brilliant statesman and in fact agreed with many of his policies and principles. She gained her political legs under Metternich.

"When Emperor Franz died in 1835 he was succeeded by his eldest son, my Uncle Ferdinand. Mother had not believed this would happen because Ferdinand was epileptic and barely functional, with a hydrocephalic head. While Ferdinand reigned, Metternich ruled, which suited him perfectly. Mama decided both had to go. It took little effort to persuade Ferdinand to abdicate. Having produced no children, his heir was my father, but the truth is, as you may have observed, Father isn't much interested in anything but hunting. According to Mama he suddenly developed a craving for possession of the imperial crown, but she was unrelenting until he agreed to

101

stand aside for me. Then she joined forces with those who wished to get rid of Metternich, and Metternich was gone."

And Sophie strode into his place. "I see." Sisi bit her lip. She saw very clearly. Franz was only eighteen when he became Emperor and, no matter how broad his education, he was a neophyte in the arena of world politics. He needed a Metternich, and there was Sophie. She had obtained the crown for him. He owed everything to her. Sisi imagined she would remind him of that fact whenever he stepped out of line.

"Do you?" he asked earnestly. "My mother is the guiding light of this empire of ours. She wants to help you become perfect in every way. You are very young and inexperienced, but if you allow Mama to instruct you, you will be an asset to the empire." He paused. "We are not ordinary people, Sisi. We are Habsburgs, chosen by God to rule. We must abrogate our own desires and always put duty first. Can you do that?"

"I will try." *I can't do that! I want to go home to Possi. I don't want to be an empress.* She felt a bubble of panic rising within her and went to the window. The curtains had already been drawn for the night, but she pulled one aside and looked out into the darkness.

Sophie was the real Empress. That was what Franz was saying. She ruled the court with an iron hand. She decided who was disgraced and who favoured. She controlled the council of ministers and they answered to her. Few decisions were made that did not have her nod of approval. And she, Sisi, was expected to obey like the rest. Her hands closed into fists. She would obey – she must, this was her life now and there was no going back, she had to adapt – but she would also, from time to time, test the limits of her own power.

"Believe me," said Franz, "I begrudge every moment I am away from you."

She turned from the window with a smile. "I will be the very best Empress Austria has ever had! And I will be the best wife and the best daughter-in-law." She sat beside him again, clasped his hand and rested her head on his shoulder. "But tomorrow I want to go with you to Vienna. It is only a little thing I ask. Will you allow me to be with you? Please."

Franz heaved a theatrical sigh. "Oh, very well. It seems I can deny you nothing." He smiled and tapped her nose with his finger. "But only if you promise to be good."

"I solemnly promise."

When Franz left the palace, almost everyone was asleep, so after dressing herself, Sisi had no difficulty sneaking out with him. She kept her word faithfully, didn't even speak until he spoke to her and was able to watch him diligently attend to matters of administration. Twice a week he gave audience to anyone who wanted to see him. Usually, these meetings were brief because the petitioners were so many, but that day he spent an hour with the Austrian ambassador to Paris, discussing the Eastern question. Sisi sat in the next room, but she couldn't hear anything because they spoke so softly.

Upon their return that evening, she was confronted by a furious Sophie. "It is unseemly for an Empress to run after her man, to gallop hither and yon like an army serjeant!"

Two reprimands in one. *I would like to tell her what is unseemly.* Sisi's inherent courtesy and natural timidity prevented her from quarrelling with her mother-in-law, as well as a dreadful suspicion that any mutiny on her part would only make things worse for her. She wanted to stay on Sophie's good side, but sometimes it was hard. So she remained silent and took her chastisement as a schoolgirl from her headmistress.

There were no more trips to Vienna for her.

Two weeks of a stultifying regime and an escalation of the conflicts between Sisi and her mother-in-law brought Sisi to the brink of despair. The worst of it was they were all trivial matters, and their very triviality made them more painful. She came to dread the moment her mother-in-law would appear. When Sophie wasn't with her Countess Esterhazy was there to correct every misstep she made, to remind her of her position and how she must greet her visitors. The Countess enjoyed relating gossip about the noble families, whereby Sisi knew the countess gossiped about her. She could do nothing right and was constantly made to feel deficient.

Sophie was an obstacle to Sisi's happiness and made it difficult for Franz and Sisi to be together undisturbed. The longer the 'honeymoon' went on, the more isolated and abandoned she felt. When she was alone, she wrote home to Possi in an effort to relieve her homesickness and keep her dear ones close, and composed poems expressing her misery.

Franz did not understand her unhappiness, still less did Sophie, and neither made any effort to alleviate it. Eventually, she begged Franz to return to Vienna.

The honeymoon was over.

Chapter 12 – May 1854-January 1855

Sisi gazed bleakly around the opulent bedchamber with its jacaranda wood furnishings. Amid the splendour and shallowness of the court, she wandered like a soul disconnected from its corporeal self. In magnificent rooms, amid undreamed-of luxury, she could not hear her footsteps on the wondrous parquet floors or the marble stairs.

She was trapped in a gilded cage. There was no escape, no breath of freedom. This was to be her life now, and it would be a lonely existence. She could no longer expect to visit friends – not that she had any in Vienna – or ride her horse or stroll in the woods whenever the mood took her, or do anything that brought her the kind of simple, carefree joy she had experienced in her earlier life. Spontaneity was anathema, if not dangerous. If she wanted to visit a museum, she would have to give notice, and the museum was closed to the public and the director would show her around. If she wanted to go to the opera, an entire regimen of protocol was mustered. If she wanted to shop in the Graben, extra police would infiltrate the crowd. If she wanted to ride, a guard escorted her, and she would trot sedately before them. She was now the Empress and expected to behave as such.

To be surrounded by beautiful and precious things brought a degree of comfort. But to know she could have almost anything she wanted only reminded Sisi of the things she couldn't have and valued: freedom, independence, her family around her, Bummerl beside her during family dinners begging for scraps. She believed even Bummerl missed Possi.

No matter who she was with, whether the imperial family or her ladies-in-waiting or during the salon for the Viennese nobility that she was required to host once a week, she was always apart, sitting quietly while the conversation spun around her, mostly gossip, often malicious. Politics were seldom discussed at family dinners. She knew there was a war going on in the Crimea, with France and England supporting Turkey, while Austria, having mobilised troops to protect her borders, had joined neither the allies nor Russia. But she knew little else. Franz was naturally fully absorbed in these matters and spent many hours with his ministers and his mother. Sisi was excluded, she presumed because politics weren't the province of the Empress.

A tap sounded at the door and a smiling Franz poked his head around before entering. "Still awake, my angel?"

Franz was a nightly visitor to her bed. She was always awake, waiting for him. Waiting for it. She did not enjoy his attentions. Franz was often rough in his lovemaking, which she found odd because he was dispassionate outside the bedroom. Afterwards, he would often cuddle her and they would talk about the details of her day. That was nicer.

"I'm sorry you didn't like the play," she said later when it was over.

"It was rather boring and silly. But you enjoyed it – that's the important thing."

They had attended the Burgtheater to see *A Midsummer Night's Dream*, her favourite Shakespearian play. Sisi liked music, the opera and the theatre; she liked to dance, walk and swim as well as ride and enjoyed reading, especially history. The stultifying atmosphere of the Viennese court had not yet smothered a fun-loving aspect of her nature but she had little opportunity to indulge it. Once, she tried to discuss with Franz the poetry of Heinrich Heine, whom her father admired, but Franz dismissed him as a subversive Jew and showed that he had no interest in any poetry. They had little in common other than a love of riding and walking. Franz was all duty, didn't particularly like music, the opera or the theatre. He did enjoy riding and hunting when duty permitted.

His rhythmic breathing told her he was asleep. She stared up at the dark ceiling, wide awake as she often was during the early hours of the night. He was usually gone when she awoke in the morning and she saw him again only on ceremonial or festive occasions or at dinner. Even family dinners were formal, certain protocols observed. He was his mother's son. From his earliest childhood, he had absorbed her political principles, her attitudes and opinions, and on the rare occasions they differed he usually gave in. Sophie had not only ensured that Franz became Emperor, but she had also made him what he was, diligent in his duty, a man of honour and decency... but, as Sisi's had soon realised, emotionally and imaginatively stunted.

Now Sophie was trying to mould Sisi into the kind of Empress she wanted.

Yes, this was to be her life. Sophie had told her that if she wanted to be happy she must learn to fit in. How was she to do that? What was to be her role? She was the Empress, strictly ceremonial, a decorative adjunct to Franz Josef. Where was she to look for fulfilment? She didn't know. But she knew she must try.

....

In June Franz and Sisi went on a state visit to Moravia and Bohemia. A large entourage but, to Sisi's secret pleasure, Sophie was not among them. Unfortunately, Countess Esterhazy was, so Sophie would be kept fully informed of Sisi's lapses.

A flower-decked locomotive called the *Proserpina* took them to Brno, the capital of Moravia, where they attended a gala performance at the theatre. A highlight of the visit for Sisi was a public festival with sack races and rope dancing at which she clapped her hands in childish glee. A torchlight parade in Moravian costume featured a bride and groom with a wedding party, while fireworks filled the sky with a brilliant display of colour.

This, too, was something she would have to get used to, Sisi told herself. The crowds, the thunder of acclaim, triumphal arches, little girls in white dresses bearing bouquets, military parades, which Franz loved, the receptions and speeches and hand-shaking, before moving on and repeating the same performance, always with a smile on one's face.

In Moravia, Sisi began to fulfil her role as Empress. Without Franz, she visited orphanages, schools and a charity hospital. She was quite comfortable talking to people of the lower classes. The *Weiner Zeitung* reported that she "made a highly favourable impression by her gracious condescension and kindness." She would have been more thrilled if she hadn't known that the Vienna newspaper was censored.

"You are a huge success, my darling," Franz crowed after reading the article. The newspaper came to him ironed, to remove the creases and destroy any germs.

Then it was back aboard the locomotive for Prague. Sisi smiled out of the window as they passed through great tracts of forest carpeted with summer wildflowers and small villages with picture-book houses and people in colourful costumes. In Prague they stayed in Hradcany Castle, perched above the Vltava River, with a splendid view of the city. A full social calendar allowed them little rest. There were the usual audiences and official dinners. They laid the cornerstone of a church, opened a target shoot, visited a home for deaf mutes, an insane asylum and an agricultural fair, where they watched a demonstration of a new centrifugal pump and inspected horned cattle.

Sisi was introduced to the Bohemian ladies who could prove sixteen generations of aristocratic ancestors and were, therefore, worthy of being presented at court. It wasn't long before she came to realise that the Bohemian nobility, just like the Viennese, despised her for her shortcomings. Franz said she imagined it, but she knew she wasn't.

She attended so many military parades that she soon understood they were an integral part of any state visit. She sat in an open carriage, trying to look interested, while Franz on horseback watched the soldiers marching past in their formations. He didn't withdraw when it started to rain, so Sisi asked for an umbrella and continued to watch while thinking about what she would wear for the tournament on horseback the following day, which would feature a joust in medieval costume.

Again she had her own duties as Empress, receiving delegations and petitioners. The common people loved her; the newspapers were generous, and she believed her first state visit was a personal success. For her, it was more of a honeymoon than their stay in Laxenburg, for the simple reason that her mother-in-law wasn't present.

As busy as they had been, there was to be no rest. They returned to Vienna the day before the Corpus Christi celebrations began. Because church and monarchy were firmly yoked, the imperial couple had a large part to play. The army too was on display, lining the processional route in ranks, massed in public squares, with a final march past the Emperor on the Burgplatz.

Tens of thousands had come to Vienna to celebrate the festival. Sisi had tried to excuse herself from further public appearances, explaining that she felt herself to be too young and too inexperienced to take the place of an Empress in full dignity during that kind of public celebration.

To Franz, she admitted: "I am afraid of crowds."

"You'll get used to them, my dear. Duty first."

Sometimes, though they might be in the same quiet room together, she had the feeling that he didn't hear her – or rather that the thick blanket of august separateness in which his mother had cocooned him did not allow the penetration of another's pain. She protested to no avail.

In full court regalia, her gown with a long train, wearing a diamond tiara in her hair, she sat through the church feast almost paralysed with nervousness. Still so new to the people of Austria, whenever she appeared, she was the principal attraction.

So occupied had she been that it wasn't until several days after the festival that she realised she had missed her courses. Franz was away on manoeuvres in Galicia, but when he returned she didn't tell him immediately, or anyone. It was too early. Then, too, she knew that things would change for her, and not for the better, once it was learned she was carrying a possible heir. No one noticed – perhaps because of all the frenetic activity of the tour and the festival. It was a secret she cherished, marvelling that it had happened, not quite able to believe that a tiny pea-sized being was already growing inside her. If she were able to give the empire an heir, surely all those haughty aristocrats who thought she wasn't good enough would have to change their thinking.

In May, less than a month after the wedding, Sophie had said to her, "I believe your courses have begun," not bothering to lower her voice.

Sisi could feel the flush stealing up her neck. "Yes, Madame Mere."

Clear as words spoken out loud, Sophie's expression said: Even in this you are inadequate. Sophie was on tenterhooks, waiting to hear the good news.

She smiled to herself now at the thought of Sophie's reaction.

When she was naked, she surreptitiously looked down on herself, expecting any day to see her belly rounding. But it remained disappointingly flat and she began to worry that perhaps the Bohemian tour had upset her cycle.

Another month passed without the appearance of her menses and then one morning as she was dressing, she urgently called for her porcelain sanitary bowl and vomited. Sophie came at once.

"How long since your last course?"

"May."

"May!" the Archduchess echoed. "Send for Dr Seeburger." She hardly ever smiled, but now a most wonderful smile softened and illuminated her features, so full of warmth and approval that Sisi melted into her open arms. "Oh, my dear, dear girl, enceinte already! You have the Wittelsbach fertility." Releasing her, Sophie said to the ladies gathered round: "Now we must be sure to take very good care of Her Majesty." Exactly what Sisi feared. She was to be smothered with loving attention.

Sisi would have liked to make telling Franz a special occasion, perhaps a private dinner, just the two of them. Was it possible? No, it was not. There never seemed to be any logical reason behind these restrictions, merely the despotism of earlier times.

She had to tell him soon before he heard of it elsewhere. In the end, she persuaded him to a walk in the parterre garden that Maria Theresa had laid out a century earlier. By nine o'clock every leaf had been swept from the immaculate lawns and paths, every weed plucked, every imperfect flower head snipped off by the large staff of gardeners.

Even then they were not alone. Members of the court strolled behind them, but at a discreet distance. Sisi had learned that protocol ruled even a walk in the garden: certain members of the nobility had the right to accompany the imperial couple, and they guarded this privilege jealously.

They were walking down the central path when Franz suddenly stopped. "Do you see that hill?"

Beyond the parterre was the fabulous Neptune fountain, which featured a marble Neptune in a shell-shaped chariot drawn by hippocampi. Surrounding him were Tritons, half-man, half-fish, and other members of his oceanic entourage. In front of the group was the pool, its balustrade crowned with flower-filled vases, and beyond was tree-clad Schönbrunn Hill.

"I had the idea of cutting the trees down and having a path made up to the crest of the hill to some kind of monument... I don't quite

110

know what but something… something to the glory of the Habsburgs."

"I thought the fountain was the crowning feature of the garden."

He turned to her. "Do you disapprove?"

"No, of course not. I'm sure whatever you create will be wonderful."

"Yes. Can you see it there? Imagine –"

"Franz."

He was looking again at the hill, drawing plans in his mind. "Hmm."

"Franz, I am enceinte."

She had felt the sudden tension in the arm under her hand before he turned to look at her, his eyes wide with – there was no other word for it – astonishment.

"Truly? Are… are you sure?"

"Quite sure. We're going to have a baby, Franz. Isn't it wonderful?"

Suddenly she was in his arms, swept off her feet and whirled around and around, both of them laughing. A smatter of applause reminded them of the presence of their entourages, some of whom had guessed the reason for this indecorous and uncharacteristic display of imperial exuberance.

Franz put her down but kept hold of one hand. Gazing at her in adoration, he said, "My lords and ladies, rejoice with us. Her Majesty is with child."

. . . .

On a lovely crisp autumn day, when the trees of the Vienna Woods were changing to their countless shades of red and gold, Sisi visited the stables. Her horse was saddled and Count Grunne was with her. As well as being Franz's adjutant general and good friend, he was also the master of the imperial stables and a superb horseman. They often rode together and Sisi enjoyed his company.

She was about to be boosted into the saddle when Sophie came rushing in looking panicked. "Your Majesty cannot think of riding in your condition!" she said shrilly.

"A gentle canter cannot hurt," Count Grunne said.

"No, absolutely not. A fall could spell disaster."

111

"But I never fall," Sisi protested. Her opportunities to ride were becoming fewer in direct proportion to her obligations.

"The jolting could…" Sophie broke off. She softened her tone. "The early months of pregnancy are perilous. I suffered two miscarriages before giving birth to Franz. I beg Your Majesty to remember that your body is no longer yours alone. You share it with a Habsburg prince."

Sisi could muster nothing to say in negation. Handing her riding crop to a groom, she allowed her aunt to escort her back to the palace.

Riding had been one of her favourite pastimes for as long as she could remember. Her father had taught her how to do circus tricks. Her seat in the saddle was as secure as her feet on the ground. Not being able to ride was a sad blow to her, but she could understand the need for caution. She compensated by spending more time with her other animals, which were kept in Schönbrunn's zoo, along with a variety of other exotic creatures presented to the Habsburgs from the heads of foreign countries. The animals were well taken care of, so their offspring survived and were then given to other zoos.

This was another pastime of which Sophie disapproved. She had warned Sisi, very seriously, that she ought not to keep looking at her parrot, particularly in the earlier months, for if she did her child might grow to resemble one! She would do better to look in her looking-glass or at Franz. Sisi could hardly contain her laughter until the archduchess had gone.

Whenever she visited her animals, she made her ladies stay at a distance. She couldn't imagine what they would say if they saw her cuddling her rabbit or talking to her parrot. He fascinated her. His feathers were all the colours of his South American homeland: the blue of sea and sky, the green of the forest, the yellow of the sun, even the reddish blush she imagined in a Caribbean sunset.

"I will get a mate for you," she murmured. "Then you won't be alone all the time. It isn't a good thing to be alone. Would you like that? Perhaps you'll become a father like the Emperor."

"Sisi," he whistled. She fed him a sunflower seed. "More," he croaked.

Her pregnancy brought out a side of Sophie that Sisi had never thought to see. On a near-daily basis, food appeared in her rooms to tempt her appetite, and sometimes there were little gifts. One was a chess set, which Sisi couldn't play. Count Grunne undertook to teach her but she found the game utterly boring, and had to admit she had no head for strategy. Sophie showed an inordinate interest in her diet and general health. She was always present during Dr Seeburger's examinations. She excused Sisi from any official engagements that required her to stand for long periods and advised her not to wear a corset, which advice Sisi was happy to take. Dancing lessons were suspended. Sisi and her ladies were encouraged to spend their leisure sewing baby clothes and Sophie made sure Sisi had her feet on a footstool. Sisi had known for a long time that whatever she did was reported to Sophie, but now the spying increased. It was as if Sophie had eyes in every room.

In her sixth month when the chill winds of autumn were stripping the leaves off the trees, Sisi spoke to Sophie concerning a matter that had been much on her mind. "Madame Mere, isn't it time we started making preparations for the baby's arrival?"

"Your Majesty is not to worry. I assure you, everything will be in order when he arrives." Sophie always referred to the baby as a boy.

"But the nursery. I thought perhaps…"

"Do not to concern yourself with such details, Elisabeth. I am perfectly capable of attending to these matters while you give your full attention to getting well and producing a healthy baby."

The solicitous mother didn't entirely eclipse the martinet. Pregnancy was no excuse to hide away in her rooms, Sophie decreed. "You must show yourself publicly as often as possible. The people want to see you in all your glorious fecundity. Take a walk in the platz, or the public garden at Schönbrunn."

Sophie had already won the first argument, that Sisi's gowns be altered to show her burgeoning stomach to maximum effect. Sisi hated her disfigurement and was horrified at the thought of parading it before the staring eyes of the public. Sophie had to take her by the hand to make her do so. As her pregnancy advanced, Sophie would drag her outside to show herself on the balcony.

"Remember that this is a child of the empire. The people want to see you growing large and in good health."

But she was not in good health. As the months passed, her health declined and she became depressed. The baby felt like a lump of iron. She was often nauseous and suffered headaches that

113

confined her to bed, only rising when Franz came and they would take tea alone together, so eager was she for his company. He always remained tender and considerate. Sisi imagined herself a fragile butterfly, and Franz's the hands that gently cupped her.

....

Christmas came and went with nothing to mark it except extra ceremonies in palace and church. Roast goose was served for dinner, with all the protocol that was such an integral part of the family's tradition that Sisi wondered if they could function without it. She had an image of them all running about without direction, falling over, crashing into one another and flailing helplessly. After dinner family members exchanged gifts. As she opened hers and tried to find new words to express how pleased she was, she thought of the jolly Christmases she had spent with her family in Munich. Gifts, although not expensive or extravagant, would be received with ecstatic shouts instead of polite phrases. Each of the children would be allowed to have a Christmas tree in their bedrooms and competed with one another in decorating it attractively. Cloves and pine spiced the air, and neighbours would draw up in their sleighs, cheeks and noses nipped with the cold, to crowd around the roaring fire and enjoy the special punch Papa claimed was an old family recipe, and the little cakes and biscuits only made at Christmas. Children would romp everywhere.

She went to bed feeling her isolation more than ever. Her only consolation was the baby growing within her. Once the child was born, she would have someone who would love her for no other reason than the love she gave in return. The relationship of mother and child was unique. No one would ever be able to take that away from her. No one would ever come between them.

Huge ceramic stoves that matched the room's decor heated the Hofburg and Schönbrunn. The stoves were once stoked using wood by the imperial court stove-stokers from passages that ran behind the walls to keep smoke and dirt out of the rooms. During the present century, they had been converted to a hot air system.

She awoke in the morning coughing. The trouble with the stoves was that when there was a sudden drop in temperature, which had occurred the previous night, it took them some time to adjust.

114

When they finally did there was likely to be a rise in temperature and they would have to be allowed to cool down again. She ordered a furred bed robe brought and snuggled down into her warm nest.

Countess Esterhazy came in with the robe, which she draped over the back of a chair. "Is Your Majesty planning to stay in bed all day?"

"No, I am waiting for the room to warm a little." She broke off to cough again.

"It is the Feast of St. Stephen. You are to proceed with the Emperor to the cathedral for Mass at nine o'clock." The countess opened the curtains with a swift flick of the wrist. Sisi could tell by the light it was snowing. She turned her face away. "After dinner, you are to give the boxed gifts to the servants. There are over five hundred servants including your own. Each is to receive a gift commensurate with his or her station. The boxes are of different sizes to avoid mistakes. Prince Lobkowitz will hand you the boxes and you will pass them on to the servants with a simple 'Thank you for your service'. Pray, do not extemporise even with your own servants. You will remain seated. I suggest, given Your Majesty's delicate problem recently, that you void your bladder immediately beforehand."

Sisi opened her mouth to protest that she certainly didn't need anyone to tell her when to empty her bladder, but snapped it shut again. What was the use? Once, on the occasion of a family dinner, and then again when she was in church, she had had to excuse herself, and now even her peeing habits were the subject of admonitions.

"The ceremony will take place in the large salon. Come along now." The bedcovers were whisked back with the same brisk hand that had opened the curtains. "Countess Bellegarde has your elixir prepared."

Throughout the day, Sisi could hardly stop coughing.

....

When she asked again about preparations for the baby in the seventh month, Sophie said, "Come. I will show you. I think you'll be pleased."

115

It was a charming room, bright and spacious, with frescoed walls featuring exotic landscapes of trees lush with fruit, water and birds that had a three-dimensional quality. The rococo ceramic stove fitted perfectly into the background with its motifs of flowers and a tiny bird perched on top about to take wing.

"It was executed by Bergl. He's brilliant, don't you think?"

For furniture, the room contained nothing but a gilded cradle and a rocking chair. Adjacent was the utility room. Here were great cupboards full of linen, a baby bath, toys, clothing, all the paraphernalia a baby could need, as well as two adult cots, an ironing board and some chairs.

"I hope Your Majesty will agree that nothing is lacking for the care and comfort of the infant."

"Yes, it all looks wonderful." Sisi's heart was beating fast and hard. She forced herself to look at her mother-in-law. Her eyes stung with threatening tears. "I only wonder why the nursery is here next to your own bedroom and not closer to my own rooms. It is such a long way for me to come."

Sophie's eyebrows rose as if she were surprised by the question. "Why, so that I will be on hand to closely supervise his care. I assure you he will not be neglected," she added indignantly.

"But, Madame Mere, I am the child's mother. Surely I should be the one to supervise its care."

"Your Majesty is too young, too inexperienced. You know nothing about the care of babies. This infant is too precious to be left to the supervision of a young girl."

At once, Sisi turned away and hurried to the door. It was rude but she couldn't help herself. The tears were spilling over and she didn't want her mother-in-law to see them. Behind her, she heard Sophie say, "It's for the best."

There was nowhere she could go to hide her distress, only her own rooms. But as she was about to enter her salon, she heard Countess Ugarte say: "She hasn't even learned court protocol."

"It is because of her upbringing," Karolin Lamberg replied.

She could not reach her bedroom without going through the salon. Nor could she hide her tears from their prying eyes. There were three of them, huddled on a sofa. They rose as she entered the room. She stared at each one in turn, until each dropped her eyes, looking shame-faced.

Pleading a headache, she remained in bed for the rest of the day with the door closed. Sophie came and tried to rally her but only succeeded in making her cry again. Exasperated, Sophie went away. When Franz came to bed, she pretended to be asleep.

Chapter 13 – March-April 1855

The great event happened one chilly morning in March. Sisi woke when Franz got out of bed after Ketterl's discreet knock.

"Franz."

"Yes, my darling, what is it?" he asked eagerly.

"Nothing. Just a pain but it's in my back, so I don't think the baby is coming."

"All right. If you're sure, go back to sleep."

He returned at seven o'clock. She was still in bed but not sleeping. He sat on the side of the bed and took her hand.

"How are you now?"

"I am still in pain, so I think I was mistaken. Our wait is almost over."

His eyes widened. He bent to kiss her hand. "Have you sent for Mother?"

Mother – not the midwife, not the doctor. His first thought was for his mother.

Sophie came at once with a piece of needlework to occupy her, both gratified and anxious, followed soon after by the midwife, who would be assisted by a chamber woman. Dr Seeburger would wait in an adjacent room in case of a crisis.

Franz left to attend to some business but returned at eleven o'clock. By that time, Sisi's pains had become much stronger, but for Franz's sake, she tried to put a good face on it. Even when she winced a little, he suffered along with her. He held her hand, kissed her repeatedly, spoke comforting words, and tried to reassure her that all was going well after glancing at his mother to make sure this was so.

Wallowing in pain as she was, Sisi was aware that her mother-in-law was giving the orders, the midwife obeying. When the pains became unbearable, when she could no longer contain her agony, Franz was so distraught that Sophie sent him from the room.

Just when she thought she was on the point of being ripped apart, a slippery mass tumbled between her thighs accompanied by vast relief. The sound of a baby's cry – the sweetest sound in the world – filled her ears. Franz came back into the room. He was weeping, and Sisi wept with him.

"It is a girl," Sophie informed him, "a big, healthy girl."

The baby was whisked away to be washed and dressed. While the women were busy, Sisi said: "Are you disappointed, Franz?"

"I am delirious with joy, my darling." His face proved his words. He couldn't stop smiling even through his tears.

But Sisi was disappointed. It meant she had to go through the whole sordid business again.

Enveloped in a long lace trimmed gown with a bonnet covering whatever hair she had, the little Archduchess was placed in her father's arms. Her name was Sophie. Her grandmother had decided that without consulting Sisi's wishes, as had the nursery staff. Baroness von Welden, who would have charge of the nursery – under the elder Sophie – had no children of her own and no experience with children. Hers was entirely a political appointment.

After Sisi had bathed, her bed freshened, and gown changed, members of the imperial family were allowed in to view the child and congratulate the proud parents. Sophie held the baby and sat next to the bed, with Franz beside her.

"Isn't she a beauty?" Franz asked his brother Maximilian, who was still a bachelor.

Maximilian stroked his handsome moustache as he pondered. "Well, now, she looks rather like a…well…"

"Like what?" asked Sisi. Maximilian had a reputation as a wit. She was afraid he would say something funny but unkind – perhaps that the child looked like a parrot.

"Like a baby. They all look the same to me."

"Your own won't," Franz said. "I have only just made the acquaintance of my daughter, but I am sure I could pick her out of a thousand others."

After a few minutes, Sophie clapped her hands. "It is time we all excuse ourselves. Her Majesty needs to rest."

"Come along, Max," Franz said. "We'll go and smoke a cigar."

The room emptied quickly. Sisi was very tired. Her eyes had already closed. Franz kissed her hands and face. "Rest well, my darling," he whispered. "I will sleep in my bedroom tonight so that I won't disturb you."

She thought he was the last to leave, but then Sophie was there. "You did very well, Elisabeth," she said and kissed her on the brow.

Sisi was grateful that she didn't say anything about producing a boy next time. But she had little reason to be grateful to her mother-in-law these days. It was her last thought before she fell asleep.

....

Congratulatory letters came pouring in, accompanied by gifts for mother and child. Sisi spent hours writing thank you notes until her hand cramped. There was little else to occupy her, as she was excused any official engagements. A week after the birth of her daughter, and four days after she had risen from her bed, she made the long walk to the apartment of her parents-in-law. Sophie was in the salon with two of the ministers. They rose and bowed to her. Archduke Franz Karl was reading a newspaper. He was a good and sweet man, but in the imperial court, he was a nonentity, entirely eclipsed by his wife.

"Your Majesty, this is a surprise." Uncharacteristically, Sophie appeared flustered.

"I came to see my daughter."

Before Sophie could respond Sisi went through into the nursery. She hadn't given notice that she was coming, because if she had, as on previous occasions, humble excuses would be sent as to why the baby was unavailable. Nor could the baby be brought to her. Carrying the precious infant up and down stairs and along draughty corridors was not permitted. Sisi could not understand this. Was the baby never to be taken out of doors for fresh air? Nor could she understand why she couldn't visit the nurseries whenever she chose.

Watched uncertainly by the two nursery women, she was reaching into the cradle when Sophie, who was on her heels, said, "Your Majesty!" in such a loud and harsh voice that Sisi, startled, snatched her hands back. "I must ask you not to visit the nursery without prior notice. It is important that the baby's routine not be disturbed."

But by this time Sisi had the child in her arms and was gazing down at her perfect little face in rapture. Tiny fingers with tiny nails curled around her forefinger and held. Slowly and carefully she sat in the rocking chair and looked up at her mother-in-law. "Are you suggesting, Madame Mere, that I must make an appointment to see my daughter?"

"I am asking that you show some consideration to the nursery staff by giving notice of your intended visit so they may have the baby ready for you."

"I have already done that to no avail. I was put off by excuses."

"That's unfortunate but unavoidable. The child has a routine, and we must all adhere to it. Any disruption may cause upset. Her well-being is paramount here."

"I do not think being held by her mother will cause her any upset." Sisi looked down at the baby and smiled. "See. She is perfectly content."

She was mildly surprised at herself for arguing with Sophie and also rather proud, but there was no question that she was in the right. And it wasn't a trivial matter – not to be compared with wearing shoes more than six times or not wearing gloves at dinner – it was a matter worth disputing. *She cannot stop me from seeing my baby. She can make it difficult, but she can't stop me.*

Sophie was angry, her nostrils flared, her mouth pinched into a disapproving line. She was entirely unaccustomed to her children opposing her, especially Sisi.

"And may I ask where your attendants are?"

"My attendants?"

"The Empress of Austria does not scurry alone through the corridors of the Hofburg. It is not fitting."

"But why not? It does not seem reasonable that I must wait for my ladies to assemble before leaving my apartment."

Sophie drew herself up. "A common housewife in the Leopoldstadt can go from room to room freely. The Empress must be representative of her exalted status at all times, with appropriate entourage. You now belong to the most distinguished family in the land. It is this adherence to proper procedure that puts us above the common herd."

"But is there some rationale for this restriction, other than that it has always been done?"

"Certainly. What if you fell on the stairs or had a fainting spell. Who would be there to help you?"

"I see." Sisi bit her lip. She supposed she would have to give in gracefully. "Thank you for explaining. I will not make the same error again. You may leave us, Madame Mere."

Sophie's mouth fell open in outraged astonishment. "Is Your Majesty dismissing me?"

"Certainly not. I am merely giving you permission to withdraw if you have better things to do, as I am sure you have."

Sophie continued to stand in front of her. Countless seconds passed while she hesitated. Then she dropped the briefest curtsy and turned away, but then turned back. Her mouth opened and closed, but it appeared she could find nothing more to say and went out. It was a treasured moment.

Sisi looked down at her sleeping daughter. "You have made me bold, little one."

One little victory changed nothing. Or rather, it changed things for the worse. Sophie became vindictive. Countess Esterhazy became more critical, Sisi more unhappy. Franz did not get involved although he must have known what was happening.

As little Sophie grew older, Sisi's opportunities to see her were even more limited than before. It was her nap time, or she had been taken for a walk, or she was receiving visitors. When Sisi was able to visit, she was never again left alone with her daughter. If Sophie wasn't present in her apartment, she came soon after, bringing a piece of needlework and chatting with Sisi about inconsequential things. If she was not able to come, Baroness von Welden stood in the doorway watching her every move. The message was clear. She was not trusted with her own child.

There was no doubt in Sisi's mind that Sophie adored her granddaughter. At family dinners, and even on more formal occasions, Sophie shared anecdotes concerning the child's care, development and adorable little habits. Sisi was able to contribute little.

Trying to see her daughter, the visits themselves, became such an ordeal that she seldom went to the nursery.

Chapter 14 – May 1856

Sisi was at Ischl, and had just come from the stables after visiting Forester, who had an open sore on his leg, and feeding him a few lumps of sugar. As she was walking back to the palace, to her astonishment, she saw a garishly painted hotel carriage draw up and her mother, brother, and sister alight.

She called, but they didn't hear her. Increasing her pace, she met them as they entered. After the joyous greetings and delighted cries of surprise, Sisi said: "But why didn't you notify me you were coming?"

"I sent you a telegram." Ludovika looked flustered. "Oh, Sisi, there was the most awful misunderstanding."

Nicknamed Gackel, Karl Theodor rocked on his heels with laughter. "Come, Mimi, it was hugely amusing!"

"The funniest thing I ever heard!" Mathilde said gleefully. Her nickname in the family was Spatz.

Sisi gave her sister another hug. "Well, let's have an early Jause, and you can tell me all about it."

In the salon, teacups in hand and cakes on a silver plate, Ludovika said, "I sent a telegram directly to you, to Empress Elisabeth. It said, 'Arriving with Spatz and Gackel. Mimi.' And I noted the time the train would arrive. When we arrived, there was no carriage. We waited and waited."

Mathilde giggled, and Karl smiled broadly, but Ludovika clearly wasn't amused. "What do you imagine happened? A servant from the hotel in Ischl turned up and approached us. He was carrying two cages. For the birds, he said, ordered by a traveller named Mimi."

It was too much. Mathilde giggled again, and Karl threw his head back and roared with laughter. Laughing with them, Sisi had to put her cup down quickly before she spilt tea on herself. Spatz and Gackel meant, respectively, sparrow and rooster.

"I suppose it is rather funny," Ludovika admitted with a smile. She reached for another slice of Sacher torte. "This is quite delicious." She looked her daughter over carefully. "How are you, Sisi?"

"A little queasy sometimes but not so bad as I was with little Sophie."

"Yes, it does tend to get easier with each one. But motherhood becomes you. You look radiant. Franz must be delighted."

"Quite the stud – our Emperor," Karl said with a smirk.

"Karl! Don't be vulgar." Ludovika admonished before she turned a beatific smile on Sisi.

"He is. So is Aunt Sophie. My productivity is one thing she can't find fault with me for."

Ludovika carefully put down her cup of tea. "Sisi, your aunt is not your enemy. Listen to her. She is very wise. She only wants to help you."

"She is like the rest of Viennese society. All they care about are appearances. She drags me outside to show my stomach so that the people can see I am pregnant. It is humiliating. She makes my condition a public spectacle! Surely it is enough to send a statement to the newspapers."

"She believes it is important for you to share yourself with the people. Besides, there's nothing shameful about being pregnant."

"I hate being stared at! I hate crowds! I ask nothing more of humanity than that I should be left alone."

"My dear, you must pull yourself together. You are a public figure now, not a private person. The greater one's social position, the less one has the right to give way to one's private grievances, or to neglect one's boring obligations."

"Does that mean I must be watched and spied upon all the time? Outside the palace, even in the garden, I see policemen lurking behind trees, peeking through bushes. When we are in the streets, they mingle with the crowds. They think they are invisible, but they are obvious. It's really too ridiculous!"

"It is for your protection. There are radicals everywhere."

"So I'm told. But we have imperial guards to protect us. Why must we be spied upon by policemen too? Even in the palace, they spy on me. Aunt Sophie chose my entire household, and they all report to her."

"Surely you exaggerate…"

"No, Mimi, I don't. I can't tell you the number of times she begins a criticism with the words 'I have heard' or 'I am told'. I dare not keep a journal because I fear the curiosity of my ladies. She

124

interferes between Franz and me and he always supports her, no matter how outrageous she is. I think she is possessive. She resents me because Franz loves me."

Feeling herself close to tears, Sisi fell silent. In letters to her mother, she had complained of Sophie's treatment of her, but she had received little sympathy. It seemed to her that her mother was in awe of her eldest sister and would never go against her. It hurt very much.

"She is possessive; I can't deny it. She doesn't lavish the same affection or attention on her other sons..." Ludovika stopped, seemingly aware she was criticising her sister. "I suppose that's only natural, Franz being the Emperor. And she made him so. He is the extension of her will."

"That's it," Sisi said. "That's exactly right."

"It is a rather sorry state of affairs," Karl put in. "An Emperor who rules millions of people tied to his mother's apron strings."

"Marriage is a hard business. I don't suppose I ever got the hang of it." Ludovika reached for her teacup and took a sip.

"I couldn't ask for a more loving husband. And yet..." It seemed love alone was not enough. Franz was neither sensitive nor perceptive; nor did he have an ounce of romanticism in him. Sisi was resentful that she was excluded from his working life, though he often complained that he begrudged every moment spent away from her. She was treated like a child and left alone for many hours of the day among strangers. Franz did not understand her at all and made no attempt to help her adjust to her role. He left that to Sophie, who was domineering and tactless and offended her on an almost daily basis.

Chapter 15 – October-November 1856

A towering wall of rock, displaying strata of different colours, hung over the path. A pleasant valley opened up in the cleavage between sheltering mountains. Bells jangling, a flock of sheep crossed the path, their shepherd shaking his crook to hurry them along. He paused to wave at the hikers.

After climbing steadily for three hours, Sisi realised she had not entirely recovered her strength after the birth of her second child that summer. Everyone was thrilled at this sign of her fertility until she produced another girl, when there was a general aura of disappointment. The baby was named Gisela, and she too was whisked away into Sophie's care. An open quarrel erupted between Sophie and Sisi when Sisi tried to insist the nurseries be moved and Sophie resisted.

"I think I had better rest here," she said to Franz. He was wearing lederhosen and a Tyrolean hat with a little tuft and looked as if he entirely belonged in an Alpine meadow. Sisi wore a heavy, waterproof loden suit and sturdy mountain-climbing boots. She sat down on the grass.

"All right, darling. Will you be able to continue after a short rest?"

"Better not. Why don't you go on? We have to make the most of the daylight. I'll just wait here and enjoy the view."

The view was of the Grossglockner, the highest peak in Austria, its crest snow-covered and soaring above them, its lower slopes clad in the deep green of pine forests. Love of the mountains was one of the few things they had in common.

"If you're sure…"

"Perfectly sure. There is no reason you can't continue without me." They had not intended to climb the formidable mountain, only to go as far as the Pasterze glacier. Sisi smiled up at him, as happy as she had been since her wedding.

"I'll only go as far as the glacier. Won't be long. I'll leave Erik here with you, and Karolin… if you wouldn't mind staying with the Empress?"

126

Count Grunne and Countess Karolin Lamberg were the only two members of their small entourage allowed to accompany them on the expedition, along with two guides.

Franz leant down and kissed her before grasping his walking stick and setting forth with Count Grunne and the other guide. What a different man he was when he shed his military uniforms and put on lederhosen, Sisi thought. In Vienna he was always serious, lacking lightness or humour. He seldom went to the theatre or opera. During Carnival, he danced because it was expected of him, not because he enjoyed it. On their holiday, he was more relaxed and even spontaneous, chatting with their guides more freely than with his ministers. He shared a love of nature with Sisi and was never happier than when he was in the mountains.

"Would you like a cup of water, Your Majesty?" Karolin asked.

"That would be nice, thank you."

The sun was mild, the breeze with a high-altitude chill. The view of the Grossglockner rising majestically above its smaller sisters was breathtaking. Turning her face up to the sun, Sisi watched an eagle circle above the valley.

They were on tour through Carinthia and Styria, a true holiday, with little intrusion of business. They had Sophie to thank for that, and Sisi was duly grateful. The trip, the private time it allowed them, had brought her and Franz closer together. As she sipped her water, Sisi wondered if the time was right to bring her own influence to bear on Franz. She had never tried to involve him in the quarrels between her and her mother-in-law, hardly ever complained to him about the treatment she received, knowing and accepting the fact that he had more important matters to deal with than women's squabbles. In March of that year, the Treaty of Paris was signed, ending the Crimean War. Franz had one less major issue on his mind.

The placement of the nursery adjacent to Sophie's suite caused Sisi great distress on a daily basis and most particularly when she was pregnant with Gisela. Once, she had said to Sophie, "I feel they are not my babies." Sophie replied, "That is true. They belong to the empire." To make matters worse, there were signs that little Sophie wasn't strong. She was often ill with fevers, which caused Sisi to want the children near her more than ever.

Karolin came to sit beside her, leaning back against her spread arms.

"Have you ever been in the mountains before, Karolin?"

"No, Your Majesty. I have only ever admired them from afar. But I'm glad we stopped here. The climb was quite exhilarating, but my poor legs aren't used to it. I wonder if they will support me tomorrow."

"I expect we will all need a rest tomorrow."

"Except His Majesty. He seems indefatigable."

When Franz returned, he was as enthused as Sisi had ever seen him. "What a pity you missed it, my dear. It was like a frozen waterfall, white and frothy! Wasn't it splendid, Grunne?"

He was still excited about the excursion over dinner in the modest hotel in Heiligenblut. After the table had been cleared and the men had smoked their cigars on the balcony, he sent Grunne to fetch the map and pored over it, preparing their next adventure.

Their bedroom was nothing like what they were accustomed to, but it was clean and cosy, and neither of them minded the creaking floor or the sloping ceiling. After they had made love, although she was tired, Sisi decided it was time to have a frank talk with her husband.

"Franz, as I'm sure you know, I am very concerned about the quarrel with your mother concerning the nursery. It distresses me greatly to quarrel with her because she has been very good to us, and I wouldn't if I didn't feel so strongly about it. Babies belong with their mother. A mother needs to have her babies about her. Our little Sophie is so often ill. It is not right that I should have to make an appointment to see my children."

"An appointment?" A frown appeared between Franz's brows.

"Yes. I have been strongly advised not to disrupt the children's schedule by visiting without first giving notice."

"Advised by whom?"

"Your mother. She rules the nursery. She decides who may visit and at what time."

"I see. Well, my mother usually knows what's best. She means only to help you with a difficult task."

"Oh, Franz! Sophie took her first steps into her arms!"

"I can understand… "

"No, you can't! You can never understand how I felt when she told me how Sophie had taken her first steps, and then she stood the child in a corner and made her walk to her." Sisi felt the sting of tears forming. She didn't want to cry, not now. She wanted to present her arguments in a rational manner, lining them up like soldiers on a drill field for Franz's inspection.

"I think not only of my own needs. You, too, are being deprived of the company of our children. We are never alone with them, as a family. I think of my own family as I was growing up... We had so much fun together, Mother and Father too... We were close. You and I, Franz, and our children are not a proper family, and that saddens me. When you were a baby were you taken away and raised by your grandmother?"

"You were so very young when you had Sophie," Franz said, repeating one of his mother's arguments.

"Old enough to be a wife and Empress! Old enough to bear babies but not to care for them? It is demeaning. Everyone knows that I am not trusted with my own children."

"It is not a matter of trust. I hope you know that." Franz pulled himself upright, took her hand in his and held it to his chest. "I would do anything to make you happy, but I don't see how I can remedy this."

Sisi took a deep breath. "I want the nursery moved to the Radetzky rooms."

Tense moments passed while Franz pondered the matter. The frown was still there. "That seems a little extreme and would cause great upset to everyone," he said eventually. "What if I were to advise Mother to allow you to see the children whenever you want? Would that make you happy?"

"No, Franz, it would not. Nor would it satisfy me. I don't think anyone should be in the position to 'allow' me to see my children. I want the nursery moved and, furthermore, I want your support in this."

"You're placing me in an awkward position."

She knew she couldn't take on her formidable mother-in-law without having Franz on her side. And she knew, too, how much she was asking of him, to defy the mother whose resolve had put him on the imperial throne and was also his chief adviser.

"I'm sorry for that. I know how much you owe her, how much we both do. But my position is intolerable, and I won't put up with it any longer."

Franz stared at her, never having heard her speak so resolutely before, and Sisi stared back, refusing to give an inch. It was such a relief to voice her opinion, though she was careful not to criticise Sophie overtly.

"I am the Empress, the first lady of the land. Yet my simplest wish is not honoured. I cannot have Bummerl at my side even during informal dinners; I can't wear shoes more than six times, or talk to anyone below a certain status; you and I can't walk outside our rooms without attendants…"

Franz sighed and released her hand. Sisi fell silent. She hadn't meant to air a litany of grievances, only to focus on the most imperative one. She picked at the lace cuff of her nightdress.

"Will you give me this gift, Franz?" She left unsaid that it was the only thing she had asked of him. "Please."

Softly, he stroked her cheekbone with one finger. "My dear one, it seems I can deny you nothing. I will write to Mother first thing in the morning. How's that?"

"Thank you, dear Franz. Thank you." She turned her face to kiss his cupped palm. "And do assure her that I have no wish to deprive her of the children and they will always be at her disposal."

It was a beginning. She could only hope his resolve would not fail when he faced his mother.

Two letters arrived in quick succession from Sophie. She was furious at Sisi's demands and threatened to leave the Hofburg. Both Franz and Sisi were nervous about confronting Sophie, but when they returned to Vienna, Franz stood his ground.

"If you think about the matter calmly, Mother, you will perhaps understand our feelings of pain at seeing our children enclosed in your apartments, while poor Sisi must pant her way upstairs, only rarely to find the children alone."

"'Poor Sisi' is a woman who climbs mountains."

Franz wisely ignored this thrust. "Often we find them among strangers because you are showing them off, which shortens the little time we have to spend with the children, and showing them off may make them conceited, which horrifies me."

"I see you rebuke me for loving my grandchildren," Sophie replied bitterly. "Sisi is more interested in her horses than her children and totally unfitted to have their care."

"That is most unfair, Mother. Sisi is a devoted wife and mother."

Sisi said nothing. It pleased her to have Franz defend her. Sophie left them, every line of her body conveying her rage. Franz lifted his shoulders in a resigned shrug.

The nursery was moved to the rooms formerly occupied by General Radetzky, who had been given the honour of an apartment in the Hofburg for his long and distinguished military career.

Sisi had won the battle, but the war entered a new phase. Sophie became more vindictive than ever and deliberately tried to come between Franz and Sisi, clinging to her influence with Franz while trying to diminish Sisi's. Sisi knew she would never win her mother-in-law's approval, but refused to be intimidated any longer and became ever more defiant.

Chapter 16 – November 1856

With her ladies in attendance, Sophie made her way to Franz's apartment in answer to his summons. Entering his study, she saw Adjutant General Grunne, Minister of the Interior, Count Bach, and Foreign Minister, Count Buol-Schauenstein, and…that provincial Bavarian.

When she thought of all the trouble she had gone to in order to educate the girl, the care she had taken over every aspect of her daily life, she felt little rewarded. At fifteen, Sisi had seemed a sweet, naïve and malleable girl. At eighteen, she had proved herself to be obdurate and demanding. Her complaints seemed never-ending, and she was always thinking of herself, rather than Franz or the empire. Her impulsiveness and inclination toward unseemly conduct were offensive, her brand of Catholicism far from true piety. She could banter easily with a coachman, but could not conduct a decorous conversation with the aristocracy. She knew little of the etiquette that governed the imperial court and cared less. As Empress, Sisi had many failings, but worst of all, most unforgivable of all, was that she had no sense of duty, which was the chain that bound the Habsburg Empire together.

Sisi truly was a most beautiful young woman with a great deal of charm, as Sophie often admitted in her letters to friends and family. But she had sensed from the beginning that Sisi wasn't the right wife for Franz. Sadly, Sophie thought back to dear, sensible Nené, who was still unmarried and would have made such a good wife, prepared to do her duty to the empire and produce a flourishing family, instead of creating scenes and exercising her body as if she was a performer in a circus.

Sophie would have liked to spare her son some of the tearful scenes Sisi indulged in, particularly when she was pregnant. Life was difficult enough for Franz, with all the responsibilities of his position. His wife ought to offer a happy and comfortable home life.

If Sophie was occasionally hard on her, it was only to help her rise beyond her provincial origins and avoid the disdain of a cruel and cynical court. After more than thirty years at the imperial court, Sophie was a Habsburg to her steel core; Sisi was a Wittelsbach, with all the wild and foolish clutter of that family.

What concerned Sophie most was that Sisi was gaining influence with Franz. Who knew what madness she might encourage in him. All the court knew she had a soft spot for the Hungarians. In her youth, Sophie had liberal leanings, but having to flee Vienna twice during the revolutions, having to call on the assistance of Russia to subdue Hungary, all the horrors of those two years had turned her into a single-minded monarchist.

After extending their courtesies, the gentlemen resumed their seats. Franz sat next to Sisi on a couch. Sophie glared at her rather pointedly. What could they possibly talk about that concerned the girl?

"Now that you are here I want to discuss the Italian question," Franz began. "We are all of the opinion that intervention is necessary."

"Italy has never settled down after the revolutions of and still chafes under our rule. I have been urging intervention for some time now." Sophie nodded briskly. "But, if I may ask, why is the Empress here? How does this concern her?"

"I will get to that in a minute," Franz said. "Minister?"

Thus invited, Count Bach said, "General Radetzky's efforts of control through repression are not working. All his floggings and hangings and firing squads have resulted in nothing more than a strengthening of resistance and the formation of an Italian unification movement."

"Stronger salutary measures are required," Buol interrupted. "We cannot relinquish any provinces under Habsburg control." He looked for confirmation to Franz, who nodded. "Piedmont, the cradle of the Italian unification movement, furnished fifteen thousand troops to France during the Crimean War, thereby earning the protection of Napoleon III. It is not only Italian unity that jeopardises our rule. The northern states of Lombardy and Venetia are under threat from French expansionism, as are the central states of Tuscany and Modena."

Bach shook his head at his colleague's first words. "Repression is not the answer. Far from restoring order, we have only succeeded in disenchanting any loyal elements and making the name Austria odious throughout the peninsula. Archduke Maximilian has made that very clear. He is on the spot and in the best position to know."

"Radetzky is on the spot too," Sophie said. "He does not favour a more lenient government."

Bach sighed. "With all due respect to the marshal, he is in his ninetieth year."

"Is he really?" Franz interjected.

"He is, Your Majesty. He knows no other way than torturing and hanging. His only concern is the safety of his troops. However, I must say that he has little choice. As a loyal soldier, he merely follows the orders that come from above. I am not alone in thinking that unless Your Majesty does something to reconcile the Italians, war is inevitable. At present, the Italians are guilty merely of unarmed hostility. I suggest reconciliation, not repression."

"We have discussed this before," Sophie said sharply. "The Italians will never be reconciled."

"But, how hard have we tried?" Bach said gently.

"These states have been warring with each other since medieval times. Piedmont will never bring them together." Sophie looked at Franz, who was gazing at the Interior Minister. She had a sinking feeling that he agreed with everything Count Bach said.

Her second son, Maximilian, to her dismay, was turning out to be a liberal. These were his views. Calm and moderation, he preached. True power doesn't need to provoke. She had one son who was a liberal and another who was a homosexual. She loved them both and both were a disappointment to her. Her eldest son, she feared, was slipping from her grasp. Allowing the child to sit in on a political discussion! Of course, she had contributed nothing; she had nothing to say.

"No, Your Highness, Piedmont could never do it. But we can. Because of our repressive policies, the sons of the Italian aristocracy are crossing the Ticino in droves to join the Piedmontese army."

Sophie sniffed. "We have nothing to fear from Piedmont. It is a pinhead on the world map."

"So was Macedon in the days of Alexander," the count replied.

The ensuing silence was broken by a loud sniff as one of Bach's cavernous nostrils inhaled a pinch of snuff, followed by the other. Snapping the lid of the box shut, he returned it to his pocket and continued. "Allow me to make one more point. The cost of the strong military presence required in Italy is vast and cannot be

134

covered by the taxes imposed. It would be an enormous saving if we could restore peace and reduce our forces."

Stroking his moustache with a forefinger, Franz said, "At the Paris conference the English and French delegates listened very sympathetically to Count Cavour."

"He should never have been there," Count Grunne said. "It was supposed to be a peace conference. He's a warmonger."

"What do we care about England and France?"

Everyone turned to look at Buol with varying expressions of surprise, indignation or disgust. England and France were world powers. They could never be discounted.

Bach rose on his toes and lowered himself repeatedly. Sophie noted it as a sign of nervousness. "I believe," he said, "a personal visit by the Emperor would soothe ruffled feathers, particularly if he were accompanied by the Empress, whose beauty would undoubtedly be a diplomatic asset. The Italians are susceptible to beauty." He bowed in the direction of Sisi, who gave him a coy smile.

Sophie felt her anger rise. Suddenly she knew that this had been discussed before – not only discussed but decided – outside her presence. Franz no longer listened to her. First the matter of the nurseries and now this. And, she had to admit it, Sisi's influence was growing. She knew the reason, and it disgusted her. Whenever Franz sided with his mother against his wife, that night he would find Sisi indisposed and her bedroom door locked. Countess Esterhazy, who faithfully reported these matters to her, who was finding it increasingly difficult to cope with the Empress's wilfulness. Sisi was learning to use her beauty and allure as a weapon.

Sophie swallowed her mortification. "I am most vehemently opposed to this. Franz, you will put yourself in danger in a useless attempt to conciliate a bunch of radicals and anarchists. Remember Libényi."

Instinctively, Franz's hand went to the scar on his neck left by the attempted assassination. "I will never forget. It happened in Vienna, in the city dearest to me in the world. Assassins are everywhere, but we must not cower from them. If, as many believe, an Italian war is inevitable, we cannot be seen as the aggressors. I do not intend to cede any territories, but I agree that our policy has not been successful. An act of appeasement is called for. It may be that a personal appearance by their Emperor and Empress will improve matters. In any case, I will go to Italy and judge the situation close at hand."

"I am willing to go. I love to travel," Sisi said.

Spoken like a child, Sophie sneered inwardly. "It will not be a pleasure jaunt," she said sourly.

"Yet, I hope we find some pleasure in it." Sisi's hand crept over Franz's. "How long do you expect we'll be gone?"

"Two, possibly three months. We'll open up the royal palaces in Venice and Milan."

"Oh!" She looked crestfallen. "In that case, we must take little Sophie along. I can't possibly part from her for so long. Gisela must stay in Vienna of course – babies don't travel well – but I want Sophie to come with us."

"I can see no reason why not," Franz said amiably, and she flashed her smile at him.

Sophie could no longer contain her outrage. "Have you lost all sense? You would take a two-year-old child into a volatile situation? She is too delicate! Travel is hard on small children. She must stay here!"

"If the Empress's beauty doesn't melt stony Italian hearts, surely the appeal of the little Archduchess will," Minister Bach said. "You will be viewed as a young family, like many another. The effect will be charming."

Smiling at the Emperor and Empress, he missed Sophie's glare. She suspected this whole plan was his idea and she would never forgive him for it. Unable to keep the bitterness out of her voice, she spoke directly to Sisi. "Italy is an armed camp, not a health resort, and hardly the most suitable environment for a delicate child."

"On the contrary, Madame Mere. I believe the climate of northern Italy will be good for her during the winter months," Sisi replied.

Sophie rose. She would not yield. She had made Franz Emperor. He owed her his gratitude. Before he left, there would be other opportunities to speak to him away from pernicious influences. She saw the way he looked at Sisi, his eyes full of love and admiration. How could she compete with the allure of a beautiful wife? All she could do for now was to make a strategic and dignified withdrawal.

"I see that you will not listen to reason. If that is all, Your Majesty…"

"Thank you for attending, Mother."

Chapter 17 – November 1856

Buffeted by gusts of wind, Sisi stood with Franz at the rail of the festive *Galleggiante* cruising the harbour to show themselves to the people. The first stop on the tour was Trieste, the fourth largest city in the empire after Vienna, Budapest and Prague, and Austria's main trading port and shipbuilding centre. Until she received the itinerary, Sisi had no idea of its importance and regretted all the geography lessons she had missed in favour of roaming the hills of Bavaria.

Wherever they went, whether in Vienna itself, or during their visits to Bohemia, Carinthia and Styria, or in Salzburg, which they passed through en route to Bad Ischl, she and Franz were accustomed to a warm welcome. Italy was very different and a shock to Sisi who was not prepared for such a level of quiet antipathy.

Although the bora was blowing, it was a beautiful day, with the sun caressing cheeks and sparkling on the blue waters of the Adriatic. The harbour was decorated with Austrian flags, stretched out horizontally by the wind, and a brass band was playing. But it was a cold welcome. The only ones cheering were Austrian soldiers. The Italians themselves demonstrated their hostility with silence.

Suddenly there was a tremendous crash. Amid shouts of alarm and the faint sound of cheers from the shore, Sisi grabbed her little daughter and pressed her into her skirts, cringing. Franz's arm went around her, as small pieces of debris peppered them. At first, she thought the ship must have struck something, but when she opened her eyes, she saw that the ship was sailing majestically on. Behind them, the huge crystal crown mounted above the deck had fallen and shattered into thousands of fragments.

White-faced, the ship's officers and Austrian officials stared at the ruin. Then they clustered around the imperial family with stammered apologies and enquiries if anyone was hurt. Sisi stooped to check her little daughter, who gazed at the debris with huge eyes. She wasn't hurt and didn't even cry. Rising, Sisi shook bits of crystal from her skirt with a trembling hand and clung to Sophie's hand with the other.

"Are you both all right?" Franz asked Sisi as he stroked his daughter's cheek.

Sisi nodded, although she was far from all right. Frightened and shaking, she wondered if this was another act of sabotage.

Franz turned to the officers. "What the devil happened?"

Only one answered, suggesting perhaps it was the wind.

"Find out," Franz snapped. "I want a full report. Now I would like to get my family off this ship."

There had been a disturbing incident earlier that day at the Municipal Palace. During the presentation of the city dignitaries, a small fire broke out among the fireworks that were intended for use that night. Sisi, Franz and little Sophie rushed outside, and the police were summoned. After an initial investigation, they determined it was sabotage. No one was hurt, and there was little damage. Franz would not believe it was anything but an accident. But how could anyone be sure? There were so many fanatics and revolutionaries in Italy.

The incident unnerved Sisi. On board the ship she waved her hand mechanically and tried to smile, but she couldn't stop thinking about it.

In their bedroom that night, Franz and Sisi discussed the incidents and the likelihood of coincidence. Eventually, Franz said, "I'm not sure, but I believe if they were sabotage they were meant to frighten rather than harm us. Well, I refuse to be intimidated by such tricks. I think we must continue with the scheduled programme."

"You're right. There's nothing else to be done."

Throughout their stay, there were no more such incidents. Nevertheless, they were relieved to leave Trieste behind.

On the yacht *Elizabetta*, they went on to Venice. Franz looked dashing in a white field marshal's uniform, young and fit and tanned. Sisi wore a blue velvet travelling outfit, and her little daughter wore a miniature copy. Her first view of the magical city enchanted Sisi, but when they arrived at the landing stage at St. Mark's, where old, bent, Marshal Radetzky was waiting to greet them, it was as cold a welcome as in Trieste. The square was packed with people, every window crowded with faces, but as she walked across the Piazzetta, holding her daughter by the hand, Sisi was intensely aware of the awful censorious silence. The few 'Hurrahs!' shouted by the Austrian soldiers only served to emphasise it.

A Te Deum was celebrated in St. Mark's Church. Brass bands played along the route as the state barge carried them to the Royal

139

Palace. In the evening the sky was illuminated by fireworks on the lagoons and the Grand Canal. The *Podesta* had done his best to provide a magnificent welcome, but nothing he did could warm the Italians toward the imperial visitors. On a daily basis, Franz and Sisi were exposed to slights and insults, shouts of 'Austrian despot!' The red and white flag of Austria was displayed with a green stripe across it, the Italian colours. At a reception given by the Emperor and Empress, only thirty of the one hundred and thirty invited families turned up. Many didn't even trouble to send excuses. As a result people of lesser status were invited to fill the gaps. Hooligans on the quay hissed at and insulted these stalwarts as they alighted from their gondolas in court attire.

Yet everywhere they went people stretched their necks and stood on tiptoes to catch a glimpse of the Empress because they had heard how beautiful she was. Sisi did her best to be gracious to all, speaking to those who showed any inclination to speak to her, although the damp air and the fetid smell of the canals made her feel ill.

"I have been warned that we may be exposed to gross insults or even an assassination attempt," Franz said on the third day of their visit. They were in a gondola, returning from La Fenice, where most of the boxes held by eminent families had remained empty. "I can't possibly terminate the tour. The Italians would see it as cowardice and failure. But it might be a good idea if you and Sophie went home. We can find some credible pretext. What do you think?"

They were closer than they had ever been, working together for the same goals, congratulating each other for their successes and commiserating over their failures. And for the first time, Franz spoke to her as if she was an adult with valid opinions instead of an ignorant girl. Such a rapprochement would not have been possible if Sophie had been with them. Sisi didn't want to give that up.

"It wouldn't work, Franz. Everyone would know I was running away. They would hold us in greater contempt than they do already. In any case, I don't want to leave. If I can help a little, I shall."

"You are a brave girl," he said kissing her forehead.

Never had she been prouder of Franz. His unruffled self-assurance in the face of public condemnation and the offensiveness of the aristocracy was admirable, and she tried to emulate it. Although she found the atmosphere of hostility disturbing, she enjoyed the challenge that Italy presented. Every time she coaxed a smile from someone she felt, rightly or wrongly, she had made another convert.

While Franz responded to the constant offences by watching troop manoeuvres, inspecting barracks, artillery, fortifications and battle sites, Sisi visited museums, hospitals and orphanages. She learned a good deal about Italy, and through Italy about the rest of the empire. And what she learned only confirmed the speculative anti-monarchy views she had absorbed from her father. She began to see that to Franz the empire meant Vienna. The problems that beset the rest of the heterogeneous empire were not only neglected but largely unexplored. The sole purpose of the limbs was to feed the gross and selfish needs of the heart.

In the short time they had been there, Sisi came to agree with her mother-in-law that Habsburg Italy was an armed camp. But she also agreed with Count Bach. The fines and sequestrations, the hangings and firing squads had alienated both the common people and the aristocracy. It was going to require a great deal more than the imperial family touring the cities to win the Italians over. In fact, she was convinced it would need vast changes in the administration headquartered in Verona, starting at the top.

As the gondola glided under bridges and past the torch-lit façades of palaces, Sisi said, "Franz, what's needed is a gesture, an act of generosity to show that an Emperor is a man of compassion."

Franz thought for a moment. She always knew when he was thinking deeply by the creases in his forehead. "I have instructed the police of Milan to give one lira to each person. I'm told the Milanese are even more inimical than the Venetians. Do you think I should do the same here?"

Sisi was thrilled that he asked her opinion. Again, he never would have done so if his mother had been present.

"I thought something that made a political statement would be better. An amnesty for some of the political prisoners, for instance, I think would do very nicely."

"Perhaps. I'll speak to the ministers."

The result was that seventy people condemned for high treason were granted amnesty by imperial decree and had their confiscated property restored. On the evening the announcement was made, Franz and Sisi went to La Fenice. To their surprise, every box was full. When they appeared in their box, they were thrilled to find themselves the recipients of sustained applause.

"Sometimes it takes so little," Sisi said, squeezing his hand.

After that, whenever they went out in public, they were greeted with cheers. They were both delighted. It had taken two weeks to conquer Venice without bloodshed.

…………..

After spending their first Christmas without the archduchess, they moved on to Padua, Vicenza and Verona, with varying degrees of success, and finally, the city they knew would be the toughest nut to crack, Milan, the foremost city of Northern Italy.

In Piedmont, Count Camillo Cavour, the leader of the Italian unification movement, had unleashed a barrage of propaganda to counter the good impression the Emperor and Empress were making wherever they went. They learned that agents had gone from house to house, persuading the owners to boycott the imperial visit. Anonymous letters warned the ladies of leading families that if they appeared at court, the Piedmontese newspapers would publish accounts of their past and present love affairs and other transgressions.

The last stop on the tour, their reception in Milan was icy. The lire Franz had distributed could not melt the stern Milanese. The insults the imperial couple suffered made Venice seem benign by comparison. At the reception, only one-fifth of those invited attended.

A night at the opera was scheduled, an event Sisi dreaded. As they made their way through the streets, the crowd was once again silent. It was not a respectful silence but so profoundly ominous that she was frightened. She couldn't wait to get inside away from those awful accusing stares. The men, she noticed, didn't even take their hats off.

As they alighted outside La Scala, with one voice, the people began to hum 'O mia patria', the chorus from Verdi's patriotic *I Lombardi*. Inside the magnificent opera house, a subdued atmosphere prevailed. To their surprise the boxes belonging to the aristocratic families were full. As she gazed covertly around Sisi became aware that the occupants were neither dressed appropriately nor behaving with the decorum one might expect from well-to-do Lombardians. One woman was laughing like a horse: neigh-hey-hey! Another stood and waved at the imperial box. A couple was actually kissing! Furthermore, all were wearing black gloves in token of mourning.

Franz spoke to one of the Austrian officials in charge of the arrangements, whose mandate was to create an illusion of harmony, to show the international commentators that all was well between the Emperor and his people. The man went off and came back during the intermission, obviously hugely embarrassed by what he had to confess. To ensure the boxes were not left empty, as in Venice, the officials had sent out letters requiring the holders either to attend or to put the boxes at the officials' disposal. All said they would use their boxes. But it was not the aristocratic families who now sat watching the opera – it was their servants.

It was a huge insult and Franz was furious. "You see how it is with these people!" he hissed to no one in particular. "Do you see what I have to put up with? Snubs! The grossest insults! My benevolence is wasted on such ingrates!"

Sisi put a hand on his arm. "Even if we cannot see the fruits at once, benevolence is never wasted."

But he would not be pacified. He seethed throughout the next two acts. Sisi had never seen him so angry, but by the time the opera was over he had himself under control and they returned to the palace without further incident.

Once again he agreed to amnesty some of the condemned. When the names appeared in the *Gazzetta di Milano*, the effect was immediately noticeable. The Milanese warmed towards their visitors. On March 1st Franz began to institute the changes he had been discussing with his ministers over the last months. Marshal Radetzky had to go. He was a hero to Franz, but to Sisi he was symbolic of the empire itself: old and decrepit, his glory days behind him, yet occasionally rousing himself to thrash about uselessly. At almost ninety, he could retire with full honours and no loss of face.

Franz's twenty-four-year-old brother Maximilian was appointed governor general. Sisi was delighted by the choice. Maximilian was charming and sensitive, cultured and clever, and he invariably enlivened the court with his presence. Sisi thought him far more a Wittelsbach than a Habsburg.

Officially the tour was a great success, but Franz said to Sisi on their journey home, "On the whole I feel happier but not entirely reassured. Everything is still very uncertain. Only God can help us and let us hope Max's tact can do some good."

Chapter 18 – May 1857

"Do you know what the Emperor said of your visit to Italy?" Count Grunne asked Sisi as their horses trotted side by side through the gates of Schönbrunn. "He said that your beauty conquered Italy better than his soldiers and cannons had been able to do. The words are being repeated all over Vienna."

Sisi smiled wistfully. "I wish it were true. I don't believe soldiers and cannon can conquer a people, only create slaves. Surely we are beyond that."

"I must respectfully disagree, Majesty. If one of your ladies were to steal your jewels wouldn't you fight tooth and nail to have them back, or at least demand punishment for the offender?"

Sisi realised she was debating the wrong person. Count Grunne being the head of the military was bound to have imperialist views. Nevertheless, he was one of the few people prepared to speak to her about political matters.

"You are oversimplifying, Count. The two situations are entirely different. I own my jewels. Neither the Emperor nor the empire owns Italy. Not in the same way. Now if I were to take my jewels back from the thief would I be considered a thief too?"

Count Grunne laughed. "But Italy is part of the empire, passed on to His Majesty by his uncle and a long list of Habsburgs before him."

"Hmm. That doesn't seem justification enough for keeping a people in chains who want to be free."

"The empire cannot survive without its subject nations."

Sisi gave him her gentle smile. "That is true. I know what the British consul said about Milan in his official dispatch: 'By far the greater part of the well-to-do and intelligent Lombardians plainly showed their dislike. This state of affairs must be regarded seriously.' What troubles me, Count, is that Britain and France, two countries I view as progressive, did away with their monarchs in bloody revolutions. I have heard it said that the empire was fortunate to survive the revolutions of '48. But nothing has changed. Might that circumstance invite revolution again?"

How far dare she go with this? To suggest to his dearest friend that the Emperor must rule with less autocracy and more benevolence, would be terribly disloyal, not to say a little arrogant. After all, what did she know of the problems that beset the empire? A snippet picked up here and there and what she had learned from her father. She could not talk to Franz himself because he seldom discussed politics with her. He seemed to want to protect her from the most unpleasant aspects of his life, not understanding that what affected him affected her also. It was always better to know than to be left toiling in ignorance.

Before Count Grunne could answer, she flicked her riding crop against her mount's flank. "Shall we give the horses a good gallop?"

It was May, and the court had moved to Schönbrunn. Sisi preferred the smaller palace with its tall windows and lovely gardens and fountains, to the chill stone walls of the Hofburg. While the good weather held she rode almost every day, often with Count Grunne, in the softly-contoured hills and deep woods around Vienna. It was unseemly for the Empress to go riding with just one man, Sophie had decreed, so now they were accompanied by six guards. Sisi didn't argue; it was no matter. They rode until she was breathless, her face flushed with the exhilaration of racing the wind. Count Grunne kept up with her but he didn't like her to ride so fast. Once he had asked: "What is it that drives you, Majesty?" She hadn't known how to answer.

She regarded Count Grunne as her closest friend, which was rather sad really: a middle-aged man whose dearest passion was the military. She liked her brother-in-law Maximilian very much, but his service to his brother meant he was seldom at court. Her old admirer Karl Ludwig had accepted an appointment as stadtholder in Innsbruck. As for the youngest brother, Ludwig Viktor, what she heard about his all-male parties disgusted her. She had been warned by Sophie not to become intimate with her ladies-in-waiting, though this was proving hard to do so far as the youngest two, Paula and Karolin, were concerned. Of the aristocratic families of the empire, only twenty-three men and two hundred and twenty-nine women had the high honour of free access to the Empress. They turned up at a formal 'salon', made correct conversation, the same words, the same stilted phrases over and over again, and then they departed. Sisi had no chance to develop a close relationship with anyone. However, she did correspond with her family and some of her many cousins. The letters she received in return were her only relief from loneliness.

Even her children were no compensation. Gisela didn't know her, and when Sisi had picked her up, the child held out her arms to her grandmother and cried until Sisi gave her up. And little Sophie was so overjoyed at being reunited with her grandmother she kept hugging her. Sisi felt excluded and jealous.

"I see Italy has done nothing to improve Sophie's health," the older Sophie had said scathingly. Sisi couldn't deny it. Her little daughter had often been ill during their stay.

As soon as they returned to Vienna, the closeness she and Franz had experienced in Italy evaporated like an autumn mist over the Danube, and he was again closeted away from her, both literally and metaphorically, only visiting her bed at night for the purpose of obtaining an heir for the empire. Sisi had begun to fear she was incapable of giving him a male heir. In court and city, people were whispering about her inadequacy, and hopes were turning to Maximilian's intended wife, Charlotte, daughter of the King of Belgium.

After her ride with Count Grunne, she was writing letters when Franz entered the room. She put down her pen and rose, ready to give him a kiss, until she saw his mother behind him. It was so seldom that Franz visited her during the day, she would have liked to have him to herself for a little while, but this, like so much else, was denied her.

"Have you seen what your wife has done?" Not giving Franz a chance to answer, Sophie quick-marched through to Sisi's dressing room, Sisi trailing behind. The room was a fantasy land, each wall decorated with murals of colourful flowers, birds and butterflies, animals peeking out through foliage, and water falling into a pool.

"What on earth..?" Franz stared in surprise at two rings hanging in the doorway. His gaze went to the adjacent wall where several horizontal bars formed a ladder.

"For exercising." Sophie pronounced the word as if it were something loathsome.

After Gisela's birth Sisi's waist measurement had gone up to twenty-three inches, but she had ridden and dieted the extra inches off. It was only by stringent dieting that she could keep them off. She was five feet seven and a half inches tall – taller than her husband – and weighed herself as much as three times daily to make sure she didn't go beyond her desired weight of one hundred pounds. Her slender figure, too, must be preserved.

In her youth she had seen acrobats at the circus, slim young men and, very occasionally, women, who could do extraordinary things with the simplest of devices, like a bar or a hoop. Why not? The court would be scandalised all over again. Madame Mere would definitely not approve. Her ladies would say, respectfully, it was not done. But she did it.

She hoped Franz would support her. He liked to keep fit by riding. "You don't disapprove, do you?"

Franz looked again and shrugged. "It is unconventional, I suppose, but I see no harm in it."

The furore caused by her gymnastic equipment was a mere upset compared to the storm that broke when it was learned she had taken up fencing, which she saw as art and dance in one, and which the court viewed as another instance of her aberrant behaviour.

"Sisi, if you have time I wish to speak to you."

"Of course, Franz."

She and Sophie sat in chairs upholstered in the pineapple red damask of Schönbrunn. One look at Sophie's thin mouth was sufficient to inform Sisi she was angry.

Franz stood before the rocaille framed mirror, his hands clasped behind his back. "My dear wife," he began, his manner very formal, "I was very pleased with the way you comported yourself in Italy. The ministers agree with me that what success we achieved was at least in part thanks to you. You made a very good impression. We hope that a similar visit to Hungary will improve relations with that troublesome province. I would like you to come along, but only if you feel you are strong enough."

"Why, Franz, thank you! Nothing would please me more than to accompany you to Hungary." To get away from his mother was one of the reasons she liked to travel.

He beamed at her. "Good. That's settled then. I know the Hungarians admire you. You shall be our ambassadress."

"I think I shall like them."

Franz winked at his mother. "Sisi is only interested in them because they are picturesque."

It was a remark that hurt Sisi because it made her seem shallow. But Franz hadn't meant to hurt her and was unaware of the effect of his words. She said nothing, for she didn't want to spoil things. In any case, she had another matter to pursue.

He was about to depart when she said: "This time I think we should take both girls with us. Gisela is old enough…"

"No! I forbid it!" Sophie burst out. Franz and Sisi turned to her with twin looks of amazement. "The children are too young for the rigorous schedule of a state visit. They need structure in their lives and stability, not to be hauled off to some barbaric country and displayed like show pieces."

Sisi waited for Franz to speak but he hesitated, his brow wrinkled.

"Madame Mere, as their parents, we are well able to care for them and ensure they get enough rest." Sisi's voice was a gentle counterpoint to Sophie's strident tone.

"Oh, you! You care more for your horses than your children!"

Sisi gasped. "That is not true!"

"Oh, isn't it? Do you know Sophie is ill again? No! But if a horse of yours had laminitis you would know about it, and you would visit every day until it recovered."

Sisi rose to her feet, her nostrils flaring in anger. "That is because Dr Seeburger reports to you. The nurses report to you." She turned to Franz in appeal. "If the children don't go, I won't go."

Sophie too turned to Franz. "If you persist in this folly, I shall leave Vienna." She had made the same threat when Sisi insisted on having the nurseries moved, but she was still here.

"Sisi, Mama." Franz's hands came from behind his back to push at the air in front of him. "This has to stop. The empire is in turmoil. Italy is fighting for unification and Hungary threatens secession. Wilhelm of Prussia is trying to form a German League against me. Britain and France call me weak because I did not support them in the Crimea. Alexander is not my friend because I didn't support Russia in the Crimea." He threw his hands out toward them and raised his voice. "Can I not have peace in my home?" And with that he strode out. With a baleful glare at Sisi, Sophie followed him.

Sisi waited until she was sure Sophie had gone and then went into her bedchamber and laid down. "Close the curtains," she said when Paula came in to see if she needed anything, "and then leave me."

Once she was alone, she turned her face into the lacy pillow and quietly wept. Her tears were not only because of Sophie's cruelty but also because of Franz's indifference. She knew he carried a great burden, and that he carried it with courage, dignity, discipline and a tireless application to work. She often excused his lapses for that reason. But today she was not in the mood to excuse him. She could hardly be expected to sympathise with his position when she knew so little of his troubles. That was his doing. When she asked a question, he always answered politely, but soon enough changed the subject or gave her a minimal answer that told her nothing. It was not part of her role to involve herself in politics. Unless it suited him. She wondered how Sophie had managed to become such a political animal that her advice was sought and respected by more than just Franz.

But he was wrong if he supposed she knew little about Hungary. Count Mailath, her Hungarian tutor, had first awakened her interest in the country, particularly its struggle for independence. During the wedding celebrations she had met many delegates from many countries, but none had impressed her so much as the Hungarians, although she hadn't had any opportunity to talk to them outside court ceremonial. Something in them appealed to something in her. She was glad she had chosen to learn the language. She spoke it imperfectly, but well enough to converse, and she read everything she could about their history. The more she learned, the more her sympathy grew.

Franz had told her that he wanted his people to remember him as a benign ruler, and he was working towards that. In Italy it had not been at all hard to persuade him to an act of benevolence, and she hoped to do the same in Hungary, in spite of Sophie's malign influence. It was well known that Sophie hated the Hungarians and Franz still listened to his mother. Sisi saw that she had a role to play: reconciling the Hungarians with their Emperor.

Thinking of this, her tears dried. She rose from her bed and went through to her dressing room where her sanitary porcelain stood on a table. The white washbasin, water jug and soap dish were all decorated with gold trim and a gold imperial eagle. She poured some water and splashed her face. Paula was too late to perform this service, but she was there to hand Sisi a towel.

150

Sisi went at once to the nursery and found little Sophie in her bed. The child was pale and listless, but she held out her arms to her mama and Sisi stooped to kiss her cheek, which she noted was slightly hot. One of the nurses brought a stool and Sisi sat. Gisela crawled over with a doll she thrust at Sisi, who dutifully kissed it too.

"What's the matter, darling?" she asked the older girl.

"I sick."

"Does it hurt?"

Sophie nodded her blonde head solemnly but was unable to tell her mother where she hurt. Sisi remained with her until she fell asleep and then returned to her salon. "Send for Dr Seeburger immediately."

The doctor was strictly bound to be on hand night and day. If he needed time away, he was to find a replacement of impeccable credentials who satisfied Sophie. Although the nurseries had been relocated according to Sisi's wishes Sophie still ruled there. It was humiliating to give the nurses an order only to find later that Sophie had countermanded it and was obeyed.

The doctor arrived within minutes and bowed low. "Your Majesty."

"Dr Seeburger, why was I not informed that my daughter is ill?" she asked coldly.

"Majesty, I…" He gulped air. Sisi watched the cartilage in his throat jump up and down. "I er… informed her Imperial Highness as per my instructions. I thought her Imperial Highness would…hmm…"

She supposed it was not his fault. Like everyone else he obeyed and reported to Sophie and expected Sophie to tell her. "In future you will inform me and while she is ill I want a daily report. Is that clear?"

"Of course, Your Majesty."

"Now, what is the matter with her?"

The doctor had never been able to diagnose Sophie's condition, whether it was congenital, or if she was one of those children prone to illness. He had once committed himself to the notion that she had a weak constitution but would grow stronger with age. Now he said, "She has a slight case of diarrhoea and a low fever, possibly brought on by teething."

"Teething?" Sisi said in surprise.

"Yes, indeed, parts of the body are intimately related. Teething often brings on such symptoms. Some doctors believe there is no connection, but I hold the view that the incidence is too common for it to be mere coincidence. The teething child produces a great deal of saliva which enters the stomach and causes the stool to become loose."

Oh, the poor child, Sisi thought. But that would explain it. When she was teething, Gisela cried robustly, but Sophie only whimpered and became lethargic. "What are you doing for her?"

"As Your Majesty no doubt knows, there is nothing to be done for teething. The teeth have to push their way through and often it is a painful process. Most teething children like to have something to chew on, but her Imperial Highness appears to show no interest. We give her cold food as this is what she seems to prefer and bathe her frequently with cold water to bring down her temperature. I am treating her with small amounts of opium for diarrhea and camphor to induce perspiration, which will cool the body."

"And you anticipate a full recovery?"

"Certainly. Your Majesty is not to worry." He beamed at her as if his permission was the only thing required to stop her worrying.

She did not return the smile. "Thank you, Doctor. You may go. But please remember what I said: I want a daily report."

When he had gone, Sisi returned to her apartment. There was some justice in what Sophie had said, she admitted to herself. Her daughter's periodic bouts of illness were something she had come to accept and to dismiss as no more than childhood ailments, which they probably were. It was only that little Sophie was more prone to them than others. But Sisi could have, should have, demanded a report from the doctor before this. Why hadn't she? Because she was intimidated by her mother-in-law and it was easier to give in? Because she didn't want to upset Franz with more quarrelling? Because she knew Sophie would neglect no part of her children's care?

Yes, there were many reasons she could admit to herself, but there was another bitter truth: she was jealous of her children's closeness to Sophie. It was painful to watch them go to Sophie to have their little hurts soothed or climb into her lap for a cuddle. The smug look on Sophie's face as she crooned over them only increased the pain. To Sisi, grandmother and children colluded to make her aware of her inadequacies as a mother.

It would be different when she got them away from Sophie, which she would do as often as possible. They would be growing up into a new world and must not absorb Sophie's entrenched beliefs in the divine right of the Habsburgs, the infallibility of empire, and the dangers of democracy or anything resembling constitutional government. Her children must grow up to love freedom.

"Your Majesty's visitors are here," Paula reminded her.

Sisi put a hand to her forehead. She could feel a headache coming on. Her guests had put their names on a list kept by her secretary. She had restricted the number to eight, so the list was quite long and most had to wait weeks. There could be no excuse; today her salon was open.

Her *valet de chambre* announced the visitors at the door. Sisi greeted them as they entered and invited them to sit in the red plush chairs that formed a circle around her own. Count von Hotzendorf asked after Her Imperial Majesty's health, which led to Countess Lutzow's complaints of her own persistent cough and guaranteed remedies and finally to the health of the little Archduchess. When that subject had been exhausted Countess von Warsburg remarked on the clock that stood on a table in front of the large mirror, which she found "charming". It had a double face so that it was visible through the mirror.

"If I might ask Your Majesty, where did it come from?"

Sisi had no idea, but rather than admitting her ignorance she hazarded a guess. "It is part of the Habsburg collection." There was an entire building at the Hofburg filled with treasures the Habsburgs had been given or bought over the centuries for which there was no room in any of their many palaces.

Her husband pointed out that they had seen a similar clock in a Parisian antique shop, but the countess would not agree. Back and forth they went. Before the issue could become a domestic dispute, maids came in with the tea trolley.

"Will you take tea?" Sisi asked.

"Sèvres!" Count von Warsburg declared. "One can always tell."

"Charming," said Countess von Warsburg.

As the tea was served, Sisi asked the von Warsburgs about Paris. Did they meet Napoleon III and Empress Eugenie?

"Nappie is enormously fat," the count pronounced.

But the Countess rightly judged that Sisi wanted to hear about Eugenie, another of Europe's beauties. "The Empress was very agreeable. She is dark and of no great height but she is beautiful, with enormous dark eyes…"

"And the mouth of a coquette," her husband interrupted.

All the ladies in the room turned their heads slowly to look at him. Count Lutzow cleared his throat. Countess von Warsburg's cup loudly rattled as she tried to replace it in the saucer. Into the silence Countess von Hotzendorf said breezily: "May I compliment Your Majesty on your enchanting gown. And the colour, that extraordinary shimmering green, so becomes you." With five ladies in the room, all dressed in their best, their newest, their most likely to be talked about, a discussion of fashion was inevitable. The gentlemen listened with well-simulated interest.

"Where are your estates, Count?" Sisi then asked the red-faced rotund Count Auersperg who so far had said nothing. From then on she had little to contribute except a smile or nod or "Really?" "How nice!" when appropriate and let her mind wander to Hungary. The Hungarians would see Franz, not as the distant autocrat who had abolished their constitution, driven their leaders into exile and initiated a reign of terror. They would see a young family man with a wife and two charming daughters. The four of them together would present an irresistible portrait. And Franz would see the human side of the Hungarians.

When the conversation waned, she put in a word about herself. "I was born in Munich on Christmas Eve. My mother used to say I was her Christmas present from Father. Our summer home was Possenhofen. The country around there is wonderful for hiking or riding. Have you ever been?"

If someone was careless enough to intrude into the arena of politics, she had been instructed to say courteously: "Such matters are not my concern."

She glanced at the clock. Five more minutes to go. There was no strict time limit, but Sisi thought an hour sufficient without being discourteous. She began to cough, and Paula hurried forward with a handkerchief.

"Dear me," Countess von Warsburg murmured.

"Do try the elixir I recommended," said Countess Lutzow. "The Queen of Bavaria swears by it."

Sisi rose. "Thank you for coming." She shook hands, and they departed, leaving her to wonder as she always did what she had given them to tattle about. Nothing much, she was sure. She was getting better at this.

When Franz came to her that night, before she would allow him to touch her, she asked, "Am I still to accompany you to Hungary?"

"Mother's objections have been heard and overruled. Dr Seeburger has said a journey by boat to Budapest could in no way affect the children's health. Your presence is essential, my angel. Your charms will force the Hungarians to give us a warmer welcome than they would otherwise. Albrecht tells me they know you are sympathetic to their cause."

"I'm looking forward to it." If only her cough didn't get worse.

Chapter 19 – May 1857

The imperial yacht sailed down the Danube to Pressburg, where Archduke Albrecht waited with a military band. Although radically anti-Hungarian, he was the military governor of Hungary. Only thirteen years older, he was Franz's great-uncle. From there, Franz and Sisi made their state entry into the capital. Franz looked splendid riding a white horse and wearing the red uniform of a Hungarian general. Sisi in a national costume, with black velvet bodice and white lacy sleeves, rode in an open coach with her two little daughters and Archduke Albrecht.

Her first sight of the city hugging both banks of the river confirmed her expectations. Flowers filled window boxes and balconies, and she could see the green spaces of parks. Beyond the stately tree-lined boulevards and grand houses, a patchwork of fields and woodlands rolled away into the distance. It was enchanting.

People lined the riverbanks, and vendors of flowers, fruit and food strolled among them. It was not a great crowd, to be sure, but it was a start. Sisi waved and most waved back.

"Is that the medieval castle where we'll be staying?" she asked Albrecht, indicating stone ramparts on a hill.

"No, Your Majesty, that's Fisherman's Bastion. It was built to warn the city of invaders coming up the river. But why does Your Majesty call the place a castle? It is a royal palace and quite grand."

"It's my imagination at play." Sisi smiled happily and lifted Gisela onto her lap. "I shall be vastly disappointed if I don't see any knights in armour."

"There are in fact some parts of the medieval buildings still in existence. I would be happy to show Your Majesty around," the Archduke offered.

"Thank you," she said noncommittally. She was quite sure she would be far too busy.

Only her imagination was disappointed. Maria Theresa had been here performing her magic. The rooms were very much like the ones in the Viennese palaces, stucco and gilt with pictures and mirrors framed in rocaille, and many-branched candelabra. Even the furniture had come from Vienna, and the ubiquitous pear-shaped ceramic stoves squatted in the corners.

Since it was late in the day, there were no official engagements to attend. Franz and Sisi were able to spend a little time with their daughters. Sisi sat on the floor to allow them to romp over her. Gisela was ten months old and unable to walk yet. Sisi hoped to have her walking before they returned to Vienna and she had to surrender her children once again to Sophie's care. Gisela wasn't cooperating. When Sisi stood her up, as soon as she let go the child went to her knees.

The little archduchesses were taken off to bed by their nurses, and Franz and Sisi enjoyed a light supper in their room, almost alone. Having been informed a Greek tycoon had commissioned the most famous pyrotechnician of the day to stage a fireworks display in their honour, they went out onto the balcony to watch. Below, the Chain Bridge that spanned the Danube glittered with a thousand lights, and across the river all the great houses and public buildings were illuminated. For fully fifteen minutes the sky over Pest shimmered and fizzed with dazzling colours and patterns, culminating in the name Erzsebet followed by a bouquet of roses.

Sisi's hand slipped into Franz's. "It's magical," she whispered.

The following day they were swept into a round of receptions and military manoeuvres. On horseback, Sisi sat beside Franz to watch a military parade. Previously she had only been allowed to watch from a carriage with a lady-in-waiting beside her. Some of the Viennese were scandalised by this further demonstration of their Empress's disregard for convention, but the Hungarians were madly enthusiastic. They took her to their hearts, and their admiration warmed her heart.

They toured the city, fascinated by the Turkish style houses of Buda, as much as the modern buildings of Pest. The horses that pulled the fiacres were the best kept Sisi had ever seen outside aristocratic stables. Her portrait was everywhere she looked. It was for sale in shops and markets and hung in the train station and schools. One of her Hungarian attendants told her that every Hungarian housewife had a picture of her hanging over the mantel, and despaired because they could never be as beautiful as the Empress. Gifts were lavished on her at every occasion: dogs and horses and jewels, making it clear they knew what would please her.

Franz, however, was even stiffer and more formal than usual, and Sisi worried that no adulation came his way. When a delegation of aristocratic conservatives presented him with a petition requesting the restoration of the constitution, he received them coldly and made it clear there was to be no change in Hungary's status in the empire. He was prepared to concede the Hungarians no greater privileges than the Poles and the Bohemians. All were to continue unified in the Austrian empire. It was obvious to Sisi that he was far more sympathetic towards the German and Slav populations than the proud, native Magyars.

The castle was festively decorated in preparation for the first court ball to be held for many years. Sisi wore another national costume she'd had designed in Vienna. It was green, with a black velvet bodice and plenty of embroidery and lace trimming. A short veil was pinned to her hair. Even Franz was astonished.

"My darling, you look ravishing."

"Like a ravishing Hungarian peasant girl?" She laughed and twirled so that the flounces at the bottom of the dress fluttered.

After Franz's lengthy titles had been called out, he entered the ballroom with Sisi on his arm. Everyone turned to look before the men bowed and the ladies sank into curtsies. Reaching the end of the room, where their chairs were, Franz and Sisi took their seats. Everyone rose. Someone began to clap, then another and soon the entire room was resounding with applause. "Brava, Empress!" a man called. "Our Empress!" from another. Franz lifted her hand from where it lay on the chair arm and kissed it

The music struck up. It was Strauss's new waltz, *The Blue Danube*. Franz danced only the first dance, because it was expected of him, and after that remained in his chair looking cold and unapproachable. Sisi had no lack of partners and was the cynosure of all eyes as she whirled about the floor. Her dress received as many compliments as her beauty. She tried to speak to her partners in Hungarian and invited them to correct her, which they were delighted to do. They were handsome and exotic, with their dark eyes and fulsome black beards, their gilded and jewelled uniforms and their leopard-skin cloaks draped with studied carelessness over one shoulder, a single heron plume rising from their shakos.

One man, Count Hunyádi, was so witty he made her laugh throughout the dance, but when it ended he became very serious, his eyes gleaming as he bent over her hand. "You are our hope, Empress. You alone."

158

Another partner, a bear of a man, somewhat of a stranger to the dance floor said to her, "Empress, Count Andrássy is in exile. He is needed. If you love Hungary, ask the Emperor to let him come home." She had never heard of Count Andrássy.

Others spoke a brief word to her, making it clear that they knew of her interest in Hungary, its history and desire for freedom, and they knew of her love of riding, which they shared. Perhaps they really did like her, she mused later, but their tribute was at least in part policy. They saw her as an opponent of Sophie and her coterie, whom they held largely responsible for the atrocities of '49, and perhaps they thought she could influence the Emperor on their behalf. Franz's bias was strongly entrenched and made all the more extreme by the fact that his would-be assassin was a Hungarian. She was resolved to try, however.

She found herself looking at the men with appraising eyes. They were so splendid, so flamboyant in dress and manners that they made even Franz look insignificant. Their admiring glances and bold flatteries told her clearer than words that she was a beautiful and desirable woman. For the first time in her life, she felt just a glimmer of the power of womanhood.

Archduke Albrecht announced that there would be a demonstration of a *czárdás*, a national folk dance for Their Majesties' pleasure. As the floor cleared, Sisi took her seat beside Franz. The orchestra began a wild, thumping rhythm and a hundred or so young people skipped into the ballroom, all dressed in white, the women with aprons of multi-coloured stripes and crowns of flowers, the men with sashes of the same stripes and feathered hats. They formed two circles, the women inside moving one way, the men the other, their feet stamping to the music. The watchers began to clap in time, and Sisi joined them. The music and the dance excited her. Even Franz was not immune: his index finger tapped on the arm of his chair.

The dancers broke apart to form an infinite labyrinth, weaving in and out, creating shapes and yet keeping the same beat. Finally, they found partners, and there was no more cohesion. Each couple performed according to their inclination and Sisi didn't know where to look. The men dominated. When the mood took them, they freed their partners who tossed their heads and turned their backs while the men strutted and postured.

"Each of these couples is from a different village. They will improvise according to their talent and mood," the Archduke leant down to say.

Sisi watched a couple who caught her eye. The man bent from the waist until his head almost touched the floor, then rose to thrust out his chest and kick his legs before taking his partner by the waist and spinning her around in an ecstasy of reunion, all the time stamping out the rhythm. Another man lifted his partner into the air and threw her from him. When she landed, she assumed a haughty expression and shook her frilled skirt. Now and then someone would shout: "*Hejje! Hujja!*"

"Ah, it's a courtship dance," Sisi murmured to Franz. "The men are displaying their peacock feathers."

When it was over and while the watchers were enthusiastically applauding, a young man detached himself from the rest and came to stand before Sisi. "Your Imperial Majesty, would you do me the great honour of consenting to dance," he said in perfect German.

"But I can't!" she protested. "I don't know how."

"I will help you." He held out his hand. "Please."

She glanced at Franz, not at all certain it was quite proper, but Franz nodded, and she could not refuse. Giving the young man her hand, she let him lead her into a cleared space.

"First we stamp," he said.

It wasn't at all difficult for her to get the rhythm; the orchestra was pounding it out, and her feet responded naturally. Then with one hand on her waist and the other in the air he whirled her round and round. When he released her, she turned her back on him, as she had seen the girls do and assumed a haughty stance. She probably spoiled the effect by peering over her shoulder to see what he was doing. Suddenly he was before her. With a gesture of the hand, he beckoned her forward, and she went to him. "I lift," he whispered. She was ready for him as he lifted her high into the air and held her there, apart from him in an amazing feat of strength while he spun and spun and Sisi laughed with pleasure. "*Hejje! Hujja!*" he shouted. The faster he twirled, the more the audience cheered. When he lowered her to the floor, he kept his hands on her waist until she was steady.

160

The applause and tributes rolled around the ballroom when the dance ended. Sisi was a little breathless, but her partner seemed unaffected.

"That was most enjoyable. Thank you," she said to him.

"It was my pleasure, Majesty. May I?" He held out his hand and escorted her back to her chair.

"You dance so well. Surely you must have Hungarian blood, Majesty." Count Hunyádi had taken up a station beside her chair.

"Do all your people like to dance, Count?"

"It has been said that to a Hungarian life is a dancing school."

A dancing school. The Viennese and the Hungarians really ought to be able to get along, Sisi thought. One loved music and the other loved dance.

She went to bed happier than she had felt in months. What joy it was to be among people who were so spontaneous and exuberant. She doubted the young man she had danced with was a peasant, as he was obviously well-educated, but still, it could never have happened in Vienna. Though the Hungarians observed the proper courtesies and were effusive in their compliments to Sisi, they affected none of the ostentatious sycophancy of their Viennese counterparts.

"What a delightful evening," she said when Franz joined her in bed. "Did you enjoy it?"

"Yes, delightful. I think I ought to be jealous. The Hungarians pay you such extravagant compliments."

Sisi giggled. "They are masters of the art!" She wished he were jealous – it would make him less contained – but such an unworthy emotion was not in Franz's nature. "That is why you brought me, remember? To charm them."

"So I did, and a grand job you are doing, my sweet ambassadress."

He reached for her. She put her hands on his chest to hold him off.

"Franz, who is Count Andrássy?"

"One of the Hungarian exiles. A firebrand and troublemaker. Why do you ask?"

"Someone mentioned him tonight. He said he thought the Count ought to come home."

"I think not. He will thwart any progress we hope to make with the Hungarians."

"Do you begin to like them a little better, Franz?"

"Don't be foolish. Liking has nothing to do with it."

"What I mean is…"

"I like you. That's all that matters."

He closed the distance between them and sought her lips. Sisi did not enjoy their coupling any more than she had on the first night and often found excuses to avoid her marital duty. But her mother was right: she had grown used to it, and she was still expected to produce an heir. Sophie reminded her of this lack often, as if the sex of the children she had produced was somehow her fault.

She wondered if she was cold, or if other women felt as she did, but there was no one she could ask about such an intimate matter. Not even her mother, or any of her aunts, and Nené wasn't yet married. Cold or not, she did her duty. Duty! The most horrid word in the language.

……….

Franz and Sisi planned to visit some of the outlying villages and agricultural areas but just before they were to leave Budapest, Gisela came down with a fever. When Gisela recovered, Sophie was ill with fever accompanied by diarrhoea. She was fretful and cried constantly.

"It is the same problem, Majesties: teething," Dr Seeburger said with utter confidence. "There is no reason to postpone your trip."

Reassured, they set off on a tour of the interior. It was a wonderful trip for Sisi. She fell ever more deeply under the spell of the beautiful country. The dreamy waters of Lake Balaton, with low hills beyond covered in the vivid green of vineyards. On the treeless plains of the Puszta, wild horses roamed and an occasional gipsy encampment squatted beside a spring. Neat little cottages with thatched roofs sat beside streams where children splashed, and herons stalked among the reeds. The fields and woods wore the tender green coats of spring, and the sweet scent of acacias perfumed the air. It all brought out the romanticism in her that had almost been smothered by the constraints of life in Vienna.

Strolling through a village with children dancing around them, and Sisi's arms loaded with flowers, Franz stopped to speak to one of the elders, trying to get a feel for the sentiments of the people. The guileless old man replied, "The people are all right, Your Majesty. It's only that wretched priest who is black and yellow up to his ears." A peal of laughter from the Empress greeted the remark.

The people came out of their cottages and waved as the procession went by, women wearing their finest embroideries, men in feathered caps. Peasants proudly offered examples of local crafts and samples of early produce. It was all very different from the reception they had been accorded in Italy. When they moved on, young men accompanied them down the road racing their horses alongside, standing on their saddles, or jumping off one side and then somersaulting over to the other without touching the saddle. Some were able to perform this feat several times in a row. Sometimes a cluster would gallop towards the Empress's coach as if about to attack, only to stop at the last moment with their horses' hooves flung into the air and waved their hats in a dazzling display of horsemanship.

The Hungarians loved their horses and gave Sisi the impression they were newcomers to cities and longed to be out on the Steppes, wild and free, their dark eyes fixed on a far horizon. She would have liked to ride too, but it was not permitted.

Five days later they arrived at the town of Debreczin, where a telegram awaited them. Dr Seeburger wrote that little Sophie was seriously ill and advised Their Majesties' immediate return.

....

The journey back was unbearably long and fraught with terror. Upon reaching the palace, they rushed to their daughter's bedside. The room stank of something vile. The windows were closed and the curtains drawn. Gisela's cradle had been moved to another room. A nurse was in attendance as well as Dr Seeburger. Little Sophie lay in her bed, flushed with fever, her eyes half-open and glazed, pitiably weak. Sisi sat on the edge of the bed and took her daughter into her arms. Sophie was like a lifeless doll, obviously insensible, her arms dangling. "Mama is here, my darling," Sisi whispered through the thickness in her throat. "Mama is here."

Franz was speaking in low tones to the doctor. Sisi gently laid her daughter down and looked their way, her eyes glittering with unshed tears. Franz sat beside her and took her hand in his. "You must be brave, my dear," he said shakily.

"No!" she screamed. "No, I won't be brave! I can't...I can't..."

She gasped for breath. The air in the room seemed poisoned. She was shaking so hard, Franz pulled her to him and held her firmly against her struggles until she subsided. "For Sophie." He choked on her name. "Be brave for Sophie."

She took a deep breath, fought for and gained a measure of composure. Rising, she faced the doctors. "Is there no hope?" The words emerged not as a question but a plea.

Dr Seeburger looked at the floor. "I am sorry, Your Majesty."

She returned to the bed and, making herself comfortable, gathered the frail little body into her arms.

Sisi spoke only once after that. "What is that smell?"

"Her Imperial Highness has been incontinent and vomiting blood," the doctor answered.

And I wasn't here to comfort her. Oh, my poor, poor child...

"Open the curtains and the windows. Let us have some fresh air in here."

Duty. She had a final duty to perform: to assist at her daughter's dying. The daughter she had failed. She could not surrender to the hysteria that threatened to choke her. Franz sat at the foot of the bed, slumped, his hands dangling between his knees. Food was brought and ignored. Franz dismissed the doctor and the nurses.

The hours slipped past and darkness filled the windows. Sophie's little chest began to heave as she struggled to breathe. Sisi held her for eleven hours while fever consumed its tiny victim. At nine-thirty that night, Sophie died in her mother's arms.

Franz telegraphed his mother. *Our little one is an angel in heaven.*

Chapter 20 – Summer 1857

Having refused an escort, Sisi was alone in the summer woods. Grooms and policemen tried to follow her, but she had no difficulty leaving them floundering in her wake. She urged Forester faster. When he showed signs of slowing, she used her riding crop on him. Trees raced by and branches flew overhead, and the horse's hooves beat a thunderous tattoo in the green silence. The only people she ever saw were herders or farmers. Sometimes she stopped to watch them. Ordinary people with ordinary lives. She was only nineteen, yet she felt she had lived too long.

Every day she drove in a closed carriage with the blinds down from Laxenburg to the Church of the Capuchins. Alighting in the Neue Markt, dressed from head to foot in unrelieved black, she descended into the crypt where Sophie was buried among her long dead ancestors, to weep and pray at her dead daughter's tomb.

After returning to Laxenburg, she ordered Forester saddled and, glutted with grief and remorse, rode off into the woods, pushing the horse to his limit as she tried to outrun the anguish that tormented her day and night.

When the sun was past its zenith, she turned back toward the palace. Her ladies smiled when they saw her. Sometimes she thought their smiles were so fixed they must sleep with them on.

"Did you have a good ride, Majesty?" Karolin asked brightly.

"Yes, thank you."

"You'll be pleased to hear His Majesty has returned. He has asked you to join him in his study."

"Very well. Get me out of this costume, please."

"What will it please Your Majesty to wear?"

"It doesn't matter."

She caught the exchange of glances between them. Franz had returned to Hungary without her to conclude the negotiations, and now he was back they expected her to take an interest in what she wore to greet him. But nothing interested her. Her Greek reader and her Hungarian tutor came and went daily without seeing her. Even her hairdresser was underemployed. Her secretaries had replied to the many condolence letters she and Franz had received from all over the world according to a standard formula. She attended no court functions or ceremonies, wrote no poetry or letters, ate little, slept badly and cried a lot. When she wasn't riding, she shut herself in her bedroom and thought about suicide. A selfish solution, she knew, to end her suffering by causing suffering to so many others. But she thought about it constantly. The oblivion of the tomb. The silence. The void.

"Your Majesty must be hungry after your ride. These are from Demel's, your favourite bakery," Paula said, offering her a plate with several rich cakes.

"You may share them among yourselves."

She couldn't eat. She was down from her usual one hundred pounds and couldn't bring herself to care.

Dressed in a dove grey tea gown, she went through the adjoining rooms into Franz's study. He was with three of the ministers.

"That will be all for now, gentlemen," he said when he saw her and held out his hands to her. His eyes searched her face.

"Welcome home, Franz." She tilted her head for his kiss. "Was it a successful trip?"

They sat together on a couch. Franz's study was a demonstration of his simple tastes. His desk was small and neat, the furniture upon which they sat plain. Beside it the Walnut Room, where Franz gave audiences was a study in formal magnificence.

"I think you will agree that it was. I was given quite a warm reception and, bearing in mind the special circumstances of Hungary and the need for conciliation, I allowed some of the exiles to return, including Count Andrássy, the man we spoke about the night of the ball. I also restored his rank and estates."

"I'm glad." But she wasn't glad. Gladness was as much a stranger to her as any emotion other than guilt and grief.

"Maximilian is due to arrive in a few days with his new bride. I think we should put off court mourning for the occasion?"

"If you wish."

"You will like Charlotte. Max says she is charming and clever."

And a far greater prize than you have in me. A king's daughter, no less. Mother-in-law must be thrilled.

Franz watched her in silence. "Sisi," he finally said gently, "I have spoken to Mother. She tells me you still do little all day and hardly eat. You cannot go on like this, my love. It is natural to grieve, but your grief is excessive and worries everyone. I have a double grief to bear: for our lost little one and you because your suffering is so great. I fear I might lose you also."

Sisi made no reply. It was hard enough to bear her own grief, let alone Franz's as well. She stared at a picture of a hunting scene on the opposite wall with dull eyes that saw nothing.

"I too have lost a daughter. I too grieve. But I can't neglect my duty for this or anything. Sisi, I want you to return to my side."

A rattle of cups came from the adjacent valet de chambre's room. Sisi turned her head towards the sound.

"I want to help you," Franz pleaded with her. "I love you so much. I can't bear to see you like this. I would do anything for you, you know that. Please, tell me what I can do."

"I want my mother," Sisi said softly.

....

Ludovika set out at once with two of her younger daughters. Sisi wept when they arrived and hugged them all tightly. It was thought their high spirits might have an effect on her, and it seemed the company of her sisters did cheer her. Settled in the salon, she heard the latest family news, including the recent development on the proposed marriage between Marie Sophie and Francis II, the Crown Prince of Naples and Duke of Calabria, son of King Ferdinand of the Two Sicilies.

At fifteen, Marie Sophie, nicknamed Madi, was becoming a great beauty like her older sisters and bore a striking resemblance to Sisi. She had the same melancholy eyes, although her temperament was anything but melancholy.

"I am already learning Italian and like you, Sister, being drilled in court manners, how to be a queen, and how to talk," Madi informed her, not sounding in the least thrilled. "I thought I knew how to do that but apparently not. I am also undergoing treatments with leeches and baths so hot as to almost scald."

Sisi turned to Ludovika in astonishment. "Leeches?"

"Her menses hasn't started. It is a treatment recommended by the doctors to bring on her flow. The Neapolitans won't commit until she is fully formed."

"Imagine, if you will, my mortification at having something of so intimate a nature discussed by total strangers in the courts of Europe." Even talking about it among female members of her family brought a blush to Madi's cheeks.

"Do you know anything about him?" Ludovika asked when the girls were distracted, having found some sheet music of Brahms. "The thought of belonging to a man she doesn't know and who doesn't know her makes her afraid."

None of the family had met him, but Sisi had asked Habsburg relatives who had been to Southern Italy and learned some disturbing facts. "I've heard he has a weak character. He fears his stepmother, the priests and the reactionary cabal at court. And I'm afraid he's not very pretty, nor well-educated."

"Well, not every girl has the good fortune to be chosen by a handsome prince who also happens to be the most powerful man in Europe," Ludovika said archly.

Sisi decided to ignore that. "But the worst is that Naples is bound to be caught up in the struggle for Italian unification."

"She will help him. She is a very resolute girl."

Another wild Wittelsbach girl to be sent into a situation for which she had not been prepared, Sisi thought, pitying her sister. At least she had known her husband and found in him a kind and loving man. What kind of man would poor Madi find?

"But what of Nené? Is there no prospect for her?" Nené was now twenty-two and spent her time painting and doing charity work while waiting for a husband. It was almost too late. Fifteen or sixteen was the preferred age, while girls were still young enough to be moulded into their new lives. Sisi still felt the occasional twinge of guilt for filching her sister's intended, even though she believed she had done Nené a great favour.

"There is. As a matter of fact, I wanted to talk to you about that. As you can imagine, Nené is very depressed by her single state. You know how it is. Once a girl reaches a certain age, everyone believes she must be somehow flawed. I am afraid if it continues much longer she will take the veil."

"But there is a suitor?"

"Your father decided to intervene and play matchmaker. He invited the Thurn and Taxis family to a hunting party at Possenhofen. Nené met Prince Maximilian. I don't know how much

168

to attribute to her long spinsterhood, but she indicated to your father and me that she found him agreeable. And, indeed, there is nothing about the prince to suggest he would not be a good husband to her. Before the hunting party was over, he approached his parents with marriage plans."

"That's wonderful. But your tone of voice suggests a difficulty."

"The Thurn and Taxis family are very rich, but that's the only thing to recommend them. King Maximilian won't agree to the match because they are not social equals of a princess of royal blood and a member of the House of Wittelsbach."

"Oh, I see." The Bavarian king had the right of refusal when it came to the marriages of his family. If a couple married without his consent, the entire family would be in disgrace.

"I was hoping you could prevail upon the Emperor to write to King Maximilian and express his approval of the match. I'm quite sure that would make a difference."

"Of course I will. I would be happy to."

"We must see Nené wed," Madi said, leaning over the back of the sofa, "if only to prove what we've always said about her."

"And what's that, dear?" Ludovika asked.

"That she will be late for her wedding!"

Everyone laughed. Even Sisi smiled.

During the following days, Sisi showed her sisters around the palace and often walked with them in the gardens or visited the zoo. Sisi and Ludovika sat together on a shady bench while the girls explored the maze, calling to each other. Accompanied by the inevitable guard, Sisi took them shopping to the Graben, and they returned laden with presents from their sister. It was the first time she had been out in public in weeks, and she hid her face as much as possible behind a parasol or a veil. In the evenings they wrote in their diaries, read to each other, played tarok, their favourite card game, or just talked, filling Sisi in on the trivial details of their daily lives that never made it into letters.

One day the two girls were taken by Count von Weckbecker on a tour of Vienna. Sisi sat on the chaise in her salon. When Ludovika came to sit beside her, she curled up and rested her head in her mother's lap with a sigh. Ludovika's fingers absently stroked the hair at her temple.

They sat for a while in a silence disturbed only by the ticking of the two-faced clock before Ludovika said, "Your Aunt Sophie tells me you hardly eat and shut yourself away all day."

"She hates me."

"That's not true. She…"

"You should have seen the look on her face when we returned from Hungary. I saw it clearly. She blames me for Sophie's death."

"Perhaps, in the beginning, she wanted to blame someone. I think that's a natural part of grief. We don't want to believe it's random, or God's will, or whatever, especially when it comes to little ones. I spoke to her. She is extremely worried about you and just wants you to get well."

"*I* blame myself! Perhaps I could bear the grief, but the guilt… Oh, Mimi, the guilt is crushing me. God gave me a wonderful gift, and I let it slip through my fingers. I insisted on taking the girls to Hungary and then I left them, knowing Sophie was ill."

"I think everyone knows who's to blame," Ludovika said heatedly. "That fool of a doctor for misunderstanding the seriousness of her condition. How could he mistake a mortal illness for teething and still call himself a doctor?"

"To vindicate himself, he has put it about the court that I persistently ignored his advice throughout the journey. And he is believed."

A maid came in carrying a tea tray with slices of Sacher torte. She was about to put it down when Sisi said fretfully, "Who ordered that? Can I not speak to my mother without interruption? Take it away."

"Very well, Majesty." The maid curtsied and went out.

Ludovika heaved a sigh. "Franz tells me you hardly see Gisela. He doesn't understand."

"I have resigned Gisela to Aunt Sophie's care. She was right all along: I am not a fit mother."

"Oh, my darling, of course, you are! What happened was not your fault."

Sisi picked at the lace on her cuff. "One day Gisela was visiting Franz and me. She sat in that little red armchair of Sophie's. We both wept, and Gisela laughed merrily. She was so pleased with herself because she could finally sit in the special chair."

"She is a dear child, and she needs her mother."

"She doesn't need me. She has her grandmama." An edge of bitterness had crept into Sisi's voice. It was the first time in the conversation that Ludovika had heard any emotion.

"I saw the poem you are writing on your desk. 'I loved, I lived, I wandered throughout the world; but never reached what I strove for.' What is it you are striving for, my dearest?"

"I don't even know. Perhaps freedom. But none of us is free really, are we? Perhaps, then, only a little more freedom. When I was a princess of Bavaria, life was kind to me. I thought it always would be. I didn't expect anything of this. I am a bad mother, and I am a bad Empress. No, it's true. I have tried, Mimi, I really have. There are so many ladies here better born, better bred and better educated than I. They envy me, and they despise me. Aunt Sophie despises me. It's all hopeless... hopeless!" There were tears in her voice.

"From what I hear you proved yourself a good Empress in Italy and particularly in Hungary. The people there took you to their hearts. They see you as more approachable than the Emperor, more human. I have even heard it said that if a rapprochement can be brought about between Austria and Hungary, it will be due in large part to you."

Sisi stirred. "I can't do it anymore, Mimi. Countess Esterhazy told me that Aunt Sophie lost five babies, but each time she bounced right back. I can't...bounce." Esterhazy had also scolded her that such excessive grief was self-indulgence.

"Yes, it's true. Then she went to Ischl and took the mineral baths. It did the trick. Astonishingly she produced four sons in a row. Imagine that. Don't pay any attention to Esterhazy, darling. She is a disagreeable woman. Your grief will always be part of you, just as the memory of that dear child will. No one can tell you to put it behind you, but we can ask that you begin to function again. Franz is beside himself with anxiety. He has so many cares; he needs you by his side. And your father and I, your sisters and cousins, all your friends in Bavaria, we worry too."

Sisi didn't believe Franz needed her – he had his mother. As in the days before Sisi came along, Sophie was on her son's arm at all official functions. How she must be loving it! First lady of the empire and surrogate mother to the empire's only child.

"I have no courage. There is nothing inside me but grief and guilt. I wake up in the mornings and the day ahead terrifies me. I don't want to get out of bed. I can't face people – the accusing eyes, the false smiles. They all know I left Sophie when she was ill. They know I'm an unnatural mother. I have no courage left to face them. I am so alone here. So alone."

"You did your duty to Franz and the empire. No one would have expected you to remain behind because your daughter was teething. That would have been absurd. I say again, it was that bungling doctor who misinformed you. Everyone knows you would never have left Sophie if you had known how serious her condition was." Voices came from the stairs. "Ah, here are your sisters. Sisi, darling, for the sake of all who love you, please learn to live again."

Sisi swung her feet down and sat up straight. Ludovika captured and held one of her hands. The two girls entered the room, looking, to Sisi, so young and carefree in their summer dresses.

"Did you enjoy yourselves?" Ludovika asked.

"Oh, yes, Mimi!" Madi unfastened the ribbons of her hat and dropped it into the nearest chair. "We promenaded in the Prater and rode the carousel."

"Count von Weckbecker showed us where they have started to build the Ringstrasse," Spatz added. "And we saw the Opera House and went for a boat ride on the river."

Franz was tearing down the old medieval walls and building a broad circular boulevard to enclose Vienna. Everyone already knew that those who lived outside it would have inferior addresses.

"We had lemonade and gugelhupf at Demel's bakery. Spatz had two pieces." Madi looked reprovingly at her youngest sister.

"My, you did have a busy afternoon," Sisi said.

I was the same age Madi is now when I met Franz. Like her I would have come running home full of exuberance, in love with life, bursting to tell everyone of my adventures. There were giants under the hills around Possi, but there never were any monsters. It is strange to think how blithe I was only four years ago.

....

It was time for Ludovika and her daughters to leave. She thought the visit had done Sisi some good, but Sisi couldn't hold back her tears at their parting. She kissed her sisters multiple times and made them promise to write.

172

"We will be leaving for Ischl soon. Please come," she said to Ludovika.

"Be sure I will if I can."

"I'm selfish, I know. You have seven other children to consider. But I need you so."

"My dear child." Ludovika hugged her again. "I will come if I can," she repeated. "In the meantime, take good care of yourself. If I come to Ischl, I shall be very angry if I don't see an improvement in your health."

Sisi could only nod wordlessly. She waved until the carriage had disappeared through the gates and then went back inside the silent palace, climbing the marble stairs slowly. In her bedchamber, she told her ladies that she would see no one, closed the door, crawled onto the bed and wept.

Chapter 21 – September 1857-September 1858

About a month after Ludovika's departure, Franz entered Sisi's bedroom at Bad Ischl. He had taken to sleeping in his own bedroom at Schönbrunn because Sisi's continual tears distressed him so much. In the Kaiservilla, as it was now called, Sisi had her own suite of rooms.

"Do you mind if I join you?" Ruler of a vast empire and millions of people, yet he sought consent to approach his wife's bed so diffidently that Sisi hadn't the heart to refuse him. She hoped he didn't want to make love. He was not very adept at hiding the longing in his eyes.

She was laid on her back and had to lift her head when he tried to wriggle his arm under her shoulders. Aware of her stiffness, he didn't attempt to draw her close.

After moments of tense silence, he said, "Sisi, I would like us to make another baby."

She turned her face toward him "You want to make another baby?" she repeated as if she hadn't heard him. "Why?"

"I think it would help."

"Babies just mean heartbreak, Franz. This one would be taken from me just as the others were."

"I don't want to quarrel." His free hand crept to her breast. "Do you think we might try?"

She sighed. "Very well."

She lay supine, while Franz ploughed on doggedly, completing an act of union all by himself.

It wasn't until January that Sisi was able to tell Franz he had succeeded. She was pregnant. After that, he returned to sleeping in his own bed. "To make sure you get plenty of rest, my darling."

Sophie had become even more unkind since the death of her namesake and no longer spoke to Sisi with any degree of courtesy in private. She had collected a coterie around her whose mandate, apparently, was to make the Empress miserable. Included in this number was Sisi's new sister-in-law, Archduke Maximilian's wife. Charlotte, the only daughter of the Belgian king, was beautiful, intelligent and rich, with the kind of impeccable pedigree that Sisi lacked. Whenever she had the opportunity, and Sisi was within hearing, Sophie made a point of praising her new daughter-in-law's upbringing, her cleverness, and most of all the true affection she showed her husband and mother-in-law. Every word, while designed to laud Charlotte, was also intended to disparage Sisi.

Instead of expressing her pleasure at Sisi's pregnancy, Sophie used the occasion to scold her. "It is about time. You are not doing your duty to my son or the empire. Your first duty is to produce children. Your second is to appear beside the Emperor on ceremonial occasions. You did not even have the grace to appear at the Christmas and New Year celebrations. How long has it been since you saw the inside of a church? You have indulged yourself far too long. In future, you will show yourself to the people. There will be no more riding, and you will eat properly. Be sure I will be watching you. The child you carry is important to the empire, if not to you. Take care of him."

Having delivered herself of this diatribe, she swept out. Sophie's words hurt because there was much truth in them, but instead of running to her bedroom to weep, Sisi continued with the letter she was writing. Perhaps I am growing a thick skin, she thought, at least as far as she is concerned.

The months ahead would include many public appearances: the two balls that Franz gave during Carnival, washing the feet of twelve poor men on Maundy Thursday, the Derby in May, the Corpus Christi procession in June, all the church solemnities that accompanied these occasions, and a charity function or two. And in between, there would come a certain day in late May when her thoughts would return to Budapest and a small girl struggling for each breath...

She resolved to get well. Specialists were called in from Berlin and Prague, and she followed the doctors' advice in every detail, forced herself to eat and gave up riding.

The news spread very quickly, and Sisi received congratulatory letters from all parts of the empire, some offering advice about what she must do to ensure the safe delivery of a male child. Paula was reading one of the letters out loud while Sisi had her hair dressed. The first Carnival ball was scheduled for that night. Paula suddenly giggled.

"What is it?" Sisi asked.

"It is a little risqué, Your Majesty."

"I am a grown woman. Read it."

"'The most efficacious method of producing a boy,' the writer says, "'is to melt some lead and drop it in water when the moon is full. If a piece takes the shape of a... you know...'" Paula giggled again.

Peering over her shoulder, Countess Esterhazy read: "'...a penis, you are to take it to the altar of the Madonna.' Why does childbirth bring out such arrant superstition in the gullible?"

But the other ladies were looking at the Empress, and her hairdresser paused with her fingers entwined with strands of long hair. Sisi was laughing.

....

Although Sisi didn't know it and would have argued to the contrary, the births of Sophie and Gisela had been easy. This one was difficult. She was at Laxenburg, scene of her miserable honeymoon, and her cries of pain echoed through the palace. After twenty-four hours of labour, her exhausted and depleted body pushed the baby out.

"It's a boy!" someone exclaimed. "A fine boy."

Sisi only wanted to sleep, but she was tugged about as her linens were changed. When someone began to fuss with her hair, she pushed the hands away. She had the impression that the room was full of people and uproar.

Then Franz was bending over her. "We have our son, my dear. We have our son." His voice was teary and joyful at once. She felt his cool lips on her brow, his fingers easing the damp hair from her face.

"Tell them to let me sleep," she murmured, too tired to share his joy.

While the Empress slept, court and citizens celebrated the birth of the crown prince. A twenty-one gun salute was fired, and flags were hoisted everywhere. Franz made generous donations to churches and the people. Every night there was a spontaneous festival in the streets and the sky was lit by fireworks. Wine and beer flowed freely, courtesy of the Habsburgs. *Health to His Majesty! To Her Majesty! To the crown prince!* Franz showed his son on the balcony to ecstatic crowds, while Sisi sank deeper into oblivion.

It wasn't until two days later that she awoke, feverish, and her breasts aching from milk congestion. She was alone in the semi-darkness of her bedroom. In the adjacent salon, she could hear subdued voices. "My son," she called, and her voice was so weak it scarce disturbed the air around her. The chattering continued. She tried again. "Ladies!"

Esterhazy came to the door, followed by two or three others, who at once began fussing around her. The curtains were opened, her pillows shaken and adjusted. How was she feeling? She needed water; her thirst was dreadful. They wanted to change her linens, but she insisted on seeing her son first.

"Of course, Your Majesty, I'll go and see if a visit is convenient," Esterhazy said.

It seemed to Sisi that she was gone a long time. Doctors came to examine her and pronounced that the fever had abated somewhat. Docilely, she drank the medicine they gave her. They ordered her bathed in cold water and fed on broth. She begged them to let her nurse the baby, but they were adamant that she must not. Then they left. The ladies removed her nightgown and bathed her, which caused her to shiver violently.

"Where is Countess Esterhazy?" she fretted. "I want to see my son." She sat in a chair while the maids changed her bed linens. When they put her back to bed, she sent Paula to see what was keeping Esterhazy.

She tried hard to stay awake but again succumbed to a feverish sleep. She did not sleep peacefully. She tossed and thrashed and had hideous dreams. One was that her son was still inside her. Everyone thought he had been born and she couldn't convince them that he hadn't. Sometimes when she opened her eyes, the room was in semi-darkness and sometimes in total darkness. Occasionally her head was lifted for a cool drink of water. She shook with chills and burned with fever. During a lucid moment, she wondered if she was dying, and allowed herself to drift away – whether to dreams or death didn't matter.

When she awoke, really awoke, the fever had loosened its hold. The room was soon full of ladies. When she asked to see her son, there was an exchange of glances. Countess Esterhazy informed her that he was gone to the nursery at Schönbrunn.

Sisi was well enough to feel the full impact of that blow. "I haven't even seen him. I haven't held him. Why was he taken away?" Slow and miserable tears leaked from her eyes.

"It was thought best to establish him in the nursery and a regular routine as soon as possible," Esterhazy said crisply. "No one knew how long you would be ill. You are far too weak to care for a baby. There now, no need for tears. You will see him soon enough."

"I'm not too weak to hold him. I should have liked to hold him just for a little while. I don't even know his name. I have a son, and I don't even know his name."

"His name is Rudolf, after a famous Habsburg ancestor." The countess could hardly keep the exasperation from her voice.

Paula came in carrying a tray. "I have informed His Majesty that you are awake. He will be here as soon as he can get away. Dr Seeburger has sent broth. Can Your Majesty manage or shall I help?"

The smell of the broth was revolting, but Sisi knew she had to eat if she was to recover her health. "I can manage."

But she couldn't. Intermittent tremors shook her. She had to be spoon-fed. After the broth, she drank some beer. Protocol permitted it for medicinal purposes.

Franz came later, sat on the side of the bed and took her hands in his. "I'm sorry, darling. I'm in the midst of audiences, so I can't stay long. How are you?"

"A little better. Franz, why did you let them take the baby away?"

"He needed to be established in the nursery as soon as possible. There aren't the proper facilities for him here."

"I haven't even seen him."

"You will. Just as soon as you're strong enough." He kissed her hands. "He's in good health and everyone says he's a handsome lad."

"He has a wet nurse, I suppose."

"Yes. Her name is Marianka, a Moravian."

Matters had not improved very much after the nurseries had been moved. True, Sisi no longer had to walk a great distance and could see the children whenever she wanted, but Sophie was still in charge, made all the appointments and set their schedules. To take them outside to play when it wasn't scheduled was to create havoc and consternation.

"Franz, I want the right to supervise the children's education."

He didn't laugh, but his mouth quirked in amusement. "My mother asked the same thing of me when you were ill. We are in agreement that you are too young and too inexperienced for such a responsibility. Who is better qualified than the mother who prepared me for the throne?"

Franz dug into his pocket and withdrew a box inlaid with mother of pearl. "I have something for you, a little gift in thanks for the wonderful gift you have given me."

Sisi opened the box to see a triple strand of magnificent pearls. "Thank you, Franz, they are beautiful." A token, a palliative, because she couldn't have what she really wanted.

"And they will look even more beautiful adorning your lovely neck. I gave Rudolf a present too. I put the Order of the Golden Fleece in his cradle and made him a colonel. I want my son, granted to me by God's grace, from his entry into the world to be a member of my brave army."

Sisi wanted to weep for her small son. It was clear that like it or not, Rudolf would become a soldier. He would be brought up with all Franz's and Sophie's regressive, destructive views of the infallibility of empire, the God-given right of the Habsburgs to rule millions of people in servitude, and the superiority of the military. Rudolf, born into a changing world, would inevitably be exposed to other views. Perhaps he was the one who would see that the monarchy must change too if it was to survive.

Chapter 22 - January 1859

Recurring fevers kept Sisi in poor health throughout the fall and into the winter. She was depressed and lethargic. She forced herself to eat, even though she had no appetite, and followed every recommendation of Dr Seeburger – in whom she had no confidence. Nothing had any effect.

The only thing that made her feel better was a visit from family members. Ludovika came again in December and brought the old family physician, Dr Fischer. The doctor ordered a change in Sisi's diet. She was to drink a bowl of boiled beef blood daily.

By the time her sister arrived in January, Sisi was feeling better, apart from a persistent cough. Marie Sophie, married by proxy to the Crown Prince of Naples, stopped in Vienna on her way to her new home. Having some notion of what awaited Madi in the future, Sisi was determined to show her a good time. They went to the Burgtheater, the Prater and the Circus Renz, always heavily veiled and followed by police. They spent hours chatting together.

After supper, on the last night of Madi's stay in Vienna, she was reading the mail that had followed her, while Sisi put Bummerl through his repertoire of tricks and rewarded him with pieces of bread, which he loved. When Madi put the last letter down, Sisi brought up the subject both had avoided so far. "Are you nervous?"

"About the wedding night?" Madi sat in a chair opposite, and Bummerl padded over for a pet. "No, Mimi says it's just something to be got through. I have heard that Francis is impotent so perhaps there will be no wedding night! Mimi says no matter what he's like, I'm not to envy you because Franz is so wonderful."

"Yes, he is." Sisi ruffled Bummerl's shaggy coat. He always looked as if he'd been pulled through a hedge backwards.

There was no point in trying to convince Madi that Franz was not quite as wonderful as everyone thought. Except for their father, the family placed the fault squarely on her shoulders; she was ungrateful, selfish and a chronic complainer. The difficult mother-in-law was so common as to be a stereotype. Many young wives had to put up with her and still managed to be happy. Sisi could never convince them of the depth of her isolation and despair.

The truth was, Franz was no longer the tender and attentive lover of Bad Ischl any more than she was the uninformed girl of those days. Now when they went to Ischl for the holidays, he preferred to spend his time shooting duck or hunting stag to spending time with her. When they walked or rode together, he no longer dismissed his aides but often had them draw close and included them in the conversation. In Vienna, sometimes she didn't see him for days.

At twenty-two-years-old, Sisi understood and accepted that the honeymoon period would not last forever. But nor had she expected to feel quite so abandoned after the first glow had worn off. In the entire court, Franz was the only one she had a close connection with, the only one she could talk to about anything meaningful, even though it seemed with the passing years that they had little to say to each other. As always, Franz was immersed in politics, which he discussed with his mother, but never with her, continuing to believe that such matters could be of no interest to her in spite of what they had shared in Italy. But for Count Grunne she would not have known the situation with Italy and France was deteriorating and the talk now was of possible war.

Sisi didn't know how far their mother had primed Madi for what was to come, but she was determined her younger sister would not go to her marriage as ignorant as she had been. "Prepare yourself for disappointments, Madi. They are inevitable in a royal marriage. Not all courts are as carefree as the Residenz, and not all ruling families are as beloved as the Wittelsbachs."

"Oh, this from the most fortunate woman in the world! Don't worry about me, Sister. I shall do well enough."

Sisi had to smile. Blessed with a sunny disposition, Madi still had all the brash illusions of youth. "But I meant are you nervous about being the wife of a man whose country is on the brink of war. You do know about the situation in Italy?"

"I know a great deal more than when I was last here. I know that Cavour wants Italy to become one nation. Piedmont is arming and Garibaldi with a Sardinian army is threatening from the south. Yes, I am nervous, but I'm not frightened. I refuse to be frightened."

Sisi bit her lip. "It is worse than that. Franz's agents have reported that Cavour, complete with false beard and a false passport if you can believe it, met in secret with the Little Napoleon at a spa where Nappie was taking the cure. They reached an agreement that France would come to the aid of Piedmont if Austria were to attack. And then Victor Emmanuel's daughter was wed to Nappie's reprobate of a cousin. With Count Buol as our foreign minister, I'm afraid there is little chance of peace."

Count Camillo Cavour, Prime Minister of Piedmont, was the effective leader of the Italian unification movement. Giuseppe Garibaldi was the sword arm, and King Victor Emmanuel of Piedmont was the figurehead around which the forces rallied. Since her sister had become engaged to the crown prince, Sisi had made a point of learning more about the Italian situation. Along with her father she had found her brother-in-law Maximilian, who was the governor general of Lombardy and Venetia, to be a fund of information. Maximilian was a voice of reason lost in the chaos. He had written to Franz that Italy had good cause for complaint, and recommended a just, sage and mild treatment. His advice was ignored because nearer at hand were Sophie and her partisans, particularly foreign minister, Count Buol, who was advising Franz that might was the best bulwark against revolution, and, in any case, little Piedmont would not dare take up arms against Austria.

Madi tugged on Bummerl's ears. "And Prussia is threatening to intervene if France does. What can France hope to gain?"

"Lands, Nice and Savoy at least, and influence in the rest of the peninsula."

What Prussia hoped to gain was less easy to understand. Perhaps only to pick up any stray pieces. The king had suffered a stroke and his brother named regent, which brought Otto von Bismarck and the Junker party to power. Their policy was to reduce Austria's supremacy in the German Confederation.

"Austria will support us, won't it?" For the first time, Madi sounded uncertain.

"Of course. Franz is already strengthening the army in the south. General Gyulai is in supreme command."

That was the purpose of the marriage. The future King of the Two Sicilies, whose father was a fervent and cruel absolutist, was now the brother-in-law of the Emperor of Austria. The regime was not only threatened from without, but also by revolts from within. Sisi wondered how her mother, who loved her children, could have agreed to a marriage that sent her daughter into such a volatile situation. But she vaguely understood that Ludovika was stuck in the past when all that mattered were pedigrees, titles and wealth. Even after so many years she still felt the stigma of being married to a man of inferior birth, but she had made the best of it. She would have seen a crown prince as an excellent catch for her third daughter, no matter what the man himself was like. Sisi could only hope that Madi would find some degree of happiness. It just seemed so unlikely.

Sisi continued the journey with her sister as far as Trieste. Along the way their eldest brother Ludwig, nicknamed Louis in the family, joined them. Upon arrival, they were conducted to the governor's mansion, where they able to rest and refresh themselves. Later they were escorted to a large hall where a silk ribbon stretched from one wall to the other to symbolise the border between Bavaria and Naples. A large table stood under the ribbon, half in 'Bavaria' and half in 'Naples'.

"How quaint," Marie whispered.

She was led to a chair at the 'Bavarian' end of the table. Sisi and Louis watched as the doors at each end of the hall opened to admit the two delegations accompanied by an honour guard of Neapolitan or Bavarian soldiers. Documents were exchanged across the silk ribbon and passed on to attendants. The delegates bowed to each other. The Bavarian representative spoke words of parting to Marie, and all the Bavarians filed by to kiss her hand. Then the ribbon was lowered, and Marie passed into 'Naples'.

A tearful parting took place in the cabin of the ship that was to carry Madi away to her new husband and a land in turmoil. She was among strangers whose language she barely understood, and the only living creature with her from her home was a pet canary.

As they descended the gangway, Louis remarked, "I thank God I was not born female."

Chapter 23 – May-July 1859

The train was huffing and puffing, as if eager to be on its way. A stream of young men in uniform climbed into the carriages, then appeared at the windows to shout goodbyes to their loved ones. The wounded and sick who had been transferred from the front on the same train had been carried off before the Emperor's party arrived.

"Train sneezed!" three-year-old Gisela exclaimed.

Franz picked the child up and kissed her cheek. "Perhaps its nose tickled."

"But it doesn't have a nose," Gisela protested, as Franz handed her to her nurse.

He looked at Sisi. "Won't you send me off with a smile, darling."

She shook her head. "Franz, don't go. Please don't go."

"I must. We are being beaten and not by superior forces. The troops are hungry and poorly organised. Whether supplies reach them is a matter of happenstance. Profiteers are syphoning off whatever they can sell. I must take control myself. I thought you understood."

"You are needed in Vienna as well. There are many generals, only one Emperor."

He turned away to take eight-month-old Rudolf in his arms. The heir to the empire didn't have his sister's calm temperament. The noises of the train distressed him, and he was crying lustily. Franz kissed his wet face and handed him back to his nurse.

"Don't worry about me, my angel. Take very good care of yourself and your precious health. You are very dear to me."

A whistle blew. The chimney stack belched out smoke. Rudolf shrieked. The two nurses held the children close together and little Gisela soothed away her brother's cries.

"I must go," Franz said, and Sisi moved into his arms, holding him as if she would never let him go. He had to put her from him. Climbing onto the first step of the carriage, he remained there waving at his family as the train chugged out of the station.

In spite of reports to the contrary, Count Buol had convinced the Emperor that France would never side with Piedmont-Sardinia, and that, if needed, Austria could count on the German Confederation for support. Goaded by revolutionary demonstrations, military preparations, and Count Buol, Austria had done what Cavour and his allies had wanted all along: declared war, showing itself to all Europe as the aggressor. It wasn't until later that anyone remembered the Lombardian railways had been sold to the French two years earlier. With no trains available for Austria's use, soldiers went into battle without food and adequate supplies. All Italy was in revolt. The unification movement was gaining momentum, and Austrian armies were being thrown back. Franz was going to the front for a personal inspection tour to see what was needed.

But Sisi asked herself: if Franz was at the front, who was in Vienna negotiating for a peaceful settlement? Sophie and Count Buol! Franz was sorely needed in Vienna, but he adored the military and couldn't resist the idea of playing soldier with the prospect of covering himself in glory. The thought of Franz possibly being in danger terrified her and had already given her some sleepless nights. She had made Count Grunne, who was going with him, promise to keep the Emperor safe on every occasion. If anything happened to Franz, she did not know what she would do. His love for her was the only good thing, the only haven, in her new life. Though she knew there were times she exasperated him, he was never anything but tender. Without him, she would be completely at the mercy of Sophie and her coterie and her life would be even more horrible than it already was.

The carriage was surrounded by people when they returned to it. There were murmurs of: "Oh, the poor children!" The Viennese were not happy about the way the war was going. Too many young men, dead or broken, were returned to their families.

"Do you have family at the front, Leopoldine?" Sisi asked the Viennese nurse as the carriage rocked into motion.

"Yes, Your Majesty, my oldest son. My brother-in-law was in the war but he was killed."

"At the Ticino?"

"He was wounded there and died on the way back."

"And your son? How does he fare?"

"He is well as far as I know."

Sisi reached across and squeezed her hand. "I am sorry for you. This is a terrible time to be a mother." Gisela, sensing that her nurse was in need of comfort patted her shoulder with a chubby hand.

"And a worse time to be a young man. I hope His Imperial Majesty will bring the war to an end quickly."

"I'm sure he will." Sisi looked out the window, her eyes stinging. Franz had no intention of ending the war. What he wanted was a glorious victory, Cavour and Garibaldi in chains, and a thoroughly subdued Italy.

In her bedchamber, Sisi unpinned her hat and sank onto the edge of the bed. Countess Esterhazy came to the door.

"Do you need anything, Majesty?"

"No, thank you, Countess."

"Her Imperial Highness asks that you join her for the *Jause* at five this afternoon."

"Be so good as to convey my regrets to Her Imperial Highness."

"Your regrets? But what shall I tell her?"

"Tell her I am unwell."

"I'm afraid she will take it amiss."

"I don't care. If I do not wish to drink tea, I will not drink tea. Kindly close the doors on your way out."

The countess left them open. Sisi closed them. The doors were well made and heavy. They shut out a lot of the noise from the adjacent room. *I should join my ladies*, she thought. *Allow them to distract me.* Instead, she lay on the bed with her arm over her eyes and thought about the train that was taking Franz further and further away from her.

....

"Good afternoon, Elisabeth." Sophie entered the bedchamber wearing the cold brittle smile she reserved for Sisi.

"Afternoon?" Sisi blinked at the light as one of the maids drew back the curtains.

"Yes, indeed. You have managed to sleep the morning away. I hope you had a productive night."

"I couldn't sleep."

"Of course not. If you sleep through the day, you cannot sleep at night. And if you don't sleep at night you will naturally fall asleep during the day. You will do much better if you remember that the daytime is for work, the night-time for sleeping."

186

Sophie came to the bedside. Sisi turned her face in the other direction. The curtain stirred gently in the breeze coming through the open window. Riding was the only thing that gave her pleasure, and sometimes she rode until she was exhausted. When she returned, she would ask not to be disturbed and lay down to rest, only to wake when it was time to get ready for bed. Then she found she couldn't sleep. Those nocturnal hours were a secret pleasure. Her apartment was empty, no one to interfere with her. She wrote letters or read, or exercised vigorously on her gymnastic equipment, enjoying the solitude.

Sophie's gusty sigh was like the snort of a horse. She clapped her hands. "Come in, ladies. Prepare Her Imperial Majesty for what's left of the day."

Sisi had fallen into a state of despondency. She cried a lot, ate little and refused all Sophie's invitations to join her for tea or family dinners. The most casual contact with Sophie was chilly. She spent most of her time alone, often staring at the miniature portrait of little Sophie she'd had commissioned and wore on a bracelet. It seemed to her that everything had gone wrong with Sophie's death. Before that, in Hungary, was the last time she had truly been happy.

Even Ludovika was losing patience with her behaviour. She wrote: *Your Aunt Sophie is well disposed to you! God grant that things will be different again.* Even the Viennese, who had always looked kindly upon her, complained that she did not meet her obligations either as Empress or woman. Sisi couldn't bring herself to care.

Once she was dressed, her hair brushed and braided but without any elaborate hairstyle, she went into her study to read the morning mail. There was a letter from Franz, and she knew at once that the usual tongues had been tattling.

I beg you, my angel, if you love me don't grieve so much, take care of yourself, distract yourself as much as you can. Go riding, drive with caution and care, and preserve for me your dear precious health, so that when I come back, I will find you quite well and we can be happy.

When she wrote to him, she begged for news about the war, but seldom received any. His letters were all about his concern for her. Nevertheless, it was impossible to remain in ignorance. Shortly after Franz had arrived at headquarters in Verona, a great battle had been fought and lost at Magenta. The blame fell on General Gyulai for having lost his nerve and ordered the retreat while the outcome was still undecided. Lombardy fell to the enemy, and Napoleon and King Victor Emmanuel made their entry into Milan. The Habsburg Grand Ducal family arrived in Vienna as refugees, with tales of how they had been abused by the people who had done them honour only a few days before.

She put Franz's letter aside and opened one from her sister Madi, now Queen of the Two Sicilies since the death of her father-in-law. A newspaper clipping fell out. In it, Madi sat with her arm linked with that of her standing husband. But her body appeared to be as far from his as she could get. Even though her head was turned from him and the camera, it was impossible not to see in her lovely face an expression of melancholy.

In the accompanying letter, Madi described Francis as mentally and physically enfeebled, a religious fanatic and anxiety-ridden. She had been unable to persuade him to come out openly in support of Austria. He had not the slightest idea of how to deal with the crisis and allowed those ministers to bully him who refused the compromise offered by Piedmont that would save his throne. *One would think* she wrote *that compromise was the same as unconditional surrender.* She also advised Sisi to take up smoking, as it soothed irritated lungs. She had adopted the habit because she found it helped her nerves.

Sisi was frantic. What would happen to Madi and her pusillanimous husband when the allies turned in the direction of Naples? They might be trapped in their capital city if they did not make their escape soon.

When she had finished the letter and filed it away, Sisi wrote a note to her chief steward, Prince Lobkowitz, and asked him to purchase cigarettes for her. It was unusual but not unheard of for ladies to smoke.

Another letter was from her eldest brother Louis. She was astonished to read that he had married his mistress of many years, an actress with whom he had a daughter. Brave Louis had ignored the dictates of society, defied his king, who had forbidden the match and married the woman he loved. Bravo, Louis – a true Wittelsbach! After she had written to Madi, advising her to leave Naples, and to Louis to congratulate him on his marriage and assure him that she would always hold him and his wife in the tenderest regard, she went into the billiards room and lit her first cigarette. Although she didn't like the taste, she found that it did indeed ease the congestion in her lungs.

....

Franz wrote: *I beg you, for the love you bear me, pull yourself together, show yourself in the city sometimes, visit public institutions. You have no idea what a great help you can be to me in this way. It will put heart into the people in Vienna and keep up the good spirit I require so urgently.*

The people of Vienna needed heart put into them. The mood was despondent. New taxes had been levied to finance the war. Food prices increased. It was said that rents in Vienna would soon equal those of Paris. Trade and business slumped. Satirists produced pamphlets excoriating the generals, particularly Gyulai and, occasionally, the Emperor himself. It vexed Sisi that the Viennese blamed poor Franz for the policies of Sophie and Count Buol.

Deliverance came for Sisi not through Franz's exhortations but from a newspaper article. She read that the ladies of England had organised a Ladies' Aid Society during the Crimean War to get necessary medical supplies to the front. And then later she read that supplies of all kinds were needed in the present theatre of war. Here was an occupation that no one could complain of and into which she could pour both the heart and intellect that were stifled in the stultifying atmosphere of the imperial court.

With the help of Countess Paula Bellegarde, she organised a Ladies' Aid Society. Her salon became the nerve centre of operations. Any number of court ladies would gather there, bringing basketfuls of old cloth to be cut up into strips and rolled into bandages. A group of volunteers met in her study, their mandate to organise collections of food, hold charity events to raise money and visit hospitals to let the wounded know they were not forgotten. In the humbler houses of Vienna, women were doing the same.

One day in June, Sophie entered the salon where Sisi was snipping and rolling with the other ladies. "Praise be to God," she cried joyously, "His Imperial Majesty has assumed supreme command of the armies! Now we shall see."

189

There was a chorus of approbation from the ladies. What else could they say? Sisi remained silent out of loyalty, but she was horrified. When Franz arrived at the front, he had relieved General Gyulai of command "for reasons of failing health". Gyulai at least had the benefit of previous military experience, but although Franz dearly loved the military, he had no experience in command. She knew when things went wrong the blame rested ultimately with the supreme commander.

Although the ladies and the doting mother might applaud, many others were openly critical. Very soon they were proved right.

Less than a week after the announcement of Franz's decision, news began to leak into Vienna that a great battle had been fought between the Austrian and Franco-Piedmontese armies. Sisi had newspapers brought to her. Viennese newspapers were carefully censored, and the foreign ones were forbidden, but there were always means of getting them, particularly for the elite. Only the common masses had to be kept in ignorance.

Headlines leapt out in bold black letters: AUSTRIA DEFEATED! THOUSANDS DEAD AT SOLFERINO! Her heart plummeted. Thousands dead – it was unbelievable.

Every day new details were reported, scrutinised and analysed by the court. Franz himself had been in the field, so had Napoleon III and King Victor Emmanuel. One hundred and thirty thousand Austrians fought one hundred and forty thousand allies in three separate battle sites for nine hours under a burning sun. Lists of dead began to appear. How fearfully those with loved ones at the front must scan those lists, Sisi thought, as she glanced through them for the names of people she knew, including that of Leopoldine's son. Viennese newspapers reported wounded and dying being shot or bayoneted by the allies. Foreign newspapers said both sides had committed such atrocities. A caricature appeared in one newspaper. The caption read: *Lions led by asses.* The lions were the bloodied Austrian soldier; the asses bore the face of Franz Josef and his generals.

Franz had always been beloved in Vienna, but now there were public appeals for him to abdicate in favour of his more liberal brother, Maximilian. The populace blamed poor policies and poor leadership equally for the tens of thousands who had died to keep a foreign province under the aegis of the Habsburg eagle. The

Viennese newspapers' coverage was reserved, but foreign newspapers placed the blame squarely on Franz. Sisi read descriptions of her husband as an 'arrogant youngster' and a 'pitiful weakling'. One man had the effrontery to write that the courageous Austrian soldiers had been beaten not by the French but by the overbearing imbecility of their Emperor. Another said that Franz Josef's system of monarchy could not survive so massive a military catastrophe.

As outraged as she was by these statements, Sisi could not deny there was an element of truth in them. Franz had such pride in his armies and implicit faith in his generals that he could not foresee defeat. His nature was such that when he made a decision, he could rarely be persuaded to change his mind. Sisi wasn't sure if this was due to overconfidence or a sense of inadequacy that prevented him from admitting, even to himself, that he was ever unsure. But now, she thought poor Franz must be feeling shocked and humiliated.

In his first letter after the defeat, he wrote:

Fortune did not smile on us on the most tragic day of my life. I have grown wiser by many experiences and have come to know how it feels to be a beaten general. The serious consequences of our misfortune will set in eventually, but I trust in God and am not aware of any blame, nor any error in judgement.

Sisi crushed the letter to her. *Oh, poor blind Franz.*

She wrote back begging him not to risk further battles but to conclude peace as soon as possible that would include peace with France and autonomy for Hungary and the empire's remaining Italian provinces. It was what the people wanted, what the newspapers called for. He replied:

Your political plan contains some very good ideas, but we must not give up hope that Prussia and Germany will yet come to our aid, and before that time there can be no thought of negotiating with the enemy.

How could he so misjudge the political attitude of Prussia? King Wilhelm would not be displeased at Austria's defeat since whatever weakened Austria strengthened Prussia's position in the German Federation. Political neophyte that she was, Sisi knew this. Why didn't Franz?

Trains packed with wounded came daily from the front. The ladies of the court were kept busy, talking fearfully about the latest

191

news as they cut bandages. One morning Countess Bellegarde approached Sisi and asked the Empress to accompany her on a tour of the hospitals. Sisi didn't want to go into Vienna. It was a city in mourning. But the two of them had become friends and allies in organising the Women's Aid Society, and she didn't want to jeopardise that. After a feeble protest, she allowed herself to be persuaded.

With an escort of smart imperial guards before and behind, the two ladies rode in an open carriage, showing themselves to the public as Franz exhorted Sisi to do, yet also exposing themselves to bitter comments. Vienna – the city of music, rivalling Paris as the gayest city in the world – was subdued. The parks were almost empty of strollers, the kaffeehäusers and sidewalk cafés had few patrons. Black was everywhere: window curtains, wreaths nailed to front doors, and on the people they passed in the street. Thousands dead, Sisi thought. Many thousands more in mourning.

Patients had been transferred to hospitals outside Vienna, to convents and churches. Even so, the Viennese hospitals were overcrowded. They were intended to accommodate the sick of a single city, not the thousands that were coming daily from a war zone. These poor men were lined up side-by-side on floors where space could be found. Men with shattered limbs still leaking blood moaned in misery. Some were already dead, Sisi saw, but left where they were because the staff hadn't got to them yet. Those who were still conscious watched the two grand ladies with dull eyes. She spoke to some, asking where they were from, thanking them for their service to the empire, and wishing them a good recovery. She could do little else. The stench was the worst she had ever encountered: a foul mixture of old blood, human waste and disinfectant. When she got outside, she gulped fresh air like one who had almost drowned.

At the *Allgemeines Krankenhaus*, the general hospital, they were shown to an interior garden, a patch of lawn surrounded by benches, a pleasant place for recovering patients to walk or sit in the fresh air. Here soldiers were lined up on the bare ground like so many logs of firewood, exposed to the elements and the flies that were crawling over them.

"Majesty, the hospital is full beyond capacity," the superintendent told her. "This is the batch that arrived yesterday. I

192

have nowhere else to put them. They are waiting here for other patients to die."

"It is clear we are not doing enough," Sisi said when she and the Countess were back in the carriage. "We must provide more hospitals. We'll start with Laxenburg."

"Laxenburg? But... Are you sure the Emperor will approve?"

"I'm sure he will. You know how he loves his soldiers."

Millions of gulden had been spent and debts incurred, to supply the Austrian soldier with the best in equipment and armaments even in peacetime. He was the best turned out soldier in Europe. And yet, in the wake of a disastrous war nothing had been done to provide medical care for him. Sisi supposed that was because to Franz and his ministers, defeat was unthinkable.

Arrived back at the palace, she sent for Prince Lobkowitz and gave him specific instructions. He was to organise teams of workmen to remove anything of value from the rooms of Laxenburg. The furniture should be pushed aside and covered, making as much floor space as possible. The Blue Court, which housed imperial suite, must be excluded. Countess Bellegarde would contact the owners of stately homes in the area and ask that they take in some of the soldiers.

When they had gone Sisi ordered her horse saddled and sat down at her desk to write a list of necessary supplies, the first being beds and bedding as there were insufficient beds in the palace.

She arrived at Laxenburg after dark to see a wagonload of men jumping down and entering the palace. Prince Lobkowitz was at the door to meet them. He had already put the skeleton staff to work. Sisi watched the workmen remove clocks, vases, paintings and pictures and carry them off to storage. There were times her heart was in her mouth, but she reasoned that if anything got broken, the Habsburgs had treasures enough to replace them.

Since she could do nothing more that night, Sisi went to bed. She remained at Laxenburg for most of the next day, arriving back at Schönbrunn in the late afternoon. She entered her bedroom through the room where her personal guards were stationed. In her salon she could hear a man and woman talking. She recognised the woman's voice as that of Rosa, her ladies' maid. The male voice she thought might belong to the head footman, who walked through the imperial chambers three times a day, straightening cushions, drawing blinds and curtains, placing footstools, and stocking letter racks with crested notepaper.

"He probably thinks he's entitled. The old *droit du seigneur*," the woman said, sounding critical. "Isn't that what they used to call it?"

"It's perfectly natural for him to have a…a companion. It is an ancient custom."

"But he won't go back to her when he returns, will he? Do you think? After everything that's happened, the war and everything."

Tattling servants, Sisi thought, as she reached up to remove her hat.

"And why not? He'll need comfort. *She* won't provide it."

There was a small silence. Sisi heard the sound of cushions being thumped, confirming her suspicion that it was the head footman. Then Rosa said, "Still, I never thought it of him. It's obvious he loves her truly."

A snort from the man. "Love has nothing to do with it. A man has needs. Even Emperors. She does not satisfy them. They haven't shared a bed for months, and that's a fact. He's not a monk. Mark me, this Pole won't be the last –"

Sisi had frozen on the word "Emperor". Her blood pounded in her head. With that single word, she understood what they were gossiping about. She even knew who 'the Pole' was, a beautiful Polish countess who had appeared at court the previous year, of whom she had taken little account. She pressed her hands to her ears, unwilling to hear more.

....

Who else knew? Sisi sat in her dressing room the following morning while Fannie, her hairdresser, braided her hair. Did Fannie know? Her ladies? Oh, most certainly! Sophie? She would have encouraged him and attempted to assuage any guilt he may have felt. It was said there were no secrets in a palace. It was also said the wife was always the last to know.

As she went about her day, Sisi asked herself the question over and over with everyone she encountered: the guards who escorted her back to Laxenburg, Countess Esterhazy, her dear Prince Lobkowitz, the palace staff. Does he know? Does she know? She looked for a knowing smirk, a sly glance, and believed she saw them.

But could she blame Franz? He hadn't visited her bed since before Rudolf's birth, and she had never tried to encourage him, nor make it a pleasant place to visit. The truth was, she had been relieved to be spared a duty that she found onerous and distasteful, particularly when she was feeling ill. No, in all honesty, she couldn't blame Franz. And yet she did. She did, because, in this world into which he had brought her, this world where she was and always would be an outsider, his love had been her only surety. His love alone had given her what little strength she had to face the ordeals of his mother, estranged children, the loss of little Sophie and the spite of a court that looked down on her as a mere Bavarian. Now it was gone, snared by a Polish countess. And she was more alone than ever.

When she looked back over the past year, she clearly saw what she had failed to see before. How Franz's attitude toward her had changed, how he more often joined his mother in criticising her lifestyle, even in his letters – *I beg you relinquish it and rest at night…And don't ride so much and so fast…* How his patience with her bouts of illness was wearing thin. How he didn't seem to mind not sharing their bedroom. But he had never been hers emotionally. A dry and humourless bureaucrat, he was bound to his cold hard, demanding desk more closely than he was to her.

But what was she to do now? There was no one closer than Bavaria in whom she could confide her misery. She had no choice but to bury it deep inside. She thought about her father. Everyone in the kingdom and many outside knew what an indiscreet philanderer he was, and she had known too. Never had she given thought to what her mother must have suffered. Ludovika would have been humiliated, but she would perhaps not have been hurt as Sisi was hurt. She had her children and lavished her love on them, and she had a warm and supportive family and still, presumably, managed to subdue her feelings and do her wifely duty. Her mother had dealt with her father's infidelities by pretending they didn't matter.

Sisi wasn't sure she could do that. What she did know was that Franz, defeated and humiliated, needed her as he never had before, and she must console him as she could when he returned.

Chapter 24 - August 1859

The next news from the front did nothing to lift the cloud of gloom in Vienna. Napoleon initiated a meeting at Villafranca for a talk with Franz that did not include either Cavour or Victor Emmanuel. The conclusion was that Napoleon was to have Lombardy and he would relinquish it to Piedmont. The other Italian states would form a federation. Austria was to retain Venetia. But for how long? Franz fought for the rights of his cousins in Tuscany and Modena but was unable to save their thrones. No one was happy about the compromise, except possibly Napoleon, with whom the Italians were deeply disillusioned. Austria had lost one of her richest and most culturally progressive provinces.

After the signing of the armistice, Franz returned to Vienna.

Sisi greeted her husband with the formality demanded of a subject. She had no opportunity to be alone with him until after dinner, where she made a rare appearance. The family had grown. Maximilian and Charlotte were back from Milan, where he had distinguished himself by his bravery.

Relatives from the Habsburg principalities of Modena and Parma followed the example of their Lombardian cousins in fleeing to Vienna, where they became permanent houseguests. Conversation at the dinner table was centred on their complaints and losses.

Archduke Ludwig Viktor, now nineteen and fond of making mischief, remarked, "All the Royal Highnesses, who are driven away from their dominions, come to us. I wonder where we will go when we are driven away."

The comment was received in a stunned silence, broken only by someone dropping a utensil on a plate. Everyone stared at the archduke, who continued to drink his soup as if unaware. Sisi had to work hard not to laugh out loud at all the outraged faces. Finally, Sophie said icily, "You have the mind of a street urchin."

Ludwig Viktor grinned around the table. Conversation started up again. The exiled royals had much to say about Franz's handling of the war but, as many other self-seekers and sycophants were doing, they blamed everything on the poor advice he had received from ministers and generals. Count Grunne along with Count Buol, had been elected as the Emperor's chief whipping boy.

Even at family dinners, protocol ruled. When Franz laid down his knife and fork, it was the signal to the servers that the course was over and plates were removed whether the other diners had finished or not. Being a considerate host, Franz held onto his knife and fork until most of the others had eaten their fill, which tended to make the dinners tediously long.

Sisi didn't enjoy these family dinners, where as often as not she would be subjected to Sophie's hard malice over some infringement or other. She now had her own cooks and kept her own mealtimes. On this occasion, she accepted a little food and moved it around on her plate, while stealing glances at Franz, unable to believe how insouciant he was about so terrible a defeat and the part he had played in it. Crushed – no! Humiliated – not in the least. It was a setback merely. He had no intention of changing his policy in respect to Italy or any of the other provinces. *Power will remain in my hands*, he had written to Sisi when she begged him to make concessions to Hungary.

After dinner Franz, as always, escorted her from the dining room. "Will you walk in the garden with me, Franz?" she asked before Sophie or any of the cousins could engage his attention.

The parterre garden at Schönbrunn was in its summer dress, the six beds planted with different coloured flowers arranged in the same pattern, not a flower out of place, not a weed or stray leaf to be seen. *As if anything could be imperfect at Schönbrunn*, Sisi thought. If a weed had the audacity to plant itself in the hallowed soil, a gardener would be there to smite it at once.

"You are too thin," Franz said, his first words of a private nature to her. "It is clear that you have not obeyed my many pleas that you take care of yourself."

She had wanted to comfort him, but obviously, he had no need of it.

"I have been ill." She took her parasol from Paula and opened it. Her ladies and the Emperor's adjutants walked at a discreet distance behind. Perhaps some of them noted that Sisi did not link her arm with Franz's.

"You must expect to be ill if you do not eat properly, ride for hours until you are exhausted and do not rest at night, which is nature's time for sleeping."

"How do you know these things when you have been hundreds of miles away for the last months?" He had nothing to say to that. "Do you have people spying on me?"

"Spying on you? How absurd! I hear from those who care about you and are concerned, as I am, about your awful way of life, because it will ruin your health. I implore you to give it up at once. Eat more. Do not ride so much and so vigorously. And most of all get more sleep. Do you still have a cough?"

"Yes. I fear I am consumptive."

"Is that what the doctors say?"

"No, they don't know what ails me, except that I have a sore throat."

Franz heaved a deep sigh. They walked in silence for a few moments before Sisi said: "If you are finished rebuking me – which I get quite enough of from your mother – allow me to say how happy I am to see you safely returned."

He was immediately contrite. "I am sorry, my dear. I do not mean to rebuke you. It's just that your poor health worries me to distraction." He caught her hand and tucked it into his elbow. "Were you anxious about me? There was no need. I was never in the battle lines, you know. As commander in chief, I was always in a place of safety."

"Yes, but there were other dangers: disease, train wrecks, assassins."

"Indeed." He directed them into the trees that skirted the labyrinth. It was pleasanter in the shade. "I cannot thank you enough for taking care of my soldiers."

Having something important to do had given Sisi a sense of fulfilment that had been lacking in her life. It gave her a reason to get up in the mornings, to be able to face each day with a sense of purpose. But already the demands on her had begun to diminish. No more wounded were coming from the front.

"How are things in Vienna?"

"Oh, Franz, the citizens are very unhappy. The new taxes have impoverished many. Businesses have closed, some only until matters improve, but others, I fear, will never open their doors again. For lack of custom the Art Society has closed its exhibition. And now the people grieve for their sons and brothers and fathers. While our soldiers were fighting and dying for the empire, profiteers were at work syphoning off supplies that should have gone to the front, so that our soldiers went into battle hungry and with guns that misfired. The newspapers say there has been malfeasance in the army and the ministries, and how it goes right to the top. They say these men are now ensconced behind their desks and planning another war."

She would have liked to say more, to warn him that if he made a public appearance in Vienna, he would find that he was no longer the idol of the populace. He would be reviled instead of cheered. He would hear calls for him to abdicate and for Maximilian to take over the government. He would see men with bandaged or missing limbs walking in the boulevards.

Franz stopped and turned to her. "How long have you been reading newspapers?"

The question took her by surprise. It seemed irrelevant after all she had said. "Since you left. I think it important that I keep myself informed. Will you replace Grunne?"

"I have given no thought to making a change for Count Grunne, and I do not consider it at all. In general, I beg you not to believe what the papers say. They write many stupid and wrong things."

"They write what they perceive to be the truth, Franz. A free press is one of the benefits of democracy that the Austrian people lack. In progressive countries like England and France, they do not fear the voice of the press. Surely after all that has happened, you must consider whether your system of government meets the needs of the times."

His mouth fell open. "I forbid you to speak such words, which are an offence against my majesty. There is nothing wrong with the system. Am I not criticised enough that I must hear it from you also? You are my wife, not some Italian revolutionary. Particularly at this time, when I am hard pressed by the victory of injustice over justice, by treachery and disloyalty, I need your support."

"You do not need my support or you would not keep me so ignorant!" Sisi whispered furiously. She glanced at their attendants, who had also come to a halt and were paying close attention while trying to appear heedless. Perhaps they couldn't quite hear what was said, but they were adept at reading lips and expressions.

Franz recognised the fact too. He took Sisi's arm again, and they strolled on. "I keep you ignorant, as you say, because I love you so much and wish to shield you from anything unpleasant, especially war. You are of such sensitive nature that such things are bound to upset you, and I want to protect you."

"Franz I am not a young girl anymore. I want to be informed."

Franz stuck out his chin. "In any case, I don't want to argue on this, my first day home."

"Neither do I. But I can't change my way of thinking. I have come to the conclusion that divine right and absolutism belong to an age long past."

"Will you at least keep your opinions to yourself?"

"How dare you ask such a thing of me?"

"I ask as your husband and Emperor."

She hardly had to think about her answer. It was clearly a great injustice to try to shut her up when his mother and those ministers who espoused Sophie's views, were free to speak their reactionary evil to him. Franz never heard another point of view. Viennese newspapers were censored, and he never read foreign newspapers if they were likely to be critical. Other rulers used the language of diplomacy. The only time he heard the truth was from dissident Italians or Hungarians. So, now that she had arrived at a political position of her own, she would not be silenced.

"In that case my answer is: No, I will not."

. . . .

Heads rolled at the *Ballhaus*, the seat of ministerial government. Foreign Minister Buol, Minister of the Interior Bach, Minister of Police Kempen, and General Gyulai, among others, were replaced. Finance Minister von Bruck slit his throat rather than face the consequences of rumours that he was involved in the embezzlement of army funds. Enquiries uncovered instances of negligence, blunders and fraud, and some men were imprisoned. Franz signed the orders reluctantly and only to satisfy public opinion. Sisi thought it a great pity that Madame Mere couldn't also be sacked since she was driving force behind Austria's failed policies.

No one received more criticism than Count Grunne, Franz's closest friend, who was accused of keeping the Emperor in ignorance of all the bad things that happened. Grunne accepted the blame rather than have it heaped on the Emperor. Sisi understood better than Franz that Grunne of all men would have to go. But she was sorry. He had been a friend to her as well.

"I wish you a happier time than the last has been," she said, when he had formally resigned his offices of adjutant general and head of the military chancellery. "I still cannot accept that everything now is so different from before, and especially to see a different person in your place. My only consolation is that we haven't lost you altogether. You know how grateful I am to you."

"I shall still be around, Majesty. I am to retain the office of chief equerry."

"Yes, and I am glad of that." But she would no longer see him in the billiards room playing against the Emperor with an unlit cigar in his mouth.

He snapped his boot heels together, leant down to kiss her hand and bowed himself away.

In spite of these dismissals and the commissions and enquiries, Vienna remained under a cloud of gloom.

Chapter 25 – July 1860-April 1861

The news from Italy was grim. In the summer Garibaldi, that French bandit, had occupied Sicily and named himself dictator. With him were only one thousand volunteers, mostly Italian, some from Venetia. From there he menaced Naples itself. The absolutist rule of Francis II was hugely unpopular, and Sisi suspected the Neapolitans would capitulate as easily as the Sicilians had. Garibaldi meant freedom.

Madi and her husband appealed for help to Franz, and Sisi tearfully joined her entreaties to theirs. Franz admitted to her privately that he was not in any position to help his brother-in-law and brother monarch. Sisi knew it was true, and she knew too how much such an admission cost him. In early September Garibaldi entered Naples amid a roar of acclaim. Madi and her husband were forced to flee. Sisi constantly fretted about the safety of her sister.

Throughout the summer months, Sisi's health declined, and her cough returned. She was nervous and depressed all the time, easily upset and prone to tears. Franz and his mother nagged her about eating more. It occurred to her that maybe they wanted to build up her body so that it could bear more children, but she didn't want more children. Her mother said she was as thin as a beanpole, but she didn't believe it. She was proud of her figure: the twenty-inch waist. She continued to drink boiled beef blood daily. But sometimes when a craving overcame her she would send to Demel's for some rich cream cakes and eat until she felt stuffed. She weighed herself as many as three times a day. If her weight went up, she would go on a crash diet and exercise even more vigorously until it was below her usual one hundred pounds.

She did her duty by appearing at her husband's side and went through the motions, whatever was required of her. She was widely admired for her beauty, and still popular in Vienna, while Franz's popularity had plummeted due to the Italian war. Sophie continued to rule the palace, the nursery, the council of ministers, and Franz. Having once been needed, Sisi felt the lack acutely. She sank into depression. Her cough worsened, and a new symptom showed itself. Her joints swelled painfully. Sisi was horrified by this disfigurement.

A new doctor was called in. Dr Skoda was a lung specialist. Sisi no longer trusted Dr Seeburger, who remained physician to the imperial family, even though he had let little Sophie die. After examining her, Dr Skoda stroked his moustache with an index finger for a while, studying her.

"What is it, Doctor?" She thought perhaps he was trying to find the words to tell her that she was going to die, and the thought held no fears for her.

"Majesty, I cannot overemphasise the seriousness of your condition. It is fragile; I would even say life-threatening. I doubt your health could endure another Viennese winter. My advice is to seek out a warmer climate at once."

Her heart bounded with joy. To get away from Vienna and Sophie... from Franz. Yes, even from Franz, with his reproachful eyes and his incessant pleas that she eat more, exercise less, his refusal to discuss politics with her and his dogged confidence in his mother's infallibility when she and her appointees were the ones largely responsible for the position in which the empire now found itself.

His mother had convinced Franz that there was nothing wrong with Sisi that couldn't be put right by proper food. The rest was in her mind. But her cough was so persistent that she had no difficulty believing the doctor's prognostication. Where should she go? The whole world was open to the Empress of Austria.

"What do you think of Madeira?" she asked the doctor.

"I know little of the place, but if it has a warm and relatively dry climate it should suit."

Maximilian had recently returned from a trip to Brazil and had stayed for some time on Madeira, an archipelago in the Atlantic Ocean. He had described it as paradise, with a mild climate all year round, rugged, volcanic mountains and laurel forests. To Sisi, it sounded perfect. And it was far from Vienna.

Franz was in Warsaw, meeting with the Czar. The Polish countess was no longer at court. Was that coincidence? Sisi didn't think so. She had said nothing to Franz about what she had overheard. She wasn't quite sure why. Sometimes she thought it was due to sheer cowardice, and sometimes pride, and, very occasionally, she thought herself wise to ignore it. There was nothing she could do about it anyway.

By this time she had no more illusions about marriage or about Franz. He was no longer the proud and confident young man she had met and been fascinated by at Ischl. His failures weighed heavily on him, and his shame made him morose and brusque. He had spent much of the summer hiding away at Laxenburg to avoid the hostility of the people of Vienna.

She waited until he returned before telling him what the doctor recommended.

"Yes, of course, you must get away," he said at once. "Your health is precious to me. We must have you well."

And again she thought: *So I can bear more babies for this decadent empire of yours, while you frolic with your mistresses?*

"What about Merano in the Tyrol?" Franz suggested. "It has a mild climate and is becoming a very popular spa."

Not far enough away. "I rather thought Madeira. The way Maximilian described it made it sound appealing."

Franz looked perturbed. "But so far... I believe Max said it had a wet climate, did he not?"

"Only in the north."

"But is it necessary to go so far? There are many ideal places closer to home. And how will you get there? Have you thought of that? It will require an ocean voyage. None of the imperial yachts is fit for such a voyage." Satisfied that he had convinced her, Franz rose to go. "I will ask Grunne to draw up a list of suitable places."

But Sisi did not give up her plan, and she informed Franz that she had to get far away from the court if she was to find peace. He tried to dissuade her, but she was adamant. She wrote to Queen Victoria, who was very sympathetic about her ill-health, asking to borrow a ship. To her delight, the queen wrote back offering the royal yacht Victoria and Albert as being the fastest and most comfortable. The ship would be awaiting her in Antwerp whenever she was ready to leave.

Franz went hunting in Ischl while Sisi organised a summer wardrobe and all that she would need in the next months. By the time Franz returned her preparations were complete.

....

205

The voyage was pleasant until the Bay of Biscay when heavy storms struck. Sisi had chosen her retinue herself. It consisted of Dr Skoda, three ladies-in-waiting and three counts, all young and devoted to her, the indispensable hairdresser, and a few servants, including her personal chef, who was too ill to cook for her. All were seasick, except Sisi, who ate food prepared by the English stewards with an excellent appetite and charmed the captain with so many questions about his beloved ship.

She loved storms. The stark white flashes of lightning, the thunder rolling across the heaving sea, called to something wild and fearless in her. As the deck swayed beneath her feet, she stood at the ship's rail and stared down into the waves rising and falling away in ceaseless motion, lashing the side of the ship. While most of her suite, including Dr Skoda, groaned in their bunks and her dogs howled in their kennels, Sisi was on deck, mesmerised by the storm.

She imagined what it would be like to plunge into that maelstrom, sail high on those towering rollers and sink down on the other side. If she didn't move, she could float there for a while, looking up at the stormy sky, with the rain on her face. In time the weight of her gown would pull her down in a slow bubbling tumble into the deep dark depths, where the water was untroubled by the turbulence of nature on the surface.

After repeated attempts by the seamen to persuade her to return to her cabin, she finally complied and continued to watch the storm from her porthole. After a while, she went to her tiny desk and wrote the beginning of a poem:
And where the sea's at its deepest, there lower me down;
Even when the storms rage above down there will be peace.

. . . .

The voyage, the sea air, maybe just getting away from Vienna – something agreed with her. By the time the royal yacht docked, Sisi already felt better than she had in months. Funchal, the capital city, rose from the water's edge along gentle slopes, towards the mountains looming above. Flowers and bunting decorated the streets. There to greet her was the Portuguese governor, with a letter of welcome from King Pedro, along with a brass band, a little girl with flowers, a company of guards and half the population of

Funchal, cheering madly. Sisi was dismayed. She had hoped to leave fuss behind in Austria.

The governor offered her the use of a princely villa, but Franz's agents had found for her a modest house on the outskirts of the capital, perched on black volcanic cliffs with a backdrop of the rugged mountains.

While her retinue unpacked, she sat on a chaise on the magnificent terrace. Before her was a breathtaking panorama of the sea – a sight Sisi knew she would never tire of seeing. Below was a wild garden of palms and laurel, mimosa and oleander and acanthus climbing the cliff. Along the cliff path stood a charming summerhouse, festooned in bougainvillea. While Vienna was a frozen landscape, tropical flowers nodded in the sea breeze on Madeira. Sisi took a deep breath of the flower-scented sea air. Here was peace. Here she could begin to dream again.

She awoke the next morning to the dawn chorus of the birds, the sound of surf breaking on the rocks below the house and an exhilarating sense of freedom. Today she could do whatever she wanted, go wherever she wished, and no one would criticise her for it.

As she and her companions were breakfasting informally on the terrace the day after their arrival, a knock sounded at the door. One of the servants came onto the terrace and bowed.

"Majesty, a gift has arrived from the governor. I cannot bring it into the house. It is too big." He grinned, showing a wide gap in his front teeth.

Sisi sighed. She didn't want gifts. But she rose and went to the door, followed by the others. Outside stood a string of eight ponies. One of the handlers gave her a note. The governor begged her to let him know what he could do to make her stay more pleasant. *Only leave me alone. Only that.*

The ponies were most welcome, though. She examined them with the eye of an expert horsewoman and chose a sturdy chestnut with white socks. The others made their choices, laughing and squabbling. That afternoon, with a guide leading the way, they explored the rugged hinterland, the air perfumed by the abundant fennel for which Funchal was named. On succeeding days they went further, into mountain valleys and deep pine forests, climbing the sides of a volcano to seek out old shrines built by the first

Portuguese settlers. They looked for birds and even managed to capture some. Sisi had an aviary built to house them.

Within two weeks her health had improved markedly. Her throat was better, her cough slight and her appetite restored. She even looked healthier and more beautiful than ever, as Count Imry Hunyádi never tired of telling her. A handsome young Hungarian, with eyes as blue as the sea, he was infatuated with her.

Although she was often bored by her companions' inconsequential chatter, she never tired of hearing about Hungary, and she urged Imry to talk about his homeland and his experiences during the reprisals. Imry's parents, loyal to the empire, had taken him to Arad to see the corpses hanging there. He had been a child of five, but he had never forgotten the forlorn sight. That his parents described them as bad men assured that they visited him in his dreams, complete with nooses and black faces.

Sisi leant over the balustrade of the sweet little summer house, watching the seabirds nest in the cliffs by Pontinha harbour, as Imry instructed her in his native language. And when she was lost in thought, when she dreamed, he stood silent and adoring at her side. She tested the power of her beauty on him, allowing him to worship her, but never permitting the smallest liberty.

It was apparent to Sisi that a romance was blossoming between Paula Bellegarde and Count Königsegg, her controller of the household. She watched them in the garden below. Paula was cutting flowers and Königsegg followed behind with the basket. The flowers were for the dining table that night. They had some special guests coming.

A Russian warship was berthed in Madeira. Sisi had invited the officers to dinner and a dance afterwards. The arrangements kept boredom at bay, and her entourage occupied for several days before the event.

When the Russians arrived, Sisi was surprised to find that a few of the officers spoke German. Some of those who couldn't used English or French and others translated for the linguistically deficient. None of the Austrians spoke Russian. Sisi had bought in what she thought would be plenty of vodka, but the Russians were fond of making toasts, and after each toast the glasses were upended. The ladies were toasted in turn, then the czar and the Emperor. They spoke loudly and laughed even louder.

But they could hold their liquor. They knew how to waltz and even managed to show off some Cossack dancing without falling over. Hunyádi wasn't so lucky when he tried.

It was a delightful evening. The next morning at breakfast, it was agreed by the ladies that all the officers, old and young alike, had fallen in love with Sisi. Hunyádi and her other equerry, Count Mitrovsky, affected jealousy. Her self-esteem bloomed. She knew she was beautiful, and all the adulation she received made her aware of the effect she had on men. It was some consolation for Franz's infidelities.

Every month Franz sent a courier out with letters and to report back to him how things were. Perhaps it was the courier who noticed the closeness between Sisi and the Hungarian, or perhaps even here on Madeira there were those who reported her every word to Vienna. Soon Count Hunyádi was recalled to his regiment.

Christmas approached, and gifts arrived from Vienna and Munich for her birthday. It was her first Christmas without her children, and it produced stirrings of homesickness. A little note from Gisela brought tears to her eyes, even though she knew Sophie had dictated it, and Rudolf signed his name when he sent kisses to his dearest mama.

She sat on the terrace drinking champagne, watching the sun go down and the sky turn to amethyst. And dreamed of Possenhofen, where snow would cover the mountains, of pine logs crackling in the stoves and sleigh rides with her siblings…

By the middle of January Sisi had to admit that freedom had its negative side: boredom. She could do anything she wanted to, but there was simply not enough to do in Madeira for a now healthy young woman. The novelty of a new place had worn off. The round of her days had developed a predictable monotony. She went walking or riding with her retinue when the weather was fine, or just sat on the terrace chattering about inconsequential things during long drowsy afternoons. In the evenings they played cards, wrote letters, or strummed their various instruments. Sisi was learning the mandolin and she often worked her werkel, a barrel organ that played arias from *La Traviata*. It was a Christmas gift from Franz. She discouraged callers, which might have enlivened the days, and she was bored with her companions. Furthermore, she missed her children, and she missed Franz. She never doubted that he loved her in his way, and even if his love was not enough to satisfy her deeper needs, she knew he was sincere when he wrote how much he longed for her return. She spent more and more time alone, reading Shakespeare or Heine, or just sitting in the summer-house, staring at the sea and contemplating the abysmal emptiness of her life.

"I want to return to Vienna," she told her companions one night. "We'll start packing in the morning."

But in the morning she changed her mind. To return, to see her children again, came at such a cruel price: Sophie's domination of the nurseries and Franz; the petty humiliations of Countess Esterhazy; the superficial milieu of a narrow-minded court; the surrender of her freedom.

"We will stay a little longer."

She wrote to Count Grunne:

That would be something for you, to live here. I don't think you could stand it for two weeks.

Letters from Grunne came with every courier. Only from him did she receive political news. Little of it was good. After Milan fell, her sister Madi and her ineffectual husband, took refuge in the fortress of Gaeta, which Garibaldi's troops closely besieged. Nineteen-year-old Madi so distinguished herself by her courage and fortitude that she aroused the admiration of even the enemy. Sisi was both proud of her sister and envious. Envious because Madi was hailed by all as a heroine, while she herself led such an empty and useless life.

There was never a letter from Madi, which drove Sisi into a frenzy of anxiety. She wept for her sister, but not for the empire's loss of Italy, and once more her health began to decline.

In February she learned that after an epic defence the Bourbon flag was lowered on the mast over the citadel, and Garibaldi's troops marched into Gaeta. To her relief, a French frigate took Madi and her husband to Rome. The Papal States had been reduced to the city of Rome itself, as the armies of Victor Emmanuel came down from the north to join up with the triumphant Garibaldi, conqueror of the South. But at least Madi was safe. In March, the first all-Italian Parliament met in Turin and the kingdom of Italy was proclaimed with Victor Emmanuel as king.

Free of nervous tension, Sisi's health began to improve.

Count Grunne wrote that Venetia was expected to rise at any time to join the new Kingdom. And matters were not looking good in Hungary. Seeing how things had gone in Italy, the Hungarians were stirring ever more restlessly. *I could help there*, she thought, *if only Franz would let me, and it would give my life a purpose.* She wrote to him that she wanted to return because she didn't want to be so far away during a time of war. In response, he assured her that no campaign was expected and there was nothing to fear.

It wasn't so much that she wanted to return to Vienna. If she didn't have the children, the life she had led so far would be unendurable. She could not think of Sophie without a shudder, and the distance between them had not decreased her loathing. Sophie would have made good use of her absence to increase her control of the children and the Emperor.

She just wanted to leave Madeira. Whenever she saw a ship pass by she wondered where it was going; she imagined some exotic place, Brazil or Africa… and she longed to be on it.

Chapter 26 – May-June 1861

Sisi's first day back at Schönbrunn was as unpleasant as she had expected. She had barely settled in when the Archduchess stormed into her salon and ordered her attendants out. Sisi resolved not to be nervous, to remain calm and not allow Sophie the satisfaction of upsetting her. To Sisi, Sophie had taken on the guise of every wicked witch or crone that she had ever read about in the fairytales of her youth.

Sophie didn't even try to hide her anger. Her eyes glittered and her mouth was a thin, harsh line. Sisi sat on her chaise in the salon. Sophie stood over her, bosom heaving even before she spoke.

"Have you any idea how utterly selfish your behaviour is? Seven months you have been away from your family and your duties, indulging your whims. You are the Empress of Austria and a Habsburg. You, an obscure Bavarian princess, are the most fortunate young woman in the world. You have a loving husband and two wonderful children, and yet you can leave them, to cavort at the other end of Europe for your pleasure."

Sisi lifted her chin, determined to be intimidated no longer. "You know very well I went to Madeira on the advice of my doctors. And, as you can see, I am quite recovered now."

"Half the court thinks your illness feigned and the other half thinks it's nothing but nerves," Sophie said waspishly.

"And you, Aunt? Do you suppose me clever enough to feign a fever? A cough?"

"I believe if you ate properly and slept during the hours God gave us for our rest, your health would benefit. You bring your troubles on yourself." Sophie narrowed her eyes as her glance swept Sisi from head to foot. "But you do look well. I am happy to see it." She nodded briskly and took a seat on a chair facing Sisi. Her face relaxed a little the stern lines of disapproval. "Now that you are back, may God grant that you will give our dear Franz a happy domestic life and the quiet enjoyment he so richly deserves after the long, sad winter. May he find in you everything he needs so urgently as balm for the painful burden of his position. He loves you so much. It is my earnest hope that you, as a result of the long separation, learn to truly value and enjoy your good fortune."

"Do you really think being Empress is good fortune? I find it burdensome and gruelling."

"Duty often is," Sophie said with a wintry smile. "You knew you were marrying an Emperor, did you not? You knew that you would be expected to dedicate your life in service to the empire."

Sisi shook her head slowly. "No. I was fifteen. I knew nothing."

"That is because your parents did not bring you up with an education commensurate with your birth and blood. You were allowed to run wild. I too was a Bavarian princess, remember. But I was raised according to my rank and in the expectation that I would make a grand marriage."

Sisi hid her smile. Being a Bavarian princess was something Sophie usually chose to forget. "I don't suppose my parents ever imagined I would marry the Emperor."

"I did not arrive at the Hofburg finished. I was a little older than you at nineteen. Pieces of me were missing. But I knew court etiquette and understood my duty, and have always done my duty no matter how 'burdensome' it was."

"I never wanted anything but Franz's happiness and to support him, to the best of my abilities, in his endeavours. I feel I could do more if only I were better informed."

"Well, now you can have no more illusions. You live in luxury; you can have everything you want. But there is a price to pay. You know what is expected of you. If you fail in your duty, it cannot be blamed on your parents or your upbringing. Do not shirk! You have a full calendar of engagements over the next week. I expect to see you at every one of them." Sophie rose and smoothed down her skirts. "And one more thing: Since you are in health, it is more than time you resumed your marital duties. I gave my husband four sons before I decided I had done my duty. One is never enough."

Sisi too came to her feet. But the words that trembled on her lips remained unsaid. She would not dignify such brazenness with a response. Instead, she said calmly, "I wish to see the children today. Shall we say five o'clock?" She hoped her words sounded like a command rather than an entreaty.

Sophie stiffened. "I am told you persuaded Franz to appoint a new governess for the children. Why do you assume that you are better able to make the best choice of governess than me with all my years of experience? Is this the sort of thing you meant when you

213

said you could do more if you were better informed? I tell you frankly, Elisabeth, that I resent your presumption in disrupting the nursery after you have ignored it for seven months!"

"The children didn't like Baroness von Welden. It is true that I asked Franz to replace her. I merely made recommendations. The choice was his."

Franz had come to meet her in Trieste. The warmth of their reunion was encouraging, as were the tears in Franz's eyes when he greeted her. Sisi was amazed at the concessions he was prepared to grant when he was away from his mother's baleful influence. They stayed with Maximilian and his wife for a few days, but Charlotte spoiled the visit. She could not hide her jealousy of Sisi. Her reception by the people of Vienna was as warm as she could have wished.

"I can do these things because I am the children's mother," she said, allowing her voice to rise just a little.

"Do not shout at me, Elisabeth."

"I apologise. I wanted to be sure you heard those last words. Please be sure to have the children ready for my visit at five o'clock."

"Very good, Your Majesty." Sophie inclined her head.

Her quick assent and the unpleasant little smile that hovered at the corners of her mouth told Sisi her children wouldn't be there to greet her at five o'clock. It had happened before. Her full calendar meant that she wouldn't have the opportunity for more than a brief visit with them over the next few days.

But she had no engagements that day, and she intended to outfox her mother-in-law. She arrived at the nursery at four o'clock instead of five. The children were there but Sophie was not. The two nurses curtsied.

"Mama!" Gisela, who was almost five, jumped up and ran to her mother. Sisi bent and swept the child into her arms to kiss her radiant little face. Sisi had written to the children often, begging them not to forget her. That her daughter had not, brought tears to her eyes.

"Rudy, come say hello to Mama," Gisela coaxed.

Rudolf, not yet three, was still sat on the floor amid a heap of different-coloured building blocks. At his sister's words, he got to his feet and toddled uncertainly over to his mother. Sisi put Gisela down and crouched to gather the little boy into her embrace. He was shy but he came to her. It was all she could do to contain her tears as she held the precious body that she had once carried within her own.

She had bought gifts for them on her travels. For Gisela, a doll that moved its arms, legs and head, and a parasol decorated all over with streamers of silk that fluttered gaily in every breeze. And for Rudolf, a rocking horse and a toy train with a circle of tracks. Looking at the shelves that contained some of the children's toys, Sisi saw row upon row of toy soldiers of different sorts including cavalry and pieces of artillery on gun carriages. By which she judged that Franz was determined to turn their son into a soldier, in fact, a replica of the man Sophie had turned Franz into.

"Would you like to go outside for a picnic?"

"Oh, yes, please!" Gisela cried. Rudolf followed her lead and clapped his hands.

"Begging Your Majesty's pardon, but the children usually have their supper here at six o'clock," Leopoldine Nischer said, looking anxious. Her son had returned from the Italian war unscathed. Sisi had sent him a gift of beer.

"I am aware of that. If they are hungry, then they will eat. If not, they won't. There can be no objection, I presume?"

"No, Your Majesty, it's just that…"

"Yes?"

"You know how Her Imperial Highness hates to have their routine disrupted."

Sisi smiled. She was going to win this one. "I fail to see how Her Imperial Highness can object to their mother spending time with her children when we have been apart for so long."

Sisi suddenly realised that the other nurse had disappeared. To warn Sophie? "Come along, my darlings."

She chivvied them out of the door, Gisela holding her open parasol in one hand and Rudolf's hand with the other. On the stairs, Sisi tried to pick Rudolf up but he wanted to walk by himself. She anxiously watched as he made his slow way down, helped and encouraged by Gisela, who kept hold of his hand. When they reached the bottom, she cried: "Well done, Rudy!" He beamed at her, as if aware that he had taken a giant step along the road of life.

There, suddenly, was Sophie. How she must have rushed to get here before them, Sisi thought in despair, imagining her running through the palace as if a horde of berserkers were on her heels.

Ignoring Sisi, Sophie said: "Children, your papa is coming to visit you in your rooms."

"Papa!" Rudolf clapped his hands and jumped up and down. Sophie bent to pick him up. He went willingly. Her glance at Sisi said: *He's going nowhere.*

"But… we were going to have a picnic," Gisela murmured, looking at the floor.

"You can do that some other day. You don't want to disappoint your papa, do you?"

Mother or father – the witch is making them choose, Sisi thought in anguish. For Rudolf the choice was easy, but Gisela was clearly unhappy. She looked from one adult to the other, and when her lip began to tremble Sisi didn't have the heart to fight over her.

She cupped the little girl's face in her hands. "Go with Grandmama, my darling. We will have our picnic another day, I promise." She kissed her daughter on the brow and watched as the three climbed the stairs, Sophie still holding Rudolf in her arms. Then she went outside into the private garden to rescind the orders she had given the servants for the preparation of a picnic.

At five o'clock, with little hope, she returned to the nurseries. Franz was indeed there. And so was Sophie.

. . . .

"Who has been consoling my husband while I was gone?" Sisi asked her youngest brother-in-law three days after her return, following a gruelling round of receptions, a charity event, a ball and a state banquet. She didn't like Ludwig Victor particularly, but he had kept her informed of events in Vienna while she had been away and was never slow to tell a blunt truth.

"I cannot say," he replied, ostentatiously brushing the sleeve of his brocade coat, and then proceeded to say, "but I've heard a whisper that he is falling under the influence of our dear cousin, the beauteous Elisabeth of Hungary. There was some talk of marriage between them before you came along but Mama put an end to that. She would rather have had a daughter-in-law from among the

216

Romani than a Hungarian. Are you all right?" Ludwig Viktor caught her hand and patted it. "Dear Sister, before you ask a question you must be sure you can bear the answer."

Without another word Sisi hurried away. She was not surprised. Why should she be surprised? She was not at all. Not shocked. Not angry. It was in Franz's nature, just as it was in her father's. Some men were made that way. It was stupid of her to ask, even stupider to ask Ludwig Viktor.

That afternoon she hosted a salon with the high aristocracy. This was particularly unpleasant because she suspected they all knew with whom her husband had dallied. During the salon, she could feel congestion building in her lungs and, although she did her best to prevent it, she began to cough. Once started it seemed she was unable to stop. The salon terminated early.

A fever so virulent that sleep and unconsciousness were indistinguishable consumed her within days. When awake, her cough returned. She could not bring herself to take any nourishment apart from a few sips of water. Sometimes when people were talking to her, she would drift off into a pleasant oblivion.

When the fever was gone, she was moved to Laxenburg. One day she sent for her looking glass, and saw that the healthy glow she had brought back from Madeira had gone, leaving in its place a sickly pallor and eyes sunk in bruised sockets. She began to cry.

She had no more idea what was wrong with her than did the doctors. Was it something in the air in Vienna? But why was no one else ill?

Doctors came, consulted with one another, and went away. Finally, Dr Skoda, the lung specialist, diagnosed galloping consumption.

"What does that mean?" Franz sat beside her on the bed, holding her hand.

"Galloping just refers to the speed with which the disease progresses through the lung tissue. What it means, Your Majesty, is that the Empress is very ill."

Franz rose from the bed and beckoned the doctor with him into a corner of the room, where they spoke at length in low tones.

When they came back, Sisi asked, "Am I dying?"

"Your Majesty's condition is poor, but I believe we can effect a cure with proper care," the doctor replied.

But Sisi had noticed the hesitation and the glance he shared with Franz before answering. She believed he was withholding the complete truth, but the thought of dying held no fears for her, only concern for those who would be left behind.

When the room had emptied of all but Franz, he sat beside her on the bed again and took her in his arms.

"I am nothing but a burden to you and the country," she said. "I am of no use to the children. I cannot make you happy. If I were no longer alive you could marry again – you must marry again."

Franz said nothing, no interruptions, no denials. He was sat behind, supporting her so that she couldn't see his face. It wasn't until he murmured, "You will get better," that she realised he was weeping. "Dr Skoda thinks you should go away to the south."

Further evidence that she was dying came when Sophie said goodbye. She too was weeping. Not for Sisi, of course, but for the heartbreak, Franz would suffer. The children came, and Sisi said goodbye as if seeing them for the last time.

At Laxenburg and the railway station, the huge crowds were unnaturally quiet apart from the sobs of some of the women. It was like a funeral, Sisi thought. They didn't expect to see her again.

The train carried her to Trieste, where Franz left her. His brother Maximilian and an entourage of thirty persons accompanied her across the sea to Corfu, which she had visited and fallen in love with on her way back from Madeira. On board the ship, she suddenly discovered she had an appetite.

Chapter 27 – September 1861-October 1862

Sisi and Nené embraced each other with heartfelt hugs and kisses and tears. They hadn't seen much of each other since Nené's wedding to the Prince of Thurn and Taxis. Now she was the mother of two small children. Spatz had recently married, but Sisi had been too ill to attend the wedding. The bridegroom was the brother of Madi's husband, the ex-King of Naples and had a deplorable reputation as a womaniser.

Finally, Nené held Sisi away. "Let me look at you." Her gaze travelled from head to foot.

"How do I look?"

Nené brushed away a tear. "Better than I expected, but you are too thin."

Sisi had to smile. She knew her face was puffy and pallid, but she didn't know why. Upon arriving in Corfu she started to get better, and at the end of July Dr Skoda went back to Vienna to report to Franz. Then an upset caused her to regress. Depression weighed her down, and she stopped eating. Once she knew Nené was coming, she improved but now there was an odd puffiness about her face and, far from being thin, she looked horridly fat.

Nené embraced her sister-in-law, Helene von Thurn and Taxis, who was one of Sisi's ladies. Leaving the servants to see to the luggage, Sisi linked her arm with Nené's and walked her out to the terrace. Two of Sisi's dogs lay in a patch of sunshine on the tiled floor. They looked up but seeing nothing amiss thumped their tails a couple of times and laid their heads down again.

"I am so grateful to you for coming. Did Mimi persuade you?"

"And Franz. He begged me so ardently I could not refuse. He is very unhappy and desperately worried about you."

"I know what a sacrifice you have made for my sake – to leave your children when they are so young. I can't tell you how grateful I am." Sisi sat on a cushioned wicker sofa and drew Nené down beside her. "Will you have some wine? Or tea?"

"A little wine, please. Oh, what a splendid view."

The house was the summer villa of Sir Henry Storks, the British Lord High Commissioner, who was helping Sisi improve her English. The veranda overlooked the impossibly blue Ionian Sea, dotted with islands ringed by white foam. In the distance, the snow-capped mountains of Albania were just visible in the haze of sea mist. Tiny wavelets lapped against a white sand beach. Sisi liked to swim in the warm sea and often walked the beach throwing sticks for her romping dogs or sat in a shady spot reading her favourite authors, while the dogs sprawled around her. Along the beach, wild olive groves with gnarled and twisted trunks flourished among orange trees and the evergreen holm oak. Aromatic bay laurel perfumed the air.

"Corfu has magnificent scenery. I prefer it to Madeira, which was more rugged."

"What is that mountain behind us?"

"The Pantokrator. It means the Almighty. Isn't it glorious? Every day in this idyllic landscape reminds me of the tales Uncle Ludwig used to tell us about Greek heroes. When I look out there, I can almost see Agamemnon's thousand ships sailing by on their way to Troy."

"Are you sure they came this way?" Nené said, just to tease, and laughed. "You always had enough imagination for the eight of us."

A servant set out a tray with chilled carafes of wine and water and a plate of olives and cheese before retiring.

"Do try these olives, the plumpest, tastiest you will ever eat. Monks in the monastery atop Pantokrator make the cheese." Sisi gestured to the plate but didn't eat anything herself. "How are your dear little ones?"

"Oh, Sisi, I'm sure I don't have to tell you what a joy they are, what comfort they can bring. They are not perfect, but they are mine!"

Sisi stared out at the glittering sea. It was impossible not to think sadly about her own children. "And Maximilian? Does he still make you happy?"

"Yes. He is the best of husbands. Sometimes I cannot believe how fortunate I am." Her words belied the expression on her face. Nené was very good at hiding her feelings, but Sisi knew something was wrong.

"What is it, my dear?"

Nené looked down at her folded hands. "He has been diagnosed with a chronic kidney disease. I don't know how long I shall have him."

"Oh, Nené! I'm so terribly sorry for you both." Sisi's heart twisted in pity. Of the four married sisters, only Nené had found love and true happiness. How infinitely sad that it was not destined to last.

"We will make the most of the time we have together and be grateful for it."

Brave Nené – she would have made a better Empress than I. Why is fate so often unkind?

"But let's not talk about me. I am charged by Franz and Mimi to provide a complete report on your health. We heard with relief of great improvement when you arrived here, but then there was a relapse. You must tell me truly how you are?"

"I was getting better and then..." Sisi rose and went to the edge of the terrace, where she plucked a hibiscus from where it was growing in a stone urn. "Do you remember Count Grunne?"

"Yes, of course. You are good friends, are you not?"

"I thought we were, but our friendship is over. He came to see me, presumably sent by Franz. He said things to me that I will never forgive."

Nené was at her side. "What did he say?"

Sisi turned away. "He implied that I had been... untrue to Franz."

"No! What a despicable rogue."

"And, as if that wasn't bad enough, he told me – in the fashion of a father giving advice to his daughter – that I could do as I liked, but I must never write so much as a word about it."

"But that's appalling!"

"I was so angry that I called him a panderer and accused him of acting as a go-between in Franz's love affairs, and that he had done his best to ruin my marriage."

"Was all that true?"

Sisi stripped the petals off the flower until only the yellow stamen remained. "I apologised later, but he never apologised to me. In any case, we shall not see each other again ever."

"Is that when you relapsed?"

Yes. And then I heard from Ludwig Viktor that Grunne was telling his friends I am mentally and not physically ill." She tossed the remains of the flower over the balustrade. "I have so few true friends in that court, and I did think he was one. Even before I

221

married Franz, he was very good to me, advising me, but in the kindliest way, answering my silly questions as if they were really quite intelligent. We used to ride together in the Prater and talk about all kinds of things. Lately, he had become even more valuable to me because he was the only one who would talk to me about politics, and talk without the least condescension. Franz won't, you see. I was deeply depressed."

"And now?"

Sisi slipped an arm about her sister's waist, and their heads leant together. "How can I be depressed with you here?" After a few moments of silence, she added. "I don't know what's wrong with me, Nené. But whatever it is, I think it's incurable."

....

They went sailing together or walked along goat paths to visit the old shrines Sisi had discovered, or explored the tidal pools along the shore looking for interesting creatures. In Madeira, Sisi had been so excited when Count Mitrovsky found a seahorse, which until then she had believed to be a mythical creature. She had sent it to Vienna to have a brooch made in its likeness

As they walked, she unburdened her heart to Nené, expounding upon her grievances against her mother-in-law, the malice of the court, her dislike of the marital duty Nené seemed to genuinely understand how it was possible to have so much and yet still feel empty, bereft.

During her stay, Nené made sure Sisi ate plenty of red meat and drank lots of beer. She coughed little and remained cheerful. The only thing wrong was the puffiness of her face, which caused her distress because it marred her beauty. Nené insisted it was only a little puffy and nothing could impair her beauty. By and large, Sisi felt her sister would be able to give a favourable report of her.

A month after Nené left, Franz arrived to take her home. He came in the imperial yacht with an escort of six battleships. Sisi heard there had been riots in Greece and an attempt to assassinate its queen. None of this affected Corfu. The Ionian Islands were a British protectorate, but the trouble was very close to home.

Instead of accompanying Sisi on her long walks of exploration to ancient shrines or picnics in the wild garden of some ruined villa,

Franz spent a good deal of his time touring fortifications and barracks and watching, incognito, the exercises of English troops. Such things fascinated him, and he gave detailed descriptions to Sisi and her ladies after each excursion.

They walked along the beach one perfect evening, accompanied only by three of Sisi's dogs. The sun was dropping like a ripe pomegranate on the other side of the island, and the water was turning into Homer's wine-dark sea. Sisi was barefoot, and the hem of her summer dress was wet because she paddled her feet in the warm water.

"I cannot go back to Vienna, Franz. Winter is coming."

"But you can't stay away forever. Sisi, I implore you. I have been so unhappy without you. The foreign newspapers are hinting that our separation is... well, more or less permanent. "

"I don't care what the newspapers say. If I become ill again, I shall be of no use to you. And I'm afraid I shall become ill again."

Franz's brow furrowed as they walked on in silence for a while. Finally, he said, "Will you at least consent to go somewhere within the empire? Venice perhaps. You enjoyed your last stay there. I can arrange to have the children sent for a visit, and I'll come as often as I can."

Sisi pondered. She didn't particularly like Venice, with its pervading smell of fetid water, and had only enjoyed it because Sophie wasn't there and she was actively engaged in a meaningful project. But at least it had a mild winter climate. It would be delightful to have the children with her, and Franz away from Sophie's influence for a while.

"Yes, that's a good suggestion."

"That's settled then." Franz grabbed her hand and kissed it. "How I've missed you, my darling angel."

Sisi wondered if she had missed him. He was so much a part of the life she had come to hate that she couldn't separate the two.

....

When she was informed, Sophie predictably protested and used every possible excuse why the children ought not to go to Venice. The water there was bad, she claimed, so Franz arranged for fresh water to be shipped daily from Schönbrunn – the 'fair spring'.

Although Countess Esterhazy had not been invited to accompany the Empress to Corfu, she came with Gisela and Rudolf and did her best to impose the archduchess's rules on the children's establishment in Venice. Sisi was having none of that, and there were frequent arguments between them. On a daily basis, letters arrived for the children from Sophie, saying little more than how much she missed them and asked when they were coming home.

After one such letter, Gisela burst into tears. "I want to go home! I miss Grandmama!" she wailed, and because they were so devoted to each other, Rudolf decided he should cry too.

They had been so stiff with her since their arrival, clinging to each other when she tried to approach them as if she were someone to be feared. Now, just when they were beginning to relax with her, this.

"Would you like to ride in a gondola tomorrow?" They had already done that twice. Something more was needed.

"We could go out to one of the islands where the people make objects out of glass. You could have them make something for you to take home to Grandmama."

Gisela sniffed, clearly tempted, but Rudolf wailed, "I want Grandmama!"

Sisi tried to wipe his runny nose, but he pushed her hand away and cuddled closer to Gisela. Countess Esterhazy looked on with such a supercilious expression on her face. Sisi fled.

In her bedroom, she paced the floor, her arms folded against her chest. What could she do? Sophie was winning this battle. No, she might as well admit it, Sophie had already won. The children were hers. Every time Sisi saw them, she had to win their love all over again. *It is because I am gone from them so much, she thought. They do not know me. But what can I do?*

When Franz came to bed that evening, Sisi had made up her mind that there was one thing she could do and she intended to do it. She was reading a translation of The Iliad. Since her stay on Corfu, she had become fascinated by the Greece of the classics.

Franz came to visit her twice while she was in Venice, but on each occasion, he used the time for troop inspections and parades. Often he took Rudolf with him. The three-year-old could already salute smartly.

Franz's silk pyjamas whispered as he climbed into bed. He smelled of cigar smoke and brandy. Sisi put her book down on the night table.

"Franz, I want to talk to you about Countess Esterhazy. I tire of her and her constant admonitions. I understand her role is to ensure I make no mistakes, but she goes far beyond her authority. For seven years I have had to tolerate this woman, who is a vulgar gossip, who spies on me and reports my activities to your mother. No, please don't deny it, I know she does. Why must I have someone I dislike intensely in such an important role in my life?"

Franz had heard her complaints about Esterhazy before and was about to say whatever he thought would appease her, when she added: "I want her replaced."

It took a moment for him to find his voice. Then he said: "Now, Sisi, you are overreacting. Countess Esterhazy has served you well..."

"She serves your mother, not me."

"My mother has your best interests at heart, would you but see it."

"I fail to see how it is in my best interests to have my children taken away from me as soon as they were born. But I don't want to talk about your mother. I want to talk about Countess Esterhazy. Your mother appointed her along with the rest of my ladies-in-waiting and my servants. I see no reason why I should not have some choice in the selection of those who serve me."

"Because to dismiss her is to insult her and the rest of her very important family."

"And so, because of her 'very important family' she can treat the Empress of Austria as she pleases? Aren't I an important person? Surely those of lower rank ought to treat me with respect, and if they do not they deserve to be dismissed!"

Franz ran a hand through his hair. It was receding at the temples and, as if to compensate, he had allowed his side whiskers to grow bushy and down to his chin. It was a style Sisi didn't like and reminded her of Count Grunne. When she looked closely, she noticed a few grey hairs in those whiskers.

"If I were to agree to her dismissal, which I should do only with the utmost regret and reluctance, who would you wish to replace her with?"

225

"Paula Bellegarde would be my choice." Paula had recently married Count Königsegg.

"Sisi!" Franz raised his voice. It wasn't a shout, but nearly so. She had never heard Franz shout. He was always unfailingly polite with everyone. "Paula Bellegarde is a mere countess."

"So is Esterhazy."

"But she was born a princess of Liechtenstein. She is of the very highest aristocracy. Paula Bellegarde is a countess by birth and marriage. As head of your household, she will take precedence over all the ladies of the land – that is all the high aristocracy. Don't you see how impossible that is?"

"No, I fail to see how impossible it is." She blew out the candles beside the bed and laid down. "Good night, Franz."

....

Sisi sat on a chaise and pulled her skirts up to reveal a new affliction. Her ankles and feet were horribly swollen. Her feet were so painful that she could only walk supported by people on each side of her. Her face was still puffy and pallid.

It was April, and Franz wanted her to return to Vienna. Ludovika had come for a visit and brought Dr Fischer with her. Sisi trusted him more than any of the Viennese doctors. After his examination, he arrived at an immediate diagnosis.

"There is nothing wrong with Your Majesty's lungs, but Your Majesty is severely anaemic, owing to which tendencies to dropsy are appearing."

Sisi had seen women with dropsy, their hands, feet, sometimes even the pads of their fingers grotesquely swollen. She did not want to go through the rest of her life looking as if she were made of bread dough. Tears leaked from her eyes.

"What treatment, Doctor?" Ludovika asked.

"This condition is caused by excess water in the tissues. It is useful to sit with the feet elevated on a foot stool or cushion to help with drainage. But then we must address the underlying causes. I suggest the first course of treatment is a visit to Bad Kissingen to take the cure."

"But I can hardly walk," Sisi protested.

"Then you shall be carried," the doctor said crisply.

To Bad Kissingen she went. By July she was walking as well as ever she had. The swelling was gone, and her appetite was good. Promenading with Dr Fischer on the Curplatz, she didn't cough or need to rest. The doctor, an old family councillor, was still able to walk briskly and carry on a conversation without losing his breath. He lifted his hat to every lady they passed.

"Has Your Majesty noticed that your periods of ill health usually occur when you are in Vienna?"

"Yes, Vienna doesn't agree with me." Sisi had remained incognito for the first weeks until a newspaper reporter had caught on to her. Now the people they passed stared while pretending not to.

"It upsets Your Majesty to be in Vienna?"

"Yes, it does. I don't want to return. I am afraid I will fall ill again."

"Would it be true to say that Your Majesty becomes ill when you are distressed?"

Sisi thought about that and realised it was probably true. "I believe so. What are you thinking, Doctor?"

"About the next course of treatment. Let me ask Your Majesty what may seem an impertinent question. Do you want to get well?"

"But I am perfectly well."

"In body, certainly, but what we must address now are the root causes of your ill health. I do not believe Vienna itself is the problem, but the court. Forgive me for trespassing on personal matters. Your dear mother confides in me, so I know Your Majesty is not happy at court and this – again, forgive me, please – is putting a strain on your marriage."

Tactfully, the doctor paused, allowing her the opportunity to reprimand him if she so wished, but she said only, "Go on, Doctor."

"Let me say at once that the medical profession doesn't know enough about the workings of the mind, particularly the subconscious mind, and what it is capable of. A growing body of medical men believe there is a correlation between the health of the mind and the health of the body. Your Majesty has a very sensitive spirit. When it is wounded, you become depressed. Depression has become a progressively existent aspect of your life in the last several years, wouldn't you say?"

"Yes," Sisi said in a small voice.

"Your Majesty becomes stuck in a destructive circle, which becomes more and more difficult to escape. When you are depressed, you don't want to eat. When you don't eat, your body becomes prone to illness. When you are ill, you become more depressed. I have consulted a friend who is investigating disorders of the mind. There is a term he uses, psychosomatic, that relates to a physical disorder caused by or influenced by emotional factors. The subconscious mind can have a powerful effect on the body. Illness can be called up, for example, as a sort of barrier, a way of not dealing with problems that seem insurmountable."

"Are you saying I am willing myself to be ill?"

"No, Your Majesty, certainly not. I use the term 'subconscious mind' very deliberately. Things occur in the mind but not in the consciousness. Beneath the conscious mind that processes our thoughts is the subconscious that influences us in minor and major ways every minute of every day without our ever being aware of it."

"Is this a new science, Doctor? I must confess it sounds absurd to me."

The doctor smiled. "I wouldn't call it a science. That there is a subconscious is generally accepted by the medical profession. How far it can influence us is the question. Can it make us do something against our will, something that is contrary to our nature? Well, there must be more investigation before we know. What I offer Your Majesty is merely a hypothesis. I believe I am correct. What other explanation supports the question I asked earlier: that your periods of ill health coincide with your visits to Vienna."

"But what can I do? Let us suppose you are correct, how do I repress this dark layer of my mind? How do I keep a bright mind all the time?"

"That, dear lady, I do not know." The doctor stopped outside a café. "Shall we have an ice water?"

Chapter 28 – July 1862

Still, she could not bring herself to return to Vienna. With the approval of Franz and Ludovika, she went instead to Possenhofen. Among her brothers and sisters, in the little castle she had always loved, living a bohemian lifestyle, she would gather her strength for the inevitable return to the Viennese court.

Abandoning all dignity, she ran through the door. "Mimi! Papa! Everyone! I'm here!"

The ladies of the court who had accompanied her on her travels trailed in after her, glancing around in amazement as doors burst open and people came running from all directions. A host of smiling faces suddenly engulfed the Empress. Adults and children alike swarmed around her, exchanging hugs and kisses and shouting greetings with no respect for the proprieties. Laughing joyfully, Sisi spied two unexpected faces.

"Madi! Spatz! How delightful! But what are you doing here?"

Explanations would have to wait, but over dinner, it transpired that Marie Sophie, ex-queen of Naples, and Mathilde, Princess of Trani, married to a younger brother of Marie's husband, had left their husbands in Rome and come for a visit to dear Possi. Madi had sent her retinue back to Rome, while Sisi travelled with some servants and six of the court ladies. The ladies would sleep in the castle, but her chamberlain had to find lodgings for the remainder of her retinue in the nearby inns.

"What is the matter with Madi?" Sisi asked her mother. "She does not look at all well."

Ludovika tried to say something but failed. With a "Forgive me, my head…" she pressed a handkerchief to her mouth and hurried away. Sisi stared after her in consternation. Ludovika had been rather subdued during dinner but had not complained of a migraine.

It did not escape Sisi's notice that the faces of the ladies, including Countess Paula's, were stiff with disapproval. Although Possenhofen had changed since she left it, with new furnishings, servants in smart new uniforms, several handsome carriages, and even an "imperial suite," dinner made no allowances for the presence of the Empress or of ladies accustomed to greater refinement. The table was overcrowded with visiting cousins, Max's friends and attending ladies. Shrieks of laughter punctuated a babble of conversation. Table manners were non-existent. Dogs and other creatures were underfoot. When a cat sprang onto Countess Furstenberg's lap, she screamed and dropped her glass. Ludovika fed a fluffy white dog on her lap. The servants chided the children. No one paid any attention to the shocked or disapproving or frequently outraged ladies of the Viennese court.

Countess Furstenberg was one of Sophie's ladies. *What stories she will have to tell Madame Mere upon her return,* Sisi thought in amusement.

"A greater contrast than between Vienna and Possi can hardly be imagined," Madi chortled, as the three oldest sisters walked arm in arm beside the lake, through flower-filled meadows bordered by massed pines. Sisi had told her ladies to amuse themselves while she was gone, which earned her some puzzling looks as if she were a shepherd abandoning her sheep when wolves lurked in the area.

"You have no idea, Spatz, how boring and uncomfortable such an exalted family circle is. There they sit hardly speaking. When they do speak, they bore each other. Everyone is glad when dinner is over. It makes you sorry to see what a sad life they lead."

"Why don't they change it, Sisi?" Spatz stooped to pick a wild violet to add to the bunch of flowers she had collected.

"I don't know. It is as if to change anything, any little thing, would undermine the foundations and eventually bring the empire tumbling down. Each one lives in isolation, bored, yes, or pursues their pleasures in private."

"That's why Sisi prefers Possi, even now. Isn't it true, Sisi?"

Sisi took a deep breath of air laden with the ineffable scents of a Bavarian summer. "My heart will always lie in Possi. My feet will always long to return. When I die they will put my body in a glorious tomb in the Imperial Crypt in the Church of the Capuchins – that's where all the Habsburgs are buried. But I would rather have a simple grave up there in the hills overlooking the lake and Possi."

"We should make a new rule, Spatz," Madi said. "Sadness must use the tradesman's entrance."

"I'm not sad," Sisi insisted. It occurred to her that her two sisters were determinedly merry. "What about you two? What brings you to Possi?"

"Shall we tell her?" Madi asked.

"We must. She is our eldest sister and a very august lady. We can have no secrets from her. You'd better start."

"No, you."

The bright flash of a kingfisher plunged into the lake and came up again with a wriggling fish in its mouth. They paused to watch Gackel pull away from the pier in the little rowing boat. Children splashed about in a roped off area, beyond which it was forbidden to go. The sisters continued walking.

"Louis never honoured his marriage vows," Spatz began. "He always has mistresses. He treats me as if I'm just another of them. In Rome, I met a dashing Spanish grandee and… well, I had an affair with him. It was never very serious. He was handsome; I was lonely. We had some happy months together."

Sisi's training at the Viennese court came to her aid, allowing her to continue walking without pause or expressing the shock she felt that her sister had so demeaned herself. She had found it was always best not to react immediately but to be sure of one's feelings first. There was shock, certainly, and disapproval, but there was also curiosity. Where had Spatz found the courage to be untrue to her husband? Wasn't she afraid of the world's censure? What would happen if Louis found out?

She was decidedly curious about how a lady in Spatz's position was able to carry on an affair under the noses of husband and household. "How did you… manage? Weren't you watched all the time?"

"Not as much as you. His Holiness put the Farnese Palace at our disposal. It is a vast place, with many unused rooms, twisting corridors and attics. We were never short of a trysting place."

"But what will Louis do if he finds out?"

"Oh, he won't care," Spatz said carelessly and buried her nose in the flowers.

"Did you know about this?" Sisi asked Madi.

It was Spatz who answered. "Of course she does. She acted as go-between, as I did for her. We have no secrets."

This time Sisi had to clamp her teeth on words of denunciation, but something must have shown on her face, for Madi said, "Don't judge me, Sisi." The sparkle was gone from her eyes as she spoke. "You have probably heard that when it came to marital love, Francis was neglectful. He never let me near his heart, though I made every effort. I discovered the reason for that. He has some condition that makes physical love impossible."

"Can it be treated?" Sisi asked.

"Yes, there is a surgical procedure that can relieve the problem. But he won't do it. He's ashamed and embarrassed."

"But that means he will never have an heir! And you, my poor dear, will never have children of your own."

Madi shared a glance with Spatz. The mood between the two of them was heavy, like thunderheads massing in the distance. "When we were in Rome I fell in love with a Belgian count, an officer in the Papal Guard. I couldn't help myself. It was as if we belonged together. I truly do love him, and he loves me. We used to ride together across the Campagna, while Francis was on his knees begging God to forgive his sins and restore his throne. We had some wonderful months together, but I always knew there would be no happy ending. There are consequences to these things." Madi came to a halt and gazed over the lake to the outline of the mountains in the distance. "I am expecting his child."

Sisi put her arm around Madi and drew her head onto her shoulder. Spatz was at her other side, an arm around her waist. It was no longer a question of judging or curiosity. Madi needed help and support, and like a wounded little bird she had flown back to the nest to get it.

The three were silent for a while, and then Sisi said, "Have you told Mimi and Papa?"

Madi choked out a little laugh. "Mimi said all the expected things. I had shamed my family and husband. Did I forget I was the sister-in-law of the Emperor? I was a disgrace. Then she fled to her room with a migraine. Papa said these things happen and there was no point in making a fuss about it."

"These things happen to his lady friends quite often," Spatz said with a giggle.

"How many months are you?"

"Seven. Fortunately, current fashions are such that so far I have been able to hide my condition. Besides Mimi and Papa, Dr.Fischer, and we three, only two of my most devoted ladies know and they are back in Rome, sworn to secrecy."

"What will you do?" Sisi asked.

Madi lifted her head. She linked her arm with Sisi's and with Spatz's on her other side and continued walking. "It has all been decided. Francis being as he is, it is quite impossible to pass the child off as a Bourbon heir. Everyone believes I am here for a rest because I am ill. Before my condition becomes obvious I shall go to the Convent of St. Ursula in Augsburg. It will be announced that I need rest after my ordeal at Gaeta. When the child is born, it will be given to its father to be raised."

"But will you see the child again, or the father?"

"No." Sisi was about to speak, but Madi cut her off. "No, it's for the best. Then I shall return to Francis. But I will tell him the truth." She glanced at Sisi uncertainly. "Spatz says I would be mad to do so. Even Mimi and Papa are frantic that he will create a scandal. Do you think I'm right?"

"You say he truly loves you, and he has good reason to be grateful to you for your conduct at Gaeta. I think he will stand by you if you are contrite and beg for his forgiveness. But in any case, you must tell him. How can you hope for a happy marriage when it is based on such a terrible lie? And imagine how much worse it will be if he should find out one day that you have deceived him. Do tell him.

"If he forgives me, I shall then do everything I can to persuade him to seek a remedy for his condition." A mere five heartbeats later, Madi said. "There, now that's out of the way we can all be merry again."

Although Madi had brought her trouble on herself, Sisi felt great sorrow for her sister. The merriment was forced. Underneath it, Madi was deeply unhappy at her separation from the man she loved, the man she was resolved never to see again. Sisi had to admire her sister's fortitude. In spite of having made a terrible mistake, Madi was determined to avoid a scandal and do the best thing for all concerned, though it meant she must make terrible sacrifices.

The sisters spent their time together, walking in the pine woods or sitting on a blanket beside the lake on an evening, watching the sunset and the stars come out one by one, whispering secrets, laughing a lot. Sisi tried to pretend she was a girl again – a girl who belonged at Possi – and that Vienna was a place of which she had only heard.

The relationship between the three had changed. Over the course of their stay at Possi, Sisi learned from her younger sisters about the procedures of carrying on an illicit affair without detection. At twenty-four-years-old, she also learned for the first time that the act of union between a man and woman, which she looked upon as something to be endured and avoided if possible, could be joyous and fulfilling. This came as a complete revelation to her.

She spent most of her time with them, readily joining the conspiracy of cheer, but when she was in bed at night, she often thought about what Dr Fischer had said. And she remembered how during the Italian War, she hadn't been ill at all; her lethargy vanished along with her symptoms. This led her to the conclusion that she needed a cause, and as soon as she thought that, she had one: Hungary.

She rose at four o'clock on the morning she was to leave Possi and wandered into the garden and down to the lake. Her eyes were still red and swollen when she bade goodbye to her family.

Chapter 29 – August-December 1862

Back to Vienna, to dwell in the gilded cage whose bars would close in until they had squeezed the life out of her.

As soon as the carriage rolled across the building site where the walls had been, and the Ringstrasse was taking shape, Sisi felt the morbid shadow of despair invade her heart. Such dread filled her that she vomited for the third time that morning and had a severe headache. Yet it was a warm welcome, the Viennese lining the route to see her and welcome her home. She was the front page headline in the *Morgen-Post: The land is glad of the recovery of its princess...*

Franz and his mother had been spending the summer at Ischl, but Sisi had adamantly refused to go where the archduchess was. So a few days before his birthday, Franz was waiting at Schönbrunn to hand her out of the carriage while Sophie remained at Ischl.

He still had the erect posture of a soldier and looked dashing in a snug-fitting uniform, but age and care and loss had marred his face with pouches under his eyes and lines scored across his brow. When he removed his cap, she noticed that his hair was becoming thin on top. Streaks of grey marred the unruly thatch of his side whiskers.

His greeting was the formal kiss on the hand, but as he escorted her inside, he murmured, "How happy I am to have you with me again after missing you for so long."

Sisi replied with a less than sincere, "It is good to be home."

Within the palace, the imperial family were waiting to greet her: her favourite brother-in-law, Maximilian Joseph, and his ambitious wife Charlotte who Sisi disliked intensely; Karl Ludwig, who was due to marry his second wife, Maria Annunciata, sister of Madi and Spatz's husbands, in Rome in October; and Ludwig Viktor, despised by all because he was an unapologetic homosexual and transvestite. There were also various cousins, all assembled for the celebration of Franz's thirty-second birthday. All the men except Ludwig Viktor wore uniforms, their breasts almost hidden beneath an assortment of ribbons and gilded decorations and medals. The women wore colourful gowns and pearls and fluttered their fans.

It was hours before she was able to get away to her apartment and lie down for a while on her chaise. The doors were closed. Visitors were told the Empress was resting. The same group would be meeting soon for one of the eternally boring family dinners. She could only hope she would sit next to Maximilian, with whom she had much in common and not Ludwig Viktor.

In fact, it was Karl Ludwig on one side of her and Archduke Albrecht, the military governor of Hungary, on the other. When the Archduke asked her about her "travels" she answered him politely but briefly and then devoted her time to Karl Ludwig and his marriage plans. Further down the table, she caught snatches of Maximilian's conversation with Archduchess Theresa about a Frenchman who had developed a theory about disease-inducing germs. She could not intrude on the conversation because protocol forbade that she speak to any but her immediate neighbours.

When the dinner was over, Franz escorted her from the dining room.

"I have been longing to talk to you all day. Are you tired? May I join you for a chat?"

"I had rather hoped we would have had dinner alone tonight. It wouldn't hurt to break with routine once in a while."

"I suppose not but…the family was eager to see you too."

Yes, they certainly were. It had not escaped her attention that she and Franz were minutely observed from the moment she stepped out of the carriage. Every glance, every nuance would be avidly discussed, and the rumour mills were already turning. Perhaps they would see that she had returned a different person. She was twenty-four years old, no longer a child, and with maturity had come a degree of self-confidence. After an absence of two years, she was determined to assert her rights in every respect. In Venice, she had already won one concession from Franz: Countess Esterhazy-Liechtenstein was dismissed and Paula Bellegarde "a mere countess" was now her chief lady-in-waiting. Even Paula herself, while conscious of the honour, had humbly pointed out that Her Majesty would cause a scandal by flouting the conventions of rank. Sisi didn't care. Her world looked a little brighter with Esterhazy gone.

Franz, she calmly reasoned, was in the palm of her hand. He would not want her to leave again and would, therefore, try to avoid discord. For that, he must pay by treating her more justly than he had in the past. She would avoid intruding on his relationship with his mother, but she would not allow Sophie to bully her any longer.

They settled in her salon. A servant poured them each a glass of brandy and left the decanter before withdrawing. *There have been too few evenings like this*, Sisi thought, *just the two of us. Perhaps if he had given me a little more attention, an emotional attachment would have developed...* But it was no use thinking like that. Franz was as he was; he would not change any more than the Danube would alter its course.

"You look beautiful," he said stiffly as if compliments didn't come easily to him these days.

Sisi had selected a gown of ivory silk with roses embroidered in silver thread and a wide belt to emphasise her twenty-inch waist. Throat and earlobes, wrists and fingers dripped diamonds. A white plume that curled down to touch her right ear crowned her hair. Her face bloomed with health and the light golden kiss of a southern sun. She had not neglected her usual beauty and exercise regimens while in Madeira and Corfu. Everything she needed in the way of creams and lotions she had sent out to her, or had them made by local people where ingredients were available.

"Thank you." She took a sip of her brandy.

"Your hair – you haven't had it cut?"

"No. How are the children?"

"Ah, they are happy and devoted to one another. Gisela is well, but Rudolf's health still gives cause for concern from time to time. He's remarkably intelligent for his age, which I suppose is a good thing, but I do wish he were physically stronger. Dr Seeburger assures me his constitution will become more robust as he matures."

Sisi had no faith in Seeburger's prognosis. "I shall see them tomorrow." She would not ask but command. She would send her directive to the nursery, specifying a time, and if the children were not there, she would take her upset to Franz. No longer would she shield him from the way she was treated.

"They aren't here," Franz said, crushing her brave resolve. "They are having a holiday in Reichenau."

Sisi was disappointed but realised that she hadn't given much notice of her return. The children's plans were probably already made and couldn't be changed. And Reichenau wasn't so far away. "Then I will visit them."

"That will be fine," Franz said, "providing you come back." He tried to smile as if making a joke, but she knew he was in earnest.

Silence fell between them, a silence that was as uncomfortable as their stilted conversation. Franz finished his brandy and rose, poured himself another glass and gestured with the decanter towards her. She shook her head.

"What's the news from Possenhofen? How are the family?" he asked, resuming his seat.

Sisi sighed. She had kept him informed in her letters. There wasn't much else they could relate apart from family matters. "Nené is happily married, though her husband's health gives cause for concern. Karl is still in the Bavarian army. When he leaves active duty, he plans to attend the University of Munich and go into the medical field. Marie and Mathilde were both at Possi for a visit."

"And what about little Sophie? Any husband on the horizon for her?"

"She's not 'little Sophie' any longer. She's fifteen. My parents are looking."

Sisi noted that he neglected to mention Ludwig Wilhelm, who had renounced his rights as firstborn to marry an actress and the mother of his daughter. Franz strongly disapproved of the union, but King Maximilian had belatedly given his blessing, and Duke Max had restored Louis as heir to the dukedom. Now it was Karl Theodor who was under a cloud of parental displeasure. They were not at all happy with his taking up a profession – even such a respectable one.

"Is this what you wanted to chat about, Franz? This family trivia?"

"Not really." He looked down at his glass, cradled in one hand and swirled the brandy in it. "I just don't know how or where to begin. I…I'm just not very good at this sort of thing."

"If you can deal with our Prussian cousin Wilhelm and the terrible Czar Alexander, you can surely deal with one lone woman."

That brought a small smile to his lips, but he didn't look at her.

Sisi took another sip of her brandy. "Perhaps I can help you. There have to be changes, Franz. I want to be heard. I want to matter."

"But you do matter! You matter a great deal to me. Surely you know that."

She believed he loved her after his fashion. But how to make him understand there was a difference. "You once said of me that the only reason I was interested in Hungary was because the Hungarians were so handsome. Would you ever say that of your mother?"

"Of course not. My mother has an entirely different feeling for Hungary."

"What I meant was," Sisi said with heroic patience, "would you ever dismiss your mother's opinion in so cavalier a fashion? You discuss politics with her because she is knowledgeable. But she wasn't born that way. She was as ignorant as I when she first came to Vienna. How can I learn if I am shut out?"

"Politics. Is. Not. The. Proper. Milieu. For. The. Empress!" Franz slapped his hand down on the chair arm with every word. A look of pain crossed his face before he resumed his usual bland expression and tempered his tone of voice. "Must we have this conversation?"

Sisi was surprised by his outburst and deeply offended. He was as obdurate as ever. "When would you suggest? Two years from now? Five?"

They sat in tense silence while the clock struck nine. Franz finished his brandy and heaved a breath. "I'm sorry. I didn't mean it to be like this."

"Nor did I, but I'm not going to apologise. I don't want to be an outsider in this court, Franz. I want to be treated as if I am the Empress, not your mother."

As if she hadn't spoken, he said: "I just wanted to tell you that I have missed you. I love you so much. I want us to be a family again."

"But that's the trouble. We never were a family. Your mother took my children from me. You are wed to your duty. I was expected to deal with these things while I was still so young and inexperienced. You, your mother and our children are the real family. You never let me share your life except as a decorative accessory on ceremonial occasions."

"I did hope that now you are home things might improve between us."

Sisi remained silent. The more she spoke, the more hopeless her case seemed. He wanted things to improve without doing anything to cause change. She twisted the bracelet that bore the portrait of little Sophie. Finally, she said, "I am not the naïve girl you married. I am a

239

mature woman, and I have needs that must be satisfied if I am to be happy."

"I too have needs," he murmured.

"Yes, and I know how you satisfy them."

His eyes came up sharply, fastening on her face, searching.

She shrugged. "I attach no blame to you." This was not something she was comfortable discussing because she accepted that she was in large part responsible for Franz's straying, and, in any case, it spared her an onerous duty. But suddenly his face was suffused with a look of overwhelming gratitude. Sisi recognised this as the time to strike.

....

She was given official leave to walk alone to the Oratorium. It was a small triumph, but contrary to court protocol. Next, she persuaded Franz to write a directive to the new adjutant general, to put an end to the constant surveillance by police agents, who were neither discreet nor inconspicuous. Even when she or Franz walked in the palace gardens, they were watched by men hiding behind trees. These methods created an impression with the Viennese that they were in fear of their lives. The habit of being constantly followed and spied upon was as offensive to Franz as it was to Sisi, to the point where he now gave a false destination to the coachman and only when they had left the palace grounds did he give the correct one.

Sisi spent the following weeks travelling back and forth between Vienna, Reichenau and Passau, where she met her mother and sisters. Franz went to Bad Ischl and spent two weeks hunting. There was harmony between the imperial couple, and now that Sisi's health was improved Franz was eager to expand the nursery.

"Rudolf's health is precarious," he pointed out. "Another son would assure the succession."

"I understand the need," Sisi said, squeezing her hands together. She was distressed that something so private was an affair of state and probably discussed with cold dispassion by ministers and court. "But I'm not sure I'm yet strong enough to carry another child. Please speak to Dr Fischer about it. If he says I am well enough, we will try for another."

Dr Fischer said the Empress must not put her body through something as arduous as pregnancy and advised a yearly visit to the spa of Bad Kissingen to take the cure. Franz was disappointed but, as Sisi knew, he was not without solace.

Sisi returned to hiking in the Vienna woods and horseback riding for hours. In the evenings she liked to walk alone in the little garden where once she had arranged to have a picnic with her children, only to have Sophie thwart her plans. Here she dreamed and tried to sooth away the cares and frustrations of the day. Even this, her solitary walks, was the cause of petty tattle in the court. When she was in her apartment, she preferred to be alone, reading or with one of her tutors.

In return for concessions received, Sisi attended the most important functions. She appeared at the court ball during Carnival, where she met Crown Princess Victoria of Prussia, the daughter of Queen Victoria, along with Otto von Bismarck, the new Chancellor of Prussia, who was trying to lead Austria into a war against Denmark for possession of two little duchies, Schleswig-Holstein. Sisi didn't understand at all what the proposed war was about, but Bismarck's misogyny was so palpable that she took a violent dislike to him and refused to attend any more functions at which he was present.

Chapter 30 – April 1864

Like a great beast waking from sleep, the frigate *SMS Novara* moved ponderously away from the dock. The whistle gave one last blast. Standing by the rail, Maximilian and Charlotte waved, and their family members on the wharf waved back.

"How can a man like Maximilian accept the throne of a country torn by strife, thousands of miles away, of which he knows nothing and doesn't even speak the language? The people – they are primitive, aren't they? Indians? Do they want a foreigner, a European, for their Emperor?" Sophie wasn't speaking to anyone in particular. Her hand raised and still, her face was awash with tears, Sophie stared at the ship. She spoke softly, as if to herself, trying to find answers to those questions that had been asked so many times.

Two years earlier, Louis Napoleon had sent an expedition to gold- and silver-rich Mexico, and liked what they reported. Capitalists and industrialists moved in and then came soldiers to guard them. The French were afraid that the United States, still recovering from their civil war, would object to European interference on their continent, and also that Spain might want to recover lost territory. What was needed to legitimise their occupation, they decided, was a monarchy. Since the Habsburgs had once ruled New Spain, Maximilian was an ideal choice. And Maximilian, to the astonishment of his family and friends, had accepted with the provisos that the Mexican people offered the crown and France guaranteed it.

But Maximilian was going to a country torn by civil strife. For years the conservative church party had fought the progressive anti-clerical party led by the Indian, Benito Juarez. While Maximilian sympathised with Juarez and his aim to free the exploited country, he would naturally be viewed by both sides as a tool of the conservatives, and of France.

"How can they believe in the promises of a man who is the very incarnation of falsehood?" Sophie wondered out loud.

Sisi dabbed a handkerchief to her eyes. She understood Maximilian, her favourite brother-in-law, very well because they had so much in common. While he was not without ambition, he had the soul of an idealist and the mind of a liberal reformer. Many another man might have accepted the role of Emperor for the cachet it gave him, but Maximilian had accepted for a number of reasons, including the good he could do the people of Mexico. His first effort would be to reconcile the warring parties. He had spoken to Sisi very frankly about his reasons for accepting. As she well knew, he and his brother had not been on good terms since the Italian War, which Max continued to believe would never have happened if Franz had not treated the people so poorly. Since then there had been a chill between the brothers, who had once been so close. He had come to the sad conclusion there was no place for him in his brother's empire. And finally there was something he shared with Sisi: wanderlust, a longing for adventure, to visit exotic places and experience different cultures.

She knew, and yet she couldn't understand why Max would want to leave his beautiful new castle by the sea and an easy life to rule over savages half a world away.

Sophie lowered her hand. "It is because of her." "Her" was Charlotte, henceforth to be known as Her Imperial Majesty Carlotta. Sophie had long since got over her initial liking for Max's wife. She turned her tear-drenched face to Sisi. "She wanted to be your equal – that's what it was. She always was ambitious."

Just the day before Charlotte had said to Sisi: "I shall be an Empress just like you."

Sisi forbore to point out that being the Empress of Mexico wasn't quite the same as being Empress of Austria. But she didn't think that Max's decision was influenced much by his wife.

The *Novara* was well out into the harbour on its long voyage to Vera Cruz, escorted by two other frigates, one Austrian and the other French. The figures at the rail could no longer be seen.

"Well, that is that," Franz said with some satisfaction. Sophie was crying quietly, without any sound. "No need for tears, Mother. It is for the best. He was becoming an embarrassment to the empire."

Sisi also suspected that Franz was perhaps a little jealous of his more intellectual and artistic brother, and remembered, too, how after the Italian War the people of Vienna – his beloved city – had called for him to abdicate in favour of Maximilian. At Max's sea-girt castle of Miramar, Franz forced him to resign all rights to the imperial throne and warned him that if he should encounter difficulties the empire could not become involved.

Franz strode off toward the carriages, Karl Ludwig following in his wake. There was another who wasn't unhappy to see his brother go, Sisi realised. Karl Ludwig was now second in line to the imperial throne, after Rudolf, who was so delicate.

For the first time in her life, Sisi found herself with feelings of sympathy for her mother-in-law. Her parting words to her favourite son were: "Farewell. Our blessing, Papa's and mine. Our prayers and fears accompany you. May God protect and guide you. Farewell for the last time on your native soil, where, alas, we may see you no more. We bless you again and again from our deeply sorrowing hearts."

Had it been anyone else, Sisi would have reached out with a consoling touch, but because it was Sophie, she only said, "He will return for a visit one day."

Sophie turned and glared at her. Not even on such a sad occasion would she accept sympathy from her despised daughter-in-law.

Chapter 31 – Autumn 1864

Busy all day with receptions, in the evening Sisi had to go to a court ball. She was exhausted when she returned to her apartment but when she was told that Countess Almassy was waiting to see her she had the countess admitted.

"I have the list Your Imperial Majesty requested," the countess said, after a deep curtsy.

Sisi had attended the ball wearing a crinoline of white tulle with camellias in her hair, and the eyes and compliments of the men confirmed what her mirror told her: that she had regained her former beauty. She had grown so used to such compliments that now they merely bored her. Furthermore, she had grown in poise and confidence, and it seemed to her that as she grew into her role, Sophie shrank. She no longer cast such a giant shadow over the Hofburg.

Sisi was having the stitches of her gown removed. Often now she had herself sewn into her gowns, so they fitted her figure as closely as possible. "Thank you, leave it on the table. You may go."

Only when she was in bed and ready to slip off to sleep did she remembered the list, which reminded her she had not done the Hungarian lesson Professor Homoky had set her. It was no easy undertaking, and she was sorely tempted to tell herself that she would do it tomorrow and go to sleep. Two years earlier, having been told that Sisi was attempting to learn Hungarian, Sophie had suggested she might learn to speak Czech instead because the Bohemian lands had remained loyal during the revolution, while Hungary had rebelled and, almost twenty years later, was still a nest of revolutionaries. She had not done very well with Czech, nor had she managed Italian, and Sophie scoffed that she had no aptitude for languages and would never learn Hungarian.

This opinion, which was prevalent in Possenhofen, only made Sisi more determined to master the language. She had someone read to her while she exercised, and studied while having her hair dressed and at every spare moment. She had advanced so rapidly as to be able to read the poems of Eötvös and Jókai in the original and now she was doing translations. She could not allow herself to shirk her lessons. It amused her to speak to Rudolf's Hungarian nurse in

Magyar, knowing Sophie couldn't understand a word, and she also wrote to her little son in that language. Using a tablet and pencil that lay on the night table, she began the translation of Josef II letters to the Hungarians.

In the morning, feeling particularly proud of herself, she presented the paper to the professor and apologised for using a pencil.

While the tutor settled himself in the chair beside her dressing table, she gave herself over to the ministrations and chatter of her hairdresser and glanced at the note. It was her Hungarian teacher who suggested that what she needed was a Hungarian lady-in-waiting, a companion with whom she could practise the language. The idea appealed to her. She had asked Countess Almassy, who was Hungarian by birth, to provide her with the names of six Hungarian ladies able to assume a position at court, to whom she could speak the language on a daily basis. It also occurred to her that if she and her new lady-in-waiting got on well together and she progressed in her studies, they could hold intimate conversations that her enemies would not overhear, report and dissect. The thought excited her.

However, there were seven names on the list. Five were countesses, one was a baroness, and the last was a Fräulein Ida Ferenczi. Sisi sent for Countess Almassy. When she arrived, Sisi pointed to the last name. "Countess, who is this person and why is her name on the list?"

"If I have displeased Your…"

"No, not at all. I'm merely curious."

"I know of her because she is the daughter of a distant kinswoman of mine married to a country gentleman." The Countess nervously twisted her fingers together and glanced around. "May I speak candidly, Your Majesty?" Only the hairdresser, Fannie, the professor and Countess Lily Hunyádi were present. Having received assent, she continued: "I included Ida's name because… because I know Your Majesty favours a compromise with Hungary, and her parents are supporters and friends of the leaders of the progressive party."

"You mean Deák and Andrássy?"

The countess started in surprise. "Yes, Your Majesty. I thought perhaps Ida could be useful."

Sisi suspected there had been some manipulation going on behind the scenes, and that Ida had been carefully selected. But she smiled at the countess to let her know she was not offended. As her intellectual horizons widened, so did her desire to accomplish something meaningful grow. She had found her cause in Hungary, and its relationship with the empire. The romantic, colourful country and its people had captured her imagination with their tragic past and their determination to achieve independence. Even the death of her daughter in Budapest had not subsumed the warm feelings she had for the country that had given her such an unforgettable welcome eight years ago. She knew from the Hungarian party in Vienna that they reciprocated. They called her Hungary's Divine Providence and believed no one but she could persuade the Emperor to accept a compromise.

There were three parties at work in Hungary. The radicals led by Louis Kossuth demanded complete separation from Austria and independence for Hungary. In opposition to Kossuth were the lawyer Ferenc Deák and Count Gyula Andrássy, who were wise enough to see that Hungary could not survive economically without Austria and, furthermore, Kossuth's unilateral demand could only result in war. They wanted the restoration of their historic rights, concomitant upon the crowning of the Emperor and Empress as King and Queen of Hungary; a dual monarchy with equal rights for both, rather than the subjugation of one by the other. The last and least popular party was the conservatives, who trod a middle ground and would be content with something short of full autonomy for the kingdom.

Sisi had been instrumental in persuading Franz to give the Hungarians a diet and Constitution, but the concept of a dual monarchy was so foreign to one who all his life had been spoon-fed his mother's reactionary policies that he was unwilling to grant further concessions.

Sisi believed that if a compromise couldn't be reached, the situation would deteriorate into war. The Hungarians' cry was the same desire that was tearing apart the empire: separation from Austria, self-determination, the demand for freedom, which was something Sisi could sympathise with mind and heart.

But what could she do? She strongly believed that only a liberal approach could save the empire from losing its largest province. So she had told Franz whenever the subject came up. But he, and his

247

mother, still held fast to Metternich's principles: "Sovereignty of the people represents the worst enemy of social order." "One cannot save the empire by ceding power to radicals." To the reactionaries, there was no difference between radicals and patriots. They were all of a kind.

Now here was Ida, a simple country girl, uncorrupted by court life, a girl such as Sisi had once been. Perhaps. And she knew Deák and Andrássy, who Sisi longed to know and wanted more than anything to help achieve a peaceful resolution.

She crushed the note in her hand. "Send for her."

....

Her first impression of Ida was of a timid creature emerging from the forest into open land where many unknown dangers awaited her. She had dark hair, vivid blue eyes and a creamy complexion.

After she had made a perfectly executed curtsy, Sisi invited her to sit on a chair placed close to her own and dismissed her ladies. "Tell me a little about yourself, my dear," she said in Magyar.

Ida glanced at her for just a moment and then lowered her eyes and her head, looking down at the hands folded in her lap. Sisi remembered the way she had hardly dared look at Franz when they first met. When Ida spoke, it was in a soft voice and perfect German. "I am twenty-three years old, Your Imperial Majesty. I live in Kecskémet on the Hungarian Plain with my parents and four sisters. I am unmarried."

"No charming gentleman has come along to sweep you off your feet?"

Her head went a little lower. "There is a neighbouring boy. His name is Kalman. We are almost engaged, but there is some difficulty with the dowry."

"Do you like living on the plain? What is it like? How do you pass the time?"

The plain was windy, Ida said. When the wind was high, housewives threw up their hands in despair at the piles of dust that gathered in crevices of doors and windows and lay in a film on their furniture. Outlying farms had planted fruit trees and grapevines to bind the soil. Sometimes the air smelled like nectar. Ida loved the wide open spaces, the big sky, and the horizon stretching away into a hazy distance in all directions. She liked to dance the country dances of her region, to draw and to take long rambling walks.

By the time she had finished, her head had lifted, and she wore a shy smile. More and more she reminded Sisi of her younger self.

"I have heard that you know Deák and Andrássy."

"My father agrees with their policies. They have visited our house from time to time."

"Is that why you are here?"

Ida looked confused. "I am here because Your Imperial Majesty invited me."

Perhaps she will report on me to them, Sisi thought, and perhaps not. But what does it matter? They will hear nothing except how sympathetic I am to their cause, which they must know already. She could not write to them personally – that would cause an epic scandal – but she could use Ida as a go-between."

"Tell me about them."

"Herr Deák is a lawyer. The people honour and trust him. He is opposed to the uncompromising stand of Kossuth and the anti-monarchists and believes complete separation from Austria would spell Hungary's death, a death without hope of resurrection, as he says. He wants to forget the past and work with the Emperor to achieve a compromise. Alas, he is an old man. His greatest desire is to see Hungary and the empire at peace before he departs this world."

"Kossuth is still in exile?"

"He is, Your Majesty, and in exile, the revolutionary firebrand has lost much of his power to inflame."

"And Count Andrássy – what is he like?"

Ida's face glowed. It was obvious that, though Deák was her hero, she was dazzled by Andrássy. "Oh, Your Majesty, he is..." She sought the right words in the framed photographs of Sisi's favourite horses that hung on the wall. "Herr Deák is the brain, but Count Andrássy is the beating heart of the movement to restore Hungary's historic rights. He is a man of strong passions. He is very handsome, too, dashing, elegant, with expressive dark eyes. All the ladies adore him."

"Including you, I think," Sisi said, and Ida blushed and ducked her head.

249

After the revolutions, Andrássy was sentenced to death. He was hanged in effigy after he made his escape to Paris, where he was nicknamed *le beau pendu*, the handsome hanged man. He was no impoverished exile, for his mother kept him in funds from Hungary. His wealth, title and background ensured that the finest families received him and, according to what Sisi had heard, he had broken more than a few Parisienne hearts. After the imperial visit to Hungary in 1857, Franz reversed the death sentences of many of the exiles and permitted them to return home, even restoring their ranks and estates. Andrássy was one of these.

"He returned from Paris with a wife, no?"

"Yes, a Hungarian aristocrat. Her name is Katinka. She was said to be the most beautiful woman in France after Empress Eugenie. But he keeps her in the country, while he goes wherever he is needed."

By the time she had finished speaking of her heroes, Ida had let her enthusiasm overcome her initial shyness and was gazing at Sisi in open adoration.

"Thank you, Ida. I am very pleased with you. We shall be much together."

That night Sisi went to bed dreaming of Andrássy. Seen through Ida's eyes, he was the epitome of the romantic, patriotic ideal, ready to devote his life to the service of his country. Although he had been sentenced to death by Franz, he was prepared to forget the past in order to forge new ties with Austria for the common good. She painted his imagined portrait on her eyelids, the brilliant blue eyes Ida had described, the tousled hair, the strong Magyar features... With a sigh and a smile on her lips, she fell asleep.

Chapter 32 – May-August 1865

To everyone's vast relief, the first day of May dawned bright and clear. A procession, with the Emperor and Empress at its head and a long tail of courtiers, aristocrats and dignitaries left the Hofburg. A fairground with tents, tubs of flowers and flags flaunting against the sky had been set up outside the Burgtor for the inauguration of the Ringstrasse. "It is my will…" Franz had declared seven years ago, and now the old city ramparts were gone and in their place was a wide boulevard with a ribbon of linden trees lining its centre. Along its length were monumental buildings of varying styles: the State Opera, Parliament, City Hall, the new Burgtheatre, the Museum of Fine Arts and the Natural History Museum, along with many splendid mansions of the rich.

"It is a link to the modern world," Franz said during his speech, before cutting the ribbon.

Gone were the hovels of the poor that had hugged the old ramparts, to add to Vienna's housing shortage. Sisi, so insulated within the walls of palaces, so far above the common masses, had no idea there was a housing shortage in Vienna. Nor did she know there were poor.

The imperial coach drove along a section of the new road to the Prater. Hundreds of flower trimmed carriages and floats followed in a long procession past gaily bedecked houses and many thousands of jubilant spectators.

Upon returning to the Hofburg, Sisi was told that Rudolf was ill with a fever. This was not unusual. Particularly in the past year, he had often suffered fevers, stomach colds and angina. She ordered a carriage and went at once to Schönbrunn. Whenever he was ill, she was reminded again of the death of little Sophie and how much harder the blow was because they were not expecting it. So she rushed to his bedside, fearful that he too would die.

A man was sitting beside him. She recognised him as Colonel Josef Latour von Thurnburg, one of Count Gondrecourt's subordinates. She knew him well. He was one of those who had accompanied her to Madeira. He moved away when she arrived but didn't leave the room.

Poor little boy. It tore her heart to see him, so thin and delicate, flushed with fever. "Fetch me a bowl of water and a napkin," she ordered.

He was seven-years-old now. When he turned six, he installed in an all-male household of his own, a Habsburg tradition. The separation from his sister had been painful for both children, and there were many tearful scenes, for they were very close. Rudolf was a remarkably intelligent child. He could make himself understood in French, Czech, Italian and Hungarian as well as his native German. His intellectual gifts did not please his father as they did his mother. Franz wanted a sturdy, bold son, who would grow into a good soldier, a mirror image of himself.

Rudolf was given into the care of Count Leopold Gondrecourt, for "toughening up". The count drilled the boy relentlessly with rigorous exercises and subjected him to hydropathic treatments that bordered on torture. One morning in February Sisi had been awakened by shouts outside while it was still dark. Looking out the window and saw Gondrecourt drilling her little boy in the deep snow. Rudolf became more anxious and sicklier. Gondrecourt's response was to increase the drills, to introduce ever harsher methods. Sisi knew he was only following Franz's orders, but Franz refused to see that Gondrecourt's techniques were harming and not helping their son.

When Latour brought the bowl of water, she bathed Rudolf's face. He opened fever-glazed eyes. At once, his arms reached out to her. She gathered his frail little body to her. He was such a delicate little boy, sensitive and needing love, and he wasn't getting any. He was far more a Wittelsbach than a Habsburg.

She held him until he fell asleep again. After depositing a kiss on his hot brow, she was about to leave the room when Latour said, "Majesty, may I speak plainly?"

"Please, do."

"I dare not speak to His Imperial Majesty, but I beg you most earnestly to do so. The crown prince is too young and too frail for the cruel methods that are inflicted on him on a daily basis. Majesty he… Count Gondrecourt shoots his guns off in the bedroom when His Highness is asleep and once shut him beyond the gates of the wild game reserve in the Tiergarten and told him a wild boar was coming toward him. He does these things to frighten the child, which, for some reason that escapes me, he seems to think will make him stronger. The crown prince is drilled until he is beyond exhaustion. Then in the morning, which is the only time he does not do military exercises, he is too tired to attend properly to his lessons. Then he is punished for his failure. I believe this is why he is continually ill."

Sisi was shocked to hear all this. She knew Gondrecourt drilled Rudolf to excess, but she had not known about his cruelty. "Thank you for caring. I will speak to the Emperor."

When Franz returned to Schönbrunn, she said firmly, "This must stop. Gondrecourt's methods are not working. They have the opposite effect."

"These are methods used in the army on young cadets. Time and trial have proved them effective. It is not Gondrecourt's methods that are at fault but Rudolf's delicate constitution. Incidentally, I have heard no complaints from him."

"That is because he wants so desperately to please you."

They had had this kind of conversation before, and Franz remained convinced he was right. He had begun his military training at the same age, but admitted that the methods used on him weren't so harsh because he didn't need "toughening up".

Sisi did not beg or weep as she might have done in earlier years. Something more was required. She thought about what she could realistically do to change his mind. *I will not let another child of mine die.*

....

Sisi rose, as usual in the summer, at five o'clock. Her first feeling was of relief, her first thought: *Good, I have no duties today. I shall write some letters and see the children.*

One of her lady's maids was there to help with her morning rituals. A rubber tub was brought into her dressing room, and two footmen carried in pitchers of cold water. Wearing a bathing shirt, she huddled in the tub while the maid poured the water over her. After the bath, she had a massage. Then she dressed in a simple black gown for an hour of vigorous exercise. Before she had completed her exercises, Fanny arrived.

"Good morning, Your Majesty." She was forced to address herself to a figure flying as gracefully as a bird through the air.

"Good morning, Fanny," Sisi replied, hanging upside down, the room swinging to and fro beneath her.

By the time she came back down to earth, the chambermaid had arrived and was arranging fresh flowers in their ceramic vases. Sisi never wore perfume because she hated the smell of it. But she loved to bring a little of the outdoors into her rooms with the scent of fresh flowers and her windows open on warm days.

After exercise, she took the time for breakfast, usually no more than a slice of toast and glass of water. Sometimes, not frequently, Franz wanted to breakfast with her, and the rest of her morning schedule was put back by an hour.

The previous year she had attended a comedy at the Burgtheater and saw an actress whose hairstyle she greatly admired. After making enquiries, she learned the artist was a young woman named Franziska Feifalik, wife of a banker and daughter of a hairdresser. Fanny, as Sisi dubbed her, was invited to the palace, interviewed and, after showing some photographs of her work, hired as the imperial hairdresser at an unprecedented salary of two thousand guldens a year. She was a lovely young woman with a surprisingly graceful, almost regal, air.

A year later, Fanny had become one of the very few people Sisi liked and trusted, even though Fanny soon gained the upper hand in the relationship. If Sisi displeased her in any way, Fanny would punish her by pleading illness and sending another hairdresser in her place. When this happened, Sisi was upset. "I am a slave to my hair," she complained. No other had Fanny's deft fingers and incomparable proficiency for creating stunning styles. Ladies of the court and Viennese society vied for her favours in the hope of having her services for special occasions. They wanted to imitate the Empress's styles, though without much luck because they did not have Sisi's strong, healthy hair. Nor were they prepared to spend the amount of time and effort, not to mention expense that Sisi did to keep her hair always looking glorious.

Fanny had already prepared the room for the regimen of the Empress's hair. A white cloth was spread over the carpet in the dressing room. One of the modern innovations Sisi had introduced into her apartment was wall-to-wall carpeting instead of the area rugs favoured by the other occupants. With a white lace robe over her black gown, she sat on a chair placed in the centre of the cloth, her hair hanging over the back. Fanny unfastened the cap that confined her loose hair then buried her hands in the waves, letting them flow over her arms as she massaged Sisi's scalp. It was the only part of the ritual that gave Sisi pleasure. After Fanny had combed out every tangle, she then brushed it vigorously until it gleamed like the parquet floor of the East Asian Cabinet. Elaborate styles were saved for special occasions, but even on ordinary days, Sisi wanted to look her best because she was always under scrutiny.

She spent two to three hours a day on this ritual. An entire day every three weeks was devoted to washing and drying her ankle-length hair. On these days the Empress was not available to anyone. Raw egg yolks and twenty bottles of cognac were used in the process to maintain its health and shine.

The hours spent pampering her hair were not wasted. She used them for reading or writing letters and for studying. She struggled with languages. Her English and French were good, but with Ida to speak with daily her Hungarian was improving rapidly.

The problem with Ida was that she was not a member of the high nobility and therefore could not serve the Empress as a lady-in-waiting. She could only work as a servant. Sisi didn't want her for a servant. She wanted her as a companion and friend. Countess Almassy suggested she should be appointed official reader to Her Majesty, with a salary and board and lodgings at the Hofburg.

Franz and Sophie were opposed to the entire idea, but Sisi had made up her mind. Ida Ferenczi was to be her bridge to Deák and Andrássy. Furthermore, their common purpose along with Ida's natural charm was such that she very soon earned the trust and confidence Sisi awarded to a very few outside her family.

After Sisi's hair had been braided and the braids arranged in some artful style, Fanny picked up all the hairs from the cloth, the brush and comb, and presented them to the Empress in a silver bowl. Sisi counted them. If there were too many, she became upset. She didn't want her hair to thin, though it was so heavy it sometimes gave her a headache. Today – six. She sighed.

Fanny sank to the floor. "I lay myself at Your Majesty's feet." The ritual was complete.

Fanny left to attend to other clients – from whom she charged exorbitant fees – but she would be back if she were so disposed, for she was an unofficial member of the Empress's entourage. Her husband, the banker, was now also a member of the palace staff.

Sisi's mode of dressing in the summer was another source of scandal. She wore only pantalettes under her light summer gowns. No corset. No petticoats. No stockings. In every way possible she let Sophie and the court know she was her own woman and would do what she pleased with her own self. If the ladies wished to burden themselves with restrictive clothing when the sun was hot and the breezes soft as a child's kiss, they were welcome to do so. She would enjoy the freedom from confinement.

Only half-dressed, as Sophie had said, she went to her full-length mirror and scrutinised herself for any flaws. What she saw was no longer the face of a shy, awkward girl, but a self-confident young woman at the height of her beauty. She had been told so often recently that she was beautiful she could no longer doubt it. At first, she had dismissed the compliments as the kind paid to anyone in an exalted position. She had never thought she was beautiful, but she had always compared herself with Nené. The childish roundness had gone from her face, leaving it not only mature but a pleasing heart-shape. Her melancholy eyes were arresting, a topaz hue, very bright and surmounted by slightly arching brows. Her nose was slender and refined, her lips full but not too full. When she smiled, they formed a perfect bow. A hint of mischief lurked in her smile but even then her eyes didn't warm. They were sad eyes. And then, of course, there was her crowning glory, her thick, shining, fabulous chestnut hair. Yes, she thought with pleasure, my face is not only beautiful but interesting. And then she thought: I can use this.

Her beauty was all she had. It was the one thing even her detractors admired, and it gave her a measure of self-assurance. But beauty was a fragile flower and took a good deal of time and effort to maintain. She exchanged recipes with other beautiful women for lotions and creams. When strawberries were in season, she had a paste made which she massaged into her face and neck. Otherwise, she applied a nightly mask of raw veal. She slept with damp cloths over her thighs and hips to preserve their slenderness and on a hard mattress without a pillow. She bathed in warm olive oil to keep her skin smooth and supple; it made her feel as if she were cocooned in liquid silk. Daily, she drank five or six egg whites with a little salt.

As her reputation grew, her beauty became a liability. The ladies of the court could not accept that a provincial Bavarian was more beautiful than any of them. When she attended a court function, she must be dressed and groomed to perfection, because any defect would be criticised and gossiped about by a court that relished finding fault with their Empress. Every minute of every day she had to live up to her reputation as the greatest beauty in the empire. But it was not a situation she relished.

Whenever she went out in public, crowds inevitably gathered to see her, to see if she was as beautiful as they had heard. She appeared so rarely in public that when she did her appearance created a sensation. Franz was virtually ignored if she was with him. It was Elisabeth the people cheered. She was their idol. Her fame provoked feelings of national pride. She could not walk anywhere, for people pressed too close. On one occasion, the curious blocked the street and would not let her carriage pass until they had stared their fill. Such incidents frightened her. Her fear of crowds had not diminished over the years; rather it had increased to the point where public functions became occasions of extreme stress, often ending in a headache and an increased longing for solitude.

After one such episode, Paula said: "How happy the people are when they see Your Majesty."

"Oh yes, they're curious," Sisi replied bitterly. "Whenever there's something to see they come running, for the monkey dancing at the hurdy-gurdy just as much as for me." That was how she saw herself: a curiosity, a spectacle.

She was known far and wide as one of the most beautiful women in the world. After she had attended her brother's wedding in Dresden, her aunt, Queen Marie of Saxony wrote to Ludovika: *You can have no idea of the enthusiasm aroused here by the Empress's beauty and grace; never before have I seen my Saxons so excited! They thought, spoke, and heard only her praises.*

But Sisi didn't care about her international reputation. It gave her no pride. She cultivated her beauty for herself alone, because it gave her a degree of self-assurance and also because it was an asset that could be used to further her interests. With ruthless calculation, she intended to use it on Franz.

....

In August the imperial family went to Ischl. Franz hunted. Sisi devoted her time to study and her copious correspondence, while exercise equipment was installed for her. Although she had an apartment in the main building, she had her own little house on the grounds, built in the English Elizabethan style, a concession to her need for seclusion.

One bright starlit evening she and Franz were sat on the veranda of the main residence when Franz leant over and said, "Do you know, my angel, I believe you grow more radiant with each passing year."

"Why, thank you, Franz."

Moving a little closer to her husband, she smiled into his eyes. "Come to me tonight, my dear little man." It was her nickname for him.

"Y...yes, I should be delighted," he stammered like any green boy.

Having established a proper relationship and having concluded that Franz would not want her to go away again, for personal reasons and also to protect the imperial house from any more scandal, Sisi sat at her desk and wrote a strongly-worded note.

I wish to have reserved to me absolute authority in matters concerning the children, the choice of the people around them, the place of their residence, the complete supervision of their education, in a word, everything is to be left entirely to me to decide, until the moment of their majority. I further wish that whatever concerns my personal affairs, such as, among others, the choice of the people around me, the place of my residence, all arrangements in the house, etc., be reserved for me alone to decide.

She put the note on his desk and walked away without a word. Within minutes he burst into her room, the note in his hand.

"I cannot believe you mean this, Elisabeth! You want the care of the crown prince. You want to choose his tutors, his household? I never heard of such a thing."

Sisi whirled on him. "And why not? You were perfectly content to put him into the care of your mother! And look what has been done to him – he is a pale and sickly shell of the exuberant little boy he was a year ago. He wets the bed. I won't be pushed aside any longer. I demand to be allowed to exercise my rights as his mother. Either Gondrecourt goes, or I go!"

Franz sat – or rather, collapsed – into a chair, and looked at her as if he had never seen her before. "I... I cannot bear the thought of being parted from you again. I can deny you nothing." He heaved a sigh. Very well. You shall have your way in this."

Sisi's heart leapt with gladness. She went to him and knelt beside his chair. "Thank you, my dear, dear little man. Thank you for understanding how much it means to me to be an important part of my children's lives." Taking his face between her hands, she drew it down for a kiss, a sweet promise of things to come.

When he had gone, she sat at her dressing table and gazed at her reflection. A small smile curved her lips as she thought about Sophie and her reaction when Franz told her. She had not only lost control of the children, but she would also know that her influence with Franz was on the wane. When she thought about it, Sisi realised she had won an astonishing victory: not just the care of her children, she had also begun the process of weaning Franz away from his mother.

It had been easy after all. Yes, it was easy, when one understood that power took many forms, and how to use it. But one must be careful not to abuse it. She would try not to quarrel with Sophie, and continue to wear gloves at dinner.

. . . .

"Please, make yourself comfortable, Colonel Latour." Sisi indicated the chair set beside hers. The colonel tucked his cap under his arm, and sat on the very edge of the seat, stiff and ill-at-ease. Sisi wondered if he thought he was on the carpet for some misdeed. She knew from the time spent with him on Madeira that his political leanings were liberal, and because of this he was despised at court and the object of many petty intrigues.

She had made enquiries of the colonel's role in Rudolf's household and was told of repeated instances that bordered on insubordination. It also became clear that he was devoted to Rudolf and looked out for him when he could. But Rudolf himself was the final arbiter. When she had asked him if he would like to have

Colonel Latour for his tutor instead of Count Gondrecourt, his little face lit up like a candle.

"Colonel Latour, it is not yet public knowledge, but Count Gondrecourt has been dismissed from his post as head of the Crown Prince's household." There was no mistaking the sweep of relief on the colonel's face. "With the Emperor's approval, I wish you to take up the post."

Latour was taken completely by surprised. He floundered a little before finding words. "Me? But, Your Majesty, I am a mere colonel. I'm not even noble. I am most unfitting for such a high honour."

"Do you love the crown prince?"

His face suddenly suffused with tenderness. "I do. His suffering and his bravery in suffering have touched my heart."

"And will you do all you can to help me restore him to good health?"

"I will always be at Your Gracious Majesty's service."

"Those are the qualifications I expect in the prince's tutor. I need hardly add that I want military drills reduced to the most basic exercises. He must, of course, learn to ride well and to shoot. But the emphasis must be on education." She paused before adding: "Liberal education. You will choose teachers to replace the present ones, not one of whom is to my liking. You need not look solely among aristocrats, military men and the clergy. The only criteria should be scholarly qualifications."

"Is Your Majesty suggesting that I may seek among the bourgeois?"

"My dear colonel, I insist upon it. Where else will we find the best liberal minds?"

"Your Majesty has quite taken my breath away."

"I suggest you get it back quickly," Sisi said with a smile. "You have a lot of work to do."

The new teachers, when they finally assembled, were bourgeois and liberal to a man, except for the religious instructor who was a cleric. They rallied around Latour and formed a small clique that was intensely disliked at court.

Gondrecourt's nose was out of joint. It was reported to Sisi that he said: "Latour has neither the desired sense of chivalry nor the uprightness and necessary distinguished deportment to exert a beneficial influence on the mind and character of the crown prince in daily intercourse." He claimed Latour was capable of only "nursemaiding" his pupil but not of educating him. The court's sympathies were with him, and he begged influential people to speak to the Emperor on his behalf. Whether anyone did or not Sisi didn't know.

She continued to champion Latour. Under his "nursemaiding" Rudolf's health improved quickly, and his mind was nurtured by a well-rounded liberal education that was the antithesis of the court system of the Habsburgs.

Chapter 33 – December 1865-January 1866

With Sisi at her side dictating, Ida wrote: *My Friend has said that when the Emperor's affairs do not go well in Italy, she feels sorry. But if misfortune were to strike in Hungary, it would be death to her. My Friend believes only a liberal attitude can avoid an open break. She wants you to know you many friends at court.*

Deák never mentioned "the friend" at all, knowing his words would nevertheless be related to Sisi by Ida. Andrássy's words made her heart flutter: *Assure Your Divine Friend that Gyula Andrássy lays his heart at her feet...* A conventional phrase, and spoken by Ida should have robbed it of any effect.

As time went by, Andrássy's letters became warmer and more personal, frequently not mentioning the political situation at all or mixing politics with extravagant compliments that brought a blush to Sisi's cheeks. Having learned that she loved the poems to Heinrich Heine, he often included a verse or two. Ida would read the words in her soft sweet voice, and they would sigh and share a secret smile. Sisi would not have wanted those letters to fall into other hands, but she cherished them and couldn't bring herself to burn them. They were kept in a casket and hidden away in Ida's room.

Ida slipped off with the letter, and Sisi summoned her maids for the ritual of her retiring. Above her bed at the Hofburg hung a portrait of Deák, which she had asked to be sent to her. With his drooping moustache and eyebrows like thickets, it was not the kind of portrait to inspire a romantic young woman. She hadn't dared to ask for one of Andrássy, but it was of him she thought as she slipped beneath the silken sheets beneath the portrait of Deák. In her imaginings she saw a horseman galloping across a dusty plain, dark hair flying behind him, white teeth bared to the wind, urging the horse faster and faster until he came to a sudden halt. The horse rose on its hind legs and pirouetted. He held the reins with one hand in a superb demonstration of horsemanship and then leapt down to sweep her up...

It was obvious that Ida was infatuated with him. Sisi feared she was too. She had never met him, but whenever she heard his name, her heart beat a little faster.

Ida had become the friend she had always wanted. She was sweet, discreet, clearly adored Sisi and quickly became indispensable. During the conflict over Rudolf, Ida had unequivocally taken Sisi's part and spoken out openly. No one had ever done that before. They were seldom apart. When Ida had asked to go home for a visit in the summer, Sisi had reluctantly agreed to two weeks and had alleviated her loneliness by writing letters and receiving Ida's replies.

Now, largely thanks to Ida, Sisi had a party of her own. Its members were mostly Hungarians, or sympathisers and all liberal. Led by the Empress they were in open opposition to the reactionary policies of Sophie's powerful clique.

The result was that Ida had become one of the most disliked and mistrusted people at court. The ladies speculated endlessly about how she had come to be so close to the Empress in such a short time that Sisi pined for her when she was absent. What hold did she have on the Empress? What did they talk about when they spoke together in Hungarian? The most virulent haters put the word about that Ida was in the pay of the Hungarian conservative party.

....

"You must talk to Andrássy," Sisi said to Franz. She could now speak with authority about Hungarian politics, and furthermore, she had the self-confidence to do so. "Bring him to Vienna. He has a plan of which I am sure you will approve."

Delegates went back and forth between Vienna and Budapest, but there was no forward motion. Sisi decided she must intervene.

Franz wore the long-suffering look of a man who has heard it all before but knows he must submit to hearing it again. "I cannot receive him at court. He is a revolutionary."

They were breakfasting together in Sisi's salon. Sisi had eaten only a *kipfel*, a roll shaped like a crescent moon, with a glass of water, but a feast had been laid on for Franz, accompanied by coffee with whipped cream. For such a small and slender man he had a hearty appetite, and he was as proud of his figure as Sisi was of hers. The crowned heads of Europe tended to corpulence.

Sisi heaved a sigh of exasperation. "He is not a revolutionary. Perhaps once he was but no longer. He is a patriot. He is not a man who wants to play a role at all costs, or one who chases glory. He loves Hungary. You must talk to him for Rudolf's sake. Do you want our son to inherit a truncated empire? Because that is what will happen if you don't come to an accommodation with the Hungarians."

"I have made concessions, have I not? At your urging, I abolished military jurisdiction and instituted civil law. What good did it do me? Tell me that."

He had been persuaded to visit Hungary in June, but it had not been a great success. Sisi wasn't permitted to go. It was not an official state visit. He told her on his return that he had been astonished at how much the people revered her.

"Because it wasn't enough. They want more."

"I know they bloody well want more! They want more than I am prepared to give!" He threw down his fork and turned his face to the window, where rain was teeming down almost obscuring the grey walls of the Hofburg. The dismal day mirrored the dismal atmosphere in the room. "My apologies." Turning back to her, he rubbed his brow as if to erase the lines there. "Here, try some of the *marillenknödel.* It's delicious." He signalled to a server, who put an apricot stuffed dumpling on her plate. She eyed it with disfavour.

"I cannot bear to watch incompetent men prompted by old and senseless hatred destroy the empire. Franz, I am convinced that if you talked to Andrássy, and at once, it would still be possible to save ourselves and the entire monarchy, not Hungary alone."

She felt sure that left to himself Franz would come to some agreement with Deák, but pulling him in the opposite direction were such men as his uncle, Archduke Albrecht, and the new adjutant general, Count Crenneville. His mother had adopted a more conciliatory stance. She wanted compromise with Hungary but not at the cost of Austrian interests. And yet, Sisi couldn't help feeling optimistic.

"I'll make a bargain with you. I will put it to the Council of Ministers if you eat the *marillenknödel,*" Franz said. "It can't hurt to speak to the fellow, I suppose. Mind you, I concede nothing more than that."

"Thank you, Franz."

Sisi was not much encouraged. There were too many opposed to any Hungarian compromise, and she believed he was merely using the ministers so he could shift the blame when he refused her.

She understood that Franz recognised no other system than the one that had been inculcated in him since birth. He could see only two conditions: rule by divine right, or anarchy. Sisi confronted a huge wall of staunch prejudice, reinforced by historical precedent and a host of those who stuck to the well-worn path of monarchism. But she had learned to be persistent. Her silence was not to be bought by a slice of dumpling. He was not permitted to forget their bargain, and to her surprise, it eventually bore fruit.

A few days later, Franz once again joined her for breakfast to inform her what had been decided. "You are to receive a Hungarian delegation. You will not receive Deák who is not noble and has no official standing, but you will receive Count Andrássy who, as vice-president the diet, will be part of the delegation."

Sisi kept her composure, but she was beside herself with joy at her victory, and even more so at the prospect of meeting Gyula Andrássy.

....

Dressed in her black gown with the white shirt over it, Sisi took her seat in the chair in the middle of the white cloth.

Fanny curtsied before her. "Good morning, Your Majesty."

"It must be something special today, Fanny. I will wear a Hungarian cap, surmounted by a tiara. I want to look my best."

"Your Majesty will look glorious even if my poor efforts fail."

In Franz's bedroom hung a portrait of Sisi painted that summer by Franz Winterhalter. It was a very sensual portrait. In it, she had her back half turned to the viewer. She wore a white gown with one shoulder bared. Her hair was loose, tumbling down her back in a gleaming cascade. Her face was in profile, yet the mystery in it and the sorrow were clear even to the sitter. She looked ethereal, like a fairy-tale princess who had lost her prince. Franz was enraptured. He declared it to be the best portrait of her ever done, and she agreed. It was always an odd sensation to see herself as another saw her. She wondered now how Andrássy would see her.

"It is for the Hungarian delegation – this special style?" Fanny asked as she massaged Sisi's scalp with long, strong fingers.

"Yes, I want to impress. What are they saying of this visit in Vienna?"

"They are fearful that His Majesty is going to make concessions, that he will form a government there and Vienna will lose its special status."

"They should fear that he doesn't."

Sisi was to receive the delegates alone. When she entered the *Rittersaal*, accompanied by eight Hungarian ladies-in-waiting, she was wearing a Hungarian national costume, a white silk dress with a lace apron, a black velvet bodice richly emblazoned with diamonds, pearls and colourful embroidery. On her head was a cap surmounted by a diamond tiara, and a diaphanous veil trailing down her back. A soft sound of indrawn breath came from the delegates before they bowed their heads in unison. They were led by the Cardinal Primate of Hungary and included representatives of all the leading families. To Sisi, they presented a magnificent sight: tall and handsome, dressed in fur-trimmed costumes and yellow boots, with spurs attached.

There was one who was taller and more handsome than the rest. As her eyes came to rest on him, she felt a jolt go through her. She knew him at once. Her heart knew him. He had wild black hair and sculpted lips between beard and moustache. He looked like a gipsy, untamed and uninhibited by the constraints of modernity, as if he had just ridden in from the Steppes and his horse was waiting outside to carry him off into the wide open spaces. His eyes met hers. Ida had said he had arresting eyes. They were beautiful and powerful. They held her gaze and wouldn't let go. She felt a warmth on the back of her neck as if the sun had slanted through one of the windows and shone on her.

The cardinal primate was making his address: "...the unbounded loyalty of the Hungarian nation to their queen..."

Andrássy stared at her. She stared back at him. He wore the gold-embroidered ceremonial dress of the Magyar aristocracy, his coat dazzling with jewels, and a tiger skin hung over one shoulder. She wanted to pull her gaze away but could not. Everyone would know where she was looking. He would think her far too forward. She could feel the heat rising in her face.

"Like every other Hungarian, it is my dearest hope that we will soon be welcoming Your Imperial Majesty to our own capital..."

Finally, Andrássy released her, and she turned her gaze upon the cardinal primate. She dare not look Andrássy's way again. When the cleric had finished his speech, she replied in fluent Magyar in her gentle voice, that she still cherished wonderful memories of the beautiful city of Budapest and nothing could give her greater pleasure than to return there. Hardly had she finished speaking than the delegates broke into thunderous acclaim: *"Eljen Erzsebet! Eljen Erzsebet!"*

Sisi took her seat while the shouts echoed through the hallways of the Hofburg and waited for them to die down. The delegates came forward one by one. Only the cardinal preceded Andrássy. She could look at him now. He carried himself proudly, almost with a swagger, flipped the edge of his tiger skin aside and went on one knee before her. When he kissed her gloved hand, she noticed how his eyes closed, and his nostrils flared as if he was breathing deeply of her scent.

"Count Andrássy." She gestured for him to rise. "It is a pleasure to meet you at last."

"Most Serene Majesty, your beauty surpasses all reports. I beg you to think kindly of your devoted slave who will always worship you." His voice was deep, caressing. It was a voice that lent itself to words of love. Then he was gone, and another took his place.

When the reception was over, Sisi retired to her apartment, but only to prepare herself for the state dinner that evening, to which the Hungarians had been invited. Ida almost pounced on her when she entered.

"What did you think of him?"

"He is everything you said he was. He made an immediate impression." It would have been more accurate to use the word "impact". To get her head out of the clouds, she added, "But I have no idea what he is like really. We only spoke for a moment." She had received many compliments in recent years. Andrássy's was more florid than most. Was that because he was so practised in the art of seduction? Ida had said he was something of a Casanova, and vain.

"Where is Fanny?"

"She is with Countess Bombelles."

"Go and ask her to return here at three o'clock. I want something different for tonight." In German, she said, "Ladies, you must help me choose a gown. Paula, my pearls – the long string, please."

She would have liked to spend the intervening hours writing letters. Her correspondence had a habit of piling up if she wasn't diligent about replying. But when she prepared her pen and official notepaper to write to her cousin Ludwig, who had become King of Bavaria upon the death of his father the previous year, she found her thoughts drifting to the reception, and she wondered why Andrássy had had such an effect on her. All she could think was that he encapsulated in his person everything she loved about Hungary and its people: the colour and vibrancy, romance and exuberance, the tragic past, the yearning for freedom and independence.

....

She had selected a white gown with a train, and Fannie had threaded pearls through her braids, which were looped to reach halfway down her back.

Franz was waiting to escort her into dinner. He bent to kiss her hand. "It seems impossible, but I think you grow in loveliness each time I see you."

She placed her hand on his wrist, and they left the apartment followed by their attendants, who would dine at a different table than the imperial couple and their guests.

"I heard the cheering," Franz said. Sisi knew that was impossible, but she smiled. "I am always amazed how much they love you. How do you capture hearts so easily?"

"It is because they know I sympathise with them. Perhaps they would love you too if you will agree to a conciliation."

Franz's bantering tone turned sombre. "I will never have the love of my people. Perhaps the best I can hope for is to earn their respect. Yes, that would be good."

"That is not true, Franz. The Viennese do love you, and I think it is because they know you love them and their city. There is bad history between you and the Hungarian people. It will take time to overcome, but it is possible with understanding on both sides."

268

Sisi had learned from Ida that there were still some houses in Hungary where no Austrian would dare show his face. The Batthyány, a prominent aristocratic family, had stood at the graveside of their beloved dead and sworn never to bow their heads to Franz Josef.

They entered the sixteenth century *Mamorsaal*. A score of uniformed and bewigged footmen stood around walls lined with artificial marble to match the appearance of the adjacent Ceremonial Hall.

Each place at the long table was set with Meissen plates painted with floral motifs, the Imperial silver cutlery, and four crystal wine glasses. It was the delight of the Court Linen Room staff to form the three feet square napkins into various shapes that defied imitation, though many tried. On this occasion, a white elephant sat on each nest of plates. Displayed on the pristine white tablecloth were centrepieces consisting of ornate candelabra featuring scrolls and rocaille work, fat cherubs, clusters of grapes and cornucopias, animals and fluttering birds, all in gilded silver. Between the gilded pieces were masses of flowers from the Imperial conservatory.

As the Emperor and Empress entered, everyone stood and bowed. Franz took his place in the middle of the table, Sisi beside him, and the company resumed their seats. Opposite them were the Cardinal and Andrássy with Countess Almassy between them. Sophie was not present. She had given fair warning that she was going to be ill during the Hungarians' visit.

It seemed to Sisi that the Hungarians were subdued, even though they did not observe court etiquette by speaking only to their immediate neighbours. Their voices were low, their laughter restrained.

When the first wine was served, Andrássy rose to his feet and raised his glass. "May I propose a toast? To Her Imperial Majesty, may the good Lord who gave her to us, long preserve her in health and happiness."

The company rose with raised glasses and echoed the toast with a shout.

Whenever Sisi looked across the table, Andrássy's eyes were on her, even when he was talking to a neighbour. She said little during the dinner, and only picked at her food. For some reason, her nerves were taut as a bowstring.

After dinner, Franz and Sisi moved about the room, speaking to each of the delegates in turn. Sisi went immediately to Andrássy and offered him her hand. He lifted it to his lips but did not release it at once. He looked into her eyes. She had the disconcerting sense that her thoughts, her deepest feelings, were revealed to him.

"Count Andrássy, I hope your welcome in Vienna was all you could have wished," she said, withdrawing her hand.

"Your Majesty is most kind. It is because of your efforts that matters have progressed so far. You are Hungary's Divine Providence."

"You give me too much credit, Count. But I am glad to have the opportunity to speak to you in person. I know you have a carefully thought-out proposal to put to the Emperor and I have spoken to him about it. One of the problems is that it takes no account of the non-Hungarian peoples of the monarchy. You are asking for parity with a larger and economically more valuable region."

"The Bohemians have let us know in no uncertain terms that they consider our demands outrageous. Well, I say, let the Bohemians take care of themselves. But, Your Majesty, my proposals are flexible. They are open to negotiation when the time comes. But first, it must be agreed that there will be a new constitution, that we will have our own government, that the Emperor wants conciliation and that he and his divine Empress will be crowned King and Queen of Hungary." If possible, his eyes became even more intent. "Will he speak with me?"

Sisi looked away. "Not at this time."

The count blew out his breath. "Then we have wasted our time coming here."

"No." Sisi laid a consoling hand on his arm. "My father once told me that diplomacy was like a dance, and I know the Hungarians love to dance –"

"I would like to dance with you," Andrássy whispered in that voice he used during the reception: deep and sultry. "I would like to hold you in my arms and whirl you away to some distant exotic playground where there is nothing but music and laughter."

Sisi glanced around distractedly to see if anyone was close enough to hear. Franz was in conversation with others. "You take one step forward and then your partner... I mean the other party takes a step forward…" Heat flamed in her face. Her father had put it so well, and now she couldn't remember what he had said.

"Would you care for a glass of wine, Majesty?"

"Thank you, no." *I have drunk enough. I don't seem able to think coherently. What was it I wanted to say?* She had a brief respite to get her thoughts in order, while he summoned a footman and took a glass of wine with a nod of thanks. "I suggest, Count, that you have the cardinal formally invite the Emperor to Hungary for a state visit. I will do my best to convince him to go. Once free of obstructive persons, he will be easier to persuade, but you must not expect too much of him." It was time to move on before she made an utter fool of herself. "Please excuse me, Count."

As she was about to move away, he laid a hand on her arm. She was wearing long gloves but even so it was a colossal *faux pas*. One did not touch royalty without invitation. He dropped his hand at once.

"Permit me to tell you one more thing. As I'm sure you know, Bismarck is preparing for war against Austria. Kossuth already has a strong following among those of my people who either do not think rapprochement with Austria is possible, or who do not want it. Now he is recruiting an army. When the time comes, he will fight for Prussia. You must ask His Majesty this: Does he want war with Prussia and Hungary at the same time?"

271

Chapter 34 – January-March 1866

Franz did not grant an audience to Andrássy, but to the great displeasure of the Viennese court party, he agreed to go to Hungary.

In late January, bundled in furs, Franz and Sisi crossed the bridge over the Danube towards the castle on the hill of Buda. Snow was falling steadily from a darkening sky, and haloes of misty light surrounded the lamps on the bridge. The people of Budapest had left their cosy houses and lined the streets to give the Emperor and Empress a warm welcome on a frigid day, but it was Sisi they cheered. *"Eljen Erzsebet! Eljen Erzsebet!"* they shouted until she thought their throats must be raw.

She wiped the mist off the window and smiled and waved. Franz was not at all upset because the acclaim was all for her. Such an emotion as jealousy was beneath him. He thought only in terms of the good of the state and had told her more than once that she was a great help to him with the Hungarians.

The warm welcome followed them across the bridge and into the castle, where the castle functionaries beamed with delight, as they escorted the Viennese to their various rooms. Tired from travelling, Sisi ate a light meal alone except for Ida, who would leave her within a few days to visit her family. Sat close to the ceramic stove, they were like a couple of excited schoolgirls on holiday.

"Last time I was here was in spring and I found it lovely. Now I am visiting a winter wonderland and it is just as lovely."

"And this time you must see the baths. Budapest is famous for its baths. The best one is the Rudas. It dates from the sixteenth century during the Turkish occupation. If the Turks left us nothing else, they did leave us with wonderful baths."

Sisi reached across and took her hand. "Oh, my sweet Ida, I shall miss you so much. Promise me you won't marry your Kalman or anyone else while you are gone."

"You have no reason to fear that. What are Kalman and Kecskemét compared to my life now in service to the kindest and most beautiful mistress in the world?"

From the door, her secretary Herr Feifalik was announced. Since Fanny travelled everywhere with her, Sisi had given Herr

Feifalik a post as one of her secretaries so they wouldn't have to spend much time apart. He entered with the official programme for Her Majesty's stay in Hungary.

Sisi glanced through it with Ida peering over her shoulder. There were the usual receptions, banquets, a state ball, and visits to various schools, orphanages and convents, concluding with an appearance at the Hungarian national diet where she was to give an address. She wondered what Franz's programme was like. Did it include an audience with Andrássy and Deák? And would she dance with Andrássy at the ball? *I would like to hold you in my arms and whirl you away to some distant exotic playground where there is nothing but music and laughter.*

"You will be kept busy," Ida observed. "Are you up to it?"

"I have to be." Whereas in Vienna, she used every excuse possible to escape the burdens of official engagements, here in Hungary she was determined to do her part towards reconciliation.

Later that night before she went to bed, Sisi visited the room where her little Sophie had died. She found it full of fresh flowers, cuddly toys and dolls. On the wall hung a replica of the portrait she still wore on a bracelet on her wrist. Unable to help herself, she wept.

. . . .

On the night of the ball, Sisi once again appeared wearing Hungarian costume. After she and Franz had opened the dancing, he sat out, for although he was a graceful and accomplished dancer, he didn't enjoy it. Sisi was free to dance with whoever asked her. When the orchestra began to play one of Franz Liszt's *csárdás*, there in front of her, extending his hand, was Count Andrássy.

"Would Your Majesty permit your slave the undreamed-of honour of a dance?"

How extravagant his language was! "It would be my pleasure, Count." Eight years ago she had danced a *csárdás* with an unknown boy and been swept away. Unhesitatingly, she put her hand in Andrassy's, but when he led her out among the dancers, she said: "I don't know this dance at all."

Andrássy showed his gleaming teeth in a smile. "Your Majesty is accustomed to leading and others to following. For the next few minutes, I want you to put yourself entirely in my hands. They are safe hands. Trust me. I will not let you down."

The *csárdás* was wild Romani music characterised by variations in tempo. It started slowly, allowing Sisi time to learn the basic steps. As the tempo increased, Andrássy led her into a series of twirls, faster and faster. The room spun around her, the faces a blur, the wall sconces a circle of light. But no matter how fast her feet flew his hand was always there to catch hers and to guide her into the next movement. His hands on her tiny waist, he lifted her into the air, and she looked down at him, smiling into his beautiful dark eyes. She remembered his words to her in Vienna; he did indeed whirl her away to a place she had never been before, a place of indescribable happiness.

Then her feet touched the floor again.

Count Andrássy tapped his hands together. "Brava, Majesty," he said softly. "You have the soul of a gipsy."

Instead of escorting her back to Franz, he led her to the side of the room where a painting of a banquet hung. It was obviously Hungarian because there was so much movement in the picture, as opposed to the frozen stiffness of an imperial banquet.

Gazing raptly at her, he said: "You are like Titania, Queen of the Fairies."

"Not Titania, but a bird that has been caught and cowers in its cage."

She longed to know all there was to know about him and urged him to talk about himself. He admitted to being a radical in his youth, influenced by his father, who had belonged to the opposition at a time when opposing the government was dangerous. An ardent patriot, he threw himself into politics as a young man. He joined the military in the war against Croatia and was later sent to Constantinople by the revolutionary government to persuade the Ottoman Empire either to support Hungary's efforts or to remain neutral. After the revolution, he immigrated to London and then to Paris, where he immersed himself in international diplomacy and learned that no country could exist independently. Upon his return to Hungary, he had been wooed by all parties, but he had given his enthusiastic support to Ferenc Deák.

274

After they had spoken together for several minutes, Sisi couldn't help noticing the looks they were getting from some of the Viennese. "I should return to my husband," she said.

"Indeed, you must. I fear there will be a riot among my compatriots if I monopolise your delightful company any longer."

"I am not concerned about your Hungarians, but about the Viennese."

"The trouble with the Viennese is that they are not a gay people, as is supposed. That is just a façade they cultivate. They have been menaced from the east by the Ottoman Empire and invaded twice by Napoleon. How can they be anything but fearful and suspicious? When may I see you again?"

Excuses were available – she had a busy schedule, after all, and she knew the wise thing to do was to use one. Instead, she said, "Wait on me anytime, Count. I will be happy to receive you."

Why was she so strongly drawn to Andrássy? she asked herself as she lay sleepless that night. She was too old for a schoolgirl crush, and he was not the only handsome man she knew. Was she starved for love – that kind of love? Or was it that he embodied for her all the romance and liberality and charm of Hungary, and of its tragic past? And what of him? She accepted that he had deliberately set out to fascinate her in order to use her to reach Franz, and did not hold it against him. But surely she was more to him than just a useful tool? Were they falling in love with each other?

. . . .

After the ball, Sisi was often in Andrássy's company. To the annoyance of her Austrian ladies-in-waiting, they spoke in Hungarian of their shared hopes for Hungary. Sisi told him about her family and children, of her struggle with Sophie that began in the nursery and had now moved to the political arena. What they did not talk about was Andrássy's wife and the feelings that were growing between them.

The high point of the visit came when Franz and Sisi attended the national diet. Sisi sensed that the members were both hopeful and anxious, as was she, as they awaited the first official word from the Emperor. In his speech, Franz thanked the Hungarian people for their good will and enthusiasm. Then he went on to say he was willing to grant some concessions but warned that they must not indulge in extravagant hopes and only put forward proposals that were feasible. There was a great deal of murmuring and head shaking when he had finished speaking. Sisi felt tears stinging her eyes. She knew he would listen; he would believe he had weighed the proposals fairly, but he would not be able to overcome the wall of prejudice his mother had built in him since he'd been a nursling. A few bricks may be knocked off. That was all.

In her address, in faultless Hungarian, Sisi too thanked the people for their warm welcome and their love for the Emperor and her. She could not speak about politics except to say that a rapprochement could be reached with friendliness and understanding on both parts. In conclusion, and barely able to hold back her tears, she said: "May the Almighty attend your activities with his richest blessings."

Her speech so moved the members they could not cry the *Eljen*. They sat in silence, old and young with tears in their eyes.

....

Early March, and a weak sun was melting rooftop snow into icicles that dripped during the day and grew in length every night. The train to Vienna huffed in the station. The imperial baggage had been taken aboard. Sisi found a moment to speak to Andrássy in a small circle of privacy.

"I shall continue to work towards the way of deliverance, which you have shown me, but I have lost all hope of seeing my activities crowned with success." In spite of all her efforts Franz had not agreed to the Hungarians' proposals.

"You did all that was possible and more. Hungary is grateful. Andrássy is more than grateful. But it is not the end of our hopes, my Queen. I shall come to Austria and have more talks with the Emperor. I shall chip away at his resolve a little at a time, like a sculptor with his chisel, until I have achieved the shape I want." He smiled.

Come soon. I will miss you. And I do love you.

Chapter 35 – May-July 1866

A circle of solemn ministers sat in Franz's study. He was at his desk, stiffly upright, his expression bland, as it always was, even when his stomach was writhing like a nest of snakes. The discussion was of war. It was plain now that the war of Austria and Prussia against the Danish held duchies of Schleswig-Holstein had been nothing but a ruse. When the fighting was over, it was agreed that Austria was to administer Holstein; Prussia, Schleswig. Not long after, Bismarck began complaining that the division favoured Austria; he wanted both duchies for Prussia. Franz responded that Austria would not tolerate any interference whatever in the administration of Holstein. Austria had nervously watched while Prussia armed for war. Then Austria too began to arm.

Count Rechberg, the new foreign minister, on his feet in front of the ceramic stove, said, "One must treat Bismarck with the greatest caution. It is hard to imagine how stubborn this statesman is, how completely he is led by his hatred of Austria."

"It would be a mercy if he were to die suddenly." This was from Sophie. "It would prevent much misfortune."

Count Crenneville, the new adjutant-general, nodded. "He wants to make Prussia great and himself great. He can achieve both by expunging Austrian influence from German lands."

"He can't do that!" Franz said. It was unthinkable. The Council of Vienna had created the German Confederation 1815 and Austria had always been its leading member. "We must negotiate a settlement." The empire was in no position to fight another war, nor could it afford to lose any more prestige.

"We are still negotiating, Majesty," Rechberg said, "but it is my feeling that as long as Bismarck remains in power, there will be no real peace. We must step up our preparations for war. We must not be caught off guard."

"And we must put the army in Italy on a war footing and provide it with a commander competent in war." Crenneville's face was as bland as a baby's. "Victor Emmanuel will not miss an opportunity to kick us out of Venetia."

Count Rechberg flipped his coattails and fastened his hands behind his back. "In fact, I have heard – although I have no confirmation as yet – that Prussia has concluded a secret treaty with King Victor Emmanuel. Venetia will be Italy's share of the spoils. If so, we can expect to fight on two fronts."

"I hear from Count Andrássy that Bismarck is agitating and fomenting trouble in Hungary. Kossuth is rallying all the dissident elements," Franz said. In fact, he had heard it from Sisi, who learned it from Andrássy.

"And France? What of France?" Sophie demanded. "We need France to remain neutral."

"So does Prussia."

"Find out what Louis Napoleon wants to keep his long Bourbon nose out of our affairs," Sophie said to Rechburg.

Franz ran a hand through his thinning hair. Sometimes he felt the whole world was against Austria. "Do we have any allies on whom we can count? Russia?"

Count Rechberg chuckled. "Hardly likely, Your Majesty. But we can hope Russia will remain neutral. She has nothing to gain by intervention. No, the German people will be our best allies. We may count on Saxony and Bavaria and many of the other states that have reason to fear a more powerful Prussia."

"Why don't we give Holstein to the Prussians," Count Crenneville said, "and avoid war?"

The others looked at him with varying expressions. "It is not about Holstein," Rechberg snapped. "For Bismarck it never was. It is about nothing less than European leadership."

"If we go to war, we must win." Franz's voice was emotionless. "We cannot afford another disaster like Solferino. If we do not win, we'll be under Bismarck's boot heel."

"Of course we will win," Sophie said heartily. "Your soldiers are brave and loyal. And we surely have numerical superiority."

Rechberg nodded briskly. "True. True. But the best of soldiers cannot fight alone. They need arms, provisions, medical equipment, and railways to get them to the front. Remember Italy? Our men complained they'd had nothing to eat for twenty-four hours before they had to fight at Solferino. Bismarck has put in new railways, and his troops have the most up-to-date weaponry and brilliant generals to lead them."

"You are unduly pessimistic, Count," Franz said sternly. "Read the newspapers, the diplomatic reports. No one in Europe gives the Prussians half a chance against us."

The reports about new railways and weaponry had been coming in for months, while Austria was at the negotiating table, not quite willing to believe that little Prussia would make war on the mighty Habsburg Empire over a trifling matter like Schleswig-Holstein. But they understood now. Rechberg had it right. It was a matter of European supremacy, and Bismarck had been aiming at war all along.

War was declared on June fifteenth.

……….

Vienna sweltered under a heat wave in June. There had been no rain for two weeks. The grass looked parched, flowers wilted, and people in the streets hurried from one shady spot to the next. Low in its bed, the Danube moved sluggishly on.

The children had been sent to Bad Ischl where the mountain air was cooler. There were few engagements to occupy the court. Whenever Franz had time, he and Sisi would stroll in the gardens or seek out the dappled green shade and dusty paths of the Vienna Woods. Sisi opened her parasol even under the arching trees.

"I hear your cousin Ludwig went off to visit Wagner in Switzerland on the very eve of mobilisation," Franz informed her. "You know him better than I. Will he support us?"

"To a man of Ludwig's temperament, war and politics are anathemas. He will spend his time listening to Wagner's latest opus and pretend the war isn't happening. I doubt we can count on him."

"Blasted fellow," Franz muttered.

Sisi smiled suddenly. "On the other hand, Rudolf is taking an interest in the war. He wrote that he has read the Prussian manifesto, and King Wilhelm lies the dear Lord in the face. He wants to know when the first battle will take place."

Franz chuckled. "He will be pestering his staff for news and information about the war."

Sisi was constantly surprised at her eight-year-old son's precocity and also disturbed by it. He was mature enough to read and understand the manifesto, and yet so much of his speech seemed to indicate that war was a game to him, such as he played with his father's toy soldiers. And he clearly believed Austria couldn't lose.

Once the subject of the war had been exhausted, they walked in silence, for nothing else occupied their thoughts.

Sisi spent hours of each day in Franz's study as he received reports, read and analysed them with various people. She refused to leave his side, understanding how desperately afraid he was of losing this war so soon after the loss of Italy. In the end, all failures rested with the man at the top. Outwardly, Franz remained calm and confident of the future, although the news was all bad. His desk was piled with reports, telegrams, letters and maps.

Only Saxony entered the war at full strength. Bismarck had won the neutrality of the other German states with the promise of a general reform of the Confederation. To Sisi and Sophie's shame, even Bavaria failed to show up in any significant numbers. Ludwig II, now King of Bavaria, retired to his Rose Island in Lake Starnberg, refused to see his ministers and spent his time letting off fireworks. The Austrian envoy wrote to Vienna: "One begins to think that the king is demented."

"Oh, no," Sisi said, "it is just that he hates war. I should have expected this." Thinking of her cousin made her sad. He might not be demented, but, even for a Wittelsbach, he was growing more and more eccentric.

"I wish he would pay more attention to the government when times are so bad," Franz complained.

Hungary had battalions on both sides. *If only Franz had acted to assure Hungary's support...*

One week after the declaration of war, the whole of north-west Germany was overrun by the Prussians. The King of Hanover had been dispossessed, and the Saxon troops were being pushed back towards the Bohemian border. The swiftness and precision of the Prussian strikes left everyone in Vienna reeling and scrambling for answers.

Sisi fanned herself rapidly. She wore nothing under her gown but pantaloons, shocking to her ladies. But to dress in layers of clothing in the summer heat – especially the kind of sultry heat that soaked garments in sweat – was to her a great foolishness.

He looked up from a paper. "It appears the needle guns are enormously successful."

The needle gun, a breech-loading rifle, was a superior weapon to anything Austria had. It could be loaded more rapidly than a conventional rifle and when its user was lying down. Adopted by the Prussian army in the Schleswig-Holstein war, it had been used to devastating effect.

The next news was more promising. "Reports of a recent battle are better than I thought they would be," he said. "Only the losses are terrible. Our troops are so brave and fiery an order was issued for them to hold their bayonet attacks until the artillery had done its work."

But early reports were always optimistic. Over the following days they learned that in a series of battles fought in Bohemia, the northern army had suffered losses of twenty thousand men. Many higher officers were dead. The Saxons also were badly beaten.

Franz put down the paper slowly and carefully aligned its lower edge with the edge of his desk. Sisi laid a hand on his shoulder. He patted it absently. After taking a deep breath, he said, "The news is bad, but one must not lose courage."

"It is not decisive then? There is still a chance?"

"With God's help, we shall win in the end." In spite of the depressing news, Franz remained calm and confident in the future.

The news was better from the south, where Archduke Albrecht had defeated the army of Victor Emmanuel at Custozza, and the Austrian Navy had won a sea battle against a superior fleet off Lissa. These victories, which would have been worthy of celebration at any other time, had little impact on the dejected mood in Vienna when set beside the defeats suffered by the northern army.

Reports contained grim tales of atrocities that made Sisi shudder with horror. Two weeks after the onset of war, trains were again arriving daily at the Nordbahnhof loaded with the wounded, the poor soldiers who had marched out with bright uniforms and gleaming arms, and returned torn and bleeding, begging for pictures of the Empress to comfort them in their distress. Once again they brought stories of poor generalship and equipment and provisions that were inadequate or did not arrive in time.

Accompanied only by Ida, Sisi resumed her visits to the hospitals. Outside the walls of the palace, the heat was oppressive. It sapped the energy and made people irritable. There wasn't a cloud in the sky to give a temporary respite from that glaring sun. The streets were almost empty. Few customers sat in the shade of awnings outside the *kaffeehäuses* that served as community centres, clubs, conference rooms and a trysting place for lovers.

The heat only intensified the suffering of the men in the wards. Flies were everywhere, despite the overwhelming smell of disinfectant, and some of the poor men lacked the strength to brush them away. Dressed in one of her simplest gowns that was nevertheless a beautiful creation, Sisi pushed up her sleeves, filled a pail with water and went from bed to bed, bathing the faces of conscious and unconscious. Ida followed behind with water to drink. Sisi was touched by the number of pictures of herself she saw pinned above the beds or sometimes clutched in a hand.

"I dreamed an angel was coming for me, and you are here," a young boy said to her. He could have been no more than sixteen. As she bathed his face, his eyes glazed over, and he died with a smile on his lips. Sisi leant over and kissed him on the brow.

"They're going to take my leg," another man told her in a trembling voice. The leg was shattered below the knee and his eyes were terrified. "They say if the enemy don't kill you the surgeons will."

What could she say to ease his terror? "The doctors are here to help you. You faced the guns of the enemy as a brave man. You can face this. I will pray for you."

"Pray for me too, Empress," the man in the next bed whispered.

He appeared to be unhurt until she saw the stains on the sheet covering his abdomen, a mixture of blood and something else. The stench arising from him was nauseating. His eyes clung to her as Sisi bathed his face.

"You're even more beautiful than I remember." His voice was hardly more than a breath. "I saw you on your wedding day. The wife said you couldn't be a real girl. You looked like a fairy princess."

"What is your name?"

"Otto. Pray for me that I get taken to Heaven soon."

"I will," Sisi said, rapidly blinking as she moved on.

A nurse came running up to her. "Forgive me, Your Majesty, but we have a man on the operating table who is in urgent need of amputation and won't allow the doctor to proceed unless you are present. Will Your Majesty consent?"

Sisi swallowed her revulsion, nodded, and hurried after the nurse. The room she entered stank of blood, disinfectant and a sweetish smell she didn't recognise. There was so much blood on the floor she almost slipped in it. The doctors all wore bloody gowns and aprons, their hands bright red as they worked over patients made woozy by chloroform, but often not entirely unconscious. Their shrieks, the shouts of the doctors, the clatter of medical instruments, all combined with the unspeakable smells to make the room almost unbearable. Sisi felt nauseous and had to swallow again before she could go forward into the chaos.

She went to the side of an operating table. A channel stained with congealed blood ran around the edge to carry away the fluids and a bucket lay underneath. Another lad in his teens lay there, drenched in sweat and his eyes wild with fear. When he saw her beside him, the look in his eyes changed in a moment to one of wonder.

She laid a hand on his good arm. "Hello. I am Elisabeth, the Empress. Can you tell me your name?"

"Stefan Karolyi. Are you really the Empress?"

Sisi smiled down at him, recognising a Hungarian name. "I am. I happened to be visiting the hospital when I was told you wanted my help."

"They're going to take my arm. I'm so afraid…" he whispered, his voice breaking.

Sisi's heart twisted with pity. He was so young, and at best he would go through life maimed. "I understand. But I also know that Hungarian men are the bravest of all. You faced the Prussian guns, and perhaps you were afraid then, but you did what you had to do. You can do this, Stefan Karolyi. Let the doctors save your life."

"Will you stay with me, Empress, please?" The panic was back in his eyes, the fear in his voice.

Sisi shifted her hand until she was grasping his tightly. "I will stay with you throughout, and when it is over you will go on to lead a happy and productive life."

A cloth saturated with chloroform was placed over his mouth and nose, and the shattered arm was strapped down. The boy's terrified eyes clung to Sisi's until they drifted closed. She turned her face away as the surgeon reached for a blood-stained saw. The limp hand in hers jerked when the saw first bit into bone and continued to jerk throughout. The rasp of the saw on the bone was about the worst sound Sisi had ever heard and it seemed to go on a long time. Only when it finally stopped did she realise she had been clenching her teeth and gripping the young man's hand much too tightly.

Sisi took several deep breaths before looking at the sleeping patient's white face and then at the limb. The surgeon had gone, and a doctor was listening to the patient's heart with a wooden tube, while a nurse bandaged the stump.

"You no longer cauterise using hot irons?" she asked in surprise.

The doctor straightened up. "No, Your Majesty, not in most cases, I'm happy to say. Cauterisation has the benefits of quickly stemming blood flow and sterilising the tissue. On the other hand, not only does the wound heal faster with bandaging but results in lower infection rates and less overall tissue damage."

"I see. Will he be all right?"

"I expect so. He is young and generally in good health. I'm sure he'll be grateful to Your Majesty for the rest of his life."

Before leaving, Sisi took a photograph of herself from her reticule and pressed it into the hand she had been holding.

Back in the carriage, at the end of a long, exhausting day, she and Ida wept in each other's arms. Those poor suffering men were so grateful, so humble. They thought nothing of their own sacrifices, only how wonderful it was that the exalted Empress had come to visit them.

....

The clock in Franz's study sounded unnaturally loud as it struck 10 p.m. on the night of July 3rd. From the adjacent room came the click of balls as the Emperor's aides passed the time playing billiards.

The night seemed even hotter than the day had been. The windows were open but no stray breeze made its way inside. The combined smell of blood, disinfectant and chloroform were still in Sisi's nostrils. She fanned herself rapidly. She would have liked to go outside and wander in the moonlit garden, but the effort to get up and go seemed too much. Besides, she wanted to be present when Franz received the news. Just in case it was bad. The latest word from the northern front was that the two armies, around four hundred and fifty thousand men, had converged at Königgrätz in Bohemia. Everyone agreed the battle would be decisive.

Franz was at his desk. He appeared to be reading the paper in front of him, but he had been staring at it for the last half hour. *What is he thinking? Is he, like me, trying not to think? After all, there is no point in speculating. When we know what has happened, we can begin to think what to do. Or is he looking back at the causes that led to the battlefield in Königgrätz, the missteps he took, the enemies he made, so that, in the end, when he needed friends, not even the German states that were so fearful of Prussia supported him. Is it that Europe is tired of Habsburg dominance?*

Her glance switched to Sophie, who was sat in an armchair doing some needlework with her fluffy little dog curled in her lap; no tremble of the hand, no discernible hint of anxiety in those stern features. She was getting old. Wrinkled skin drooped over her once sharp eyes, the flesh of her cheeks was sunken and the corners of her thin mouth sagged. Her hands, when she exposed them, as now, were blue veined and speckled with brown spots. And what of her? Had she yet realised that, as Victor Hugo pronounced, 'Kings are for nations in their swaddling clothes.' The Habsburg empire was old and tired, with a rigid ruling class, mistrusted by other rulers, overburdened with bureaucracy, enormous debt and the pointless adherence to protocols and procedures that served no purpose save to promote the illusion that all was well with the Habsburg world. Whereas Prussia was a young nation, vigorous, ambitious and adaptable to the changing times.

I should not cast blame, Sisi told herself. Franz is a conscientious ruler – more so than most. And whatever Sophie has done, she truly believed it was for Franz's good.

Sophie laid her sewing in her lap. "Max ought to have been crowned Emperor of Mexico by now," she said out of the blue.

Franz turned from his reading to look at her. "Mama, Max will never be crowned now. The best he can do is abdicate. Under pressure from the United States, the French are pulling out of Mexico."

"But what will Max do then?"

"Come home, I should think." Franz's gaze returned to the paper on his desk.

"Well, I warned him. That country is unstable, I said. And uncivilised." She paused, sucking on her teeth, a habit which irritated Sisi. "He did good work there. It is too bad he is unappreciated, but what can one expect of such savages?" Sophie picked up her sewing again.

The clock struck 10:30.

Just as Sisi was thinking of going to bed, Count Rechberg was announced. Her heart began a rapid beat. Her fan stilled in mid-flutter. It must be the news they were awaiting. The count entered, followed by the aides who paused in the doorway to listen. He bowed in turn to the Emperor and then to the ladies. His face was grave. But of course it would be, Sisi thought frantically, no matter the outcome.

"Your Majesty, I regret..." He could not go on. Instead, he handed a telegram to Franz. Franz stared and stared. His face didn't change. He didn't blink. Sisi glanced at Sophie, who was as rigid as a statue.

"Franz?" Sophie whispered.

He lifted his eyes from the telegram but looked at no one. "The battle is over. Our army is in full retreat. All is lost."

No one spoke. The disaster was too enormous to take in. Franz was the first to move. All eyes followed him as he dropped the telegram on his desk and went into his bedroom, closing the door behind him. Sisi rose and approached Rechberg.

"Count, please tell me. What have we lost?"

"We have lost the war, Majesty. We have lost the leadership of the German Federation. Bismarck will form another led by Prussia. We have lost our standing in Europe, and European governments will recognise Prussia as a new power. Venetia will be handed over to the Italians. But most fearful of all, Majesty, the road to Vienna is now open to the enemy."

"Can nothing be done?"

The count shrugged wearily. "At this time, at this moment, I cannot think what."

Sisi felt the greatest pity for Franz. She wanted to go to him, but that closed door shut her out too. The aides bowed as she went with dragging footsteps to her apartment, not yet fully understanding the enormity of what had happened. Sophie remained in the study with her sewing.

....

It was very strange to watch the palace being dismantled a piece at a time. Under the direction of her chamberlain, Baron Nopcsa, servants had invaded Sisi's rooms, removing from the places they had occupied for at least twelve years priceless paintings, urns, clocks and hangings. Her ladies were packing her gowns and other clothes into huge travelling chests. Her jewels had been entrusted to Baron Nopcsa for safe transport.

No one knew what would happen. Franz said, "We must trust in God." But God had been present at Königgrätz.

In the nurseries the maids were also busy, packing Gisela's little dresses and the toys she hadn't taken to Bad Ischl. *My poor Rudolf, what is his future to be?*

Wherever her footsteps took her, there were bare walls where paintings had hung since Maria Theresa's time, and servants hurrying to the doors carrying boxes and bundles and chests, rolls of paintings that had been removed from their frames. The same thing was happening at the Hofburg. The valuable gold and silverware, the porcelain and fabulous table centres, the treasures of the Imperial House, the crown insignia, all were being carefully packed in crates ready for shipment, along with important papers from the ministries and the most valuable manuscripts from the Court Library. She wondered if this was what it was like in '48 when the revolution came to Vienna, and the imperial family had to flee. Or perhaps there had been no time because the enemy was already in the city – their own beloved citizens turned against them like a pet dog suddenly become rabid. Today their enemies were not yet at the gates, but they were coming. They had swarmed across the border, ever closer to Vienna, wanting an end to Austrian hegemony.

Sisi wandered as if in a dream because it all seemed so unreal.

She had been with Franz when he signed the order to surrender. Even then she had not understood the enormity of the catastrophe that had overtaken them. Only now, seeing the palace denuded of its treasures, hearing how the people of Vienna were fleeing out the gates, clogging the railway station with their moveable belongings, did she begin to realise that the centuries-old Habsburg Empire was in danger of crashing down with the one devastating defeat at Königgrätz.

Five days after that decisive battle, a ministerial council advised that the Emperor and the ministers move to Budapest. But the question was, given the strained relations between the two lands, would Hungary receive the imperial fugitives? From his exile in Italy, Kossuth was exhorting the Hungarians to throw off the Austrian yoke and Bismarck promised them great rewards. Now, in defeat and shame, Austria had little to offer.

"Once again I must ask you to be our ambassadress to Budapest," Franz said to Sisi. "I fear the Hungarians will take the opportunity of our defeat to remove themselves from the empire. Go and make sure of their loyalty and support. Only you can do it."

"No! I won't leave you."

Franz placed his hands gently on her upper arms and looked into her eyes. "Dearest, these are the most critical days of my reign. I have always felt... the stability of the empire, those centuries behind me that somehow... gave me strength and resolution. I have always believed in my Divine Right to rule. Now I find the very principles of my life undermined. I can no longer envisage the future." He swallowed painfully, and Sisi saw tears in his eyes. "I need all the help I can get. I beg you to do this for me. I'm not asking you to run away, but to do what you can to ensure the Hungarians remain loyal."

A new thought struck Sisi, and she hesitated. Should she speak of it? Would it be very wrong to take advantage when Franz was so demoralised, even though it was in a good cause? After a pause, she said, "The matter would go easier if I could... If I could offer them something to counter Bismarck's promises and Kossuth's threats."

His hands slid down her arms, and he turned away, the portrait of dejection. "Sisi, please. I cannot think about the Hungarian problem right now when the Prussians are streaming across our borders. That is all I can think about and all I can deal with."

"You're right, of course." She went to him and leant her head on his shoulder. "I will go to Budapest if you think it's for the best."

Franz accompanied her to the railway station. It was the unhappiest trip they had ever taken together. In the streets, the populace booed and hissed. The newspapers had carried the rumour that Maximilian was about to return from Mexico, and there were

288

shouts of "Viva Maximilian!" and "Abdicate!" Sisi could feel Franz's humiliation as if it were a cloak he wore. She had never seen him looking so distraught.

"Franz, come with me, please," she begged, knowing it was useless at this late hour.

"My place is here. I will not abandon my people or my duty. But you must go. The people there love you so. They will remain loyal for your sake. The radical and revolutionary elements will have no chance against you!" He smiled briefly at his little joke.

Too late, Sisi thought. But she couldn't reproach him, not now in his most desolate hour. "I'm worried about Rudolf's future. And you – what will happen to you if the Prussians enter Vienna?"

"There is no need to fear on my account. France or England will intervene. There will be an armistice. They will not want to see Frederick Wilhelm and Bismarck dominant in Europe any more than we do."

Sisi took his hand in hers and kissed it. Then she went into his arms, and they held each other in silence for a long time, while the train chuffed impatiently and porters and attendants looked on. Finally, Franz urged her away. His hands slipped down her arms to hold hers.

"Go now, my angel, and God be with you."

Releasing his hands slowly, she climbed aboard the train. She watched him through the window as the train pulled out of the station until she couldn't see him anymore. Only then did she begin to weep. Ida held her and rocked her with the motion of the train.

Chapter 36 – July 1866

The railway station was crowded with thousands of people, and they were cheering even before the train came to a stop. Sisi spotted the handsome figure of Andrássy from the window. As usual, he was wearing full Hungarian regalia, with his coat emblazoned by gold and jewels, his tiger skin cloak and his hat topped by an ostrich plume. His left hand rested on the hilt of his sword. Sisi smiled when she saw him. It always seemed to her that Andrássy held his chin an inch higher than other men. She had seen him in Vienna, but only on ceremonial occasions, and her heart never failed to skip a beat when he was near.

Accompanied only by Ida, she descended to the platform to a great roar from the crowd. Andrássy bowed before her. "Hungary rejoices that her Divine Providence has returned," he said, before raising her hand to his lips.

It was only then that Sisi realised Deák was also present. The unassuming little man bowed. "Welcome back to Hungary, Your Majesty."

"It is always a great pleasure for me to return to a land I hold dear." Sisi bent to accept a posy of flowers from a little girl. "I had no idea when I left that I would be back so soon and in such sad circumstances."

She had not come to Hungary to hide from the horrors of war. She was determined to continue her efforts along with Deák and Andrássy to persuade the Emperor to accept terms reasonable to both parties. Now was the time to make Franz see that he could not afford to lose Hungary as well.

Against Sophie's furious objections that the humid air and bad water could harm the children, she insisted on having them sent to her. Sophie, of course, was even more annoyed that Hungary had been chosen for their refuge, and refused to join them, preferring to go to Bad Ischl with her valuables. But Sisi remembered a story she had once heard about Maria Theresa and how in a similar crisis she had appealed for help to the Hungarians in Pressburg, holding the little heir to the throne in her arms. Having Rudolf and Gisela with her was a political gesture that Sisi felt would attract a good deal of sympathy at this time of Austria's desolation.

Crowds of cheering people lined the route from to her rented villa from the railway station, waving little Austrian flags and straining their necks to catch a glimpse of their Queen, who still looked like an eighteen-year-old girl. It was such a warm contrast to the palpable panic and hostility she had encountered in the streets of Vienna. After the castle staff had warmly welcomed her, Andrássy begged leave to wait on her the next day, and the two men left her to rest and settle in.

....

Ida was in a froth of excitement the following day. Sisi was excited too, but dare not show it even to her dearest friend, and decided to go for an early ride in the hills behind Buda. Dressed in a handsome green habit with a perky black hat, and with Ida similarly attired, she went to the stables and found, to her delight, some of the horses given to her during her earlier trips to Hungary, which she had left at Buda Castle. She had a preference for black horses. There was one all black, apart from a blaze on her nose, that Sisi had named Gypsy Girl. Her name was engraved on a brass plaque on the gate. Sisi gave the mare a lump of sugar and stroked the velvet muzzle. "Hello, Gypsy Girl. Do you remember me?"

Walking past the stalls, she looked the other horses over. "Which do you fancy, Ida?"

"I like this girl. She looks frisky."

Ida, a good rider, had chosen a chestnut mare. When the two horses were saddled, a groom helped Sisi mount, and Ida arranged her skirts before gaining her own saddle. They rode along the trails, dust rising under the horses' hooves from the baked earth. The heat wave continued, a torrid ominous presence that sucked the sweat from pores, but the trees were thick with summer foliage and the early morning air was still cool in their shade.

Gypsy Girl pulled on the rein, eager to run. Sisi was delighted to be on a horse again, to feel that strong, steady rhythm beneath her, free of guards and spies, with only Ida and the birds twittering in the trees for company. She was tempted to let the mare have her head, but she didn't know the trails and what hazards might lay in wait. "Later," she told the horse. "Later we will race the wind."

Hoofbeats sounded behind them. Sisi turned to see a rider trotting through the dappled shade. In a moment she had recognised Andrássy and was not surprised. They had not planned to meet like this, but it seemed as natural as the birdsong that they should meet out of doors under the friendly oaks and beeches. She brought her mount to a halt to wait for him. Her heart did its familiar somersault.

"Good morning, Your Majesty." Today he had forsaken his usual Hungarian costume in favour of a buff riding jacket and black trousers. There was a faint sheen of sweat on his forehead, under his unruly hair.

"Count Andrássy, welcome. I didn't expect to see you so early."

"I trust my eagerness has not inconvenienced Your Majesty?"

"Not at all. Will you join us?"

"I should be delighted. I hear Your Majesty's riding skills are quite the equal of any Hungarian's. This I must judge for myself."

He drew his horse alongside Sisi's. When they set off, Ida dropped back, so they had a private space in which to talk.

"You will not see any great skill from me today. It is too hot, and the horse and ground are unfamiliar. I have been accused of being reckless, but it's not true. I would never do anything to risk hurting a horse."

"The Magyars have always been excellent horsemen. We came from the Steppes, east towards the Carpathians, a place of vast spaces and long distances between settlements. We brought our pride and spirit with us. Our spirit can never be broken. For a couple of centuries, we raided far into Western Europe, as far as France. We were great warriors too, shooting our bows from the back of galloping horses…"

"I think there is still something wild about you today."

"Yes, civilisation is but a thin veneer. Scratch a Magyar, and you will find a fierce horseman from the Steppes underneath."

"It makes for an interesting dichotomy." Although Andrássy was speaking in general terms, Sisi was thinking specifically of him.

"It pleases me that you think so." He turned to smile at her, his teeth gleaming in the sun between the dark hair of beard and moustache. In a moment the smile was gone, replaced by a frown that wrinkled his brow. "Majesty, as pleasant as the day is, and as divine the company, we must talk about unpleasant matters. This war

292

must change things. The Emperor must see that he is vulnerable and needs Hungary."

"It is too soon to say how the war will affect his thinking. These are such difficult days for him. He has many things on his mind right now."

"Even before the war, Bismarck had agents seeded throughout our country, offering our people concessions that the Emperor had refused. His aim is to start a national uprising and separate Hungary from Austria, and he spares no expense. The revolutionary elements are very strong, and Kossuth's supporters mean to take full advantage of the Emperor's vulnerability. Only Deák and I, and the belief that Your Majesty loves them as they love you, are holding the people back. But I don't know for how much longer. They are on the verge of rebellion. They have been patient throughout the years while Italy rebelled, and now this with Prussia. The empire needs us. We need the empire. Together we can grow strong. Apart we can only be swallowed up by the Prussian king's greed."

"You are right about the Prussians. They will overrun Europe if they aren't stopped. It is rumoured that the Prussian general staff have had plans for the invasion of France for years. Wilhelm intends nothing less than European domination."

"What we want is a dual monarchy, distinct and autonomous, partner rather than subject. If the Emperor wants to keep Hungary attached to the empire, he must compromise, and do so quickly. There is no time to lose."

"I do understand, Count. I will do all that I can but do not be too optimistic. The archduchess and the conservative element at court influence him still."

"I count upon the friendship, which I perhaps only imagine Your Gracious Majesty feels for me... Be my voice with the Emperor. Make him aware of all the dangers into which he will irrevocably fall if he persists in refusing us concessions. Be our saviour, I implore you, in the name of our unhappy fatherland and for the sake of your son. If we do not succeed now, we never will." Andrássy bowed his head as he rode beneath a low branch.

"Like Margaret in Goethe's *Egmont*, I foresee much, but cannot alter it. I fear I will live to see the sun set on the Austrian Empire."

Andrássy dropped the reins and seized her gloved hand, holding it between his own. "No, Majesty, don't be sad! I, Gyula Andrássy, will not permit it! Hungary has placed its faith in you."

As if suddenly aware that he was holding her hand, he let it go. They continued walking their horses in silence until Andrássy said: "One thing more I would ask of you. If you could prevail upon the Emperor to make me minister of foreign affairs I would be in a position to influence imperial policy towards Hungary."

Sisi kept her eyes between her horse's ears. There wasn't a hope in heaven that Franz would agree, nor that the Austrians and Bohemians would accept him. And what effect it would have on Archduchess Sophie she couldn't bear to think. She would probably drop dead of apoplexy. The trouble with Andrássy was that he was so thoroughly a patriot that he thought only in terms of what was best for Hungary, without consideration for the rights or opinions of other nations or people.

"I will talk to him about it," she conceded, and she would, but the time would have to be right.

Andrassy's white smile flashed out. "Together, Majesty. *Together* you and I may be able to make a better future for our respective countries." After a moment, he said, "Enough of politics. Shall we ride?"

Riding to Andrássy meant racing, letting the horses have their heads and galloping until both riders and mounts were tired. Grinning at her over his shoulder, he dug his spurs into his horse's flanks. Gypsy Girl leapt forward at the touch of Sisi's riding crop. The trees had thinned; open country lay before them. The ground of firm sand and loess was perfect for racing horses and rising only slightly. She had no difficulty keeping up with Andrássy, but she never could catch him.

They brought their horses to a halt atop a slight elevation and paused to look around at a wide landscape. It was only then that Sisi realised they had outrun Ida.

"These are the hills of Gödöllö," Andrássy said. "As you see, they are a transition between mountains and plain."

In the misty distance to the north Sisi could see the Hungarian mountains rising; to the south and east the plain, dotted with copses of oak and maple; to the west was the Danube and the hills bordering Buda. Circling above it all was a golden eagle.

"What is that?" Sisi pointed to a great house, surrounded by lush parklands and with a small village of scattered houses nearby.

"That is the village of Gödöllö and the palace."

"A palace! I must visit it."

As they set their horses walking down the gentle slope, Andrássy said, "It was built for the Grassalkovich family and is still privately owned. The architecture is unusual, being a double U shape, with eight wings. It has extensive parklands as well as a riding hall."

The closed gates were guarded, but to the guards, they were only two more tourists gawking at the beautiful palace.

"If only I had a palace like this," Sisi said wistfully, "I would feel I truly belonged to Hungary, instead of being just an occasional visitor."

"Your Majesty deserves nothing less. Shall I enquire if the owners would be willing to sell?"

"Thank you, but no. I doubt the Emperor would agree – not now when we are forced to economise." Sisi sighed and turned away from the gleaming white walls and red tiled roofs. "We have ridden a far distance, Count. We should start back."

Taking the same route back, they came across Ida waiting patiently for them. "I'm sorry, Your Majesty, I couldn't keep up." But Ida was an excellent horsewoman. Sisi wondered if she had fallen back purposely.

Arrived back at the villa, Andrassy said, "If I may be permitted to enjoy your company a while longer, I will take the horses to the stable and make sure they're given a good rub down."

Sisi was quite tired from their long ride, but the prospect of spending more time with Andrássy enlivened her. "I should be delighted, Count."

His hands on her waist, his eyes on hers, he lifted down. When a groom performed the task, it meant nothing, but when Andrássy did it… There was that somersault of her heart again.

....

The Prussians were at the gates of Pressburg on the Austrian-Hungarian border. Cholera and typhoid fever decimated the allied army. Many exiled kings and princes from Italy and Germany had taken refuge at the Viennese court, each with his own programme that required help from Franz. Fighting still continued in Italy, to what point Sisi had no idea because Venetia had been handed to Napoleon III. Hungary had suffered nothing in the war; in fact, the country was being rewarded by Bismarck in hopes of detaching it from the empire. In the occupied provinces, on the other hand, the Prussians were wreaking havoc, and cries for help were heard in Vienna where Franz could do little. The Bohemian lands had suffered worst; they needed food immediately. Famine was likely in the winter. Sisi suspected Hungary was the last thing on his mind.

Nevertheless, after a long talk with Deák and Andrássy, she wrote a strongly-worded letter to Franz stressing how urgent it was that he receive Andrássy and not to let this opportunity pass.

I beg you, send me a telegram the minute you receive my letter whether Andrássy should take the night train to Vienna. I am asking him to come again tomorrow when I will give him an answer. If you say "No," if you are unwilling at the final hour even to listen to disinterested advice any longer, then you are in fact acting unkindly to us all. I can do nothing further but to reassure myself with the knowledge that, whatever happens, I will one day be able to tell Rudolf, 'I did all in my power. Your misfortune does not weigh on my conscience.'

If that doesn't move him, she thought, nothing will.

Andrássy wasn't the only one putting pressure on her. Visitors, even the staff, named her the saviour of their country. Deák often came with Andrássy. He lacked Andrássy's passion, but he was pragmatic and quietly persuasive. What none of them understood was the pressure Franz was under.

....

"Count Andrássy is here, Majesty," Ida said from the door. "Shall I summon your ladies?"

"No. You may stay with us."

The Emperor had summoned Andrássy to an audience with the Emperor. There was a quiet but heartfelt celebration when the news came. Hopes were high. Sisi had hardly slept the night before, so anxious was she. That morning she had received a letter from Franz, which she read with trembling eagerness.

296

Andrássy spoke very frankly and cleverly and developed all his views. I was impressed by his great frankness and level-headedness. For the rest, I found him as always without consideration of the other parts of the monarchy. He wants a great deal and offers too little at the present crucial moment... I fear he has not the means in his country to carry out his intentions.

Her hopes crumbled to the floor. They lay around her feet like ashes.

"Please be seated, Count. Can I offer you some refreshment?"

"Thank you, no."

He was moving about the room like a force of nature, driving his fist into the other palm, as he told her what he had said and what the Emperor had said. "An hour and a half I spent in the audience and at the end all I could wring from him was: 'I will study the matter thoroughly and think it over.'"

Finally, he sat down and leant over with his elbows on his knees and his face in his hands, the very portrait of despair. Sisi wanted to go to him, to put a consoling hand on his shoulder... No, what she really wanted was to take him in her arms, to hold him to her breast until that proud head lifted, that gleaming smile flashed out...

But she could not console him except with words. "We will not give up, Count. I know we must succeed eventually. You must not despair."

His head came up slowly. He rubbed his hands over his face and then dragged them through his hair, making it look wilder than ever. He heaved a deep sigh. "Frau, a whisky, if you would be so kind," he said to Ida.

"Two," Sisi said.

Andrássy rose and moved closer to her. "Do you think there is any reason to hope at this point?"

"We cannot let Kossuth gain the upper hand in Hungary. He would hand it to the Prussians. There would be another war. We must persist. I think the problem is that the Emperor is focusing his attention on the peace process at the moment. Louis Napoleon has agreed to mediate, but so far he has done nothing with the Prussians. Once peace is established, I am quite sure we will have better success."

Franz had written that the Prussians were so close that the light from their campfires was visible from the heights of the Kahlenberg, a popular recreation place in the Vienna Woods. The only comfort was that they would not easily get across the Danube. One of the nightmare scenarios he lived with was the prospect of King Wilhelm Friedrich making a triumphal entry into Vienna, and Franz himself being forced to receive him.

His letters made such sad reading that she was constantly torn between pity for him and exasperation at his refusal to see reason.

"It is certain that if the matter is successful Hungary will be beholden to the Beautiful Providence. A toast then," Andrássy said, taking a glass from the tray Ida held. "To our future success." He tossed his head back, and the whisky went down his throat in one draught.

After dinner, where her ladies and others were present, Sisi took Andrássy to meet the children. It never occurred to her to ask if he had children of his own – perhaps she didn't want to know – but seeing him interact with Rudolf and Gisela, she was almost certain he had. It was evident even at the first meeting that Rudolf thought him excellent.

Chapter 37 – October 1866

Since the peace process was well underway and Prussian troops no longer threatening Vienna, it was deemed safe for Sisi to return. Franz was pathetically glad to see her.

At a formal dinner for the Hungarian delegation that followed soon after, Sisi found herself seated next to Andrássy. Franz was across the table with Sophie between him and Archduke Albrecht, who was presently highly popular because of his success against the Italians. The victory was meaningless, as Italy was already lost and, as part of the peace, Venetia was to be handed over to Victor Emmanuel.

With Sophie fading into the background, eclipsed by Sisi and dispirited by recurring bouts of illness, Archduke Albrecht, Franz's great-uncle but only thirteen years older, had come to the forefront as the champion of the court conservative bloc. There was a time when the fearsome Albrecht so intimidated Sisi that she retreated into silence when he was near. But these people could do nothing to her that they had not already done. With that understanding came strength. She had exchanged heated words with him on more than one occasion. During the meal, he overtly watched her and Andrássy through his gold-rimmed spectacles.

Next to him was Sophie, wearing the scowl that had been a permanent fixture ever since Franz announced he would receive the Hungarians again.

Sisi spoke to Andrássy in Hungarian. "The Prussians have put forth their demands. They have annexed Hanover, Hesse, Schleswig-Holstein, Nassau and Frankfurt. Blind King George of Hanover supported us in the war, contrary to the wishes of his parliament. Prussia has annexed Hanover, and the King has fled to Austria. Saxony has been spared thanks to Franz's personal intervention with King Wilhelm. I do not know what the Prussians are doing to the rest of Germany, or what they will steal. Bismarck wishes to form a North German Confederation, which will exclude Austria. We are no longer to be part of Germany. The last link with the old Holy Roman Empire will be severed. They are asking that we pay twenty thousand thalers as a precondition for the withdrawal of the Prussians from our lands. It will mean stringent economies. Even the

Habsburg holdings have been terribly devastated by the war. It will take years for them to recover. Franz says we must sell half the stable. He wants to pay the Prussians as soon as possible and get them out of the country they are ruining. The newspapers are all saying that the terms are generous."

"Bismarck is too shrewd a statesman to want to humiliate Austria. If what everyone says of Wilhelm's dream of building an empire is true, he may have need of Austria's support or neutrality in the future."

It was being called the Seven Weeks War. Seven weeks – that's all it had taken to send the mighty Habsburg empire reeling. Bohemia, the stage of several actions, had suffered the most. Villages were destroyed, and hundreds of thousands of people were homeless. The broad fields had been trampled by the combatants until not a blade of grass stood, and nothing would grow on them for years. Famine was a certainty. On the battlefield at Königgrätz, twenty-three thousand soldiers and four thousand horses were interred. The stench of decaying flesh was said to be so overwhelming in the area that a process of disinfecting had begun.

Andrássy took a sip of his wine. As Sisi knew, his thoughts, always, were only of Hungary. "All of this is going to require a reorganisation of the government. Is that why the Emperor has agreed to receive us?"

"I think so, yes."

Overhearing a snatch of conversation, they fell silent and looked across the table at Franz. He had just celebrated his thirty-sixth birthday, yet he looked much older with his receding hairline emphasising the lines on his brow.

"In any case, we would have withdrawn from Germany entirely, whether it was demanded or not, and after what we have learned through bitter experience about our dear German allies, I consider this a fortunate turn of events for Austria."

Still staring at Sisi and Andrássy, Albrecht replied, "At first the prospect of peace gave me no joy. But now I think we cannot carry on any longer since the troops are too worn out and discouraged. Furthermore, it is very necessary to make peace because of Hungary. We need to deal with that country."

Franz made no reply. He was staring at a telegram handed to him by one of the servants. Without reacting, he folded it and slipped it into his pocket.

"I think if the Archduke dealt with us as he would wish, I would not be hanged in effigy but in reality," Andrássy observed. Popular as Albrecht was in Austria, he was hated in Hungary for his part in the reprisals after the revolution.

"I would never let that happen. Never!" Sisi said vehemently.

The count turned his head to smile at her, such warmth in his eyes that she quickly looked away. They must not share such looks, not in so public a setting.

....

Restless, Sisi left her apartment to take a walk in the garden, a solitary figure and her faint shadow, cloaked against the chill of the night. She crossed the paths of the parterre into the concealment of the trees. An earlier rain had released the dead and decaying smells of the earth. This was her time to be alone with her thoughts, her phantoms. Here, during her walks, she visited places of the past and places that had never been, but she never looked towards the future. The future was a kindly blank. Sometimes she whispered lines of poetry or something she had read in a letter, things that moved her. Ludwig: "It is my wish to remain an eternal enigma to myself and to others." Heine: "I cannot explain the sadness that's fallen on my breast. An old, old fable haunts me, and will not let me rest."

She believed she was alone on this occasion until she caught a whiff of cigarette smoke and a voice spoke out of the misty darkness. "'Well met by moonlight, proud Titania.'" Count Andrássy leant against a tree, his face illuminated by the fiery brand of his cigarette.

For a moment, just a brief moment, she resented the intrusion, but then she accepted it. "My favourite Shakespeare play."

"I know. I know more about you than you can imagine."

As I do about you. But what she didn't know was if he loved his wife, if she loved him, how many children they had… "You saw the Emperor today?"

"Yes. It did not go well. He seems convinced that our aim is to strip him of power."

"He has lost so much. You must understand." But she had come to realise that Andrássy was not the man to understand a point of view that opposed his own.

"We offer him a peaceful resolution, yet he treats us as if we are still the revolutionaries of '48. Does he love war so much he wants to become embroiled in another?" He was becoming angry. Sisi wondered if he had shown temper to Franz. "Deák arrives by train tonight. Perhaps he'll have better luck."

"May I?" She indicated his cigarette.

With a lift of one brow, he produced a case and offered it to her, then lit a match. "I didn't know you smoked."

"It's not becoming in an Empress."

He smiled. "That's why you do it."

"Occasionally. I'm not consistently rebellious."

They walked on, away from the friendly trees that lined the parterre on that side. The moon was almost full, the stars a dusting of silver powder against the infinity of blackness. The windows of the palace shone with the lights of thousands of lamps and candles. They turned away toward the Neptune fountain.

Andrássy threw his cigarette down and crushed it underfoot. "Why are you so melancholy, Empress?"

"I…Oh, Andrássy! When I was little more than a girl, I would awake in the night with a sense of relief thinking it was all a dream. But it would last for just a moment, and then I would realise, this was my life now. This was all there would ever be. There would never be any awakening from it. I would never escape except into death."

"There are those who believe life is only an illusion, and therefore nothing matters. I am not one of those. I believe we must live life to the fullest before we come to an end, and who really knows what follows."

"Whether what we have accomplished at the close of our earthly existence appears little or great – how quickly is the empty spot refilled! What difference does it make to the ocean – a drop or a wave less?"

Andrássy halted. With a hand on her arm, he turned her to face him. He was close enough that his legs her gown encased his legs and she could smell the cigarette on his breath. She dropped her own on the path.

302

"You are my happiness. When I see a smile blooming in the lovely face of my queen, it brings such a glow to my heart. I wish it were my privilege to make you happy." He took a step towards her. She took a step back.

But now you are part of my melancholy. Because this is all there will ever be.

"Your Majesty!" A voice broke in on them. Andrássy dropped his hand. Sisi turned. Ida was hurrying down the path. "His Majesty asks you to join him in his study."

"I will come."

She hurried away with Ida toward the palace, leaving Andrássy on the path. She looked back at him once, silhouetted against the shining white waters of the Neptune fountain. What would have happened if Ida hadn't come at that moment – at that moment of stolen intimacy? Perhaps he would have tried to kiss her. Perhaps she would have let him – just one little kiss. What could it have hurt? Now it was too late. She would never know what it was like to be kissed by Andrássy.

. . . .

Franz was not alone when she entered his study. To her surprise, Sophie and Franz Karl were with him.

"What is it, Franz?" Sisi took a seat distant from the Archduchess.

"I have received a telegram saying Charlotte –" he pulled a wry face "– Empress Carlotta, as I suppose we must call her, has had a complete mental breakdown during an audience with the pope and requires expert medical care."

Sisi had never liked her sister-in-law, but now her heart went out to the poor woman. She knew how it was to live in a nightmare world and face an abyss of despair. "Can we do anything to help her?"

"I won't have her here," Franz said. "At the present moment, that is all we need. God knows we have exiled relatives enough without adding a raving madwoman."

"Franz, don't be unkind!" Sisi reproved. "She is your brother's wife and has been a good wife. What of Max? Should we be concerned?"

"His letters are always optimistic," Sophie said, and Sisi noticed her eyes were red with tears, and she was tugging at a handkerchief. "But it takes six to eight weeks for mail to reach us from Mexico. Who knows what might have happened in the meantime. And I begin to think he has been painting the conditions in Mexico in a rosy light for our sake. Or perhaps because he is too proud to admit the truth. The fact that Carlotta has left to get help from some European power suggests there is greater trouble than he has led us to believe."

Sisi looked at her husband. "Franz, ought you not to advise him to abdicate? Return home immediately?"

"He is making the sacrifice for his country of remaining there," Franz Karl said, "which at the moment is an urgent necessity. Were he to leave, the country could immediately become the prey of party anarchy. By staying, he acts honourably, in contrast to the bad behaviour of Louis Napoleon. And if one day he is forced to yield to the machinations of the United States and leave his post, he will do that with honour, too."

"But with Carlotta's collapse, he has lost his last support!" Sisi glanced at Sophie, who turned her face away as tears leaked from her eyes.

"I fully approve the fact that he has stayed in Mexico..." she said staunchly. "Since it is his great love and sympathy, besides the dread of the anarchy which would follow his departure that keeps him in his new country, I can only rejoice in it and hope profoundly that the rich people in the country will make his remaining possible."

She certainly doesn't sound as if she rejoices in anything. She wants him home with every fibre of her being, but she is being staunchly Habsburg instead of passionately Wittelsbach.

Yielding to the bullying of the United States, the French had pulled out of Mexico leaving Maximilian without military protection or financial resources. He had used his position to do much good for the poor and downtrodden, but Juarez and his followers refused to accept a government imposed by foreigners and wanted nothing to do with a monarchy.

There was no help to be had from Belgium, for Carlotta's doting father had died, succeeded by her indifferent brother. Franz was in no position to help him either, and, in fact, having yielded his hereditary rights, Max no longer had any standing in the empire.

304

Carlotta had gone first to France – to Louis Napoleon, the man who had persuaded Max to accept the imperial crown and had then abandoned him. Everywhere she turned she was rebuffed. Even in Paris, a letter from Prince Metternich had described how Carlotta had made embarrassing scenes and appeared to be on the verge of nervous collapse. She had gone on to Rome in spite of his advice. The pope's refusal of help had obviously sent her over the edge.

"There must be something we can do to help," Sisi implored Franz.

"You must understand. Max is no longer an archduke of Austria. Outside Mexico, he is no more than an ordinary gentleman. While crowned heads might put themselves out for an Austrian archduke, they are not going to want to become embroiled in the troubles of that savage land on behalf of a simple gentleman."

"Can he be reinstated?"

Franz stroked his whiskers. "I doubt it has ever been done, but I don't see why not. It will require the consent of parliament."

Sophie delicately touched her handkerchief to her nose. "It distressed me greatly when you forced him to renounce his hereditary rights, Franz. After that, I always felt that he was estranged from the family."

Not allowing Franz to respond to this reproach, Sisi said: "I will write to my sisters, who are still in Rome, and see if I can find out more about Carlotta's condition."

"I am sure it is only temporary, and she will soon be well. I think I will retire now." Sophie held out her arm to Franz Karl, who helped her to her feet. As she was passing Sisi, she reached out a hand to clasp her arm. "Thank you, dear. I feel a little better now."

Sisi took the liver-spotted hand in hers and placed a kiss upon it. "Rest well, Madame Mere."

When she had gone, Franz turned to Sisi with a sad smile. "I thank you with all my heart for returning to me. Perhaps soon we can bring the dear children back. I am so melancholy and lonely without you and in need of some cheering up, especially in these bleak days. My sense of duty alone keeps me going, as well as the hope that perhaps, after all, better days will emerge."

"I am sure that is true, my dear. Things can get no worse." She went to him and rested her hands on his shoulders. Defeated and despairing he might be, but his shoulders were still straight. "It is for that reason and not for my own satisfaction that I begged you to talk to Andrássy. Did you listen to him? They are asking for nothing more than they asked before Königgrätz. They are not attempting to profit from our situation."

"It would go counter to my duty for me to adopt his exclusively Hungarian point of view and to discriminate against those lands which, in unswerving loyalty, have endured unspeakable suffering and which now more than ever require special consideration and care. If Germans and Hungarians alone share power it will disadvantage all other nationalities. Other solutions, which would include Bohemia, will have to be found."

"Yes, so you have said, but you must see that compromise must be made if we are to avoid outright war." *And so I have said. We keep using the same tired words.* "The great necessity at the moment is for the country to be calm and induced to place all the strength it can command at your disposal, by a man who is himself a guarantee of a better future. The situation is becoming critical. The longer we delay, the more the people are ready to listen to Kossuth. It may be that tomorrow Andrássy and Deák will be in no position to deliver what they offer today."

"I know what you think, my dear. But things of that nature should not be done in too much of a hurry. The Hungarian constitution must be settled with reference to the rest of the monarchy."

Sisi paused, seeking the words that could persuade him. "I am convinced that if you will trust Andrássy and trust him implicitly, we may still be saved – and not only Hungary but the monarchy too. But in any case, you must talk to him again. Any day now matters may take such a turn that he would not be in a position to provide what we need. I know what you fear, Franz. In granting duality to Hungary, you would be knitting the empire together, and otherwise, it will inevitably fall apart. I want Rudolf's inheritance to include that rich and beautiful and precious land. For Rudolf's sake, will you receive Deák? He arrives on the train tonight."

Franz nodded wearily. He looked drained, almost shrunken. "Andrássy does not consider the other provinces at all. Deák at least can see the other side. He has some thoughts on that."

"That does sound promising. We must build on it." She leant down and kissed him on both bewhiskered cheeks. "My dear Franz, I also am very sad when we are apart. I find I expect you to walk through the door at any moment. I firmly hope that when the Hungarian question is settled and now that the war is over, we can think about having another child." He tried to hold her, but she slipped away and left him, not the least ashamed of her blatant attempt at manipulation.

But Deák failed to impress. "He is honest and genuine in his devotion to the empire. I found him ready to take the other parts of the monarchy into account. On the other hand, he is too cautious and lacking in confidence. Resolution and endurance in misfortune have simply not been granted to the man."

When Sisi heard these words her heart sank, her hopes once more crushed. It seemed to her that Franz couldn't work with Andrassy or Deak simply because they were Hungarian. He could not overcome the prejudices of his youth.

She resolved to go back to Hungary as soon as she could pack.

Chapter 38 – Nov. 1866

Sisi turned her face towards the window where snow was drifting lazily down to settle on the shapeless mounds that in spring would revert to shrubs and urns. She was back in Budapest. During the past months, she and Andrássy had spent so many hours together and had come to know each other so well, that he probably saw the tension in her.

"I have received a letter from Franz. The peace has been signed. Vienna is no longer under threat. He wants me to return."

It was not a demand, but a humbly worded request. *I should like to ask for something very nice. If only you would pay me a visit, it would make me endlessly happy. I simply cannot get away from here at present, much as I would like to come to you… I long for you so and perhaps you too would be glad to see me again at such a sad time.*

Andrássy came to her side. They stood together looking out at the snowy landscape. He didn't say anything for a long time, and finally, he turned to her. "You must go."

"I don't want to. The thought of returning to that awful place depresses me." She had been away for months. Everyone now knew of her preference for Hungary and resented her for it. Nor did she want to leave Andrássy. He was chivalrous and romantic and passionate, possessing all the qualities she admired and once thought she saw in Franz. His poetic speeches stopped short of a declaration of love, but she knew he loved her as she loved him. She didn't want to leave him and was jealous of the time he spent away from her.

"But you must!" He seized her hands to turn her to face him. "The moment has come. Austria no longer need fear Prussia, and the Emperor is free to turn his attention to Hungary. You said it yourself. This is our opportunity. All that is required now is for our divine queen to apply some sweet personal pressure."

'Sweet personal pressure'. His meaning couldn't have been clearer had he winked. Very well, she could do this – for Andrássy and Hungary.

. . . .

It is the children, and only the children, that make Christmas bearable, Sisi thought, as she watched them scampering around the Christmas tree on their knees among a jumble of presents. They were a delight, lifting the gloom that had settled on the Hofburg in the aftermath of a disastrous war and uncertainty about Maximilian, making everyone merry as only children can do. Along with Gisela and Rudolf were their cousins, the two sons of Karl Ludwig, Franz Ferdinand, who had just turned three and Otto Franz, still tottering around on unsteady legs. Gisela played mother hen to them all.

Franz, who loved children, got down on the floor and pushed Otto in his shiny new sleigh, while little Franz sat next to Sisi on a sofa and looked through a picture book with her.

Sophie was in her most sanguine grandmotherly mood, rocking little Otto to sleep in her arms when he became irritable, rather than turning him over to his nurse to be taken away. There was no doubt where her thoughts were when the big clock suddenly struck. "That's the one with the works Max brought from Olmutz," she said. "It is as if he is sending greetings from afar to the family circle."

Tears came into her eyes and everyone looked away. No one spoke beyond the prattling of the children. The Habsburgs were no good at dealing with emotions. A little later, she said, "I have sent gifts to Carlotta and ordered them to be arranged in her room on Christmas Eve. I do hope they lift her spirits a little."

Madi and Spatz had paid a visit to Carlotta at her villa in Miramare, where she was under the care of the celebrated Professor Riedel of the Vienna Asylum. In a letter to Sisi, they described how they had found her haggard and dishevelled, fearful of being poisoned by agents of Louis Napoleon who she saw as the Antichrist. Sisi did not show the letter to Sophie, who continued to believe that Carlotta's condition was only temporary, and with rest and medical care she would soon be well enough to return to her husband.

The mother of the two little boys was Maria Annunciata of the Two Sicilies, a sister to the husbands of Madi and Spatz. Into the awkward silence, she said, rather too loudly, "Sisi, shall you visit Zurich when your sister has delivered her child?"

Sisi smiled. "Yes, I shall, certainly. I have been invited to assist at the christening." It came as a great surprise when Spatz and her husband reconciled, and an even pleasanter one when she announced her pregnancy. Madi and her husband would be there too, which would be delightful, and Zurich was a new place for her to explore. "But first I will stop in Munich to congratulate the happy couple. I am so glad that Ludwig has finally been conquered, and by our own dear Sophie."

It had come to Sisi's notice that the King of Bavaria had said in the presence of his future wife that what attracted him most to Sophie was her resemblance to her lovely sister, who epitomised for him the ideal of womanhood. Yet the news had given Sisi great pleasure.

"Your mother must be delighted," Sophie observed. "Another daughter married into royalty."

Sisi sensed a barb there as if her mother ought not to presume so far, but she kept her smile in place. "Yes, she is, as am I. Ludwig is one of my favourite people in the whole world."

Maria's shapely brows rose. Her face lent itself well to disdain. "Let us hope that Sophie can distract him from that mystifying obsession with Wagner. I have never understood it. Wagner's music is... Well, I don't know quite how to describe it, except that it is gloomy and not at all uplifting."

"Music touches different people in different ways, sometimes in ways others can't understand. Wagner's music suits Ludwig's temperament."

"I suppose that's true, but still... His obsession with the man is unhealthy and unnatural."

"A love of the spirit is a rare and beautiful thing, and difficult for most people to understand," Sisi said, gazing at her sister-in-law coldly.

Sophie began to croon to Otto. Franz wandered over to the seat next to Sisi that little Franz had vacated. Karl Ludwig put a hand on his wife's shoulder and gave it a hard enough squeeze to cause her to look up at him. Maria had made a *faux pas*. There were rumours that Ludwig was a homosexual, but there was no doubt that Ludwig Viktor was, and unashamedly. Franz was so disgusted by his aberrant brother that he would no longer allow him to live in the palace.

There were so many topics that were off limits in a family gathering. They must avoid any reference to Bismarck or Prussia or Germany or Hungary or France, for these were all subjects that

310

depressed the spirits. Mention of Maximilian invariably upset Sophie. And Ludwig Viktor's lifestyle was taboo.

Thank heavens for the children, Sisi thought. Their endless prattling and excitement filled the silences that otherwise would have become intolerable.

....

Seeing a new face at dinner one day, Sisi said, "I do believe that is Baron Beust. What is he doing here?" The Baron was the former foreign minister of Saxony. She had met him at her brother Gackel's wedding in Dresden the previous year and judged him to be an unprincipled opportunist.

"He is our new foreign minister," Franz said, rather sheepishly.

Following Andrássy's advice, Sisi had returned to Franz's bed, and although she didn't refrain from mentioning the Hungarian situation when the opportunity arose, she avoided arguing with him. Hiding her disappointment that Andrássy had not been chosen for the post was difficult.

She remembered something else about Beust. "He loathes the Prussians. You must take care he doesn't lead you into another war." In fact, Bismarck had insisted upon his dismissal before he would agree to any terms with the Saxons.

"I will admit that is one of the reasons I chose him. He wants vengeance. I don't intend to make things easy for Bismarck. Would you believe he is already making friendly overtures? As if the war had never happened! As if..." He broke off and blew out his cheeks. "Well, it is certain now that he has designs on France and wants a docile Austria at his back."

"Appointing Beust was a mistake," Sisi said, not to be diverted. "No foreigner is capable of infusing new life into the monarchy. I am convinced that only Andrássy can be of use at the present moment."

"I take it you don't like him?" Franz said, still looking unaccountably smug.

"It has nothing to do with liking. I feel he is the wrong choice."

Still holding his fork, letting the servers know the course wasn't yet finished, he leant his head towards her. "Would you change your mind," he whispered, "if I were to tell you he has stated his first job in office will be to come to a settlement with Hungary."

"Oh, Franz, really?" Sisi cried joyfully, drawing the attention of those around them.

"Yes, and I feel he can succeed because his is an unbiased opinion. Being a 'foreigner' his judgment is free of the bias that clouds the judgment of our Austrian statesmen and our Hungarian patriots. You have convinced me that the dual system doesn't endanger the position of the monarchy but, on the contrary, our only salvation lies in making Hungary happy."

"I know Deák will not seek a place in the new government, but will there be a role for Andrássy?"

Franz chuckled. Sisi thought it must be for the first time in months. "You are getting a little ahead of us, my angel. Nothing has been discussed yet, but I think the position of minister for Hungarian affairs would suit. Don't you?"

"Yes! And richly deserved." She sighed happily. "Oh, Franz, won't it be wonderful to lay this matter to rest finally."

"We have a long way to go before that happens, but I think now we can begin to look forward to it." He laid down his fork to take her hand under cover of the tablecloth. "This has been the most terrible year of my reign. Let us hope the next will be better, a year of peace and harmony between nations."

The servers came forward to remove the plates.

Chapter 39 – April–June 1867

"Do I have you to thank for this?" Sisi indicated the room with a sweep of her hand, but what she really meant was Gödöllö, the palace she and Andrássy had passed on one of their rides. Now it was hers. Now, finally, she had a home of her own – her very own Possi. It had eighteen hundred acres of parkland, as well as an indoor riding hall, so she would be able to ride in all seasons and all weathers.

"No, Your Majesty, for this you have only yourself to thank. The people of Hungary are so grateful to you they are pleased to gratify your every whim. You once told me if you had a palace of your own you would feel you belonged to Hungary instead of being an occasional visitor. It is my dearest wish that you to stay among us a long time."

They were alone in the room, apart from Ida who sat in a window seat, apparently engrossed in a book. The windows were open to the garden, and the sweet scents of spring and flowers drifted into the room.

Andrássy was looking at her appreciatively, his dark eyes gleaming in the way that made her heart lurch. "Your Majesty looks radiant."

"Thank you, Count, I am wonderfully well." She tore her eyes from his gaze. "How does it go in the Chamber?"

"The radicals are doing their best to disrupt proceedings. And Kossuth has sent an open letter to Deák accusing him of being a traitor. His followers threaten to prevent the coronation from taking place, but they can do nothing. Because of your presence here, Kossuth has little support."

"Then it goes forward?"

He moved a step towards her, removing his gloves as he spoke. "That is what I came to tell you. With His Majesty's approval, the coronation will be June 8th."

Sisi caught her breath. "Oh, Andrássy! Then we've done it! We've really done it."

Andrássy grinned. "It goes forward like a locomotive."

She reached a hand out towards him, then drew it back when his own hands reached for hers. She spun about towards the woman in the window seat. "Do you hear that, Ida? We've done it!" She laughed joyfully as Ida looked up from her book. Suddenly all three were laughing.

"Champagne, quickly. We must celebrate."

"Yes, Your Majesty."

As Ida hurried from the room, Andrássy moved close to Sisi. "Have I not always told you that if there were ever to be a rapprochement between Hungary and Austria, it would be thanks to you? For three centuries we had faith, we had hope, until those things were extinguished. But only you with your courage, conviction and your love of Hungary that called to the Hungarian people in the depths of their heart to love you in return, only you could have saved us. On behalf of Hungary, I thank you. May I kiss your hand, Majesty?"

"Of course." Sisi's breath caught in her throat. His eyes held hers trapped, as he gently held her hand and tugged on the fingers of her glove one at a time, until it came loose and slid off. Then he bent his head and placed his lips on her soft white hand. *Too long*, Sisi thought. She could have withdrawn her hand, but she did not. The contrast of soft lips and rough beard and the sensations that so personal a contact awoke in her were too erotic to curtail. She wanted it to go on and on.

When he raised his head, there was such tenderness in his eyes. "I am impertinent, yes?"

"Yes," she said softly.

"I will not so trespass again. But when I am a very old man, with a bent back and few teeth, you will still be in my heart. Elisabeth, Empress of Austria and Queen of Hungary."

Her sisters had taught her that physical love could be delightful and fulfilling when it wasn't a duty but a choice, when there was mutual attraction and fire in the blood. But Sisi understood that the kiss on the hand was all she was to have of him. She knew he would like to make love to her, if only she weren't Franz's wife. And she would like him to. But it was necessary that he remain in Franz's confidence. He wouldn't risk all for her, and she wouldn't let him.

....

The volley of a twenty-one gun salute from the Citadel of St. Gerhardsberg echoed over the rooftops of the palace on Buda Hill. Sisi awoke, stretched and savoured for just a few moments the joy of the day to come, before the shadow that blighted her happiness made itself felt. Maximilian. Franz had arrived in Budapest bringing the news that Maximilian, her dear brother-in-law, had been captured by his enemies, put on trial and sentenced to death. Sentenced to death!

How could an Austrian archduke be sentenced to death like a common criminal? But, of course, he was not an Austrian archduke. Shocked and distraught, Franz scrambled to have him reinstated, and the heads of European powers wrote to Juarez asking for an armistice. The United States ambassador to Vienna was entreated to do whatever he could to procure Maximilian's release, but the United States were covertly backing Juarez.

Even as she lay there in her bedchamber in Buda Castle on the day of her greatest triumph, she imagined him sitting in some filthy airless Mexican jail cell with only flies and rodents for company. How fearful he must be, how heavy his heart. She forced him out of her mind, knowing he would return again and again, a shadow over the festivities.

Today was the climax of months of often volatile negotiations: coronation day when Franz and she would be consecrated as King and Queen of Hungary. This was her apotheosis, her triumph; she had worked indefatigably to bring it about and in doing so had won the hearts of the Hungarian people. Upon her return to Hungary, Deák had said to her: "Firmly as I believe that never before has a country had a queen more deserving of it, I also know that there has never been one so beloved."

Credit too, she thought, to Andrássy and Deák, who had never given up despite all the setbacks, Franz's ambivalence and the enmity and malice of the Viennese court party. They had travelled back and forth between Budapest and Vienna, holding often heated negotiations with Franz and the ministers, and keeping in constant communication with Sisi. Andrássy's letters were in the custody of Ida – Sisi couldn't bear to part with them. They were not quite love letters, but often they were more intimate than was quite proper.

She went to the window and parted the curtains a little to look out across the river to Pest. It was four o'clock in the morning, but the windows of many houses were already lit, and she could see

315

people in the streets. They would be hurrying to cross the bridge and climb the hill to the church of St. Matthew to get a favourable spot from which to watch the procession arrive and depart. Many more had come in from the country, squeezing in with relatives, some sleeping in the parks or railway station. They were there, Sisi knew, principally to see her.

The culmination of the conciliation process occurred in February when the old Hungarian Constitution was reestablished. The Habsburg Empire became the dual empire of Austria-Hungary, with two capitals, two parliaments and two cabinets of ministers. To Sisi's delight – and his own – Gyula Andrássy was named the first prime minister of the new Hungary.

In a throne address before the Imperial Council, Franz had promised the western half of the empire – the greater part – amendments to the Constitution to provide the same security for the other kingdoms and provinces as Hungary had been granted. And he promised every extension of autonomy that accorded with their wishes and could be granted without endangering the total monarchy. The reorganisation, he said, was a work of peace and harmony and begged that a veil of forgetfulness be spread over the recent past, which had left deep wounds in the empire.

Then began the weeks-long work of preparing for the coronation. More than a thousand guests were expected. The old castle would have to be properly equipped to receive the imperial court.

Not everything had gone smoothly. There were inevitable clashes between Austrian and Hungarian. Franz Liszt had composed music specifically for the occasion, but he was not allowed to conduct his own composition. That a non-Hungarian had been chosen as conductor and the music to be performed by the Viennese Imperial Court Choir caused a major upset in the coronation preparations. It was a matter of "strict ceremonial".

All controversy would be put aside today, Sisi thought as her ladies and hairdresser, arrived promptly and fluttered around her in a state of great excitement. The wonderful coronation dress was carried in on a dressmaker's dummy, its layers smoothed by envious hands. Worth of Paris, the most famous couturier of the day, had made it, but it was a Hungarian design, with a skirt and ten-feet-long train of white and silver brocade and a black bodice smothered in embroidery and pearls and other jewels. A veil of exquisite lace would be attached to a diamond tiara.

By six o'clock the suspension bridge across the Danube was clogged with pedestrians and the carriages of noble families. Sisi's hair was styled, and she was sewn into her coronation gown. The sky was lightening in the east, promising a fair dawn and a day of sunshine.

Seven o'clock and the newly risen sun was as warm as a beneficent hand. When Franz arrived to escort her, he was so overcome that he took her in his arms and kissed her on the mouth in front of all their attendants.

His face was lined and sad-eyed – Maximilian standing at his shoulder – yet he had overcome his political doubts and seemed relieved that the decision had been made and the 'Hungarian question' settled without more bloodshed.

He too looked resplendent in the uniform of a Hungarian Hussar, his breast glittering with decorations and orders. The last year had taken its toll on him. His hair was thinning on the crown as well as at his temples. He once joked that he was tearing it out in frustration. Sisi wondered if in the privacy of his bedroom he ever indulged in tears, or whether such solace was not in his nature. The latter, she suspected. Tears she had seen, but never of sorrow or self-pity.

The procession formed outside the castle. Eleven standard-bearers, chosen from among the high aristocracy, preceded Count Andrássy who looked, to Sisi's eyes, more splendid than ever in a military uniform and wearing on his chest the cross of the Order of St. Stephen. As prime minister, to Andrássy went the honour of carrying the crown of Hungary. Following him, were gonfaloniers bearing the state insignia on red velvet pillows. Then came Franz.

Sisi heard the people up ahead cheering for him, and she noted how the cheering swelled when she appeared. She kept her head and her eyes down. This was taken by the newspapers to signify her humility, but it was, in fact, to avoid looking at the people who jammed the area between the castle and St. Matthias Church. Even after so many years of being at the centre of attention, she still could not get used to the presence of so many people pressing close to her.

Aristocrats, diplomats and representatives of other states packed the church, all wearing their finest, the men flashing with insignia

317

and decorations, the women glittering with jewels. The churchmen were almost as splendidly dressed. Amid all the jewelled splendour the unassuming Deak was somewhat conspicuous in his civilian clothes. He was entirely happy to leave all the honour and glory to Andrassy.

Hanging from the walls, the banners of Austria, Hungary and Bavaria stirred in the waves of rising hot air as Sisi took her place beside Franz. The Primate of Hungary draped the thousand-year-old mantle of St. Matthias over his shoulders and anointed him with holy oil. Then Andrássy placed the crown on his head. For just a moment, as the music of Franz Liszt soared in the background, Andrássy's dark, gleaming eyes met Sisi's in a look that burned with its intensity. If this was her day of triumph, it was also his: the day he had fought for, worked for, suffered exile and the excoriation of enemies to achieve. He was a man who had stared death in the face and had now realised the dream that for so long had seemed hopeless. Sisi tore her eyes away to look at the wrinkled face of the primate. Andrássy moved to stand at her side, holding the queen's crown over her right shoulder as the primate anointed her.

With Sisi's hand resting on Franz's wrist, they emerged from the church into a new day, as King and Queen of Hungary, monarchs of the Austro-Hungarian Empire. The roar of the crowd, as Sisi wrote later to Rudolf, almost blew the roofs off the houses.

***

Thank you for reading my book. If you enjoyed it, I hope you will take a moment to leave a review at your favourite retailer.

Thanks.

Susan Appleyard

A note from the author.

Sisi was a complex character. She was taken at a young age from a carefree lifestyle and placed in an environment that was both alien and hostile, with no time to adjust. I believe most of her problems stemmed from that simple fact. She was undoubtedly selfish and self-absorbed, but that's understandable given that she had no one else to focus her love on, not even her children. When she had a 'cause' that engaged her heart or intellect, she was a different person, generous and unreservedly committed. She was also at times anorexic and suffered serious bouts of ill health. In my research, I frequently read that contemporaries described her as 'nervous" and often her illness was attributed to 'nerves'. I feel sure there was a little hypochondria in her makeup and suspect that many of her symptoms were psychosomatic, which is why she quickly recovered when she left Vienna. But it is true that before she went to Corfu, she was believed to be dying. Some things just defy explanation.

I have tried to be faithful to the historical Sisi, at least as I see her, without making any attempt to romanticise her or her life. She was an unusual woman and a challenging character.

About the author

I was born in England and learned to enjoy English history at an early age. I also enjoyed writing stories, so I am able to combine two of my passions. Now I spend half the year in Canada with my children and grandchildren and the other half in Mexico with the sun and sea. What a life!

Read more books by Susan Appleyard

Queen of Trial and Sorrow
This Sun of York
The Remorseless Queen
The First Plantagenet
Dark Spirit
The Forsaken Queen

Connect with me:

Check my author page at: http://www.amazon.com/Susan-Appleyard/e/B00UTVMT5Y
Visit my blog: https://susanappleyardwriter.wordpress.com/
Facebook: https://www.facebook.com/susan.appleyard.9
On Twitter: @susan_appleyard
Please feel free to contact me at sue.appleyard@hotmail.com. I respond to all emails.

Printed in Great Britain
by Amazon

22571394R00178